RAVE REVIEWS
FOR JULIE KENNER!

APHRODITE'S KISS

"Adorable characters and hilarious story lines set Julie apart.
. . . *Aphrodite's Kiss* is pure delight!"

—Trish Jensen, author of *Against His Will*

THE CAT'S FANCY

". . . charming and magical."

—*Romantic Times*

". . . funny, witty, and unbelievably erotic."

—*Affaire de Coeur*

"120% pure delight!"

—*Rhapsody Magazine*

"*The Cat's Fancy* deserves a place on any reader's keeper
shelf!"

—*Wordweaving*

"Add Julie to your authors to watch list."

—*HeartRate Reviews*

MORE PRAISE FOR JULIE KENNER!

"Ms. Kenner is an up-and-coming author with a bright future ahead of her."

—*ReaderToReader.com*

"A fresh new voice in humorous romance."

—Sandra Hill, bestselling author of *Truly, Madly Viking*

"Kenner has a way with dialogue, her one-liners are funny and fresh. Her comic timing is beautiful, almost Jennifer Cruise-esque."

—*All About Romance*

"A writer undoubtedly on her way to the top!"

—*New Age Bookshelf*

TOUCHED

Oh, Apollo's apples, his touch. A firestorm of shocks ricocheted through her. Her chest constricted, her body warmed, and she felt faint. Then her body finally remembered that little detail about breathing and she exhaled in a *whoosh*. Mildly mortified, she opened her mouth to say something, then shut it again when she realized it wasn't too keen on sounding out vowels or consonants.

Sucking in air, she slipped her arm through his, trying not to jump from the electricity that zinged through her when her skin brushed against his. Sooner or later, she'd get used to his touch. Sooner, hopefully, because if she waited for later, all her nerve endings would likely be fried.

She frowned, realizing just how much she wanted to be with this man. He made her laugh, he made her insides flutter. He made her want to take risks.

Huge risks, actually. She nibbled on her lower lip, worried. Did she really want to lose herself to this mortal? Could she? Or was it more likely she'd lose her mind since just the slightest brush of his skin against hers sent every one of her super-senses zooming into super-charged mode?

Insanity seemed like a small price to pay.

Other *Love Spell* books by Julie Kenner:
THE CAT'S FANCY

Aphrodite's Kiss

Julie Kenner

LOVE SPELL NEW YORK CITY

A LOVE SPELL BOOK®

April 2001

Published by

Dorchester Publishing Co., Inc.
276 Fifth Avenue
New York, NY 10001

ISBN 0-505-52438-4

Visit us on the web at www.dorchesterpub.com.

*Some things are worth repeating,
and some friends should be reminded of how much they
mean along the way, even if they already know it so well.
So, this book is dedicated to
Kathleen Panov and Dee Davis.
Y'all know why. Thanks for everything.*

Aphrodite's Kiss

VENERATE COUNCIL OF PROTECTORS
1-800-555-HERO
www.superherocentral.com

Protecting Mortals Is Our Business!

Official Business

Ms. Zoë Smith
Halfling
Los Angeles, California

Greetings and congratulations on your upcoming twenty-fifth birthday:

Enclosed please find your application for membership to the Venerate Council of Protectors (487 pages, excluding affidavits and attachments) and council publications numbers 1758-A(3) and 2987-

Z(9), respectively titled "So You're a Halfling!" and "The Venerate Council: A Brief History in 1,200 Pages."

Please complete the application and return it in triplicate to the council by no later than one month prior to the twenty-fifth anniversary of your birth.

As part of the application process, you may be evaluated through field testing during your birthday week. Such testing is random, and applicants are not informed in advance.

You will be advised of your application status the morning following your twenty-fifth birthday. A decision as to your denial or acceptance will be based on your overall skill level and performance during the tests.

If you are accepted to the council, you will be informed at that time of the date and location of your swearing-in ceremony. If your application is declined, you will be escorted to the Bureau of Registration, where you will be required to either register as an Unlicensed Protector (Outcast) or forfeit your Protector heritage and undergo mortalization, at which time all memories of your Protector relatives will be removed. (For more detailed information on the mortalization process, including limitations of liability, warranties, and disclosures, please visit our Web site at *www.superherocentral.com*.)

Failure to register as an Outcast or to select mortalization is a violation of Section IV, subpart 2(a)(ii) of the Mortal-Protector Treaty of 1970.

In addition to your formal application, you must submit—by no later than sunset on your twenty-fifth birthday—the enclosed Affidavit of Mortal Disclosure affirming that you have disclosed to your mortal parent your status as a halfling and your decision to apply for council membership.

As you are aware, your Protector parent filed a Notice of Halfing Nascence contemporaneously with your birth, and such information has been periodically updated. Your file currently states that, in addition to the speed, strength, and agility inherent in the Protector genetics, you have also demonstrated a propensity toward the following skill(s)/power(s)/characteristic(s):

heightened five senses (including X-ray vision)

As the anniversary of your birth draws closer, you will most likely experience significant oscillation in your ability to control/utilize such skills(s)/power(s)/characteristic(s). Such fluctuations are an unfortunate by-product of your halfling status and are considered normal.

Our records further indicate that you have not yet mastered the following necessary skill(s):

matter manipulation (a.k.a. telekinesis)

Form 82-C(1)(a), on file with the Office of Halfling Registration, reflects the issuance of the following council-controlled articles:

propulsion cloak, model C-14A (training model)
and
X-ray blocking glasses, tortoiseshell variety
(regular and sunglasses)

Please be advised that at any time prior to the anniversary of your birth, you may formally announce your intent not to submit the affidavit and to select mortalization. Please use Form 93B, enclosed, Intent to Select Mortalization.

Upon submission of such form, you will be immediately escorted to the Bureau of Registration for processing. Please arrange return transportation in advance. Following the mortalization process, you will have no memory of the council of your Protector relatives. A stranded mortal is an unhappy mortal!

Thank you for your attention to this matter—and happy birthday!

Sincerely,
Phelonium Prigg
Phelonium Prigg
Assistant to Zephron, High Elder

jbk:PP
enclosure

Chapter One

Zoë Smith stared at the chocolate bar, wondering if it was going to attack. She'd confiscated it an hour ago from one of the students, who knew better than to bring food into the library, and she'd been contemplating the dastardly thing ever since. It looked innocent enough— sitting there on her desk surrounded by children's book catalogs, order forms, and manila folders.

Zoë knew better.

That smooth, creamy milk chocolate mixed with chewy caramel had it in for her.

One bite, and *Riverdance* would begin tap-tapping away inside her mouth. Two bites, and her head would start spinning while smoke came out of her ears. Three bites, and those urban legends about spontaneous human combustion wouldn't be legend anymore. Her whole life, Zoë'd had to watch what she ate. Too spicy, too tangy, too *anything* and she'd be jumping up and down, trying to put out a fire on her tongue or otherwise calm her taste buds.

And she'd thought *that* was inconvenient. . . .

Ha!

That was nothing compared to what her ridiculous senses had been doing recently. These days her senses had been shoved into the touch, smell, sight, taste, and sound version of *The Twilight Zone*. Sometimes perfectly calm, perfectly stable. Other times more unstable than a psychopath on a bad day. In other words, totally whacked-out.

At least her X-ray vision could be blocked by simple glasses. So far at least, Zoë hadn't discovered any easy way to wrest back some control of the rest of her senses.

Her brother Hale had said she just needed to get used to it—that after a while she'd become more acclimated.

Yeah, right.

Zoë was pretty sure that Hale's ability to understand animal-speak and turn invisible didn't hold a candle to what she went through if she tried to eat spicy Mexican food. Or the noise when a hundred or so conversations popped into her head unannounced. The unexpected drone of voices was bad enough; trying to sort them out and hear just one conversation was exhausting.

Besides, since Hale was a full-fledged Protector, he'd never had to deal with this sudden increase in powers. Instead of sporadically peaking like an adolescent boy's voice, his powers had developed calmly and slowly as he'd grown up. So Zoë doubted he had any idea just how overwhelming her megawatt senses really were.

As far as Zoë was concerned, at the moment her life was in a state of total chaos. Her senses were whacked-out, she still couldn't levitate worth a darn, she could barely steer her propulsion cloak, and in just a few days she had to tell her mother that she was a halfling and about to join the Venerate Council. *You see, Mom, I just never got around to telling you that I'm a superhero.*

Oh, yeah. That's *gonna go over big.*

She tapped her fingers on the desk, considering the candy bar. Maybe Hale did have a point. She needed to start somewhere, and she'd certainly never get used to this new hyperaware state if she lived on rice cakes and oatmeal. Maybe she should put a little effort into acclimation.

Squinting, she leaned forward until she was nose-to-wrapper with the devious confection. "Okay, Mr. Goodbar. It's you or me." Slowly, ceremoniously, she peeled the wrapper away, waiting for her nose to start twitching as the decadent smell of chocolate surrounded her.

Nothing.

A good sign, maybe?

Experimentally, she touched the tip of her tongue against the candy. It was chocolate, all right. Yummy, delicious, fattening chocolate. But—so far, anyway—not in the least bit spaz-inducing.

Well, in for a penny and all that.

Before she had time to think about it, she opened her mouth, shoved the candy bar in, and bit down.

Heaven. Pure heaven in a bite-size package.

She closed her eyes, letting the chocolate melt on her tongue, the sweet sensation of caramel mixing with the pure, rich decadence. Delicious and wonderful, but not overwhelming. Just your average, everyday choco—

Uh-oh. Big-time, major uh-oh.

The world tilted on its axis, spinning faster and faster

as the superfragilistic taste of chocolate grabbed hold of her taste buds and refused to let go.

Colors. She was tasting colors. Pinks and purples and yellows exploded in her mouth, forming and re-forming into kaleidoscopes of sensory delight, seeping into her blood and making her entire body flush. She tried to look around, tried to tell whether anyone could see her, but the rainbow blocked her vision.

She thought the library was empty, but what if someone came in? What if someone saw her losing her mind because of a chocolate bar?

What if someone thought she'd spiked a brownie?

Frantic, she dropped to the floor and scooted under her desk, pressing her hands against the solid wood as vibrant sensations ricocheted through her body. Deep breaths. That was what she needed. Lots and lots of deep breaths and no more chocolate.

Ever.

The worst of it passed, and she dug in her pocket for a tissue and tried to wipe any remaining chocolate off her tongue. The procedure left little bits of paper in her mouth, but since paper was a heck of a lot blander than chocolate, she couldn't exactly complain.

Finally feeling normal again—well, normal for her, anyway—she leaned her head against the desk, closed her eyes, and let the sounds of the empty library surround her. At first she heard only a cacophony. She squinted, urging her ears to filter the auditory mess into something she could get her mind around.

Then, slowly, something happened. Sounds emerged. Sounds she knew. The whirr of the ancient air conditioner, the patter of footsteps in the hallway, the irritating buzz of the clock over the door. The gentle rasp of breathing.

Breathing?

She stiffened. It was very low, not audible to normal ears, but there it was. Well, wasn't that just great? Probably Principal Dorsey, come to approve this week's library book orders.

"Ms. Smith?"

Zoë exhaled. Not Mr. Dorsey. A kid. Probably one of the sixth graders.

"Ms. Smith?" he repeated, but this time a head popped around the side of the desk, and big eyes behind Coke-bottle glasses peered at her. "Oh. There you are. Do you want to buy some PTA candy?" he asked, as if it were perfectly normal to find the school librarian hiding under her desk.

With as much dignity as she could gather, Zoë climbed out from her hiding place and brushed off her skirt. She gave the kid a stern look and tried to look authoritative. "Do you have a hall pass?"

"Uh, yeah." He dug deep into the pocket of his over-size jeans, then pulled out a mangled piece of paper. "I'm using my study period to sell the candy." Once again he waved a box of chocolate bars toward her. "Want one? They're only a buck."

Not in a million years. Aloud, she said, "No, thanks."

"Oh. You're sure? It's for playground equipment."

Then again . . . there was that whole acclimation thing. Maybe it was best just to jump in with both feet. She cocked her head as the kid stood in front of her, doing a good job of looking like Oliver holding out a porridge bowl. She sighed. "How many come in a box?"

For just a second, the kid looked confused. Then his

salesman instincts kicked back in. "Uh, twenty-four. But I've already sold five."

"I'll take the rest of them." She reached into her purse and started rummaging for her wallet. "A buck apiece, right?" At the kid's nod, she pressed a twenty into his hand. "Keep the change."

Alone with her nemesis, Zoë placed the carton of chocolate on her desk, turning it this way and that until she'd angled it just so. She didn't intend to eat one. Not now. Not after the little fiasco just moments before. This chocolate thing was going to require some serious pondering and planning.

What was that saying? Keep your friends close, but your enemies closer.

At the moment, Zoë wasn't sure whether the chocolate was friend or foe. But either way, she wasn't letting it out of her sight.

George Bailey Taylor steered Francis Capra into the parking lot of South Hollywood Elementary and tried to ignore the enormous ball of lead that seemed to have settled in his stomach. It was just a job, after all. No matter how distasteful. And right now he needed all the damn jobs he could get.

The simple fact was, he was in trouble. The kind of trouble that had pesky credit card agents calling during dinnertime. The kind of trouble that kept him up at night. The kind of trouble that left a big, smoldering lump in his stomach.

Money trouble.

And that, in a nutshell, was why he'd taken such a stinker of a case. Taylor needed to keep reminding himself of that. Harold Parker or starvation. Parker or a long, slow death from hunger with big, black buzzards circling him from above.

Okay . . . so maybe it wasn't *that* bad. After all, peanut butter and macaroni were cheap. But without this job he sure as hell wasn't going to make his rent. And he'd be damned if he'd bum a couch off somebody or go crawling back to the department and trade the bullet in his leg in for a nice, fat disability check. No way, nohow.

Time to get down to it. He parked the car in a visitor space, pitched his sunglasses onto the dash next to the box of flowers, then started digging through the pile of papers on the passenger seat until he found his notes. Emily Parker. Forty-three. Elementary school head librarian. Unlucky enough to be married to Harold Parker, who now wanted a divorce, along with a chunk of Emily's family money.

Which meant that the man wanted Taylor to track down a scandal—any scandal—so he could force a hefty settlement. So far Taylor had come up with zip, which was particularly unfortunate since Taylor had a sinking suspicion that, unless he brought Parker some juicy gossip, the man was going to stiff him for fees.

So much for the glamorous life of a Hollywood private investigator.

When he'd hung out his shingle six months ago, he'd fantasized about a Remington Steele lifestyle. Or at least Magnum, P.I. Instead he'd gotten Mike Hammer on a bad day. Hell, he was thirty-four years old, supposedly in the prime of his life. But here he was, working two-bit cases and struggling to pay his rent.

He should've paid more attention when he was a kid

and the social worker had told him that bit about life not being fair.

With a groan, he angled himself out of the Mustang, reached back inside for the flowers, then headed for the front doors. With any luck, the library would be empty and Taylor could take a quick peek at the inside of Emily Parker's desk.

And if luck wasn't with him . . . well, there was always the fire alarm.

"But Miss Smith," came the high, nasally voice, "I really, really, *really* need *A Wrinkle In Time*."

Sighing, Zoë kept a hand on the stack of books she was reshelving and looked down from the ladder into the face of little Patricia Something-or-other. "Patty, I told you yesterday. Both copies are checked out."

"But it's my turn." The little girl placed her hands on her hips. Her wiry red pigtails smelled of Johnson's baby shampoo and sprang out from the sides of her head like bent pipe cleaners. With that unruly red hair and an attitude that wouldn't quit, Zoë couldn't help but like the kid.

"How about I make you a deal?" she asked, and Patty squinted at her warily. "I'll bring my own copy tomorrow, and if the school's copies aren't turned in, you can borrow mine. Okay?"

Suddenly the girl was all smiles. "You're the best, Miss Smith."

"I bet you say that to all the librarians."

Patty frowned. "Huh?"

"Never mind," Zoë said.

She shoved her glasses back up her nose, intending

to go back to her reshelving, but as Patty swung her Powerpuff Girls backpack onto her shoulder, the girl managed to bang it against the ladder. The stack of books on it teetered, and Patty's eyes went wide as the volumes tumbled toward her perky little head.

In that very same instant, Zoë aimed her full concentration at the books, not thinking, just reacting. Time seemed to slow as she gripped them in her mind, testing their weight, their shape. And then—still not quite believing she was actually doing it—she gave the books a teensy little mental nudge . . . and sent them crashing harmlessly to the ground at Patty's feet.

Hopping Hades! She'd done it. She'd actually done it.

Below her, Patty tugged on her skirt, pulling Zoë back to the present. "Miss Smith? Did you see that?"

"See what?" Zoë asked.

"The books. They moved."

Zoë sucked in a deep breath, hoping she sounded calm. "Yes, they did. They fell. It's called gravity. You'll learn all about it in sixth grade, I think." She kept her words measured. "And that's why you should never, ever stand under ladders."

Zoë stepped down, then led Patty toward the door. She could barely keep the smile off her face. As Patty would say, she really, really, *really* wanted the library to herself.

"No, Miss Smith. I mean they moved . . . *sideways.*"

She pulled open the library door and aimed the girl into the hallway. "You're going to be late for third period, young lady. Come back tomorrow and I'll give you *A Wrinkle In Time* and a book on optical illusions. Okay?"

Patty didn't look convinced, but what could she say? There was no instant replay feature at South Hollywood Elementary.

As soon as the little girl was in the hall, Zoë shut the door and leaned against it. *She'd really done it!*

True, it had just been an itty-bitty bit of mind-over-matter—nothing like what some Protectors could do. Her dad and Hale, for example. They could do the most amazing things simply by focusing a blast of mental energy. But this was a start—and a good one.

And it called for a celebration. A definite champagne-and-roses moment. Except . . . her nose wrinkled as she thought about the effect sparkling wine and fragrant flowers would have on her sometimes supercharged senses. Better to go with a rice cake and bottled water. But she needed *something* to mark the moment.

A very auspicious moment it was. Every year she'd been tested with her cousin Mordichai, and he'd always, *always* beaten her. Her whole life, she'd been the halfling who couldn't do anything right, who didn't really fit in. And now, when she'd least expected it, she'd finally managed to levitate something! That meant she could amend her council application to check the "yes" box for telekinetic skills, and that put her one step closer to acceptance.

Of course, she still had to get her senses under control. Plus, she had to submit her Affidavit of Mortal Disclosure. Which meant telling her mom everything. Which was terrifying. For as long as she could remember, she'd wanted to join the council and go on missions. She wanted to rescue people from avalanches and kittens from trees. She wanted friends who understood her and didn't think she was weird.

24

The problem was that she wanted her mother, too.
And twenty-five years ago her mother, a pregnant Tessa
Smith, had walked away from her one true love about
two seconds after she'd found out his secret. Her mother
never even knew that her father had started visiting Zoë
when she was still a toddler, and Tessa certainly didn't
know that Zoë had inherited quite a few traits from him.

Overall, it wasn't exactly a typical childhood, though
by Los Angeles standards, she supposed it wasn't too
out of the ordinary.

She blinked, trying to force herself back to the issue
at hand—her newfound telekinetic powers. The question
of the hour was, could she do it again? Or was she going
to have to endanger a child every time she wanted to
levitate something? Clearly that would not do.

Well, no time like the present to find out. She tipped
her head down, then peeked over the frames of her
glasses and through the rows of shelving to make sure
the coast was clear. Then—satisfied that no kids were
sitting behind the bookshelves and no Application Com-
mittee members were hovering around to see if a mere
halfling was breaking the carved-in-stone rule against
power exploitation—she aimed her concentration at the
canister on her desk filled with yellow number two pencils.

Steady, steady . . .

Her faced tightened, muscles straining as she focused,
visualizing it rising in the air. There, in her mind, it
hovered a good foot off the desk.

Unfortunately, it was hovering *only* in her mind. In
reality, the stupid can was still planted firmly on the
wooden desktop.

Just relax, Zoë. Remember what Hale said. Her half

brother had this levitation thing down pat. True, things came a lot easier for him, but he was also her very best teacher. *Just do what he said and let it flow.*

She tried again, aiming her eyes toward the pencils, but looking past them. Focusing, but not. Concentrating, but not. Urging, coaxing, *wanting*.

The canister moved.

At first it was just a little jiggle, the pencils shaking a bit in the cup.

Focus . . . focus . . .

Then, yes, finally, it rose—a bit wobbly—off the table.

She'd done it again! So what if she'd broken some rules; the point was she'd really—

Whump! The library door slammed inward against her butt and the pencils went crashing to the floor.

She spun around—ready to deliver a stern lecture about slamming through doorways—and stopped short, her mouth hanging open as she stared into the deep brown eyes of a truly spectacular man. Unruly chestnut hair, a chiseled face with a thin scar dividing one eyebrow, a five o'clock shadow well before lunch, and fabulous shoulders that filled out a not-so-fashionable suit. Even in the wrong clothes, this guy had the right stuff.

With a bit of effort, she managed not to drool. With a bit more effort, she kept her glasses on, resisting the urge to take a peek and see if he looked as good out of those clothes.

"Sorry," he said, shifting the flower box under his arm.

"Mmm?" It would be so easy. After all, what was the point of having X-ray vision if you never got to use it?

All she had to do was tilt her head and peer over the frames. *Easy. So very easy . . .*

No, no, no. She shoved her glasses into place. She needed to get her mind out of the gutter, to stop thinking about—

"Sorry," he repeated. "I'm—"

"Sex."

"Excuse me?"

Oh, mother of Zeus. Had she really said that? "Six. I said *six.*" He probably thought she was a total ditz. "You're the sixth person who's done that to me today."

"Oh." He glanced behind him at the heavy door. "Maybe you shouldn't stand so close."

"Right," she said, moving away from the actual place of mortification. "Good idea." She smoothed her jumper, then fiddled with the end of her braid.

"So how can I help you, Mr. . . . ?"

"Taylor." He grinned and held out his hand. "And you are?"

"Zoë Smith." She shook his hand, his solid, warm fingers curling around hers. It was a nice, normal handshake—at least until he pulled his hand away, his skin gliding against hers. She inhaled sharply as the friction of his touch sent a billion sparks of electricity rushing through her fingers. Her entire body tingled, and she was pretty sure her hair was frizzing. *Oh, wowza.*

She tried to catch her breath, tried to act normal. "I . . . I'm the assistant librarian."

"Ah," he said, stepping closer.

She stumbled behind a table, feeling oddly safer with a buffer zone.

"Well, Zoë Smith, I could have sworn you said 'sex.' "

27

"Don't be ridiculous. Why on earth would I say that?" Other than the fact that lately she'd been worrying about the whole sex thing, of course. She could barely handle chocolate. How the heck was she supposed to handle an orgasm?

In the throes of total sensory overload, she could lose her grip completely. And that couldn't be good. If she didn't end up revealing her secret, she might end up hurting someone.

The thought of losing control so completely, so *intimately,* terrified her. And yet . . . and yet there were times—like now, if she wanted to be perfectly honest—that she really wanted a taste of forbidden fruit.

All of which made sex just one more frustration in her already confused and frustrated life.

Once again she gave her glasses a good shove, ensuring that they stayed squarely on her nose. No matter how good-looking this Mr. Taylor might be, she absolutely, positively wasn't going to sneak a peek.

Really.

He cleared his throat, and she sprang to attention, realizing then that his eyes were still aimed right at her. She frowned. "You're staring."

The smile that spread over his face was one of pure, devious pleasure. "Well, I thought you might be getting ready to answer your own question." The grin made it to his eyes. "About why you'd say I'm *sex.*" He stepped closer, clearly favoring one leg.

"Not that I particularly mind the endorsement."

"I told you. I didn't say that at all."

"No?" He moved closer to the desk and propped a hip against the edge. "Too bad. I was hoping to investigate all those stories about how wild librarians are after they whip off their glasses." Mischief danced on his face. "So. Are they true?"

The smooth timbre of his voice tickled her senses, and she pursed her lips, trying to stay focused. She should be annoyed, not intrigued. "Do you believe everything you hear?"

"No, but in this case, I'd be happy to believe." He held his arms out to his sides in a gesture of surrender. "Wanna take off your glasses?"

Oh, my. Her cheeks warmed. Trying to be nonchalant, she leaned against her desk, her heart pounding in her chest, her palms starting to sweat. She could run the Boston Marathon without getting this worked up. What on earth was this man doing to her?

She fought to keep control, and was pretty sure she was losing the battle. He was just so very . . . male. Every luscious, testosterone-laden inch of him. So very sensual, so very yummy, so very, very—

Pop!

Zoë jumped as the bulb in her desk lamp blew out, the noise dragging her back to reality. With renewed determination, she firmly quashed thoughts of lust and testosterone and raging hormones. By Zeus, she was going to be cool and distant even if it killed her.

"What do you want, Mr. Taylor?"

He upped the wattage on his smile, and *cool* and *distant* suddenly seemed extremely foolish. *Red-hot* and *close-up* held much more appeal.

Which, all things considered, was rather inconvenient.

Because, this casual flirting aside, she was pretty sure he hadn't come into her library wanting sex.

Chapter Two

The brow over one pale gray eye lifted, and Taylor realized that the other eye was blue. The contrast was somehow alluring. Hell, everything about this woman was alluring, from her prim-and-proper braid to the boring little jumper she wore over a plain white T-shirt.

Zoë Smith, elementary school librarian and average, everyday girl next door, was just about the sexiest woman he'd ever laid eyes on.

Lately, all the women he'd met had seemed rather surreal. Actress wanna-bes whose biggest thrill was discovering a new all-day mascara. Women with so many obvious piercings it scared him to think about the hidden ones. Women who thought discussing the NASDAQ was a really keen way to break the ice. Every one of them was somehow unreal, phony. This enticing librarian was a welcome change.

With a start, he shook his head. For reasons he had

no intention of examining, he was strongly drawn to her. And he wasn't at all sure he liked the sensation. He was here on a job, plain and simple. He was having enough trouble paying the rent; getting involved with a person of the female persuasion was the last thing he needed. *Right? Right.*

Nodding, he mentally dug in his heels.

"Yoo-hoo? Mr. Taylor?" She waved a hand in front of his face. "What are you doing?"

With a start, he realized he was still nodding. He stopped, smiled, and felt like a total idiot. "Just thinking."

"Uh-huh. I'll try again. What do you want? Are you looking for one of the students?" She frowned. "You really should have a visitor's badge if you're going to roam the hallways."

"I'm not roaming. I'm looking for Emily Parker." He tapped the flower box he'd brought. "I've got a delivery."

She frowned. "Fake roses?"

"They're not—" He cocked his head. "How'd you know they're fake?"

Her cheeks flushed pink. "Sensitive nose."

"I guess so." He cleared his throat as he tried to come up with a plausible lie. "Anyway, these are what some folks order if they think the person may be allergic."

She looked a little dubious, but didn't argue. "Emily's not here until after lunch."

"How about I leave them on her desk?" He looked around at the sturdy desks behind the checkout counter. "Which one is it?"

"She's got her own office," Zoë said, and Taylor let

31

loose with a mental cheer. A private office meant privacy—for snooping.

"Great. I'll leave them there. So where is it?"

Zoë pointed to the area behind the counter, and Taylor noticed a closed door to a private office completely blocked by a bright yellow Spring Read-A-Thon banner.

"Kind of hard for Ms. Parker to get to work, huh?"

"We didn't have enough wall space, so you can't get there from here. There's another entrance off the hallway, though." He followed her to the main doorway, then into the hall. She pointed to another door. "That's it."

"Thanks," he said, smiling, and feeling absurdly pleased when she smiled back. "Uh, well, I guess I'll go now."

Her cheeks colored again, and she stared at the floor. "Right. Guess so."

"Right." He took a step backward, wondering if he should just bite the bullet and ask her out for coffee.

" 'Bye, then," she said, then slipped back into the library. *Another lost opportunity. Damn.*

Not that it mattered. He was here on a job. And it was time to get down to it.

The office was unlocked, and he was inside within seconds.

Emily Parker was a neat woman. She was also a chaste woman, if everything he'd learned so far was true. Still, Parker wanted dirt. If the woman had anything sleazy going on in her life, maybe Taylor could find a hint of it in her office.

Careful to not make any noise, he started methodically going through each of her desk drawers, feeling like a jerk for doing it. *Rent, remember.* With a sigh and a silent apology to Emily, he kept on looking.

Nothing incriminating. Nothing at all. Not even any papers that indicated that she thought her husband was a slimy worm, which suggested that Mrs. Parker wasn't the brightest bulb in the lamp, but certainly wasn't going to satisfy Harold's desire for divorce court ammunition.

"Well, hell," he whispered. He sat back in the woman's chair and glanced around the office, wondering if Emily Parker kept secrets hidden in picture frames behind photos of her wedding.

The sound of paper ripping broke the silence, and the door to the library whipped open.

"What in Hades are you doing?" Zoë stood there, furious, hands on her hips, glaring down at him. The ripped ends of the Read-A-Thon banner hung limply in the doorway behind her.

He shut the bottom drawer with his foot, hoping she couldn't tell from where she was standing that it had been open. "How'd you know I was still in here?"

He asked the question to cover the noise, but he was also curious. The blinds were closed and he'd been as quiet as a mouse.

She rolled her eyes. "As much noise as you were making, rifling through drawers and cursing under your breath? It's a wonder the whole school doesn't know you're here. So? What *are* you doing here?"

"Just dropping the flowers off," he said, wondering when he'd made enough noise for her to hear.

"Try again. And it had better be good or I'm calling security."

He sighed. Better to take the high road. "Information," he said, shifting into professional-investigator mode. "I'm looking for information on Mrs. Parker."

She frowned. "I've heard of going directly to the source, but breaking and entering seems a bit over the top."

"Considering the way people gossip, it seemed more tactful than asking questions of her coworkers."

The frown deepened. "Is she in trouble?"

"Not at all," he said, trying out his smooth salesman voice. He passed her one of his fake business cards. "That's why I didn't want to start the rumor mill flying. I'm just doing a little background check."

Her eyes flicked down to the name printed on the card, then back up to meet his. Her mouth twitched. "*Buster* Taylor?"

"That's me," he said, suppressing a cringe. His foster sister had been with him when he'd ordered the cards. She'd thought Buster sounded more like a tough-guy name than George Bailey.

Since he'd wanted a fake name to go with the fake business card, he hadn't had the heart to argue.

Amusement danced in her dual-colored eyes as she looked him up and down. "You really sell insurance?"

"You sound surprised."

"I just expected something more . . ." She trailed off, her hand circling as she searched for words. "Macho. Like a cop."

His gut twisted. "Yeah, well, close but no cigar." He couldn't fault the woman for her intuition, but his serve-and-protect days were over.

"Close? What's that supposed to mean?"

He plucked the card out of her hand and tucked it into his pocket. "I investigate. Claims, potential insureds." That was not exactly a lie. He did all of those things.

Just not for some insurance company. Instead, for jerks like Harold Parker.

"So what are you investigating Emily for?" She crossed her arms over her chest.

"Insurance," he said, resisting the urge to reassure her he wasn't the scum of the universe.

She scowled. "Duh. I think we've already covered that."

"Right," he said. That they had. Unfortunately, just being around this woman had turned him into a tongue-tied idiot. "I'm talking about . . . beneficiaries." He flipped open his notebook. "My information indicates that her husband's name is Harold, and she has two children."

"Yeah, so?"

"Well, the policy she applied for identifies another male, not a relative, as a beneficiary," he said. "We're trying to confirm the relationship."

"I hardly think Emily's sleeping around." Her voice rose, irritation and incredulity obvious in her tone.

"I didn't say that." He didn't believe it either. But Harold Parker had paid him to find dirt, and that meant turning over stones. "So do you know who else she might have named as a beneficiary?"

She put her hands on the desk and leaned toward him, her eyes flashing, the floral scent of her hair making him a little nuts. "Mr. Taylor, I think it's time for you to leave."

Aw, hell. "I'm not trying to insinuate anything."

"Could've fooled me."

"I'm just looking for the facts."

"Yeah? Well, the fact is, the door's that way." She held her arm out, her finger aimed at the door to the hallway, and he had the queerest sensation that the door actually jiggled.

"Leave?" he asked, all innocence. "You want me gone?"

" 'Fraid so."

"Say it ain't so," he said in his most charming voice.

"It's so," she said, but she was fighting a smile, and he held his breath. Then her face hardened, the amusement disappearing. "Don't make me call security."

Just leave, Taylor. There are other ways to find dirt on Emily Parker. True, but suddenly he didn't give a flip about Mrs. Parker or her nutso husband. All he cared about was making sure Zoë Smith didn't think he was the world's biggest creep.

"Look, Zoë—"

She glared at him.

"Ms. Smith, I mean," he said, backpedaling. "I'm just trying to do my job."

"Why? You can't tell me you like prying into people's personal lives."

"Maybe I do," he lied.

"Funny. I used to be better at first impressions."

"It's my job," he said tightly. "The only job I have at the moment, and I like to eat."

"Peanut butter's cheap," she said. "As for the job, do it somewhere else."

"You can't blame me for trying to be thorough." He was practically pleading, wishing he could start over again. Only this time he wouldn't even mention Emily Parker.

"I'm not blaming you. I'm telling you to leave. Again."

He had the feeling she was disappointed in him, and

damned if he didn't feel ashamed. "Well, thanks anyway," he said. "I can show myself out."

He left without looking back, and stepped into the polished hallway. As Emily Parker's door latched behind him, Taylor sighed. He'd spent maybe five minutes with librarian Zoë Smith, and already she couldn't stand him.

Which was a damn shame, really.

Because, given the opportunity, Taylor could handle spending a little bit more time around the feisty librarian.

"Damn," he muttered, pushing open the doorway to the outside world. "I really hate this job."

An entire continent away—in a penthouse apartment sixty floors above Manhattan—Mordichai watched his father pace in front of twelve huge monitors. As usual, one was tuned to the local news, one was playing a tape of *Superman II,* and nine were showing various financial programs.

Also as usual, Hieronymous was pointedly ignoring his son.

What wasn't usual was the fact that on this particular day, Mordi doubted his father would even notice if the market crashed. Today, Hieronymous's attention was focused on the twelfth screen—the one illegally displaying his cousin Zoë and her library.

Hieronymous pulled the red silk robe he wore tighter around himself, then turned to face his son. "I trust this does not concern you?"

"Of course it concerns me," he said, hating the thought that Hieronymous was probably monitoring his house, too. "If Zephron finds out you've tapped into the council's circuitry, he'll have a fit. You know that only council elders are allowed to monitor halfling home and work activity. The privacy laws—"

"I meant the girl. But I appreciate your concern." He pressed a button on his desk and the twelfth monitor went dead. "Your cousin's skills are increasing. Despite her pathetic lack of practice, the girl is finally developing some control."

"Zoë's an amateur," Mordi said with conviction. "I'm not."

Since Hieronymous was an Outcast, Mordi had been permitted only limited visits with his father over the years. Now, though, he was council age, and that meant he had options: join the council, or join his father. And the amazing, surprising fact was that Hieronymous *wanted* him. Needed him, even, and the feeling thrilled him. No matter what, he intended to prove to Hieronymous that he was worthy.

"I've been training all my life," he continued. "Zoë's mother doesn't even know Zoë's a halfling." He paused at that. His own mother had known all along. And at the first sign of his powers, she'd passed him off to Hieronymous. He'd gone back to see her only once, right after his twelfth birthday.

She'd called him a freak.

"Your mother was a mortal and a fool," Hieronymous said, and Mordi concentrated on the floor, ashamed he was so transparent. "Like so many mortals, she does not have the proper respect for what we are."

Mordi nodded, gathering his resolve. He wanted—no, *needed*—to make his father proud. "Zoë's not a threat," he continued. "Uncle Donis and Hale work with her occasionally, but there's no way she'll be strong enough to beat me if it comes to that." He stood up straighter. "No way at all."

"Everything depends on the stone," Hieronymous said. "My plans. Your future. *Our* future."

His father made it all sound so simple. The council's archaic philosophy needed to be swept aside so that someone with vision could step in. Hieronymous was simply ahead of his time, and the moment of change was fast approaching.

Right now, the council spun its wheels in a futile effort to protect mortals from their own stupidity. Instead of being gods, council members were practically slaves to mortals, running around saving them from burning buildings or runaway trains. Soon, though, that would change.

Hieronymous aimed a steady stare at Mordi. "You spent much of your youth with the girl. If it becomes necessary for you to face her, are you sure you won't be adversely affected by some pathetic sense of familial loyalty?"

He considered the question. They were cousins, but they'd never been particularly close. Zoë, after all, had her family. And, truth be told, Mordi had always envied her for it. That little bit of envy had always sweetened his inevitable victories over her in each of the frequent tests during their training. "No, sir," he said finally. It wouldn't pain him at all to defeat Zoë again.

He frowned. *Still* . . .

"There is something you wish to say?"

Mordi took a breath. "It's just that . . . Well, it is only a legend, after all."

Hieronymous swept his arm, indicating the room lined with bookcases packed with rare, leather-bound editions and glass cases filled with odd archaeological finds. "I have spent half a lifetime pursuing this question. Aphrodite's girdle is real, as is the gemstone that forms its centerpiece."

"But the girdle's been missing for centuries. Just because of that story you believe the stone's going to somehow end up with me or Zoë?"

Hieronymous sighed. "Must you be so frustratingly pragmatic? There are too many coincidences not to believe the legend. You and your cousin are both halflings, both born on the same day. Your twenty-fifth birthdays fall on the day of the eclipse. And this, too." He plucked a plastic box from his pocket and handed it to Mordichai. "The stone is in Los Angeles."

The box blinked in his hand. "A tracking device? How?"

"Generations ago, the stone was set into a necklace that has certain unique properties, the characteristics of which remain a family secret. A legacy, if you will. I was able to create a device that honed in on those characteristics. This week, finally, the device detected a signal."

Mordi nodded, silent, as he stared at the blinking green light.

"You will not fail me."

"No, sir."

"Excellent. When the eclipse comes, you will prevail," Hieronymous said. "Little Zoë will have to continue her life as a mortal." A slow smile graced his lips, and Mordi shivered. "An unfortunate existence, considering what we intend to do to the mortal population, but, hey, those are the breaks."

*   *   *

"Well, if it isn't George Bailey Taylor." Harold Parker chewed on the end of his unlit cancer stick. Beside him, Tweedledum and Tweedledee shifted, practically snarling. *Stupid oafs.*

"You owe me eight hundred dollars, Mr. Parker." Taylor had made up his mind to quit this case even before he'd backed out of the parking lot at South Hollywood Elementary. Now it felt good to finally be turning his decision into action.

"I can't give you what I don't have, Georgie-boy." Parker leaned back against the worn vinyl of the circular booth and lit his cigarette.

"Taylor," he said. "I go by Taylor."

Parker waved a hand in front of his face. "Whatever. You know I'd help if I could. But I ain't got a dime to my name. And your snoopin' around hasn't exactly helped me out there, now, has it?" He tilted his head back and belched.

"Look," Taylor said, his fingers digging into the edge of the table, his biceps burning with the effort not to lash out at the little slimeball. "I did what you asked. But now I'm done with you. And it's your turn to pay me what you agreed."

Parker snorted and took a long drag on his cigarette. He exhaled toward Taylor, who stood his ground as noxious menthol smoke curled over his shoulders. "What I agreed? I think that bullet in your leg worked its way up to your brain." He aimed a self-satisfied smirk toward his moronic bookends. " 'Cause you're talking pure rot, Georgie-boy. You didn't do shit for me."

The perpetual ache in Taylor's thigh intensified to a dull throb. Eight years on the force, five commendations, a handful of awards, and a front-page spread in the local

41

paper, and this was where he'd ended up. One mistake and he was reduced to spying on a perfectly chaste woman with a husband from hell.

"She's not cheating on you."

Parker took another drag on his cigarette, then ground it into the tabletop. "Maybe you oughta look a little harder."

"Just give me my fee," Taylor said, measuring each word.

He settled back into the booth, the Tweedledumdums snickering beside him. "You bring me the goods, *capicse?* You find some dirt; then you get your money."

Taylor rubbed his thigh, forcing himself to stay calm as every cell in his body screamed at him to beat the little worm into a pulp. He should have avoided Parker like the plague. Dammit, he knew better. But like a damn fool, he'd let the need for cash suck him into a sucker's deal.

He counted to ten, clenching and unclenching his fist. Just one misstep, and instead of looking at him like a hero, women like Zoë Smith thought he was lower than slime. "Forget the fee. I'm not interested in money that's crossed your greasy palm."

"You think you're hot shit? Got your name in the papers back when you was a cop? Think that hero bullshit's gonna keep you in clients? You're a fool, Georgie-boy. A damned gimp fool," Parker sputtered, his prune face turning red with his rising blood pressure. "I let on that you welshed on me, and ain't nobody else gonna darken your doorstep again. You hear me, Georgie? You hear me, boy?"

The rubber band holding his emotions in check snapped, sending Taylor lunging forward. He plowed over the tabletop, arms out, hands ready to close around Parker's oh-so-smug neck. He slammed on the brakes just before he touched him, his fingers hovering over Parker's ring-around-the-collar. The Tweedle twins scrambled out of the booth and hightailed it for the kitchen.

"I should do it, you know," Taylor whispered, the itch in his fingers seconding his words. "But I don't think you're worth the effort."

Slowly, slowly, he backed away. *Nice, even breaths. Nothing wrong here. Nothing at all.*

Then, with one last look at Parker cowering alone in the booth, Taylor stepped out of the diner and into the heavy Los Angeles air. For someone who'd just told his one and only client to take a flying leap, he felt remarkably calm. Uplifted, even.

And he was absolutely certain that—if he ever saw her again—a certain elementary school librarian would be quite proud of him.

Chapter Three

She didn't want to think about him. She had no reason to think about him. Which was why it was particularly annoying that for the last three days, thoughts of Buster Taylor had been filling her head—the sexy scar that marred his eyebrow, the sparkle in his eyes when he smiled. The cute way he'd tried to backpedal when he'd realized how furious she was.

And her heart had just about melted when her ears had tuned in to his gripe as he was leaving the building: "Damn. I really hate this job."

In fact, she'd been so preoccupied with the irritating insurance investigator that she'd inadvertently shelved *The Lion, the Witch and the Wardrobe* with the arts-and-crafts books, and had completely blanked when a fifth grader asked if the latest Harry Potter book had made it to the library yet.

Ridiculous. She needed to get over this. Whether he

hated his job or not, he'd still pawed around in Emily's things. She shouldn't waste another thought on him.

Right. Absolutely. She should just get up and get back to work filing or reshelving.

Sure thing. That was what she should be doing. Not fantasizing about some mortal, no matter how gorgeous he was, or how intriguing he'd seemed at first.

The man was mortal, after all, and what could come of that?

Mortal and a jerk.

Right.

Then again, maybe she wasn't being fair. After all, he'd only been doing his job, and he felt really bad about it, too. Maybe she'd been thrown so off balance by the fact that she was, well, *attracted* to him that she'd overreacted.

Wheels turned in her head and she tried not to smile as the idea took root—if she'd overreacted, she should apologize.

It wasn't as if she'd be tracking him down for a date. After all, she didn't date. Actually, *couldn't* date was more like it. Considering her . . . *unique* lifestyle, latching on to a guy—especially a fully human, flesh-and-blood kind of guy—just wasn't in the cards.

Besides, hadn't Hale warned her a million times about getting involved with mortals? Weren't her mom and dad the perfect example? She wasn't stupid. She knew her limitations.

No, she simply wanted to apologize. Perfectly innocent, nothing wrong with that.

And the fact that he'd been gorgeous and amusing— exactly the kind of man she'd so often found herself fantasizing about—had absolutely nothing to do with anything. Nothing at all.

Okay. Sure. Now all she had to do was call him. . . .

She fumbled around on her desk looking for the business card, then remembered that he'd taken it back from her. *Well, no problem.* His name was Buster Taylor, and the card had said he worked for Atlas Insurance. She just needed to look him up.

She tried the phone, but the operator couldn't find a listing, and the yellow pages weren't any help either. Zoë scowled at the computer. She wasn't supposed to use the council search engine, but surely it would be okay this one time. It was a silly rule, anyway. And she did know Hale's password. . . .

Before she could talk herself out of it, she flipped her computer on and pulled up her Internet browser. She'd just get on and off. Nobody would even know. She'd find out where Taylor was, and that would be the end of it. *Easy-squeezy. No big deal.*

The browser opened and she headed for *www.super-herocentral.com* and typed in Hale's password, wondering just how much trouble she was bringing down on herself. Then she shook her head. *On and off, remember? No big deal, remember?*

Besides, if she wanted to find Buster, she needed to venture into the off-limits pages.

She picked up a pencil and gnawed on the eraser, thinking, as the banner headlines flashed:

Crack council team foils international kidnapping ring! Click here to view exciting video footage!

Undercover operative hired at NASA; expected

to pave the way for mortals to implement manned Mars missions. Protectors debate—should the council force technology on mortals? Click here for point/counterpoint.

Legend of Aphrodite's girdle surfaces! Rumors of Outcast uprising abound!

Zoë grinned at the headline. She'd seen statues and heard plenty of stories about her great-great-great-etcetera grandmother Aphrodite, and there was one thing Zoë knew for certain—that had been one woman who did *not* need a girdle.

Her eyes skimmed over the next headline, and she groaned.

Tax Office alert—all Protectors working in the United States are reminded to timely file form C-290 (Disclosure of Mortal Income Earned) with the Mortal/Protector Liaison Office by their deadline. To calculate individual deadlines, please see Schedule C, part 2 (b) 5 (a) (ii) of the Council Handbook.

Apparently death and taxes were pretty much the same in the mortal and the Protector worlds.

She tapped the eraser against her teeth one more time and then, before she could talk herself out of it, she jumped from the main area to the council's search engine.

There were no alarm bells, no Instant Message warnings. No council members swooping down to take her off to the Hall of Justice.

So far, so good.

She pulled up the southern California directory and searched for Buster Taylor. Nothing.

She searched for Atlas Insurance. Still nothing.

Odd. The council's records were more complete than the IRS's. Why couldn't she find him?

She tried for a few more minutes, searching the more obscure directories, pulling up old case files, generally snooping around where she didn't belong.

Zilch.

She couldn't believe it. Buster Taylor didn't exist.

Which meant two things. First, he'd lied to her.

And second, she'd probably never see him again.

Well, darn.

Lane Kent had a problem. Not a huge problem, but as a general rule, she tried to avoid huge problems. She had enough trouble keeping track of all her little problems, and Lord knew she had plenty of those lately, all decked out in tiny George Washington outfits.

From her perch on the Mustang's hood, she looked up at the green-gray sky, wondering if it was going to rain, and hoping it would. Rain in Los Angeles was like no place else. Like millions of little scrub brushes, the raindrops would attack the smog, polish the mountains, and leave the city crisp and clear and sparkly.

She could really use sparkly. These days her mood was anything but bright, and it was way the hell and gone from shiny.

Nope, these days she was worrying. Worrying about her car, her kid, her job—or, rather, her lack thereof. About the only thing she wasn't worrying about was her rent. And that only because her foster brother, George

Bailey, had managed to sweet-talk Mr. Timmons into letting her stay another month.

On one hand, that was good. On the other hand—the hand holding her checkbook—it was bad. Bad because George had worked out a deal with her landlord, and now she ought to pay him for a job well done.

So here she was, camped out on the hood of his classic red Mustang, waiting for him to come out of his apartment so that she could present him with the whopping sum of two hundred and fifty dollars, an amount that would pretty much clean out her checking account.

She saw him the second he rounded the building, then watched as his face changed from bland to pleased to annoyed.

"Would you stop, already? I'm not taking your money, Lane," he said, shouting to be heard over the traffic behind them. He finished crossing the parking lot and stopped in front of her, looking pointedly at the hood. "And don't sit on Francis Capra. You'll scratch her."

"Sorry," she said, slipping off, feeling as if she were twelve again. "Thanks for working all that out about my apartment."

"You're welcome," he said, but he still looked wary.

Lane almost giggled. It wasn't every day she had to sneak around just to give someone a check.

"But I'm still," he said, walking past her to the side of the car, "not," he added, opening the door, "taking your money." He slid in and started to close the door.

She grabbed it. "That's not fair. I asked you to. I want to at least pay your hourly rate."

"We grew up together, Lane. Family gets a discount."

"Fine. So knock some off your normal price." She

49

held out her wallet. "But I should pay the rest."

"It's your lucky day. Fifty percent off."

"Terrific. One hundred and twenty-five. No problem."

"It's double-coupon day. Guess you lucked out. No charge." He slammed the door, which—since the car was a convertible, and the top was down—didn't really go a long way toward cutting off her arguments.

"George," she said, sure she was whining.

He cringed. "Taylor, okay?"

"I'll call you Taylor if you let me pay you."

"Lane . . ." His voice was firm, no-nonsense.

"George . . ." she answered, sure she sounded equally dug in.

He rolled his eyes skyward. "I said no. You've got a two-year-old." He glanced down toward her legs, where her son usually clung. "Where is Davy, anyway?"

"A friend's watching him."

"Well, use the money to buy the kid a Happy Meal or something, 'cause I'm not taking it."

"But you're broke, too, and I know it."

She thought he flinched, then decided it was a trick of the light.

"Business is picking up."

She raised an eyebrow.

"I can take care of myself, Lane."

"Tayl—"

"And so long as I can, I'm going to take care of you, too." He put his hand on hers, his smile tender. "So keep your money. You and Davy need it more than me. Stick it in his college fund." He glanced at her yellow Gremlin. "Or buy new tires and I'll put them on for you. Something."

She nodded, part annoyed and part relieved. The re-

lieved part made her feel a little guilty. Her fingers
drifted to her neck, closing around the odd-looking green
stone she'd picked up at the Hollywood thrift store next
door to the bookstore where she worked. "Maybe we
can sell this." She pulled it over her head and pressed it
into his hand. "We could split the money."

Taylor looked at it, his face a mixture of confusion
and . . . well . . . more confusion. "Well, sure. If we each
want to buy a piece of bubble gum."

"You think it's just junk, huh? Oh. That's what I was
afraid of."

He glanced at her through narrowed eyes. "Why are
you wearing it if you think it's junk?"

She shrugged. "I bought it."

"Ah," he said, as if she'd explained everything. Then
he said, "Why?"

She sighed. "I don't know. I just did." She bit her lip.
"I thought it was worth something."

He held out his hand, the stone sitting on his open
palm. "You have got to be kidding me."

"No, really. The guy in the store said it was some sort
of artifact or something." Actually, he'd said it was her
destiny, but that seemed a little too bizarre to admit.

"Give me a break. How much did you pay for it?"

"Only a dollar." She shrugged. "It's so ugly, I didn't
really want it at all, but he kept insisting. And when he
finally said I could have it that cheap, I took it just to
shut him up."

He pressed the necklace back into her hand. "If we
sell it, we might hurt his feelings. Sounds like he's got
a thing for you."

Lane pictured the old proprietor's weathered face,
white hair, and brown teeth. "I don't think so. He just

seemed . . . befuddled. Kept going on and on about how things weren't really what they seemed, and how those whomp-'em, stomp-'em television shows didn't know the half of it."

" 'Whomp-'em, stomp-'em'?"

"I'm guessing *Buffy* or *Xena*."

Taylor's eyes opened wide. "To think I thought those shows were the height of realism."

"Guess not." She grinned. "Can't I do anything for you?" She racked her brain, trying to come up with some way to show her appreciation to a guy who wouldn't take her money. "What about a party? My friend's having a get-together next Saturday. You really need to find a girlfriend." She looked down at him, and his expression told her everything she needed to know. "No, huh?"

"Nothing personal, kid. But I'm not exactly in a date-of-the-week mind-set these days. More of a scrape-to-keep-my-business-alive state of mind." He looked annoyed as he continued. "Which translates into pissing off the only woman I've found even remotely attractive in a long time."

"So there is someone?"

"There's no one," he said, in that *the-topic's-closed* tone she knew so well. His fingers tightened on the steering wheel, and she knew he was lying.

"Fine," she said, trying to bait him. "Then you can meet someone at the party."

"Lane . . ." He sighed and shook his head. "Besides, I've seen your friends. You've set me up with your friends."

Lane winced. "That was a misunderstanding." In college, Allison had been perfectly normal. Dean's list, dorm resident adviser, total straight arrow. How was Lane supposed to know that Allison had gone on a piercing and tattooing frenzy about three seconds after she got her Ph.D. in economics?

"Right," Taylor said, sounding more than a little dubious. "My point is that if and when I decide to jump back into the dating game, my female of choice is going to be someone a little less"—he twirled his hand in the air—*"colorful."*

"There's nothing wrong with a little color." Heck, in Lane's opinion, Taylor's life needed some.

"My life has so much color I could open a crayon factory."

She peered at him over her sunglasses. "Oh, sure."

He started counting on his fingers: "I quit my job at the force. I'm barely surviving doing the private-eye gig. My biggest client to date is the scum of the universe. And I've got a sister who wants me to set up house with the tattooed lady."

"That's not color. That's ookey life stuff. And if you're barely surviving, you should take my money. I'm a big girl. You don't have to keep protecting me from the world."

Taylor gave her one of those looks, then cranked Francis Capra's engine. "I'm not taking your money," he said. "I don't need your money."

She pasted on an innocent smile. "Great. Then you can afford to take a girl out on a date."

"I'm not interested in dating for the sake of dating. I spent my childhood bouncing from house to house with no roots, nothing tying me down. I hated it, and I don't want to spend my adult years bouncing from woman to woman."

"But how will you ever meet the right woman if you won't—"

"Listen to me, Lane." He hit the clutch and shifted into first. "I'm *not* dating your friends. I've had it up to here with wacko women. The next girl I date is going to be the quintessential girl next door, complete with a dog, a pitcher of lemonade, and a white picket fence. Hell, she might even be a librarian." He glanced pointedly at her hands resting on his door, and she stepped back as he inched the car out of the parking spot.

"Normal, Lane," he said, raising his voice as he pulled farther away. "The next girl I date is going to be so normal she could pose for a Norman Rockwell painting."

Zoë sat alone on the far side of the cafeteria, away from the overpowering odor of fried fish fillets, plastic-textured pizza, and lime Jell-O. She was also away from the other teachers, who'd never quite managed to find room at their table for Zoë. For almost twenty-five years it had been pretty much the same—everyone else sticking together, knowing without being told that Zoë was somehow different. By now she was used to the seating arrangements.

What she wasn't used to was the torrent of Buster lust ricocheting through her brain when she should be thinking chaste lunch-monitor thoughts.

She'd gone her whole life without mooning over some guy. They weren't part of her agenda, her plan. So how had this one man so completely and totally infiltrated her thoughts? It wasn't fair. She was going to be twenty-five in a few days. She needed to be worrying about her council affidavit, about what she was going to tell her mother . . . about what she was going to do with the rest of her life. But was she worrying, considering, planning, anything-ing? *Nope. Not at all.* Instead she was acting like a mortal teenager with a high-school crush.

She sighed. This newfound obsession with Buster Taylor was incredibly distracting, to say the least.

With massive effort, she lassoed her thoughts and shoved them to the far corner of her brain. She had decisions to make, and so long as the cafeteria remained distraction-free, this was the perfect time to make them.

First . . . her council application. For over a month, the massive packet had gathered dust on her kitchen table. She'd finally sucked it up and sent in the main forms, but so far she hadn't worked up the nerve to submit the Affidavit of Mortal Disclosure. Considering how Tessa had reacted to her husband's revelations about his superpowers years ago, Zoë wasn't real keen on telling her mother the same thing.

But she had to tell her soon. The one thing Zoë had wanted for as long as she could remember was to be on the council, to work with her father and Hale. She reached into her tote bag and pulled out her wallet, sliding out her insurance card to peek at the photo she'd hidden underneath—her and Daddy after the first mission she'd been allowed to go on. Hale had gone, too. But since he'd turned invisible, he hadn't made it into the picture.

The mission hadn't been any big deal—just some reconnaissance work so the mortal police would find some missing children—but after, on the steps of Olympus, she'd felt proud, special. Like she belonged.

But that had been years ago. Since she was a halfling, if she wanted that feeling ever again, she had to formally apply for council admission. And that meant telling Tessa that—

"Kyle Martin eats worms!"

Zoë blinked, doubting the truth of the statement, but curious about the speaker. He was easy enough to find. Joey Tannin, the sixth-grade bully, was standing on a table, hurling Jell-O at poor Kyle, who probably didn't eat worms, but looked like he'd gladly swallow one or two if it would get him away from the bigger kid.

"Leave me alone!" Kyle howled, throwing his arms over his head to ward off bits of gelatin and marshmallows.

"Joey!" Zoë stood up and headed toward the fray, armed with her best don't-mess-with-the-lunch-monitor scowl. "What do you think you're doing?"

Joey turned, his foot landing in a clump of Jell-O before shooting out from under him. Jell-O went flying, along with a half-eaten slice of pizza, a pint of milk, and something that looked like a cookie but smelled like chicken.

Joey yelped. Zoë lunged.

His arms windmilled. Zoë focused, ready to perform some kid-saving levitation.

But nothing happened. Nothing good, anyway.

As Joey started to fall, tumbling off the table in a flurry of arms, legs, and Jell-O, Zoë started to panic. Her newfound telekinetic powers apparently weren't putting in overtime.

But she wouldn't give up that easily. In the last few milliseconds before Joey and the Jell-O went *splat*, Zoë lurched forward, aiming every smidgen of concentration right at the boy. She only needed a little bit—just a tiny levitation. Just enough to break his fall, but not enough to be noticed.

Focus . . .

She leaned forward.

Focus . . .

Just a little more. And then . . .

Ker-thunk!

Both she and Joey hit the ground. Zoë because she tripped; Joey because her levitation skills sucked.

Sally Simmons, who taught kindergarten, rushed to help Joey, who was glaring daggers at Kyle. Across the cafeteria, Mrs. Wilson, the gym teacher, crossed her arms over her chest, stared down her nose at Zoë, and shook her head.

Zoë blinked back tears. *Hopping Hera.* Why did she have to be such a klutz? All she'd had to do was levitate Joey—just for a second—and she couldn't even manage to stand on her own two feet long enough to do that.

And now she was sprawled out on the cafeteria floor, bits of lunch stuck to her, while all the other teachers stared at her as if she were a loon.

It was absurd to think the council would want her. Even if she did work up the courage to tell Tessa, she wasn't exactly a prime candidate. For one thing, she was an incompetent klutz. Hadn't her little stunt just now proved that? Her senses were wacky, her aim was sporadic, and she couldn't levitate worth a darn.

Besides, as a halfling, she already had one huge black mark against her. And considering the 487-page application, it was pretty clear the council wasn't into affirmative halfling action. They'd never approve her membership, not in a million years.

She sat up and hugged her knees to her chest, letting

57

her gaze drift over the other teachers, who very pointedly had not rushed to help her. She might as well face the truth: her dream of joining the council—of belonging—was just that, a dream.

If she knew what was good for her, she'd forget all about it. She'd rush home, rip the affidavit to shreds, formally withdraw her application, and put herself up for mortalization.

That was what she *should* do. Tessa would never be the wiser and, considering they'd erase her memory, neither would Zoë.

Sighing, she stood up. In front of her, teachers rushed to clean up Joey and Kyle and calm the other students. Zoë just stood stock-still, watching the hullabaloo.

Darn it, she wanted to belong. Wanted to be part of the council. Wanted to be like her dad and Hale.

And she certainly didn't want to forget her family— divided and offbeat though it was.

No, the affidavit wasn't going anywhere. Not without her signature, and certainly not in pieces.

Chapter Four

South Hollywood Elementary was actually in the heart of Hollywood, right between a bail bondsman and the new Tripoli Tower. The folks who lived nearby had raised havoc when developers had proposed the tower—apparently looming buildings ruined the neighborhood's atmosphere more than did loitering criminals—but Zoë loved it. She'd fallen into the habit of hanging out on the roof after school, enjoying the afternoon and listening to the buzz of conversation thirty stories below. . . . Not eavesdropping exactly, just letting the flow of words swim around in her head.

That was how she'd met first met Deena. She'd been eating Oreos—the insides, anyway—when the volunteer art teacher suddenly appeared, a devious grin matching her out-of-control mass of blond curls.

"I'm Deena," she'd said, stripping off her shirt to reveal a bikini top. "I've seen you around."

And then she'd plunked herself down next to Zoë, hiked her gauzy skirt up so her legs would get some sun, and grabbed a handful of cookies. "That bat who teaches gym said you were an odd bird, so I figured we'd hit it off," she added, then shoved an entire Oreo into her mouth.

For about two seconds, Zoë had considered leaving and finding a new tall building. But she'd always wanted a friend—a real one—and this Deena person seemed pretty open-minded.

So she had taken a risk; she'd stayed, and they'd fallen into a pattern. Zoë brought the cookies, Deena brought the beer, and every Friday they'd meet on the roof of the Tripoli Tower to compare their weeks. By the end of a year, two things had happened: Zoë finally had her first close friend, albeit one who didn't know *all* her secrets. And—despite liberal application of superstrong sunblock—she'd developed her very first sunburn. All of which made her feel that much closer to normal.

On this Friday before spring break, Zoë was already camped out on one of the patio lounge chairs they'd stowed when Deena arrived, schlepping a cooler, a tote bag, and binoculars.

Binoculars? Zoë sat up, tilting her head until her sunglasses slid down her sweat-slicked nose. She shoved them back into place and peered at her friend. "What's up with those?"

"My new project," Deena said, tossing Zoë a light beer.

"Ah," said Zoë, dread brewing somewhere near her stomach.

Deena sat on the edge of the lounge chair, her back

to Zoë, and began rummaging around in her bag.

"And exactly what is your new project?" Zoë asked Deena's back.

"You, of course."

Uh-oh. "Could you be a little more specific?"

"Sure," Deena said, turning around to face her. "Zoë Smith—school librarian, recluse, probable virgin, and perpetual single gal—is my new project."

Zoë rolled her eyes. "Thanks so much for clearing that up. But I'm still a teensy bit fuzzy on the 'project' part."

"Oh, *that*," said Deena, making a great show of sliding a pair of Ray-Ban sunglasses onto her face. "It involves a guy."

Major uh-oh. "Look, Deen, I like being alone."

Deena crossed her arms over her chest. "Are you actually telling me that you never fantasize about meeting Mr. Right?"

Zoë swallowed, remembering some particularly vivid fantasies about one very fantasizable man. "Fantasy and reality aren't the same thing. I'm happy being single."

"You just think you are because you haven't met the right guy." She brushed a loose curl off her forehead. "And you never will if you don't get out there and circulate."

"No, really. I don't want to do the dating thing." The response was not exactly true. Lately, she'd begun thinking that dating would be great. So would sex, for that matter in theory. But in reality, they would be very, very, very bad things. The whole concept of making love was rather terrifying. Instinctively, Zoë crossed her legs, wondering just how wild the wild thing would be for someone with her particular traits.

Besides, even if she could get a handle on her senses,

dating a mortal was out of the question. She needed to keep reminding herself of that. In addition to the super-sense thing—and on top of the whole "I'm not like other girls" speech—there was still her little problem with Hale.

Throughout her high school and college years, when-ever a mortal boy had so much as looked at her, Hale had made it absolutely clear that he intended to make sure she kept her virtue intact. It was bad enough for a mortal girl to have a big brother playing watchdog. Zoë had to put up with a huge brother who—when he threat-ened to pound a boy into a pile of mush—could really follow through. And the fact that he could turn invisible at will put a whole different spin on having someone looking over her shoulder.

Which was why it was just as well she hadn't found Buster Taylor, despite having spent two full nights look-ing for him on the Internet.

"Trust me, Zo." A bright smile flashed across Deena's face as her eyes widened. "Hey, I've got an idea. A really cute guy subleased some office space from Hoop a few months back. Maybe I could set you up with him. He used to be a cop," she added mischievously. "He's sweet in a 'me Tarzan, you Jane' sort of way."

Zoë had no idea what Deena was talking about, and her confusion must have shown, because Deena went on.

"I've met him once. I was painting Hoop's office—to surprise him, you know?—and this new guy wouldn't even let me move a file cabinet. Had to drop everything he was doing to come help me." She grinned. "Guess chivalry isn't dead, huh?"

"I'm not going out with your boyfriend's friends."

She aimed a stern look at Deena. "It's just not happening."

Deena shrugged. "Have it your way." She held up the binoculars. "We'll just have to find some fresh fish."

"No, no, *no*." Zoë shook her head, trying to emphasize the point. "I don't want to date fish. I don't want to date men. I'm perfectly happy."

Deena shot her a "yeah, right" look. "You spend your days cavorting with kids. You need some adult interaction."

Zoë gestured between the two of them. "We're interacting."

"Stimulating conversation."

"We're conversing."

"Sex."

Oh. Well. She couldn't really argue with that. "I'm really not ready for a commitment right now. I have a lot of issues." *There.* That was a highly plausible, millennium-gal kind of thing to say.

"Issues? You're about the least issuey person I know."

Zoë grimaced, mentally awarding herself a Best Actress Oscar.

"You sound like an eighties self-help book. And who's talking commitment, anyway? You just need to get out there. I mean, look at you. Except for your really stinky taste in clothes and that braid you wear, you're like some Greek goddess. If you'd just get out once in a while, you'd probably have your own fan club."

"What's wrong with my clothes?" Zoë asked, purposefully ignoring the Greek goddess comment.

Deena raked her eyes over Zoë, scoping her out from the top of her discount-store jumper all the way down to her formerly white Keds. "Boring. And shapeless. You've got no sex appeal going at all."

"I'm a librarian in an elementary school. I don't think a red Lycra tube dress is appropriate."

"I'm not suggesting a tube dress," Deena said, although the glint in her eye suggested otherwise. "And you're changing the subject. We're trying to figure out how to get you a guy."

"No, we're not. We're talking about—"

"What?"

Zoë threw up her hands. "I have no idea." That was the trouble with Deena. She set Zoë reeling even more than did jalapeño peppers.

"Well, there you go." With a little nod, Deena opened the binoculars case. She pulled out the glasses, went to the ledge at the side of the building, and focused on the street below.

Zoë tried to ignore her, but failed miserably. "What are you doing?"

"Scoping out potential men."

Hopping Hades. Zoë rolled her eyes skyward and thought of Oreos. She needed Oreo insides, and she needed them now. Comfort food. The itty-bitty flecks of cookie that stuck to the creamy goodness were as close to chocolate as she could come and not get knocked completely off-kilter. And she really needed some comfort now.

Leaning her head back, she cracked open an Oreo and dragged her teeth across the filling, enjoying the way the sugar tickled her tongue like a million tiny feathers, and letting Deena's comments—"Now there's a guy worthy of you!" . . . "This one's a loser." . . . "Uh-oh, check out the biker dude!"—swirl around her.

Deena was just starting to rattle off the attributes of a denim-clad cowboy—"Maybe he's a Texas oil man."—when Zoë heard the scream. Loud, high-pitched, and utterly desperate, it accosted Zoë's eardrums, rattled around in her head, and set her muscles twitching.

She bounded to her feet, dashed to the edge of the roof, then looked over. Focusing her superkeen eyesight, she saw, deep in the shadows on the far end of the side street, a grimy man with a beard and a jagged scar on his cheek. He gripped a woman around the waist and was tearing her purse from her shoulder. He shifted his victim, and Zoë caught a brief glimpse of vivid green eyes.

Mordichai? But that didn't make any sense at all.

Sense or not, Mordi pressed the barrel of a gun against the woman's throat with such force that Zoë could hear her sharp intake of breath.

Now or never.

Hurriedly she yanked her midnight blue training cloak out of her pack and swung it around her shoulders. She'd never once bested Mordichai—for that matter, she'd never once flown from more than six stories—but she could do this. She had to.

With a gulp, she slipped the fitted hood on, then did a nearly perfect swan dive into the mildly polluted Los Angeles air.

She was trying to steer the cloak when she saw the little boy. He'd run to escape and was now standing stock-still in the middle of the street. A Porsche veered sharply, horn blaring, barely missing the child, as Zoë tried to urge the cloak to move her faster.

"Well, there's nobody interesting on the Boulevard," she heard Deena say from somewhere above her. "I'm gonna scope out the side street." A pause, then, "Oh, my God!" Zoë somehow knew the binoculars were now aimed right at her, and she wondered if she'd lost her best—and only—friend. No time to think about that right now, though. She had a little boy to save.

A muddled cacophony attacked her ears: the whoosh of air past her head, screams from below, the blare of a car horn, Deena's feet pounding on the gravel, the slam of a door as Deena headed into the stairwell. She tried to focus, to sort it all out, and still to keep her goal in mind. On the street below, maybe-Mordi was pawing at the woman's throat, and Zoë heard the snap of metal as the chain of the woman's necklace broke.

The stoplight at the end of the street changed color, and a flood of cars started moving toward the child.

Approaching the ground, Zoë tried to remember the basics from Propulsion Cloak Training 101, but she must have overcompensated. Instead of gliding to a halt, she was now turning somersaults in the air.

Okay, everything is going to be fine. No need to panic. If she could just keep from tossing her Oreos, everything would be just dandy.

With supreme effort, she managed to slow herself and twist so she'd—hopefully—land on her feet. She aimed for somewhere between the kid and the oncoming traffic.

She missed her target, instead careening headfirst into maybe-Mordi's gut, knocking the man down and freeing the child's mother. His loot spilled onto the sidewalk, and he grappled for the money and jewelry as Zoë half flew, half ran for the kid. Still zooming, she scooped the shell-shocked boy up just as the car roared by, leaping backward with the kid squirming and squealing in her arms.

Not the most elegant rescue in the history of the world, but who cared? She'd done it! She'd set out to save the woman and her little boy, and she'd actually done it!

"Davy!" With a delighted cry, the woman held out her arms, tears streaming down her face.

Considering how many eyes were now watching her, Zoë wished she could come to a stop with even a smidgen of grace. Hardly. Instead her feet skimmed the ground, her legs frantically pumping to keep her upright and failing miserably. She and the child ended up in a heap right in front of the boy's mother—just in time to see maybe-Mordi running off down the sidewalk with the woman's purse tucked under his arm.

Oh, no, you don't.

Zoë was on her feet in seconds, sprinting after him.

"My purse!" the woman yelled.

That, too. But mostly Zoë wanted some answers. Not only that, but if she was going to get in trouble with the council, she wasn't about to go down alone.

"Mordichai!" she yelled, but he didn't even slow down as he turned the corner into a dark alley. She sped up. He might be stronger, but his speed and agility always decreased when he shape-shifted. She could maybe just catch up with him—

She whipped around into the alley, then leaped, managing to grab the back of his jacket. The two of them went down in a heap. "Give me that!" she yelled, grabbing for the woman's purse.

His smile was smug. "You can't win, Zoë. You know you can't."

Zoë gasped, realizing that until that moment she'd been clinging to the possibility that this villain really wasn't her cousin. "Why, Mordi? What are you doing?"

He leaped backward, taking her with her as he soared skyward. They spun—once, twice, three times—in midair before he landed in a perfect crouch.

Zoë landed with a thud on her rump.

She grimaced, wondering why the devil her powers had to come and go like people in Oz, when Mordi seemed to have completely reined his in. It really wasn't fair.

"Times change, Zoë. Gotta go with the flow."

He moved backward, and Zoë clambered to her feet, pacing him. "I don't think I'm up for any change that means I have to dress like a bum and attack mortals."

Mordi shrugged. "To each his own." He smiled and held up the woman's purse. "I'll just be running along."

She leaped as he spun around, her hand managing to close on his. He looked at their clasped hands and a slow grin spread across his face. "Why, cousin, I didn't know you cared."

Beneath her fingers, his flesh warmed, growing hotter and hotter the longer she held on. Her own sense of touch kicked in—exaggerating the heat generated by his flesh—and too late Zoë remembered Mordi's other special skill: pyrokinesis, the ability to conjure living flame.

The sickly sweet smell of seared flesh surrounded her as heat scored her palm, pain stabbing through her hand and up into her arm. She writhed in agony, fighting the pain and gagging against the smell, but not letting go. She had to hold on, had to keep him there. Had to find out what he was up to.

Red hot and throbbing, her hand blistered and charred from the heat of his skin, his touch so hot it was icy-cold. It was too much . . . too much, and she ripped her hand away as tears stung her eyes.

She stared, amazed, at her unmarred hand, and then remembered—Mordichai could summon both real and illusory fire. He was toying with her. Just as he always had when they were younger.

"You'll never win, Zoë. I know it; you know it." Mordi flipped her a little salute and took off running again.

"No!" Zoë cried, reaching once more for his clothes, bracing herself for the pain of the fire.

As she caught the hem of his jacket, he turned slightly. "It's no use," he said. "You know I'm stronger. I'll alwa—"

His eyes went wide with surprise as his body shimmered, and suddenly Zoë's hand was clutching the tail of a large sewer rat with Mordi's vivid green eyes. The woman's purse plopped onto the ground, and her wallet and necklace spilled onto the street.

Zoë snatched the Mordi-rat around its middle. "Annoying the way our powers fluctuate these days, isn't it?" she said, unreasonably happy to discover she wasn't the only one. "You may be stronger, but I'm bigger."

The rat's mouth clamped down on her hand, and she yelped as needle-sharp teeth pierced the tender skin, shaking her hand wildly to get loose. It worked, and he fell to the ground—right into a gutter labeled NO DUMPING. DRAINS TO OCEAN.

She let out a groan of frustration as she massaged her sore hand. In that gutter, he was gone for good. At least for now. And she was left with a million questions and no answers.

She collapsed onto the curb and dropped her head to

her knees, letting out an exhausted sigh. Whatever the heck Mordi thought he was doing, he hadn't gotten away with it.

She heard the patter of approaching feet and looked up. A small group, led by the woman clutching the little boy, was rounding the corner. *Uh-oh.* She really needed to get the heck out of Dodge.

The woman knelt beside her, breathless, as she scooped up her purse and jewelry. "I don't know who the hell you are, but thank you."

"You're welcome." Zoë put her hand to her face, relieved to find her hood was still in place. A police siren sounded in the distance, and Zoë stood up. Behind them, the crowd applauded and snapped pictures. *Oh, sweet Hera, the newspapers.* Zoë cringed. "I should really get out of here now."

"Wait!" The woman grabbed Zoë's arm.

Zoë glanced around, frantic, wondering how the heck she was going to get away.

"Please," the woman said.

The siren drew closer, and she stumbled backward, needing to get away from the flashing camera bulbs and the siren. She was afraid that if she stayed too long, she'd somehow be recognized.

"No, really," she said, stepping back again. "I need to—"

"That's a wrap, everyone!" That was Deena's voice, breathless from running, and Zoë flashed her a grateful smile.

"We hope you all enjoyed watching our rehearsal for *Boopsey Saves the World.*" Deena waved at the small crowd gathered on the far sidewalk. "We'll be running through the space alien segment in ten minutes, five blocks that direction. Go early for the best seats." She gestured toward the end of the street and, with cameras and tote bags in tow, the herd of tourists moved down the side street toward Hollywood Boulevard.

As the crowd stampeded away, Deena flashed a triumphant smile, and a wave of relief washed over Zoë. Deena hadn't disappeared. In fact, just the opposite. Deena was pretty much taking charge, and now she grabbed Zoë's arm and tugged her the wrong way through the tower's emergency exit.

Zoë was so relieved, she didn't even realize that the woman and her toddler had followed until the door closed behind them.

"A movie?" the woman asked, incredulity in her voice. She looked from Zoë to Deena, then back to Zoë again, all the while balancing the little boy on her hip.

"Uh," Zoë said stupidly, then looked to Deena for help.

"We've got some bigwig backers," Deena said, and the woman turned to look at her. "Some heavy-duty product placement."

The woman shifted the child. "Uh-huh."

"No, really," Deena said. She pointed to Zoë's propulsion cloak. "It's specially designed. Works like a hang glider. Has microthin, superstrong wires in there."

"Really?" the woman asked, almost sounding like she was actually buying Deena's wacko story. She took a step forward, and Zoë took a step back, keeping Deena's microthin superwires just out of reach.

"Absolutely," Deena said. She turned to Zoë, her eyebrows riding high above her Ray-Bans. "Right?"

"Oh, yeah," Zoë said. "I was up there getting ready to shoot my scene. And, uh, I saw that guy, and I figured

I could help." She nibbled on her lower lip, wondering if she sounded like a total idiot or just a partial one. "But it's top secret. You won't say anything to the, uh, newspapers, will you?"

"Please," Deena added. "If other special effects companies knew . . ."

"I won't say anything," the woman said, snuggling close to her little boy. "I mean, I owe you, after all." She squinted. "A movie, huh? I didn't even see a camera."

Zoë looked at Deena. "On top of the tower," she said, only barely making it a statement rather than a question.

"We were hoping not to draw too much of a crowd."

"Exactly," added Zoë, getting more into the spirit. "We're taking a huge risk not filming on a closed set."

"Oh," said the woman, still looking bewildered. "Well. Lucky for me you took a chance."

"You have no idea," Zoë said.

The woman caught her gaze and smiled, holding out her hand. "Thank you. For saving Davy, and for getting that creep off me."

"Do you know him? What did he want?" Maybe this woman had the answer, because Zoë couldn't think of one reason why Mordi would be robbing mortals.

"I don't have a clue." She bit her lip. "I'm just glad it's over."

"Money and jewelry," Deena said, pointing to the purse and necklace the woman still held in her hand. The chain was wrapped around her palm, and the stone pendant swung free. "Your basic mugger staples."

"He's a stupid mugger," the woman said. "I'm flat broke, and I bought this thing for a buck at a thrift shop." She grinned. "I thought it was so ugly that it was fun."

"Ugly?" Zoë asked. "It's fabulous."

The woman raised an eyebrow. "Really?"

"She has lousy taste," Deena said with a laugh. Zoë scowled at her, but she just shrugged. "Well, you do."

The woman pressed the stone into Zoë's palm. "Take it."

"Oh, I couldn't."

"Please. It's the least I can do."

Zoë closed her fingers over the smooth stone. It seemed to fit her hand, and the stone pulsed warmly in her palm. "Okay, then. Thank you."

The little boy yawned, and his mother smiled. "It's nothing compared to what you gave me. I thought Davy . . ." She blinked, her eyes moist. "Anyway, thank you again." She cocked her head. "I don't suppose you want to tell me the name of your production company?"

"No," said Zoë.

"Can't," added Deena, flashing Zoë a glare. "Top secret, remember."

"Right." Then, with a wink and a smile, she slipped out the emergency exit, leaving Zoë and Deena staring at each other in the service area.

As soon as the door clicked shut, Deena put a hand on her hip, and Zoë braced for a barrage of questions.

"So," Deena finally said. "I'm guessing those issues you mentioned run a little deeper than just not wanting to share a bathroom with a guy, huh?"

Chapter Five

Deep beneath the Washington Monument, the American base of the Venerate Council of Protectors hummed with activity, computers churning, viewscreens displaying precise layouts of the nation's cities. In the ops center, Donis and Hale sat in front of a static-filled image of Zephron, the high elder.

Hale drummed his fingers on his knees, waiting for the holographic transmission to clear. He had no idea why he'd been summoned to the center, and he hoped like Hades it wasn't going to interfere with his vacation plans.

On his shoulder, Elmer stretched and yawned. *Well, this is fun—not! I thought you said we'd be in Greece by now. . . .*

Hale scowled. The little ferret had a heck of a mouth on him. "Quiet," he whispered. "Do you want to get me in trouble?"

Donis shot them both a look. "If you insist on bringing your furry sidekick, you should teach him some manners."

"Have *you* ever tried to teach a ferret manners?"

Hey! I've read Miss Manners. I know which fork to use. What do I look like? A heathen?

"He's talking back, isn't he?" Donis asked, eyeing Elmer suspiciously.

Hale rolled his eyes, wondering for the umpteen-millionth time why he had to have been born with the ability to talk with animals. At least Zoë and Donis got some peace and quiet once in awhile. Even in the park, when Hale was alone . . . well, let's just say no one knew all the really nutty jokes the squirrels tended to shout out.

Elmer nipped at his earlobe. *Yo, Hale, my man. You're not really mad, are you? Not at little ol' Elmer. Are you?*

For about half a second, Hale considered letting Elmer stew. Then he shook his head. Elmer had been his buddy for three years, and before that, Elmer's dad, Ercel, had been his constant companion. They were family, he and Elmer. And he couldn't stay mad at family. "But stay quiet," he whispered. "We don't want to irritate Zephron."

As he was laying down the law to Elmer, the holograph shimmered, coming into focus.

"Hieronymous is attempting to rally the Outcasts," Zephron announced, and Hale's stomach twisted. He turned to look at his father, and saw that Donis's eyes were wide, confirming what Hale already knew—this was bad. Very bad.

Hoo-boy. This sucks big-time.

"But the new treaty—" Donis began.

"Exactly," Zephron said.

The council Web site had recently been filled with news about the negotiations between the council and the mortal heads of state. The original Mortal-Protector Treaty had been in place since 1970, the year Hale was born. Under its terms, only a select few mortals who worked for the top-secret Liaison Office knew of the existence of Protectors and their governing body. Under the newly proposed treaty, council members would take a more open role in society, aiding mortals as always, but abandoning the need for absolute secrecy.

Hieronymous and his Outcast followers, however, didn't belong to the council, and had no intention of working for mortals.

"Surely you don't think—" Donis began.

"If he does manage to rally the Outcasts, they can wreak enough havoc that the mortals will fear us. Everything we've worked for will break down. Our relationship with the mortal governments will be destroyed, our hopes for a broader treaty will be squelched, and we will likely end up in a war with the Outcasts." He paused, his image flickering. "How many mortal lives would be lost in the battle?"

"But what can he do?" Hale asked. "He's an Outcast. He's under constant supervision. He can't even communicate with other Outcasts without using a monitored device. He's forbidden to use his powers except in private. So how can he possibly interfere?"

"He is forbidden, true. His offspring, however, is not." Zephron's image shimmered. "You have heard of Aphrodite's girdle?"

Hale and Donis exchanged a look. "Who hasn't?"

Hale asked, confused by the change in topic. "It's a bed-time story."

"The belt worn by Aphrodite centuries ago," Donis added. "She forged it with her powers, and when she wore it, anyone she desired fell hopelessly in love with her."

"Exactly," said Zephron. "And there's more. The belt has many unexplored properties. Its centerpiece, for example, has many mysterious characteristics. For one, that stone can act as a transmitter under certain circumstances. At the right time, at the right place, a skilled Protector could speak directly to all Outcasts, circumventing all our efforts to forestall communications among the Outcasts."

"And what exactly are the right circumstances?" Donis pressed.

Zephron looked him straight in the eye. "A lunar eclipse coupled with a certain planetary alignment."

"When?" asked Hale.

"Next Wednesday. Midnight exactly."

Hale's head was spinning. "I'm still confused. Are you saying Hieronymous has this stone? Hasn't the belt been missing for centuries?"

"He does not have the stone. Yet. But I'm certain he is aware of the legend."

This was the part about being on the council that drove Hale nuts. No one would just come out and say what was on their mind. Everything had to be riddles and legends. Mysticism was all well and good, but a little straight talking would surely move things along.

What legend? Elmer asked.

"My question exactly," Hale said. "What legend?"

Donis closed his eyes. "Mother of Zeus, now I remember." He turned and faced Hale. "There's a legend that says that prior to the night the moon vanishes from the sky, the stone from Aphrodite's girdle will find its way to the hand of a halfling, who will then be welcomed to or shunned from the council."

"Zoë and Mordichai," Hale whispered. "They have the same birthday. Next Tuesday. Right before the eclipse."

"Two halflings, born on the same day, both nearing their twenty-fifth birthday." Zephron paused. "One has not yet completed her application. The other seeks admission to the council, and yet is the child of Hieronymous."

"Okay. I know Zoë hasn't turned in the Affidavit of Mortal Disclosure. She doesn't want to freak out her mother. But you don't really think Mordi's gonna chuck it all and throw in with his dad? I mean, I grew up with him. I helped train him. Zoë used to play with him. He's a bit of a weasel, but he's okay."

Zephron's lips thinned. "We shall see, won't we? It appears, gentlemen, that the council admission tests for young Zoë and master Mordichai have been determined."

Hale swallowed. "So where will this Outcast ceremony take place? Here? On Olympus?"

Zephon shook his head. "No. The ceremony must take place at a certain longitude and latitude."

"Where?" asked Hale, dreading the answer.

"The grounds of the Griffith Observatory."

Hale swallowed. "That's in Los Angeles."

"So it is."

"Zoë's in Los Angeles."

"It would appear the legend is accurate."

Hale rubbed his temples, trying to stave off the beginnings of a monster of a headache. "So basically, what you're saying is that the fate of the world rests with my sister or Mordi. And if either one fails their test, we're in big trouble."

"That is so. Unless you recover the stone first, of course."

"Excuse me?"

"You will look for the stone as well," Zephron said. "It is far too dangerous an artifact to be lost in the mortal world." He looked straight at Hale, who saw his vacation go flying out the window. Except, of course, there wasn't a window this far underground.

"Why Hale?" Donis said.

"Why me?" Hale asked at exactly the same time.

Why not you? This fits right in with your undercover mortal job. Elmer said, an obvious snicker in his squeaky ferret voice. *Fashion accessories, I mean.*

Hale scowled. Despite his sister's, his father's, and his ferret's teasing, Hale's assignment suited him just fine. Of course, being a romance novel cover model wasn't a typical disguise. It wasn't like he was a cop or a mild-mannered reporter. Still, it had some perks—good hours, good pay, gorgeous women. Plenty of time to search out and battle evil.

But that hadn't meant Elmer teased him any less frequently.

"Why me?" Hale repeated.

"Hieronymous has minions everywhere, and this mission requires the utmost discretion. Hieronymous won't think it's odd that you are visiting your sister. Especially if the apparent purpose of your trip is to remind her of proper council protocol and procedure."

Hale squinted. "Huh?"

Zephron's image shuddered, shifting and shimmering until he was gone, replaced by video footage of a news program—"Witnesses say the hooded female actually flew thirty stories from the roof of the Tripoli Tower. . . ." The reporter's voice faded out, and Hale cringed as Zephron's image reappeared.

"You're her mentor, after all," Zephron said. "It's only natural that you travel to Los Angeles to discuss such indiscretions."

"Maybe she had a good reason," Hale said, trying to suppress a smile. He should be annoyed, he knew. After all, she could've gotten hurt. But she'd actually flown. Which meant things were definitely shaping up in the fate-of-the-world department. Plus, he was going to California. Maybe he'd have a day or so to do some thong watching after all.

"Hale," Donis said, a note of warning in his voice.

Hale shrugged. "Or maybe we should just dump old Uncle H. into the pit and get on with our lives." It seemed like a reasonable enough solution. Hieronymous bad. Punishment good.

"There is the small matter of proof," Zephron said.

"So you're not even sure Hieronymous is planning this Outcast-a-thon?"

"There are changes afoot, my friends," Zephron said, which didn't exactly answer Hale's question. "Donis, you will travel with me to Olympus. We must prepare for the possibility that Mordichai will deliver the stone to Hieronymous before the eclipse."

"Thanks so much for the vote of confidence," Hale muttered.

"We hope for the best, but will prepare for the worst."

Zephron's smile was grandfatherly and genuine. "The fact that I am sending you to recover the stone is all the proof you should require of my faith in your abilities."

Hale sighed. He never could handle compliments. "Fine. Forget Greece. California, here I come."

Woo-hoo! screeched Elmer. *Maybe we can work in a trip to Hollywood Boulevard or even Disneyland. Maybe watch a taping of* The Tonight Show! He started humming "Hooray For Hollywood," and Hale rolled his eyes. Los Angeles wasn't high up on his list. The smog made him sneeze, and when he sneezed, he tended to turn invisible. Which was never easy to explain—even in a town like L.A. that had seen it all before.

He pulled his thoughts back to the problem at hand. "So I'll just tell the Zoëster what's going on. We can scour the town and get this wrapped up in no time." And maybe he could still work in some beach time.

"No," said Zephron.

"Excuse me?" Hale said.

Donis leaned forward and stared at the head of the council. "Don't you think my daughter would have a better chance at succeeding if she knew what she was doing?"

"She is a halfling," Zephron said. "And from what I understand, her skill level leaves much to be desired."

"She's my daughter."

"I cannot bend the rules out of friendship. As a halfling, she must finalize her application, and she must demonstrate that she is worthy. Fairly. It appears that her test will be to protect the stone. I can think of no better demonstration of her worth."

"But if she doesn't know she's supposed to protect it . . ."

81

"If she is truly worthy, she will sense the nature of her mission. She will protect the stone not because she has been told to, but because she *has* to."

"What a crock of—"

Donis closed his hand—hard—over Hale's arm.

"Ouch!" Glaring at his dad, Hale flopped back in his chair, then immediately bounced forward when Elmer squeaked.

Zephron ignored him, focusing on Donis. "Until young Zoë submits her affidavit, she must not be told of the legend of the stone. Her decision to abandon the mortal world must not be tainted."

Hale frowned. "Even if that means risking Mordi's getting the stone and turning it over to Uncle H.?"

"Even so," said Zephron. "Her safety—*our* future—depends on it."

"Zoë'll do fine," Hale said, hoping he sounded optimistic. The truth was, Mordi was almost as powerful as a full council member, and Hale didn't want Zoë fighting the little weasel. After all, Zoë could barely control a propulsion cloak, and she still hadn't managed to rein in those damn senses of hers. Hell, the girl hadn't even mastered telekinesis.

And now some ancient legend had gone and dumped the fate of the world into Zoë's lap. How absurd was that?

If Hale ever met the head dude in charge of legends and portents, he intended to give the fellow one very stern talking-to.

Taylor banged his fist against Francis Capra's steering wheel and wondered when he'd lost his grip on reality. Just what the hell was he thinking? He ran a hand

through his hair. Of course, the answer was obvious—
he wasn't thinking at all. Or, rather, he'd quit thinking
with his head and started thinking with certain other
parts of his anatomy. Parts that really shouldn't be running his life, thank you very much.

Which explained why he was now parked in front of
Zoë Smith's Studio City apartment complex at nine
o'clock at night, trying to work up the nerve to ask her
out for a drink.

Not that he had a chance in hell. She might be a ten
on his perfect-woman scale—pretty, smart, lacking in
obvious tattoos—but she still thought he was the devil
incarnate.

And maybe for a few seconds there, he had been.
Except now he'd fixed all that. He'd dumped Parker, and
he wasn't sniffing out dirt on Emily anymore. So maybe
if he just let Zoë know . . .

For the second time, he banged his fist against the
steering wheel. *Taylor, you are pathetic.*

He put his hand on the key, ready to crank the engine
and get out of there, but couldn't quite do it. Dammit,
he wanted to see her. Wanted her to know he wasn't the
creep she'd pegged him for. Wanted it so much it was
making him crazy.

And then—as if his thoughts had conjured her—there
she was, heading down the stairs right in front of him.
His hand froze on the key, and for a moment he just
looked at her.

Her trademark braid was still there, keeping tight control of a mass of coppery hair that would likely stir up
a shower of sparks when released. Her plain-Jane jumper
was gone, replaced with truly ugly orange gym shorts
topped by a sweatshirt that looked to be at least five

sizes too big. But despite the horrible clothes, Taylor was even more convinced that she was the loveliest creature he'd ever seen. He'd done quite a bit of daydreaming over the last few days, and she more than fulfilled every one of his Technicolor fantasies.

No doubt about it: the woman was sexy. Sexy yet innocent. The kind of woman who'd one day have a little house with a picket fence on the outside and a dresser full of red lace underwear on the inside.

Interesting, said his heart. *Dangerous,* warned his head.

Yes, indeed. Zoë Smith was exactly the kind of woman who could get under his skin. Who'd already managed to do just that.

She fidgeted with the keys in her hand, then glanced to her left. Taylor followed her gaze, realizing that she must be looking at the line of mailboxes.

Tires squealed down the block, and Taylor turned to see a polished black Ferrari convertible make the turn, then career down the street, sliding at the last minute into the loading zone in front of Zoë's apartment. Zoë took the last few stairs at a run, looking happier than a kid at Christmas.

Fighting pangs of green jealousy, Taylor squinted, trying to get a better look at the driver, who was now half standing and hugging Zoë over the closed car door. He was tall and dark, with perfect pecs and a perfect tan. Hell, the guy looked like he should be on *Baywatch* or something. He was the quintessential Los Angeles guy—with a hot car, no less. And he was hugging Zoë. *Well, shoot.*

Still . . .

It could be nothing. He could be a friend from work.

Her personal trainer. A traveling encyclopedia salesman.

As he watched, the guy sneezed—and then he was gone.

Taylor blinked. The car was there, but no guy. He blinked again, then squinted, trying to get a better look. Was the guy on the floorboards? Probably, because Zoë was still chatting away, looking perfectly happy to be carrying on a conversation with air.

Okay, this is very—

The guy was back.

Taylor pulled off his sunglasses and rubbed his eyes. He really needed to get more sleep.

Zoë jumped back from the curb as the *Baywatch* guy pulled away with a wave, then took off down the street, his car humming like a dream. She just stood there looking after him, then turned so that she was looking in Taylor's direction.

He cursed.

Without thinking, he ducked down. Not exactly the world's most comfortable position, but at least he was hidden behind Francis Capra's door frame. And being hidden was key. Because the last thing he needed was for her to see him and blow all his good intentions to smithereens.

Zoë wiped her face with the little gym towel draped around her neck, but couldn't wipe the grin off her face.

Hale was in town. What a wonderful surprise!

When he'd zipped up in the Ferrari, she'd assumed he was just dropping by on his way to the Mediterranean. But instead of Greece, he'd told her he was camped out in a suite at the Beverly Wilshire, and would see her tomorrow after he'd had his share of room service and a few other accoutrements of high living.

She lifted her braid and ran the towel along the back of her neck, stifling a grin. Her brother liked to live well. For that matter, he liked the whole Protector lifestyle. She didn't need to wonder what he'd think of her silly pseudocrush on a mortal—he'd be mortified.

He'd also be mortified that tomorrow she'd promised to tell her deep, dark secrets to a mortal who wasn't her mother. It was a conversation Zoë wasn't exactly looking forward to. Fortunately, Deena'd had plans with Hoop, and that had bought Zoë some time before the these-are-my-issues conversation. In the end, though, Zoë had promised she'd give Deena the skinny. So now she had one evening before she had to reveal all. No wonder her stomach was twitching so much.

And Deena was the least of her problems. The big problem was Mordi. She should have reported him to the council right away. She knew that, but she hadn't done it. Ratting on Mordi would mean confessing to interfering, to using her propulsion cloak, to revealing herself to a mortal, and to getting her picture in the newspapers.

All those confessions would mean big, ugly black marks on her application. Her application was already on shaky ground; she wasn't too keen on messing up her chances even more.

Still, she really should tell. For one thing, the council probably already knew. And even if her stunt had gone unnoticed . . . well, the council needed to know if Protectors—even halflings—were running around mugging innocent women.

It was all so very odd. And she hadn't a clue what her cousin was up to. Mordi'd never been mean. A little moody, maybe, but never cruel. Also, council members swore an oath to protect mortals, not attack them.

Of course, Mordi wasn't a member yet. But, like Zoë, he was getting close. Closer, even, since he'd surely already submitted his Affidavit of Mortal Disclosure. After all, unlike Tessa, his mother had known for years. But this mugger stunt would be a definite black mark against him. Not to mention it was just plain rude.

She frowned, frustrated by the thoughts running through her head. Maybe she should go put in another thousand or so sit-ups. Or chin-ups. She hated chin-ups, but if that didn't get her mind off Deena and her punishment and Mordi—not to mention those ever-present thoughts about that Buster Taylor—nothing would.

Armed with the promise of an evening free of Buster-Mordi-punishment-Deena-revelation thoughts, she headed for her mailboxes, humming the theme from *Rocky*. She'd left her glasses in her apartment, and now she checked out her mail, trying to decide if it was even worth bothering to get—a few bills, a Pottery Barn catalog, and a "you could be a winner" letter from Publishers Clearing House. *Boring.*

She took a peek at the mail inside Mrs. Callahan's box, wondering if hers was any better. It was probably some sort of felony offense to examine someone else's mail that way, but Mrs. Callahan was forever forgetting to pick up the stuff, and Zoë hated to see the sweet woman do without something important.

Junk, junk, junk, Victoria's Secret catalog, junk, AARP magazine, junk, junk, check. Aha.

She circled the staircase and peered through the woman's door, not wanting to wake her if she was asleep. No worries there; the woman was up, watching

Wheel of Fortune. Zoë rapped on the door.

"Well, hello, dear," Mrs. Callahan said, after she'd checked through the peephole.

"Hi, Mrs. Callahan."

"Mary, dear. I've told you a hundred times."

Zoë smiled. "Hi, Mary."

"You're all dressed up. Do you have a date?"

"Uh, these are my workout clothes."

Mary patted her hand. "A man who'll love you when you look like hell will love you always."

Somehow that didn't make Zoë feel better. Especially since there was no man. No boyfriend, no dates, no social life whatsoever. Except for throwing herself off a thirty-story building, the high point of her day was this: chatting about her less than trendy wardrobe with her eighty-something neighbor.

Mary opened the door wider. "Would you like some spice cake and tea? I was just having a snack and watching Vanna. That woman's outfits, well, I tell you . . ."

"No, thanks." Spice cake sounded, well, too spicy. And Zoë didn't need to have one of her food moments in front of the woman. "I just wanted to let you know that I got a glimpse of the mail earlier while the postman was filling the boxes. I think your check's in there."

"Oh, that's lovely." She smiled, her eyes crinkling behind Coke-bottle glasses. "I don't suppose you saw my"—she lowered her voice—"*catalog*."

"Your catalog?"

"You know," she said, her voice still in a whisper, "Victoria's Secret."

Zoë stifled a giggle. "Yeah, I think I saw it there."

The woman let out a sigh. "Marvin would have loved that store. Back in my day, all we had was Sears Roebuck." She leaned closer. "That's just not the same."

Zoë nodded, sure that if she spoke, she'd laugh.

"You're sure about the cake?"

"I'm sure," Zoë said. "Would you like me to bring you your mail?"

"No, thank you, dear. I'll get it tomorrow when the postman comes." She patted Zoë's hand. "He's quite a hunk, you know."

"Right." She'd never considered Mr. Davidson a hunk, but then she wasn't over eighty.

She said good-bye, then headed back toward the staircase, sure she was grinning like an idiot. If she was that spunky when she hit eighty-five, she'd consider it a victory.

She headed back up the stairs, mentally ticking off all the things she needed to do before going to bed. She was debating whether or not the dishes could wait until morning—she was on spring break after all—when she felt it.

Someone was watching her.

She whipped around, her head cocked, trying to focus her hearing. She heard the gentle, sandpaperish sound of the cat in 4B bathing, Vanna White and Pat Sajak chit-chatting on Mary's television, someone cooking in the apartment behind the mailboxes. She sniffed . . . fettucine Alfredo, garlic bread, Caesar salad, and red wine. The guy in 2A must have a hot date.

None of the sounds or smells seemed threatening, yet something wasn't right.

She listened again, this time picking up sounds from the street behind her. Teenagers laughing and smoking in front of the liquor store down the street, crickets chirping in the dark, the wind whispering through the bushes. And something else. Someone breathing.

Who? Her gaze roamed the street. All was quiet, no people around at all. Even the teenagers were out of her line of sight. And this sound was close by. She didn't know why, but she had a funny feeling. She shivered, her eyes drawn to a perfectly restored Mustang convertible parked right across the street from her building. She frowned, sure it didn't belong to one of the residents.

Curious, she took a step toward it, and the breathing seemed louder. *Odd.* The top was down. It wasn't as if there was anyone *in* the car. She cocked her head. Or was there?

Feeling a little silly for being paranoid, she concentrated on the door panel. Metal was always the most difficult to see through, but not impossible, and after she'd taken a few deep breaths, the door shimmered, then became transparent.

Zoë gasped, her fingers flying to her mouth and a dozen butterflies suddenly decided to perform the Dance of the Sugarplum Fairies in her stomach.

Buster Taylor.

She was thrilled.

She was pissed.

He was spying on her.

What did he think? That Emily was going to bring some young lover over to Zoë's apartment? That Zoë was running a love nest for wayward teachers?

Sinking down to sit on the front step, she balanced her chin on her hand, trying to stay calm. This was the man she'd been fantasizing about, remember? The man she'd hoped would call her, ask her out for coffee, proposition her for a wild night of living out X-rated fantasies.

The mortal man she'd hoped she'd never see again so she wouldn't have to make hard decisions.

Well, she should be grateful. He'd just made her decision for her. She certainly wasn't going to entertain fantasies of some lying, spying mortal. No matter how intriguing he might have seemed.

Time to teach him a lesson.

She stood up quietly, then checked the street for witnesses. Empty. *Good.*

She ran forward, then sprang up, landing on her hands and whipping up and over into a flip—finally ending up right on the hood of his car. It was a landing worthy of at least a 9.5—*and the crowd goes wild!* She stifled a self-satisfied giggle. Too bad Hale had missed it. He would have been impressed.

As the car shook, Buster sat up, his eyes wide. Zoë dropped into a crouch, which put her face-to-face with him. Just a single thin piece of windshield glass separated them.

Her heart upped its rhythm, and Zoë shivered, wondering if she'd just made her eight zillionth huge mistake of the day.

His face clearing, Buster smiled, and her body started to melt.

"Where the devil did you come from?" he asked, standing up to look at her over the windshield.

All of her intentions to be firm and no-nonsense headed out for coffee, leaving her with a fuzzy, funny feeling in her stomach and the overwhelming desire to throw herself over the windshield and kiss him senseless.

Which was probably not a good idea.

"Does it matter?" she asked, trying to be nonchalant

as she climbed over the windshield and settled into the passenger seat. "I'm here now."

"No kidding you're here. But how'd you get here? What are you? One of the Flying Wallendas?"

"Not exactly." She steeled herself, trying to ignore the way his eyes burned into her, the way the scent of his after-shave tickled her nose. He was spying on her, after all. Trying to find dirt and sneaking around to do it. "What are you?" she asked. "A professional jerk, or just an amateur?"

She mentally congratulated herself—at least until he grinned. Then she wondered if maybe her zinger wasn't all that zingy after all. "What are you grinning about?" she asked, not even trying to keep the irritation out of her voice.

"You."

"Me?"

"You're so damn sure I'm here doing dastardly investigator things." He'd lowered his voice, hunching his shoulders and waggling his fingers like an evil magician.

She grimaced, refusing to be amused by his silliness. "Why are you staking out my apartment? Emily and I don't hang out together."

"I'm not looking for Emily." He stretched his arm out, hooking it over the back of her seat.

"Oh." Zoë sucked in air and tried to keep her composure despite his proximity. "So what are you doing? Looking to interview kids she went to kindergarten with? Find out if she ever showed off her underpants?"

"Not a bad idea," he said. "Except that that would be sleazy. And I'm off the case."

Her breath quickened. "Really? Why?"

"Emily's clean and her husband's a jerk. Do I need a better reason?"

"No. Those are good reasons." Gutsy, too, if what he'd said about needing the work had been true. Without planning to, she smiled at him, wide and genuine. "So why are you here?"

He leaned toward her, close enough that she could feel his heat and smell the lingering scent of soap on his skin. "You," he said simply. "I'm here because of you."

"Me?" she repeated, sure her voice was squeaking. "Why?"

One shoulder rolled slightly. "I came by tonight hoping to ask you out."

"Oh." He wanted to go out with her? This incredible man? The man who had taken up residence in her dreams? This man wanted to go out on a date . . . with her? "Really?"

"You've been on my mind all week. Constantly. Pervasively. Hell, I can't do anything without thinking about you." He smiled, his eyes dark, dangerous. Dangerous to her heart, to her head. "You've become my obsession."

She smiled, unreasonably delighted at the thought of being someone's obsession. That wasn't exactly status quo for her.

But he's a mortal, Zoë. Dangerous territory, very dangerous.

She took a deep breath. *Righto. That it is.* She shouldn't get involved, *couldn't* get involved. No matter how tempting he might be . . .

"I should go."

"So you hate me, right?"

"What? No." Hate him? Her feelings were a heck of a long way from hate. "Why on earth would I hate you?"

93

He shrugged, looking sheepish and adorable. "That stuff about Emily. All of this." He spread his arms, indicating the car, the street. "I mean, most men use the telephone."

"I have a feeling you're not most men."

The smile that touched his lips just about brought her to tears. "No," he said, reaching for her. "I'm not."

She gasped as he took her hand, the pad of his thumb caressing her palm. Like a phoenix, she burst into flames, only to be reborn over and over and over from his touch. She squirmed, trying to settle her insides, trying to block the wonderful sensations shooting down the tips of her fingers all the way to the ends of her hair.

She was on fire. She was *alive*.

She was anxious and fascinated and oddly at peace, all at the same time.

Oh, mother of Zeus. How she wanted his touch, wanted his hands on every part of her body. Wanted more than that, so much more.

But she couldn't handle it, shouldn't even try.

Every cell was singing, every atom in her body spinning out of control. She'd left his car and was floating on a rainbow of colors, electricity zipping through her, leaving her gasping for breath. Leaving her wanting, needing.

Terrified.

She summoned her strength and pulled her hand away, the loss of contact leaving her hollow, a shell of herself. She couldn't do this. She couldn't get involved.

She clasped her hands in her laps and tried not to cry.

"Are you okay?" Real concern shown in his eyes.

"I'm so sorry. But I'm . . . I'm . . ." She took a deep

breath, grappling for an excuse. "I want to, so help me, I do. But I can't. I'm not. . . . There's some—"

"I know." His jaw tightened.

"Know?"

"You're already seeing someone." He said the words like a curse. "Right?"

In a way, he'd pegged the situation just right. She was taken. Not by a man, but what did it matter? The bottom line was still the same.

"Yes," she said, the words costing her everything. "I'm not available."

From the far end of the street, Mordi watched Zoë talking with the investigator. That made twice he'd seen her with the man—first at the library and now here. And from the look in her eye, Mordi doubted this would be the last time they would be together.

Interesting.

And potentially useful.

His mind turned over the possibilities. The stone was lost in the mortal world. True, he had use of Hieronymous's tracking device, but it was proving sadly unreliable. All it seemed to be able to determine was that the stone was in Los Angeles. But L.A. was a rather large haystack.

Good old-fashioned legwork had led him to the thrift store where the stone had turned up. And through good, old-fashioned luck, he'd seen the woman who bought the gem. But when he'd tried to snag it, Zoë had interfered. His target had retrieved her purse, and Mordi had lost track of the gem. It could be with the first woman, it could be with Zoë, or it could be lost somewhere on the streets of L.A.

If he had to go poking around in the mortal world, what better way than to enlist the aid of a mortal? Especially a mortal who would, quite likely, be in a position to know if the stone reached Zoë.

Mordi smiled. Tomorrow he would engage the services of Mr. George Bailey Taylor, private investigator.

Chapter Six

The ringing phone woke Taylor from a particularly pleasant dream. He groped for the handset, finally grabbing it and pulling it to his ear. "What?"

"Pardon me, Mr. Taylor." The cultured voice was smarmy and definitely not that of the librarian of whom he'd been dreaming. "Did I wake you?"

Taylor glanced at the clock. Almost noon. "No. Up for hours."

"I have a job for you, if you have the time to take it on."

Taylor sat up and swung his feet to the floor, trying to ignore the dull ache in his head. "Um, yeah, sure. What kind of case?"

"A stolen gemstone. A family heirloom. I'd like it located and returned. To me." The polished voice paused. "I'm prepared to pay your hourly rate, plus ten thousand dollars for finding the item."

Whoa! Fully awake, Taylor shot to his feet, then winced as his leg throbbed.

"Mr. Taylor? Is that acceptable?"

He looked around his apartment, noting the empty Chinese food take-out containers and the empty cans of beer. Since ditching Parker's case, he'd been living on leftovers and avoiding his landlord. Except for a few skip traces—checking up on people who'd skipped out on bills—work had pretty much dried up. A neat little infusion of cash was exactly what he needed. "Uh, yeah. I think I can work you in."

Ice-cold milk, Oreos, her quilt, and the remote control— pretty much all Zoë needed for a perfect Saturday at home.

Too bad this wasn't a perfect Saturday. It was pretty dismal, actually.

Scowling, she eyed the phone she'd dragged to the coffee table—the same phone that had refused to ring all morning. No calls at all, and definitely no calls from Buster. Of course, he had no reason to call. Not any- more. Not since he thought she was involved with some- one else. But even though she'd lied, even though she'd pushed him away, even though getting involved with a mortal was bad news—*oh, sweet Hera*—how she'd hoped he'd ignore her rejection.

She shifted on the couch and focused again on the phone, willing it to ring, but the darn thing remained stubbornly silent.

Well, heck.

And she still didn't know Buster's phone number, so she couldn't even recant her lie.

But that was for the best. She needed to keep telling

herself that. Getting involved with Buster Taylor would be a mistake. A big, huge, hairy mistake.

She clicked on the television, turned the volume way down, and started surfing, determined not to think about Buster Taylor.

She'd done the right thing. No question about it.

It just happened to suck that the right thing left her so darn miserable.

Absently, she picked up the odd green necklace the woman she'd saved had given her, twining the chain through her fingers as she tried to collect her thoughts. On top of her serious lack of phone calls, in just a few hours Deena was going to be rapping on her door. And since Zoë had made a promise, she couldn't go back on her word. She'd tell Deena everything, even though by telling she'd be breaking yet another set of rules.

The doorbell rang, and Zoë jumped. She turned around, dropping the necklace as she knelt on the couch cushions, then shoved her glasses down her nose to look through the door.

"Zoë? Are you home? It's your mother."

So it was. Standing right outside Zoë's door holding a shopping bag. *Odd.* Zoë shoved her glasses back into place. "Just a sec, Mom."

She opened the door and Tessa brushed in, pushing the bag into Zoë's arms. "I thought we were going shopping today. Did you forget about the Andersons' party tomorrow?"

Yup. She'd completely forgotten. "No, of course not."

"Zoë . . ."

"Maybe I sort of forgot."

Tessa sighed, long and drawn out. "Sweetheart, you need to get out. Go on dates. Have fun."

She moved to put her arm around Zoë's shoulder, but Zoë eased sideways, not looking her mother in the eye.

"Yes. Well." Tessa cleared her throat. "I just worry about you. Sometimes you remind me so much of . . ."

"Who, Mom?"

Tessa lifted one shoulder in a delicate shrug, then moved the rest of the way into the apartment. She dropped onto the couch and nodded at Zoë, still standing in the hallway clutching the bag. "I hit the sales racks. I thought you might like these."

"Mom. Who?" She took a step into the living room, wondering if now was the time to take care of that Affidavit of Mortal Disclosure requirement. She took a deep breath. "Do I remind you of Daddy?"

Tessa flashed a weak smile. "Yes."

Zoë released a breath she hadn't realized she'd been holding.

"I'm sorry you never knew him," Tessa began, then stopped.

Now. She should tell her mother now that Donis had introduced himself when Zoë was only three. That he'd been a secret part of Zoë's life for as long as she remembered, and that she loved him as much as she loved Tessa.

She opened her mouth, but the words wouldn't come. "Why didn't I ever meet him?" she asked instead.

Tessa nibbled on her lower lip, and her gaze didn't quite meet her daughter's. "I . . . I sent him away. I made him promise he would honor my wish—that he'd stay far away from me." Her eyes met Zoë's. "I didn't understand . . . I didn't realize."

She shook her head as if shaking off a mood. "Your father always took his promises very, very seriously."

She smiled, but the sadness never left her eyes. "It was for the best, though."

"Why?"

"He was . . . different."

"How?" Zoë pressed, hoping her mother would reveal the truth and open the door for Zoë's own confession.

"He . . ." She trailed off, her eyes moist. "No, it doesn't matter." She lifted her hand to brush Zoë's cheek, but Zoë moved backward, pressing herself against the soft cushions. It wouldn't do for her senses to go haywire in front of her mother. How on earth would she explain *that?*

"He would have adored you," Tessa added, pulling her hand back and holding it primly in her lap. "But I couldn't live with his . . . with *him.*"

Which meant Tessa could hardly live with Zoë any more easily. She'd loved Donis—her father had always been sure of it—and yet she'd pushed him away. Tessa would push Zoë away, too, if she found out her daughter could see through walls, hear a whisper a mile away, put a karate black belt to shame, and do all the other odd little tricks her father and Hale had secretly taught her.

"At any rate," Tessa said brightly, "why don't I fix you up with a date for the party?"

Zoë rolled her eyes. "No, Mom," she said, wishing she had the nerve to explain why dating was out of the question. "Between you and Deena, it's a wonder I'm not engaged five times over. But I'm really, really, *really* not looking to date anyone right now."

She picked up the remote control and started idly flipping channels, waiting for the "you need to get out and find a husband" speech to start.

"You need to at least get your feet wet."

"Bad analogy, Mom. You make dating sound like drowning."

"I just don't understand why a pretty, bright woman doesn't get out more."

"Maybe I'm shy."

Her mother cocked an eyebrow. "Maybe you're not telling me something?"

That was an understatement. Not to mention an opening. But Zoë just couldn't make the words come. This was a nightmare. Her own personal nightmare.

Sometimes she wished Donis had just bitten the bullet and told Tessa the truth himself. But all along, he'd said it was Zoë's decision to make—join the council and tell her mother, or choose mortalization and Tessa would never need to know. Darn her father for being so righteous when he could have made everything so much easier for her. At least then she wouldn't have to make her own decision.

Tessa leaned closer, her face intense. "Sweetheart, you used to tell me everything. Is something the matter?"

Zoë shrugged, feeling guilty. *Never* had she told Tessa everything. But lately she'd been sharing less and less. "I just don't see what's the big deal. I mean, you never dated after Daddy—I mean, my father—left."

For just an instant, a cloud crossed Tessa's face. Then it cleared, and she sighed. "True. But I retired from the game. That's different from never playing."

"So maybe I'm not into sports," Zoë said, cringing at how glib she sounded when her mother only wanted to help.

Why did this have to be so hard? She wanted to tell

her mother everything—about Buster, and how he made her tingle all over even without her wacky senses. But how could she explain why she was terrified of dating without telling her mother the whole story?

When she'd been a little kid, she'd kept a few secrets from her, but mostly her mom had been her best friend. The other children had picked up that she was different—it was hard to fool kids—and had cut a wide berth. Even Donis and Hale would disappear for weeks at a time. But Tessa had always been there.

Zoë couldn't bear to lose her now. Even if she couldn't share the details, she could still draw strength from knowing her mom cared.

But once she told her . . . then Tessa would be gone. And nothing in the world would be able to bring her back.

"Zoë, sweetheart, you know you can tell me anything." Tessa scooted closer on the couch. This time, when she took Zoë's hand, Zoë didn't jerk away. Instead she mustered all her concentration to keep her sense of touch from going nuts.

"I do read *Cosmo,* you know," Tessa said. "And . . . well . . . I watch *Maury Povich* all the time. So if there's anything you want to discuss . . ."

Zoë squinted, clueless. "I'm not following you, Mom."

Tessa's forehead crinkled. "It's just that I want you to know that it's okay if . . . well . . . I'll understand perfectly if . . ." She took a deep breath while Zoë watched, her mouth hanging open and absolutely no idea where the conversation was going. "Sweetheart, you do like *men,* right?"

"Mother!" Zoë leaped to her feet. "Of course I do!"

This keeping secrets thing was getting way out of control. "Men are great. Men are way up there on my top-ten list." Especially certain adorable dark-haired men. "In fact, I even have a date for tomorrow."

Tessa blinked. "A real date?"

Zoë frowned. In Mom-speak, there was a big difference between platonic buddy for her possibly lesbian daughter and potential son-in-law material.

"Of course." She mentally crossed her fingers. "Definitely real."

"Have I met him? What does he do? How long have you been seeing him? Why didn't you tell me?"

"This is exactly why I didn't tell you." Zoë swept her hand, indicating the room now filled with her mother's excitement. "You're gonna terrify the poor guy. Not to mention making me incredibly nervous."

"Sorry," Tessa said, but she didn't look it. Instead she looked like the cat who'd just swallowed the canary. "You just date so rarely." She grinned. "Are you nervous?"

Zoë pictured Buster. "A little."

"Do you want to talk about it?"

Yes. "No. Thanks, Mom, but I'm fine. And Deena's on her way over, so I should—"

"I get the message." Tessa stood up, tucking her purse under her arm. "I'll meet him tomorrow, then. Six sharp. Don't forget."

"We won't," Zoë said, then coughed. "He's looking forward to it."

Hoo-boy. She followed her mother to the door, then held her breath through a quick peck on the cheek. She shut the door, flipped the lock, then sank to the floor and hugged her knees to her chest. She hated lying to

Tessa, but lately it was getting harder and harder not to. The council, boyfriends, the whole shebang.

The affidavit might be major problem number one, but she didn't have to turn it in until Tuesday night. Compared to the few hours she now had to find a date for tomorrow, that was an eternity. Which meant that—at least for the evening—her serious lack of male companionship had been bumped to the number one trouble slot.

Sighing, she rested her chin on her knees and eyed the phone again, hoping Buster Taylor was the telepathic sort. She'd been an idiot last night for not getting his number. Now she knew better. *When confronted with the object of your lust, forget the cool and distant approach. Always take down the vital stats.*

Now, unless Buster picked up the phone and dialed, he wasn't in the running for potential date material. Which raised a whole new problem. Where on earth was she going to find a date in time for the Andersons' party?

"Come on. Give." Deena slammed through the door, then slapped her hand over her mouth when she saw that Zoë was on the phone. "Sorry."

Zoë held up a finger, silently promising she'd be off in a minute, and listened as vice principal Tandon explained, in excruciating detail, why he couldn't take her to the Andersons' party. "It's okay, Billy. Thanks anyway." Finally she hung up and leaned back against the wall, shaking her head. "Billy Tandon talks more than anyone I know."

"Is he helping with the library?"

"No. I need a date."

"I knew that. We had this conversation yesterday."

She drummed her fingers on the countertop. "Yesterday. *Remember?* Explanation? Full disclosure? I want to know everything. Can you fly without that?" She nodded toward the cloak on Zoë's kitchen table. "Can you fly with me? Do you have laser vision? Superhearing? Can you leap tall buildings? Are you from another planet?"

Zoë laughed. "You've been watching too much television."

"Well? Are you?"

"No."

"What about the laser vision?"

"Not that I know of." Her mouth twitched.

"What?" Deena asked, but Zoë just shook her head.

"X-ray vision, then?"

Zoë smiled. "Only if I don't wear the glasses."

A wide grin spread across Deena's face. "Oh, wow. That is unbelievable. Superhearing?"

Zoë nodded, just slightly, and Deena whooped.

"I knew it," Deena said. "So tell me everything."

"You'll get your explanation. I promise. But I've got Mom issues right now. I need a date for tomorrow."

"Mom issues, huh? Well, that takes precedence over explaining how you managed to jump off a thirty-story building . . . and survive."

Zoë frowned, in no mood for sarcasm, but Deena held up her hands.

"I'm serious," she said. "Mom issues come first. It's like a cardinal friendship rule. Right up there with 'Thou shalt return all borrowed clothing' and 'Thou shalt not flirt with thy best friend's boyfriend.' There's also 'Thou shalt not keep secrets about jumping off tall buildings,' but we've already been over that. Anyway, your explanation can wait."

106

Zoë grinned, realizing she was truly glad she'd decided to let Deena in on her secret.

Her friend picked up the cloak and ran it through her fingers. "I'm not gonna wait long, though. And I gotta say, you're making lousy progress on the date front. For one thing, Billy's gay, so you're fishing in the wrong pond."

"I know he is," Zoë said. "That's why I asked him." She needed someone temporary and attractive. No strings, no commitments, no attraction. Someone safe. As much as part of her wished Buster was her date, the rest of her knew that would be a bad thing.

"Sweetie," Deena said, crossing to the coffeepot. "I don't think you completely grasp my full meaning when I say you need sex." She poured herself a cup, then turned around, leaning against the counter and eyeing Zoë.

"Sex is totally out of the question," Zoë responded. Sad, but true. At least until she could manage better control.

Deena's eyebrows raised. "You *are* an alien. And this is just a disguise. You're really just a glowing mass of energy, and for you, sex is sort of like cell division."

"What?" Zoë shook her head, blinking. "No. Ick. Where do you come up with this stuff?"

Deena shrugged. "Seems perfectly reasonable. I mean, why else would you avoid sex?"

Zoë felt her cheeks blush, and she stared at the ceiling. "What?"

"My senses," she said, mumbling. "I can only control them when I concentrate."

"Your *senses?* I'm not following you."

Zoë sighed and looked at Deena, feeling a little foolish. "My hearing, my vision. Remember? Well, all the rest of my senses are like that, too. Hearing, sight, smell, taste." She caught Deena's eye. "Chocolate pretty much sends me on a trip wilder than what I expect was going on at Woodstock."

"Wow," said Deena. "But what does that have to do with—" Zoë knew the moment realization struck. "Oh. *Touch.*"

Deena nibbled on her lower lip. All her life she'd known she was a magnet for odd things. She'd talked with fairies, made wishes on stars, and had a sister-in-law who had a truly amazing secret of her own—so Zoë's little demonstration of superpowers hadn't rocked her world. But Deena was dying to hear the details. The concept of supersex blew her away. Flying through the air was one thing, but superhero sex sounded pretty damn cool.

"But, Zo," she said, "that's *great.* I mean, everyone wants to feel the earth move during sex. You really can."

Zoë frowned. "Trust me. This is not a good thing."

Not a good thing? Deena would be willing to debate that point. She was no stranger to sex, and hyperaware sex sounded, well . . . super. "Are you sure you've thought this through?"

"Deena . . ." Zoë raised an eyebrow. "Think about it."

Deena did . . . and came to exactly the same conclusion. "I wouldn't mind borrowing those supersenses of yours for a night with Hoop. It sounds a lot more erotic than body paint or feather massages. And why not lose control if you're with the right guy?"

Zoë shrugged and started inspecting her fingernails. "I haven't found a Mr. Right, remember?"

The kid had a point. "And I guess the odds of finding

him in time to solve your Mom problem are pretty slim."

"Of finding him again, anyway," Zoë mumbled.

"What?" *Again?* What was the girl talking about?

"Nothing."

Deena couldn't help but grin, and it was all she could do to keep from putting down her coffee and rubbing her palms together. "Okay. Come on. Give. Who is he?"

"No one. Really."

"Zoë, I heard you. Tell me about the guy."

Zoë's face turned red, and Deena tried not to laugh. She'd read her share of comic books growing up, and never once had she pictured a blushing, Oreo-eating, library-tending superhero.

"I don't know how to get in touch with him, so it doesn't matter anyway."

"For crying out loud, Zo, do I have to beg? Just *tell* me."

"Okay, okay." She leaned over the table, and Deena leaned closer as well. "He's gorgeous. Dark hair and a light beard. And his eyes are brown—almost gold."

"So he's a hunk. That doesn't really help a lot. How do you know him?

With a sigh, Zoë sat back. "That's the problem. I don't. He came to the school a few days ago. We actually flirted a little." The blush deepened and Zoë looked down at the table. "But then he started asking about Emily and I kicked him out."

Deena's head was swimming. "Why would you kick him out? Were you jealous? You didn't even know the guy."

Zoë rolled her eyes. "No. He was some insurance investigator, and he thought Emily was sleeping around."

She shrugged. "He was poking around in her desk, so I kicked him out."

"And you haven't seen him since." Deena sighed. "It's so sad, but so romantic."

Zoë started inspecting her fingernails again. "Actually, I saw him last night."

"Oh, really?" Deena bit back a grin. "The plot thickens."

"He came by to ask me out for a date."

"Well? What did you say?"

"I said no, of course."

"The man of your dreams asks you out and you say no? Are you insane?"

"I told you. The touch thing."

"Maybe it won't be as bad as you think."

Zoë shook her head, her eyes wide. "He held my hand."

"And?"

"And I pretty much felt like the power of the universe was ripping me apart from the inside." She smiled, shrugging a little. "But in a good way."

"Hoo-boy." If this wasn't one of the weirder situations Deena'd ever run across . . .

She regrouped, studying Zoë. "Was that the first time he'd touched you?"

"Like that, anyway. I shook his hand in the library, but it wasn't like this."

"Well, there you go," Deena said, throwing her hands out to her sides and sloshing coffee on the floor.

"What?"

"You were a touch virgin."

Zoë's eyebrow shot up over her glasses. "Excuse me?"

"You know. Your first time and all. I bet the next time will be calmer, less intimidating." She smiled wickedly. "But still fabulous."

Zoë nibbled on her lower lip, obviously considering the possibility. "I'm not sure. You really think so?"

"Absolutely. It's like the superhero, supersense equivalent of being sixteen and groping in the backseat of a Pontiac."

Zoë grimaced. "I'm not sure about that, but I get your point."

"Then go for it."

"Even if I wanted to"—she held up a hand—"and I'm not saying I do, there's still another problem."

Deena quit bouncing and flopped back in her chair. "Hit me. I'm on a roll." Hell, at the rate they were going, she'd have Zoë ruling the dating world by the time spring break ended.

"He's a mortal."

"Can't do anything about that," Deena admitted. "Why does it matter?"

"I can't get involved with a mortal."

"Oh. Why not?"

"My brother, the council, this whole big thing." She waved a hand in the air and let out a breath. "Too complicated. Just trust me. Relationships. Me. Mortals. Won't work."

"Well, there you go," Deena said, not sure what Zoë was talking about, or why she wasn't picking up on the obvious answer to her little problem.

"What?"

"Relationships. Who said anything about relationships?"

"But . . . this guy . . . and his touch . . . it makes me all crazy."

"Virgin touching, remember? Hell, this guy could be your Lenny Potts."

"Who?"

"Lenny Potts." She slid into a chair and propped her elbows up on the tiny kitchen table. "My first backseat fondle. Sweet guy. Went out for a whole year. When he kissed me, I thought he hung the moon. I mean, I saw fireworks." True, it'd been the Fourth of July, and Deena had been only thirteen, but she didn't see the point in mentioning that. "*Now* I wouldn't go out with him if you paid me."

"Oh." Zoë's forehead creased, a little vee appearing on the bridge of her nose above her glasses. "So you're saying—"

"A fling. A date. I mean, it's not like you have to marry the guy."

For a moment Zoë looked doubtful. Then her face cleared. "Doesn't matter anyway, because there's still another problem."

"Well, you're just boiling over with good news, aren't you?"

Zoë scowled, ignoring her. "I don't know how to find him."

"Did the guy tell you his name?"

"Deenie, it doesn't matter. I've looked everywhere for him. Trust me. I've got resources. If I can't find him, neither can you."

"I just want to know his name, Zo. It's not like I'm gonna hire Hoop to track him down."

"He gave me his card at the school. His name's Buster Taylor."

"Taylor?" A wave of suspicion smacked Deena upside the head. Surely Hoop's officemate wasn't Zoë's Mr. Right—was he? She frowned, taking inventory—an investigator with dark hair, a light beard, and brown eyes. It had to be. She barked out a laugh, then slapped her hand over her mouth. "S-sorry." She swallowed, gathering control. "Silly name."

Zoë's brow furrowed. "Yeah. About as silly as *Hoop.*"

Deena shrugged. "True. I'm not dissing your man's name. It just surprised me."

"He's not my man."

"I know. And I can—"

"And even if I could find him, I wouldn't."

Deena closed her mouth with a snap. "What? Why?"

"I told you." She held up a hand before Deena could get a word in. "And everything you said about Lenny Potts makes sense, but I'm just not sure. I just don't think . . ." She trailed off, then shook her head. "I like him, but . . . no."

She looked up at Deena with misty eyes. "Besides, I just can't take the risk. I mean, he was, well, nice."

Yes, he was. And Deena was more than willing to play matchmaker between Hoop's officemate and Zoë. But if the girl was relationship-shy, then Deena seriously doubted that Zoë would take the bait if Deena confessed to knowing good ol' Buster. Which meant that she had to go the creative—otherwise known as devious—route.

"None of this matters right now, anyway," Deena said. "We need to find you a date for tomorrow."

Zoë deflated. "I know. Any ideas?"

"Basically, you want some incredibly attractive guy to be your escort for the night. No strings. No need for niceties. A purely business arrangement."

"Right."

"So you'd be willing to pay him."

Zoë frowned. "Yeah . . . I guess."

"So you're looking for a good-looking guy so desperate he'll drop everything when you offer to pay him to go out with you." Deena nibbled on her lip. Taylor might not appreciate it, but he did need the money. And Zoë needed an escort.

"Never mind," Zoë said. "I'll just tell Mom—"

"Not so fast," Deena said, unable to help the huge grin that spread across her face. "I know this guy named George Bailey." She leaned back in her chair, thoroughly pleased with herself. "And I have a feeling he's just what you're looking for."

Chapter Seven

Hale didn't need this. He really, really didn't need this.

With a groan, he leaned his forehead against the cool door of the refrigerator in Zoë's kitchen. "What kind of an idiot agrees to chase down missing fashion accessories?"

Beside him, tiny toenails skittered toward him on the formica countertop. *Your kind of idiot, that's who.*

True enough. Not that he'd had a choice. For one thing, Zoë might be in danger, and he wanted to keep an eye on her. For another, saying no to Zephron wasn't a viable option.

In a perfect world, he'd be lying on a beach right about now without a worry in the world. No council duties. No photo shoots. No responsibilities whatsoever. Nothing to do except kick back and soak up a few Mediterranean rays. Maybe bounce up to council headquarters for an unbelievable meal or two. A little wine, a little ambrosia. Watch half-naked mortal women running around sun-bleached beaches in barely-there thong bikinis.

In other words, all the normal, typical, run-of-the-mill perks of being a young, virile, kick-ass superhero.

At least, that had been his plan. But did he get to do any of it? Any rays? Any thongs? Anything at all?

No, sir. No way. Nohow.

Instead he got stuck with helping his sister save the world.

A dirty job, but somebody had to do it.

Thank goodness for room service. At least there were *some* perks on this trip.

"I don't even know where to begin looking for this stone, not to mention keeping an eye on Zoë." He scowled at the empty apartment. She'd known he was going to drop by, where in Hades had she run off to?

Lucky you. Your sister's a disaster waiting to happen.

Hale glared at Elmer, who managed a little ferret shrug.

Not that I don't adore the girl...

Hale closed his eyes and thumped his head three times against the fridge. "This sucks."

The food selection? Your klutzy sister? Or were you referring to a philosophical state of suckiness?

Hale scowled at Elmer, who scurried back until he could jump from the counter to the floor. He balanced on his two rear legs, looking up at Hale with a supercilious expression.

"Being a superhero is supposed to be about stopping out-of-control trains, rescuing beautiful maidens, seeking out evil and squashing it like a bug under my thumb. It is *not* supposed to be about tracking down oversize green pendants that look like rejects from the Home Shopping Network."

Where'd you hear that? The superhero handbook?

"The Web page, actually."

The ferret's mouth opened, but nothing came out. Amazing. He'd actually stumped the furry little guy.

"I'm kidding," he said. He ran his fingers through his hair. "I'm just worried about my sister."

Annoyed about missing your vacation, more likely.

Hale couldn't help the small smile that tugged at his mouth. "Maybe. La-La Land doesn't exactly compare to Greece."

Speak for yourself. I, for one, prefer Hollywood. The whiskers twitched. *Do you think I could get a commercial? Maybe a sitcom?* His voice went wistful. *I could be the lovable but rambunctious family pet.*

Hale groaned, then stifled a sneeze. "No." His sister was living with mortals and quite possibly held the fate of all of them in her back pocket, and his ferret friend had picked this opportunity to go mental. Not what he needed today. "Besides, we're not going to be here long enough for you to strike up an acting career."

You said indefinitely.

"Well, not that indefinitely. If this legend's right, then everything will come to a head by next Tuesday at midnight."

Wednesday.

"What?"

I knew you'd get confused. It's the midnight between Tuesday and Wednesday, not Monday and Tuesday.

Hale rolled his eyes. "I think I can keep the days of the week straight."

Elmer didn't look convinced. *Whatever. Either way, the point is the eclipse, right?*

"Exactly." A rather rare and mystical event.

And His Supreme Uppityness says that whatever dastardly deeds your uncle and Mordichai are up to will happen then.

"Zephron'll make me put you in a petting zoo if he hears you call him that."

Yet Elmer was right. The bottom line? For the time being, his vacation was MIA. Instead of being in Greece, he was hanging in his sister's apartment. Instead of soaking up the sun, he was going to raid Zoë's cabinets in search of more breakfast. He'd had Eggs Benedict at the hotel but that had been two hours ago and he was starving. Superheroes needed to eat to keep up their strength.

He flung open the cabinet over the coffeemaker. Tupperware. Tiny little Tupperware containers. And all of them empty.

Frustrated, he yanked open another cabinet and started plowing through the bottles and boxes. He found some really old crackers. A box of plain Quaker oatmeal. Four bags of rice cakes.

Clearly he should have had lunch at the hotel.

"How does she live on this stuff?" He shoved aside a box of Earl Grey tea and—yes, finally—found a bag of Oreos. "I'm amazed she hasn't died of starvation."

Perhaps she has a more discriminating palate.

"Perhaps she's a wimp."

You might have more sympathy if you shared her particular trait. It can't be easy experiencing each sense so . . . vividly.

Hale frowned, ignoring Elmer, who probably considered his silence a victory. But Hale just wasn't going to get into this with the little rat. He'd already done it too many times with Zoë herself.

With the bag in one hand and a diet soda tucked under his arm, Hale headed back to her living room, his nose twitching as he tried to stave off a massive allergy attack. He dumped Elmer into the recliner—

You could try *to be a little gentler.*

—then crashed on Zoë's couch. Across the room, Elmer turned in a circle three times and settled in for a nap.

With a sigh, Hale glanced at the council-issued backpack he'd tossed onto Zoë's coffee table earlier. As he crooked his finger, the pack opened, and the picture of the stone he was supposed to be tracking down floated out, finally landing on his stomach.

Hard to believe such a trinket could wreak so much havoc. Elmer was up, his whiskers twitching, his fur a spiky mess.

"I thought you were napping."

How can I nap when the fate of the world rests with a big rock?

Well, he might have a point there. "Just don't call the damn thing a trinket. It's a council artifact. Pay it a little respect."

One wouldn't expect a ferret to be able to make an effective snorting sound, but Elmer managed. Hale grinned, then pitched the photo into his pack. He leaned back, ready for a little feast of Oreos, but instead ended up in a massive sneezing fit.

A key jangled in the lock, and he heard the front door open.

From his prone position, he lifted his soda in greeting, only then realizing that he'd sneezed himself into invisibility. From where Zoë stood, the can must look as if it were floating in midair over the back of the couch.

"Hale!"

He grinned. Fortunately his sister was used to the way he came and went. "I let myself in."

He heard her running through the hallway; then suddenly she was there, bounding over the couch—

"Don't sit! I'm lying down!"

—to settle on the padded armrest opposite him. He concentrated on becoming visible again while she smiled down at him in her raggedy jogging shorts and grungy T-shirt, practically quivering with excitement.

"Hey, Zoëster," Hale said with a wink.

"Hey, Halester." She winked back as Elmer pulled himself up the side of the sofa and onto the seat. "I'm so glad to *see* you! I didn't think you'd be back 'til after lunch."

Hellooo? What am I? Chopped liver? Elmer nudged Zoë's hand with his nose until she stroked his fur and kissed the top of his little head.

"I wish I knew what you were saying, Elmer. If it's 'hello,' then hi right back at you. You're looking good."

"Better than you," Hale said. "What are you wearing?"

"Workout clothes. I just did nine hundred push-ups, eight hundred sit-ups, and spent two hours on the treadmill." She grinned. "It's taking longer and longer for me to work up a sweat. Pretty soon I'll be as good as you."

Hale laughed. "We'll see."

Elmer's nose wiggled, his whiskers vibrating. *Is that . . . ? It is! Perspiration!* He craned his little head backward, aiming his deep black eyes at Hale. *You never perspire,* he said, making it sound like an insult. *Mr.*

Perfectly Pure Protector. I guess only the halflings have to put up with—

"Enough, Elmer." The little guy really had a knack for getting out of control.

Zoë raised an eyebrow. "What's he saying?"

"He's just glad to see you."

"Uh-huh," his half-sister said with a knowing smile. She slipped off the couch, ending up sitting on the edge of the coffee table. "It's funny you came into town now. I was just thinking about you the other day."

"Oh, yeah? Why?" he asked, ready to be entertained. "Did you lose one of your kiddies in the stacks and have to look through a bookcase to find him? Did you manage to eat a pepper without freaking out?" He held out a hand. "I know. You levitated the cat."

"You shouldn't tease me about that. Poor Miss Kitty hates me!"

"No comment."

Zoë grimaced. "She does hate me, doesn't she? She probably told you."

"Well, let's just say you're not on her favorite-person list. She didn't mind the levitating part. It was the dropping part that annoyed her."

"She can spit and howl louder than any cat I've known."

"Well, I can't blame her. Maybe you should stick with inanimate objects until you get this levitation thing down."

"I'm doing better." She plucked Elmer off the couch and settled him in her lap, stroking his fur.

Ah, heaven, he squeaked.

Hale rolled his eyes as Elmer let out a human-size sigh.

Yup, this is the good life. Guess I'm the only one who's going to get stroked by beautiful women this vacation. The little beast closed his eyes and let his head loll back.

"You're a talker today," Zoë said to him. "Why's he so chatty?"

"Just can't keep his mouth shut," Hale snapped, scowling. Unfortunately, Elmer was right. Hale *wasn't* on a beach, and wasn't having suntan oil applied by a gaggle of luscious females out to make his every dream come true. Instead, he was stuck with his sister and a smart-mouthed rodent.

Some ferrets had all the luck.

He blinked, pulling himself back to the conversation. "So what made you think of me?" he asked.

Her nose crinkled, but she didn't say anything.

"Zoë?" he prodded. She nibbled on her lower lip, and he wondered if she was about to confess to the leaping-from-the-tower stunt.

"Nothing. Really. Can't I think about my wonderful brother without having some huge reason?"

She'd always been a lousy liar. He tapped a finger against his temple. "Umm . . . I'm gonna go with no."

She grimaced, then lifted one shoulder in the barest of shrugs. "I was at Mom's and she was reading your latest book." She grinned and waggled her eyebrows. "Nice pose."

"Very funny." When he'd first taken the assignment, no one—not Hale, not the council—had realized just how well suited he was for the job of romance cover model. His popularity sneaked up on them, and by the time the council realized that he wasn't exactly *incon-*

spicuous, Hale's face—not to mention his arms, chest, back, waist, and thighs—was gracing the covers of countless novels in bookstores and supermarkets across the world.

Hale loved the notoriety, though now, unlike his council brethren, he didn't fade easily into undercover anonymity. It was a great thing that he could become invisible. Still, the odds that Zoë's mother's romance novel had reminded her of him were pretty darn slim.

"I'm not buying it." Especially not, knowing what he knew.

"What?" she asked, all innocence.

"Give it up, kid. What are you up to?"

"Not the cat . . ."

He sat up straight. "But you levitated something? Why didn't you tell me?"

"Not that big a deal." She shrugged. "Just some books."

"Are you kidding? That's great news." Zoë needed to get her skills under control. She'd need a firm handle on them if she was going to pass her tests—if she was going to defeat Mordi. "You were practicing?"

"Not exactly."

He squinted. "What then?"

"I was reshelving. Some books fell. I . . . uh . . . caught them."

"Well, that's no big deal. No one saw, right?"

She nibbled on her lower lip. That was not a good sign.

"Zoë? Who saw?"

"Just one of the kids."

At least that was a relief. "That's not too bad. It's

revealing yourself to a mortal, true, but since it was a only kid, I don't—"

"Interfering."

"What?"

"I interfered. They were gonna whomp her on the head."

He exhaled. This on top of flying from buildings. His sister certainly knew how to make his life complicated. "You know halflings aren't supposed to use their powers in public until they've been approved by the council! I'm supposed to be mentoring you. You screw up enough and they'll take it out on me! Not to mention that rule violations get counted against you on your application."

Not that the council would really turn her down for protecting a kid from falling books. Or even for the tower stunt, for that matter. Saving mortals was their sworn duty, after all. But she would probably end up getting a stern lecture about protocol and procedures— and have to spend a full day in a Surreptitious Defense course.

Zoë's nose crinkled as she scraped her teeth along her lower lip. "The books would have hurt her. And I didn't actually try to levitate them. It just . . . happened." She caught his eye. "I'm sorry," she said, but he doubted she really meant it. Hell, he would've done the same thing.

"Don't worry. The council isn't going to get that upset because you tried to save a little girl."

"Well"—she looked up, meeting his eyes—"the council won't care about *that*. . . ."

Hale cocked his head, looking at his half-sister's face. Her eyes were wide, her lips slightly pursed, giving her that bee-stung look that was all the rage—and a hint of color tinted her cheeks. All in all, she looked damned innocent. With Zoë, that had to mean trouble. Was it something he hadn't already heard about? "Okay. Give."

She looked a little sheepish. "I worked in some extra practice with my cloak."

"And?" he asked, urging her on.

"The thing is, I kind of practiced right off a thirty-story building."

He laughed, breathing an inward sigh of relief. "I was wondering when you'd get around to telling me."

Her eyes went wide. "You knew?" She hurled a pillow at him. "Why didn't you say anything?"

"I'm a man of mystery."

She cocked her head. "So this isn't really a social call. You're here to lecture me on rules and stuff."

Hale hated lying to his sister. Instead he dodged. "Do you need a lecture?"

She shrugged and scrunched down into the corner of the couch, hauling Elmer into her lap. "No. I just couldn't watch that little boy almost get hit and that woman get mugged and not help. And when I realized it was Mordi—"

"What did you say?" A chill slivered down Hale's spine and he leaned forward.

Elmer's whiskers twitched. *The Mord-man?*

Zoë peered at him. "Are you okay?"

"I'm fine," he said, knowing he didn't sound fine at all. "Mordi was there?"

"He mugged the woman. It's so strange. I mean, Mordi's always been a little odd, but he's never been criminal." She shrugged. "I figure it must have something to do with our testing, but I don't know what. It's weird."

125

Julie Kenner

Not weird at all, but he couldn't tell Zoë that. "Very weird," he lied, wishing he could tell her she was part of a legend that he was only beginning to truly believe.

Weird? What are you talking about? Have those sneezes rattled your brain? Elmer climbed up the armchair and perched in front of him. *If that boy is here, he's already got a bead on the stone.*

"I know that," Hale said, flashing Elmer a look he hoped telegraphed *Be quiet.* It must've worked, because Elmer looked insulted, then crawled off to hide under the couch. Hale sighed. He'd deal with the sulking rodent later.

"What do you know?" Zoë asked as Elmer's tail disappeared under the furniture.

"How weird it sounds," he answered quickly. He couldn't tell her the truth about Mordi, not until Zephron gave approval. "I know your story sounds weird, but I believe it." *And I'm very, very interested, in the details.* "So did he get the purse?"

Zoë shook her head, beaming. "Nope. I got it back from him."

"Way to go, Zoëster! What about the woman? Did you catch her name?"

"She left before I thought to ask." Her brow furrowed and she cocked her head to look at him. "So why *are* you here? Just to lecture me on rules? You totally surprised me yesterday. I thought you were catching rays in *Greece* this week."

"Don't remind me. But as long as I'm here, why don't we do dinner? I can have Wolfgang Puck's latest culinary masterpiece while you eat white rice."

"Um," she said, then pressed her lips together.
"Um?"

126

"I can't."

"Why not?"

"Well," she began, drawing out the sound and reminding him of Samantha on *Bewitched*.

"What?"

"I've got a date."

"A date?" he repeated, aghast. "For the love of Zeus, Zoë. A date? With a mortal? What in Hades are you thinking?"

"I was thinking I needed to find a date or else I'd end up spending the day with some dweeb my mother picked out."

"Dweebs are good. Dweebs don't ask questions." *And you're not likely to* fall *for one.*

"For crying out loud, Hale, it's just one party."

"But a mortal—"

Let the girl have a little fun.

Zoë squinted toward the couch, from under which Elmer's disembodied voice chittered. "What did he say?" she asked.

"Nothing. He's on my side."

No, I'm not. I'm—

"You don't need to be dating mortals," he said firmly.

Domineering jerk.

"I don't even know the guy," Zoë said, looking suspiciously at the space beneath the sofa. "I'm even hiring him, okay? Besides, don't you think you're overreacting just a little?"

"Let *me* fix you up with someone," he suggested, almost begging.

She scowled at him. "Like who? Like Snydley, the man who can turn his body into rubber? Do you have any idea how hard a guy like that is to fend off when he decides to get frisky?"

Hale held up his hands. "At least he liked you."

"No, he didn't. Not really. And that's the problem. Even if I wanted to go out with a Protector, they don't want to have anything to do with a halfling."

"Sure they do. They just—"

But he couldn't finish. She was right. Only a handful of Protectors would go out with a halfling.

"There's nothing wrong with mortals," Zoë protested. "I'm half-mortal, remember?"

"You're different," he said, knowing it was a cop-out answer, but unable to put into words just how much . . . well . . . *better* Protectors were than mortals. And, full-blooded or not, his sister was a Protector. Or would be soon.

Hale might indulge in occasional flings with mortal females, but that was completely different. They were good for his psyche. They kept him on his toes, kept his juices flowing. And there was no way that Hale was ever going to get suckered into thinking that the mundane, humdrum mortal existence was even remotely appealing.

But Zoë.

Well, as . . . she herself had admitted, she was half-mortal, and a fling was just plain dangerous. What if she decided she *liked* being with a mortal? What if she wanted more than a fling? With a Protector, sure. He could get behind that. He'd even set her up with a buddy.

But a *mortal?* He stifled a shiver. Zoë could do so much better.

Saving mortals was one thing. Getting into relationships with them was something entirely different. For one thing, mortal-Protector relationships just didn't work. Take his father and Zoë's mother for example. Hale had been five years old when Tessa had sent Donis packing, making him promise to leave her alone forever. And a Protector's promise to a mortal was a sacred thing. So Donis had walked away, even though the entire year before, he had told Hale over and over that the woman would adore him the moment she met him. That Hale would have a mother again, after his had been killed in a secret Protector mission when he was just a baby.

But at the end of the day, there hadn't been any new mother. Tessa had shut Donis out of her life and never looked back.

Work with a mortal, yes. Bed them, sure. Protect them, always.

Trust them with your heart? Never.

And Zoë needed to learn the hard truth. He spoke in a no-nonsense tone: "Go easy on the mortals, okay? You need to concentrate on your application. On your tests. Now's not the time to suddenly get distracted by all your wacky senses. Or some good-looking mortal."

She rolled her eyes. "I told you, I'm fine. You don't have to get all protective and weird on me every time I mention the word *date*. I know everything you think would happen, and I'm not going to do anything."

Hale nodded slowly, wishing he could believe her, but it was hard, and the fact was, he was afraid of losing his little sister. If she got involved with a mortal, she just might decide to give up her heritage—to forget about turning in the affidavit—and submit to mortalization.

The possibility was more than a little disturbing. She'd lose her memory, and Hale would lose her. Not only that; there was that whole fate-of-the-world thing to worry about, too.

A mortal Zoë wouldn't have any chance at all at keeping the stone from Mordi.

No, he'd have to keep a close watch on her. After all, he wanted the best for his little sister.

And the best was definitely *not* a mortal.

The problem was, if Hale was out looking for the stupid stone, he couldn't run interference between Zoë and this mortal. He needed an early-warning device. Some way to know if she was falling too hard, too fast.

Some way to get good information on the state of his sister's love life.

He thought of Elmer, curled up under the sofa.

Looks like his sister was in the pet-sitting business.

And Elmer was back in the sister-watching biz.

Saturday started out rainy, which matched Taylor's mood. Ever since Zoë had said she was taken, he'd been under a cloud. Now, after almost twenty hours, all he wanted was to chow down on some really unhealthy food and try to forget about her.

Unfortunately, he'd emptied his checking account to pay Lane's rent. And his credit card wasn't any help. *Declined* seemed to be the word of the day. He finally scrounged up a dollar and eighty-five cents in Francis Capra's glove compartment. Not enough for lobster, but it would get lunch.

He bought a hot dog from a convenience store and topped it with a cheese-food product, all for the bargain-basement price of a buck. Which left him with just enough for a soda to wash the stuff down.

It was just as well Zoë'd turned him down for a date.

It wasn't as if he could afford to take her out, and tap water and crackers didn't exactly make a stellar impression.

Still, he would have liked to just spend time with her. Maybe drive around the mountains. Take in the view. Ride bikes along the beach.

Taken. He should have known, should've guessed. But the thought hadn't even entered his mind until he'd watched Zoë laughing with *Baywatch* boy in the Ferrari. He'd seen her, and his testosterone level had skyrocketed. *Woman-mine* had pretty much been his Neanderthal way of thinking. And it depressed the hell out of him to know that some other caveman had already claimed his female.

Now, with Zoë on the brain, he headed for the Beverly Hills Hotel to keep his meeting with his new mystery client. He parked out front, and was just finishing his not-so-gourmet lunch when someone rapped on the window. Taylor rolled it down, ignoring the light rain that blew in. It was probably someone wanting him to move his car. "I'm not blocking traffic. I'll be out of here in less than five minutes."

"Mr. Taylor? I'm your appointment."

The cultured voice was familiar, and Taylor groaned. "Sorry. Hop on in."

The man circled around to the passenger side. The door opened and a slightly damp man with a hangdog expression slid into the car.

"I thought we were meeting in the hotel."

"I saw you and decided to grasp the opportunity."

Taylor grimaced, not sure he liked this guy's style. Still, if the guy really had a job for him . . .

He sighed, giving in to curiosity. "So tell me about this jewel, Mr. . . . ?"

"Mord—Mordon." He held out his hand. "Mr. Mordon."

Taylor shoved the last bite of hot dog into his mouth and took Mordon's hand. It was cold and clammy. On top of that, he almost felt certain he'd seen this guy's green eyes watching him before. They were creepy eyes, the kind that seemed to look straight through him. But that was crazy.

And yet Taylor didn't trust the fellow. He was just about to open his mouth to say "Thanks, but no, thanks," when the guy pulled out a wallet and withdrew five hundred-dollar bills, laying them on the dashboard.

"An advance on your fee."

Taylor looked from the money to the guy, then back. He shrugged. Trust was highly overrated in the investigator-client relationship. So what if the guy was a little smarmy? He could live with smarmy so long as the bills got paid. And this guy was only looking for a jewel, not dirt on a perfectly nice woman.

"Okay. I'm in. You got a picture or something?"

"I tracked it to a thrift store," the man said, "but was . . . unable to catch up with the woman who purchased it." He pulled a Polaroid out of his jacket and passed it to Taylor.

"*This* is the stone?" *Lane's ugly pendant? Oh, man.* This was just priceless. Lane would freak when she found out her necklace was going to pull down ten grand.

"That's right. As I said, a young woman bought it from a thrift store, but I was unable to obtain the necklace from her."

Taylor tapped his fingers on the steering wheel.

"You're really planning on paying me ten grand to find this?"

"I certainly am."

His eyes narrowed. "Why?"

"I told you. It's an heirloom." He smiled. "I assure you there is nothing nefarious. The stone has been in my family for . . . well, let's just say even a museum would be interested in a piece like this."

"And the ten grand is for locating it?"

"Correct."

"*Just* locating it." Maybe this client—for a change—did come from a family that could trace its roots back to Cro-Magnon man, but that didn't mean he wasn't going to try to pull one over on Taylor.

"As I said, correct."

"So how are you going to get it after that?"

"Why, my dear Mr. Taylor. I will purchase it, of course."

Bingo. If Mordon here was willing to pay ten Gs just to find the thing, he'd surely pay even more to Lane to get it back. This was a man with some serious cash. And he wasn't proposing anything too shady. . . .

"Do we have a deal, Mr. Taylor?"

"Yup. I think we do."

"Fine." Mordon turned in his seat to face Taylor more directly. "I might suggest you begin with the shopkeeper and try to track down the woman who bought it."

"You might," Taylor snapped, then waved away the smart-ass comment. "Sorry." The guy might be pushy, but he was paying the bills. "I mean, it's a good idea, but I have a feeling I'll have your necklace back to you sooner than you imagine."

Mordon inclined his head, and Taylor had the uncomfortable sensation that he was being sized up. "I see." The man opened the passenger door. "Then I'll leave you to it, Mr. Taylor."

"You got a card or something? A phone number?"

"I'll be in touch."

Taylor shrugged. The guy already gave him the creeps. If he wanted to play the dark and mysterious client, Taylor wasn't going to argue. "Whatever."

"Excellent." Mordon stepped out into the drizzle and shut the door behind him.

Taylor exhaled and watched him go. In just a few days, he'd have ten grand in his bank account. He should be ecstatic. He should be on the phone to Lane, or at least on his way to her apartment.

Instead he had the overwhelming urge to scrub down the passenger side of his car.

Chapter Eight

Baubles & Beads was Deena's favorite thrift store, and it just happened to be conveniently located in Hollywood, right across the street from Hoop's office. Over the past year she'd wasted a lot of time there, blown through several paychecks, and found some pretty keen bargains. Where else could she find semitacky costume jewelry, vintage dresses, and pink umbrellas with purple fringe? Not that she'd actually used the parasol yet, but one never knew when one could come in handy.

"Are you sure this is a good idea?" Zoë looked at her over a round rack displaying a variety of leather outfits.

"It's the best idea I've had in a long time," Deena said as she plowed through a box of belts and scarves.

"Hiring this George guy, I mean. Not our spur-of-the-moment shopping spree."

Deena looked up. "It's a great idea. You hire a date, your mom thinks you've got a guy, everyone's happy."

"I suppose." Zoë ran her finger down a leather bustier. "It just seems like cheating."

"Well . . . it is. But it's either that or find a real date— or go out with some dweeb your mom sets you up with."

Zoë's nose wrinkled. "Will you come with me to ask him?"

Deena sighed, then held up a black scarf with gold sequins. "What do you think of this?"

"Deena . . ."

"Look, sweetie, it's just a business deal. All you have to do is go across the street, take the elevator to the seventh floor, walk in the door, and ask George to be your escort for one night. Simple."

"So you're not coming."

"Can't. I have to teach a class in Santa Monica. I'm going to be late as it is." That was a teensy lie. She did have a class, true. And she was going to be late. But mostly she didn't want to catch hell when Zoë realized that George Bailey was none other than Buster "the object of lust" Taylor.

She held up the scarf and raised her eyebrows.

Zoë shook her head. "Too flashy."

"Probably right." She tossed the scarf back in the box and pulled out a gold mesh belt. Tacky, but fun in a retro-sixties kind of way. "You'll do fine. It's not like you're interviewing for a job. You're just hiring an escort."

"I suppose."

"Or you could tell your mom the truth."

Zoë took a deep, loud breath. "I'm just stalling."

"I know you are, sweetie."

"I've never hired a man before."

Deena grinned. "With your looks, you shouldn't have to."

"You think he'll agree?"

"Honey, I'm betting good money he'll jump at the chance." She wrapped the belt around her waist and fastened the clasp. "What do you think? Should I buy it?"

"Well . . . it's incredibly ugly, but for some reason, I sort of like it."

"Sold." Deena smiled. "Now go hire yourself a man."

The trip to Lane's would have proved more productive had she been home. As it was, all Taylor did was sit in her living room for an hour watching bad television and wondering where she was on a rainy Saturday afternoon.

The day didn't improve after he left. First, he ended up stuck behind a three-car pileup on the Santa Monica freeway. Then, when he finally managed to exit, it took him an hour on surface streets to get from her tiny Venice Beach apartment to Hollywood.

By the time he pulled Francis Capra into the pay-parking lot five blocks from his office, his already shaky mood had completely deteriorated. Even the possibility of ten grand wasn't enough to put a silver lining in Los Angeles traffic.

The rain was falling with a vengeance now, turning the city eerily dark for early afternoon. Holding his empty briefcase over his head, he strode down the street and pushed through the revolving door into his office building, ignoring the hawkers trying to make a fast profit with cheap umbrellas.

He jabbed at the elevator call button. Nothing. He punched it once more. Again, nothing. The needle above the antiquated box showed it was stuck on the tenth floor. *Oh, well.* He hadn't been to physical therapy in over a month. He could probably use the exercise.

Only silence greeted him as he stepped into the run-down office suite, his thigh throbbing. Not that he'd expected a rip-roaring welcome. Holding only two PIs, a part-time secretary, and a teenager who ran errands, the office was never exactly hopping. And on Saturday, the cockroaches even took the day off.

A vague noise floated from the back of the suite, followed by a crash, then a groan.

Hoop.

Taylor grinned. Looked like he wasn't alone after all. He headed for the file room sandwiched between his office and Hoop's, pitching his briefcase onto the reception desk as he passed by.

More of a storage area, really, the file room was chock-full of banker's boxes piled ceiling-high, stacks of paper covering every surface, and surveillance equipment teetering precariously on the metal shelves that lined the back wall. A retro Formica table dominated the center of the room, complemented by vinyl-cushioned chairs. Boxes and papers littered the floor. And there was Hoop in the center of it all, rumpled and unshaven—as usual.

Taylor leaned against the door-frame. "I think the files are escaping into the hallway."

"Just trying to make some room to eat." Hoop swept his hand over the table, sending the last three folders flying. "Twinkie?"

"No thanks. I'm giving up health food."

Hoop grimaced. "Hey, man can't live on pizza alone."

"I'm probably going out on a limb here, but maybe it's time to organize the file room."

Hoop twisted in his seat, surveying the mess. "Looks organized to me."

In the six months since he'd subleased space from Hoop, Taylor had learned two important facts about his old academy buddy: One, Hoop was a slob. Two, he was one of the best investigators Taylor had ever known. All of which probably illustrated some huge cosmic principle, but Taylor was damned if he knew what it was.

"If you want to organize it, though, knock yourself out," Hoop said. "Deena's helping out around here next week. She can give you a hand if you want."

"I've only met her once, Hoop. It's bad enough she's going to answer my phones for free. I'm not about to make her schlepp boxes."

Hoop waved the thought away. "Oh, please. She likes to do stuff like that. I'm surprised she hasn't already moved all the boxes to one side of the room and painted some frou frou mural on the wall." He finished off his Twinkie, then washed it down with a slug of orange soda. "Trust me."

Taylor shrugged. The file room was the least of his worries. "I'm mostly concerned about the money thing." That was putting it mildly. "Between the two months' rent I owe you and the rent on my apartment, I'm a little tight." A lot tight, actually, but he didn't need to share that little tidbit. Especially since that problem should be remedied soon.

"Parker screwed you for fees, huh?"

Taylor tapped the side of his nose. "Bingo."

"What a horse's ass."

"I was using stronger language the other day." He straddled one of the chairs, resting his arms on its back.

139

"Besides, it's my own damn fault. You warned me." He lifted a shoulder philosophically. "I would've done better to buy a lottery ticket than to bank on Harold Parker paying his bill."

Hoop ripped open another package of Twinkies. "Maybe the check's in the mail."

"Nope. The bastard was just trying to screw over his wife. I told him to forget about paying me. Right after I told him to go hell."

Hoop wiped a glob of Twinkie innards off his chin. "I knew you had a knack for client relations."

"Very funny," Taylor muttered.

"I know you're good for it, but if your landlord's getting antsy, you could always sell your Mustang."

"In your dreams," Taylor scoffed, forcing out a laugh. He'd spent four years rebuilding Francis Capra. If he had to choose between his car and his apartment, he'd be sleeping in the car.

"I'm pretty overloaded right now. I could use a second set of legs."

Taylor shook his head. "Thanks, but no, thanks." Playing sidekick wasn't his style, and neither was taking charity. For half his life he'd been shuttled from foster home to foster home. The day they set him free and sent him out on his own, he'd made up his mind to take care of himself for the rest of his life.

"There's nothing wrong with accepting a little help, you know. You don't have to be the lone wolf out fighting for truth and justice."

Taylor brushed the comment away, trying to pretend Hoop hadn't hit the nail on the head. "I'll be fine. The fact is I just met a guy with a job that'll refill my bank account." He shrugged. "Ten thousand bucks, assuming I get the job done."

Hoop took another slug of soda. "Can you?"

He laid the photo on the table and gave Hoop the rundown on Lane's thrift-store necklace, ending with a shrug. "Piece of cake."

Hoop's eyes widened. "A guy hires you to find your foster sister's necklace? What, are you leading a charmed life?"

"Dead broke with a bullet in my leg, and the only woman I'm interested in already is taken . . ." He paused for dramatic effect. "Oh, yeah. I'm charmed."

The corner of Hoop's mouth raised. "Yeah, you're right. Your life pretty much sucks."

Taylor scowled.

"I'll ask about that love triangle later. Right now, what's the story with this trinket? Is it stolen? Is it the Hope diamond?"

"The guy says it's a family heirloom. I made a couple of calls. Nothing like it has been reported stolen."

"Lot of money just for an heirloom. Why?"

"I dunno. If I had a family memento that was centuries old, I might go a long way to get it back." Of course, a thirty-four-year-old orphan who could trace his family tree back all of thirty-four years wouldn't exactly be an expert in the family heirloom department.

"Ten grand covers a lot of sentimentality."

"That's just my finder's fee. He's still got to buy the necklace back from Lane. And if he's throwing ten my way, I figure Lane can negotiate quite a deal."

Hoop shook his head and let out a low whistle. "This guy look like he was rolling in the dough?"

Taylor remembered his finely cut clothes, his cultured way of talking. He shrugged. "Yeah."

"Well, hot damn, boy. I repeat my earlier comment—you're charmed."

Hell, maybe he was.

The phone rang, and Taylor scooped it up. It was Lane.

"I got your message," she said. "What's up?"

"You know that necklace you wanted to sell? I'll take it off your hands after all."

A pause, then, "Why?"

"Long story." He couldn't wait to see her face when she found out her thrift-store necklace was going to get them both out of debt. "Can you bring it over?"

"Um . . . well, no."

He heard Davy crying in the background. "Fair enough. I'll come get it."

"Uh, Taylor, I don't have it anymore."

He closed his eyes. When he opened them, Hoop was staring.

"Well?" Hoop hissed.

Taylor waved the question away. "How can you not have it anymore?"

"I gave it away. This woman saved Davy from getting hit by a car, and I gave it to her. Like a fee."

"*Saved* Davy?" He tried to keep his voice calm as the rest of him wanted to crawl through the phone line. Across the table, Hoop tensed. "Is he okay?"

"He's fine."

Relief washed over him, and he nodded at Hoop, who relaxed.

"Why the hell didn't you tell me?"

"You worry too much. And it turned out okay. I told you, this woman saved him."

"What woman?" He should find her. Thank her. Buy back the damn necklace.

"The one who jumped off the building."

Whoa, there. "What?"

"The one who saved us. I don't know her name."

"She *jumped* off the building?"

Hoop looked up from the Hostess package he was opening. Taylor lifted his free hand in an I-don't-know sort of gesture.

"Yeah. It's been all over the news. Happened right by your office."

"Who is she?"

"Nobody seems to know. Some mystery woman."

"Well, hell."

"She told me she was filming a movie or something."

"What movie? Think, Lane. It's import—"

"I gotta go," she said. "Davy's crying."

"Wait, Lane," he said, but she'd already hung up. *Damn.*

"Did you say some chick jumped off a building?" Hoop asked.

"I didn't say it. Lane did. And she gave the necklace to this mystery woman."

"I was wrong, man. You're not charmed; you're S.O.L."

Taylor sighed. "So much for an easy ten grand. I guess tomorrow morning I start looking for the mysterious flying woman."

"Hello? Mr. Bailey?"

At the distinctly feminine voice, Taylor jumped, then

looked at Hoop, who shrugged. "A client?" Taylor whispered.

"Not for me. I don't work on Saturday."

Taylor considered arguing—after all, Hoop was at the office, and it was Saturday—then decided not to split hairs. If Hoop wanted to hand him all the Saturday walk-ins, so be it.

"Have a seat," he called out, plucking at the damp slacks clinging to his legs. So much for an aura of professionalism. *Oh, well.* If Saturday didn't qualify as casual day, nothing did. "Be right there," he added, calling toward the main room.

He stepped into the reception area, then stopped short. *Zoë Smith.* She was standing right in front of him, eyes wide, mouth hanging open, looking every bit as surprised and delighted as he felt. For just an instant, he allowed himself the pleasure of seeing her again.

His Zoë.

Another man's Zoë.

Her lips thinned and she lifted her chin. Behind those lenses, her eyes flashed lightning, the quiet joy he'd just seen replaced by anger.

"George Bailey, I presume." One eyebrow lifted, and she crossed her arms over her chest. "Or am I mistaken, *Buster?*"

"Buster?" Hoop repeated from behind him. Taylor whirled to see his friend leaning in the doorway to the file room, an amused expression playing across his face. "She's pissed at you, man," he said under his breath. "Buster's the polite girl's word for *asshole*. 'Or am I mistaken, *asshole?*' " he said, mimicking her. "See how that works?"

"Got it," he said somewhat ungratefully and shot Hoop a look.

"Why shouldn't I be mad?" she asked. "He told me it was his name."

"Asshole?"

"Buster," Taylor corrected.

"Right," said Hoop. "Why?"

"Funny, I was going to ask that very thing." Zoë put one hand on her hip and waited.

Taylor opened his mouth to say something clever and pithy, but nothing came out.

He tried again, finally managing an "Uh . . ."

She scowled.

"Look," he said. "Pretend I said something so incredibly clever that you were blown away by my wit and charm."

Her smile was reluctant, but it was still a smile, and it took every ounce of his willpower not to run around the room doing a victory dance. Instead he just grinned like an idiot. "Maybe we should do it right this time," he finally managed. "I'm George Bailey Taylor."

"Nice to meet you, George. I'm Zoë Smith."

"He prefers Taylor," Hoop said from behind him.

Zoë gave Hoop a smile—did they know each other?— and a nugget of something remarkably close to jealousy rattled around in Taylor's gut.

"Good to see you again, Hoop," she said, answering his question. He frantically tried to figure out how on earth she knew Hoop. Then he put it all together. Deena volunteered at the school. Zoë knew Hoop through Deena. The bead of jealousy melted.

She trained her eyes on him. "So, *Taylor,* you want to tell me why you lied?"

"Yeah. Explain to the lady." Hoop hooked a leg over the reception desk, apparently enjoying the show.

"Twice," she said.

"Twice?" Hoop repeated, before Taylor could get a word in.

"At the school, and then last night."

"Last night?" Hoop's voice rose, and a devious grin spread across his face. "And so the pieces of that triangle we were discussing fall into place. . . ."

"Hoop," he said in what he hoped was a threatening manner.

His friend held up his hands. "I'm not saying a word, buddy. You're the one who's supposed to be doing the talking."

"Talking?" he asked dumbly.

"The lie?" she said. "Your explanation."

"Oh. Right. Well, I didn't exactly lie."

Her eyebrows rose above her glasses. "You said your name was *Buster.*"

"I was undercover."

She crossed her arms over her chest. "Exactly."

Damn but he hated seeing that look in her eyes. "Okay. So I lied. But I was working a job."

"Not last night you weren't. Last night you were looking for a date."

"Yeah," Hoop agreed. "How do you explain that?"

Taylor turned to scowl at him, then focused his full attention on her. "I didn't think about reintroducing myself."

"Why on earth not?"

"I wasn't thinking clearly." He caught her eyes and

looked deep into them. "Beautiful women make me nervous."

"Oh." She dropped her gaze to the floor. "Thanks."

"So why are you here?" he asked, hoping to change the subject while he was ahead. He held his breath, knowing the odds that she'd rushed to find him and tell him she was no longer taken were pretty damn slim.

She grazed her teeth over her lower lip as she looked from him to Hoop, then back again. He didn't know what, but something clearly had the poor girl agitated. She pulled her braid over her shoulder and started fidgeting with its end. Without thinking, he moved closer, wishing he could calm her fears. He knew he was unreasonably drawn to this woman, but he couldn't help it. He could only follow the path cut by his rough-edged emotions.

"Zoë?" he asked when she remained silent, starting to get concerned. "What is it?"

Biting her lower lip, she avoided meeting his eyes. "The thing is," she said, "I kind of need . . . well . . ."

She took a deep breath. "I need a man."

Chapter Nine

A man? Taylor frowned, not sure he'd heard correctly. Was Mr. Wonderful out of the picture? And if so, what exactly did she want a man for?

"Not like that," she hurried to add, a slow blush creeping up her cheeks. "I need an escort for a lawn party tomorrow. Just one night, and Deena said you needed clients." She squinted at him. "Of course, that's before I knew you were *you.*"

He tried out a weak smile. Apparently they were back to his little misrepresentation about his name.

"I was right, my man," Hoop said, with a cocky smile. "You do lead a charmed life."

Charmed? The very woman he'd been fantasizing about for days waltzed into his office and set her sights on him, but not because she wanted *him*, but because she needed a paid, *platonic* escort. Somehow, *charmed* wasn't the word that leaped to mind.

True, he might be really close to losing the quick ten grand he so desperately needed, but he hadn't sunk so low that he was getting paid to schlepp another man's woman to parties. "I don't think—"

"It's just the one night." Her eyes darted to Hoop, silently pleading.

"Well, that's part of the problem, isn't it?" Taylor said.

She squinted. "What is?"

"One night," he said. "Just a temporary gig while Mr. Wonderful's away. *That's* my problem."

"Mr. Wonderful?" she repeated.

"What are you talking about?" Hoop asked at the same time.

Taylor held up a hand. "I just think—"

"I'll pay your usual rate," Zoë cut him off.

"It is not the rate, dammit. It's the principle. I just—"

"Please?" Her eyes widened behind those studious frames.

"Jeez, man. What the heck." Hoop spoke before Taylor could cut him off. "Help the lady out for a night, and you're that much closer to financial freedom."

Taylor glared at both of them in turn. "Would you two let me finish a sentence?"

She glanced at Hoop; then the two of them both shrugged.

"Sure," she said.

"No problem," Hoop agreed.

"Thank you." He turned to face his friend. "First off, in case you missed the sign on our door, this isn't an escort service."

"So pretend a little." Hoop casually pulled his wallet out of his back pocket and flipped through it. "Unless

149

you've already found a buyer for that Mustang . . ."

Taylor scowled. "Now you're hitting below the belt."

"Me? Never."

Taylor ignored him. "Besides," he added, "I already have a case I need to be cracking on. Remember?"

Hoop snorted. "Like one night's gonna make a difference."

Zoë glanced at Hoop, nodding vigorously, then turned back to Taylor. "He's right. It's just a cocktail party. Then you can get back to detecting or defecting or annoying or whatever you do." She grinned at him, her arms crossed over her chest.

"Investigating," Taylor said, rubbing his temples. The woman made his head spin in more ways than one. "And that's my point. I don't do the paid-escort gig. Especially not with another man's woman."

"What the hell are you talking about?" Hoop asked.

"She's got—"

"A problem," Zoë interrupted. "Please. I need your help."

"Sorry. I can't."

She pressed her lips together and gave him one curt nod. "I guess I'd better get going, then."

She turned, heading for the door, and his gut clenched.

Was it his training as a cop that always made him want to help a lady in distress, or was that instinct why he'd become a cop in the first place? Either way, his soft nature was about to set him an entire half day behind on his plan for financial freedom. Not to mention what it was going to do for his level of sexual frustration. An entire evening with a woman he craved who belonged to another man? He must be an idiot to even consider it.

Oh, hell. "Wait," he called.

Hoop smirked, an "I knew you'd cave" expression spreading across his face.

Zoë turned back, her head cocked and her arms crossed over her chest. "What?"

"Gratis," he said. He'd be her date, but he wasn't going to stoop to playing *American Gigolo.*

"Excuse me?"

Hoop jumped to explain, pointing to Taylor. "He'll do you—sorry, *it*—for free."

Taylor shot Hoop full of holes with his eyes.

"For free?" Zoë asked in an odd tone.

"Right," Taylor said. "Plain, old-fashioned, simple. No money changing hands. Everything normal."

"Like a real date?"

He frowned, pushing back a wave of rising irritation. Wasn't she supposed to be grateful? In his script, those gorgeous eyes would look at him in gratitude, thrilled he was sacrificing a day's wage. Not in hers, though. This girl's baby blue—and gray—looked anything but grateful. "Isn't that what you asked for? Or is Mr. Wonderful the jealous type?" He fought to keep the annoyance out of his voice. For some inexplicable reason, he wanted to razz her about this boyfriend, as though she'd somehow cheated on him. It was stupid and juvenile, but that was how he felt.

"I don't think—"

"Look," he interrupted. "You need an escort, a date." He pointed to himself. "I'm willing to do it. But I won't take money for it." He ran his fingers through his hair. "So. Do we have a deal?"

She blinked.

He waited for her to say something—anything—but nothing came. He sighed. "I think 'thank you' is the traditionally accepted response."

She didn't answer, just fingered the earpiece on her glasses, which had slid down her nose. Then she scowled and pushed them back up, looking every bit like a kid eyeing a candy jar.

He frowned, wishing he had a clue what was going on in her mind.

She tapped her glasses, then shook her head. "No. I don't think that would be a good idea. It's nothing personal," she added, and he silently cursed her mysterious boyfriend. "It's just that I don't feel . . . comfortable having you do this for free."

"And I don't feel *comfortable*," he said, mimicking her, "being paid."

Hoop hopped off the desk and came to stand between them. "Children, children. I think you're missing the big picture." He aimed a grand wave toward Zoë. "The lady needs protection."

Her brow furrowed. "I do?"

"You *do*," said Hoop meaningfully. "You definitely do."

Taylor saw the lightbulb flash on over her head.

"Oh! Right. I need protection." She nibbled on her lower lip. "Just for the one night, of course."

Hoop grinned. "Our door *does* say 'Investigative and Protective Services.' "

"Uh-huh." Taylor tried to fight his laugh, but lost. "So who exactly do you need protection from?"

"Good question," she said, holding up a finger. "I'm working on it." Her eyes darted to Hoop, who shrugged.

"I'm hiring you because of the . . . the . . ." She trailed off, her hand twirling in the air.

"Thugs?" Taylor suggested.

"That's good," said Hoop. "Thugs." He shoved his hands into his pockets and leaned back against the wall, looking so smug that Taylor would almost believe his friend had just disproved Einstein's theory of relativity.

"Thugs?" Zoë repeated, then, "Oh! Right. *Thugs.*" She moved infinitesimally closer, and his awareness of her jumped exponentially. Once again she twisted the end of her braid around her finger.

He fought the urge to reach out and stroke her cheek, to see if her skin was as soft as it looked, then surprised himself by saying, "So tell me about these thugs."

She looked at Hoop, then back at him. The bridge of her nose crinkled as her eyebrows drew together. Then she sighed, a long, drawn-out sound. "There're these guys. Big guys. Huge." She threw her arms out, illustrating their girth. "And they've been harassing me. And they know about the party tomorrow, and I think they might try to do something."

He sighed. This was so obviously fake. She was still paying him to be a date, and Mr. Wonderful was still hanging in the background.

He wanted her. And she wanted a business deal.

Then again, what did he expect? Beautiful redheads sashaying in, looking to hire a guy . . . that was Philip Marlowe's staff, not George Bailey Taylor's.

He should tell her he had another job lined up, and just walk away. He'd be an idiot to get distracted by this girl.

Thanks, but no, thanks. And please come again.

"Taylor?" She looked up, waiting.

All his life he'd been a sucker for a damsel in distress. But this damsel *caused* distress, and he needed to get clear, to leave her to her boyfriend and focus on the ten grand he could be making.

And that was just what he intended to do.

He stuck out his hand. "Congratulations," he said, blowing every one of his intentions into a billion tiny pieces. "Looks like you've just hired yourself a man."

A rainbow of sparks zinged through her arm as he grasped her hand, sealing their bargain. In that moment, Zoë had one coherent thought—that she was making a huge, walloping, change-your-destiny-forever kind of mistake.

The absolute mother of all mistakes. Which brought her full circle to why she couldn't back out of this deal. Her mother.

Zoë needed a date, and this man—this P.I. whose touch made her body snap, crackle, and pop—had stepped up to the plate.

She concentrated, unwilling to let the magic of his touch overwhelm her control, urging her nerve endings to quit singing. *Breathe in, breathe out, in, out.* And slowly, slowly, she felt her faculties flood back, the sparks a sweet undercurrent to the warmth of his hand on hers.

With a little moan, she ripped her gaze away from him. She couldn't get involved with a mortal. Couldn't, wouldn't, shouldn't. It was too dangerous, and no matter what Deena claimed, Zoë just didn't believe that she could share something intimate with this man and then walk away. She'd made up the boyfriend story, and she intended to stick to it.

With a tug, she pulled her hand away, hoping the break in contact would clear the last bit of fuzz from her brain.

Still, a little demon kept urging her to tilt her head down . . . to take a quick gander over the rim of her glasses. . . .

"Zoë?"

She jumped, blinking, and shoved the glasses up her nose.

Get a grip, Zo. He is just the hired help. This isn't a real date.

Of course, considering how crazy he made her feel, even a pretend date was dangerous, but at least by paying him there was that extra distance. It could be purely professional. And he thought she had a boyfriend, which doubled the safety factor.

No risk of heartbreak, no risk of revealing her secret.

Just a guy helping a girl pull one over on her mother.

"Zoë?" Taylor asked again.

"Hmmm?"

"You okay?" He was staring at her, his brow furrowed.

She snapped to attention. "Yes, thank you. I'm fine."

She flashed him a smile, knowing she was flirting with the man, but unable to help herself. "Just a little distracted, what with those thugs hounding me and all."

"Right." He grinned. "Those nasty ol' thugs."

She stifled a giggle and saw the corner of his mouth twitch. This was dangerous. Already she was having too much fun with this guy, and that had to be a bad thing.

Just being around him was making her head spin and her skin sizzle, every little tiny hair on her body practically vibrating with electricity—incredible sensations that had nothing to do with her supersenses, and everything to do with this man.

She was kidding herself to think that this bodyguard malarkey meant that their "date" would be a purely business affair. She almost snorted. Like *she* needed a bodyguard.

What she needed was a swift kick in the libido before she threw herself at this man, this handsome hunk who was standing in front of her, an amused expression playing across his face as though he knew how much havoc he was wreaking in her head.

She propped a fist on her hip. "What are you looking at?" she asked teasingly.

His eyes twinkled. "Apparently I'm looking at a woman fleeing in terror from a gaggle of goons."

"Are you suggesting I've been less than truthful?" she asked in mock disbelief, even as she wondered how furious Hale was going to be when he found out she'd been flirting with a mortal. "Because if you are, then I guess you're in the paid-escort business after all."

"Not necessarily."

"Well, if there are no thugs . . ." She trailed off, watching his eyes to make sure he got it.

The corner of his mouth curled up. "Ah. I see."

She waited expectantly for a moment, then said, "Well?"

"Well, what?"

"Say it."

"Zoë—"

"Ah-ah," she warned, waggling a finger, and fighting a grin.

"What?" he asked, amused.

"Come on. Say it. I have to know you know what you're up against."

A muscle in his cheek twitched. "Fine. There are thugs. Big, ugly thugs. Gangly goons. Creepy crooks. And they're chasing you all over the city."

"Thank you," she said, dropping into a little curtsy as Hoop laughed. "That's much better."

Taylor inclined his head, pretentious butler-style. "You're very welcome." He looked up and caught her gaze, his dark eyes flashing with something more than just amusement.

She broke eye contact, making a show of fumbling in her purse, hoping he couldn't tell that her pulse had sped up crazily. "Pick me up tomorrow at five, okay?"

"Sure thing," he said, and she nodded, wondering if it was a good or a bad thing that she'd already started counting down.

Twenty-two hours, thirteen minutes, thirty-nine seconds and counting.

She sighed. *A bad thing. This is definitely a bad thing.*

Chapter Ten

"How could you have let her get away?" Hieronymous leaned against his desk, his fingers drumming a slow rhythm on his desktop, his eyes narrowing. "One mortal female. How much simpler could it have been?"

Mordi cringed and backed away, overcome with a sudden urge to shape-shift. How very nice it would be to simply change into a rat and scurry away. He smiled at the thought, closing his eyes, and imagining a little rat life where he could preside over all the other rats without his father's incessant criticisms. *Ah, such a lovely image.*

"I've called you here to explain this blunder," Hieronymous raved. "So *explain.*"

"I had it, Father—right in the palm of my hand. But Zoë was there—"

"Why? Did she know about the jewel?"

He shook his head. "An unfortunate coincidence, I think. But she was there nonetheless."

"And she managed to defeat you." Hieronymous looked down his nose at his son, his eyes dark and cold. "A few days ago you stood here and told me such a thing was not possible."

Mordi swallowed. "My powers. They blipped."

"Blipped?" Hieronymous repeated, scorn lacing his voice.

"The fluctuations. I had it, but then . . ." He trailed off, ashamed that he had no control over the changes that were upon him.

"I see." He tapped louder on the tabletop. "You are a halfling, of course. I suppose we must make do."

Mordi sighed. Truly, there were times when he despised being the son of the self-proclaimed soon-to-be high ruler of the mortals and usurper of the council.

Still, once he defeated Zoë—once he had the stone—then he'd be the son of the high ruler of the mortals and usurper of the council. Surely that would earn his father's respect.

"Mordichai!"

"Yes, sir," he said, jerking his head back up to face his father's coal black eyes.

"You will return to Los Angeles and redouble your efforts. You will obtain the stone before the eclipse so that we may perform the ritual and gather the Outcasts."

He glanced at the monitor, which was scrolling through his current portfolio. "The market closed up last week. That's good news for you." He smiled, all teeth and jowls. "It improved my mood considerably."

Thank goodness for small favors, thought Mordi, as

he desperately wished for an amazing performance by the Dow and NASDAQ for the rest of the week.

"As for the stone, I'm already on the trail, sir," he said.

"How?" asked Hieronymous.

"I've hired a detective, sir," Mordi mumbled.

"Yes. I am aware of that." He settled himself into his chair and propped his feet on the mahogany desk. "I can't say that I approve bringing a mortal into these affairs, particularly when his help is not necessary. What does a child of an Outcast need with mortal assistance?"

"The tracking device isn't sufficient," Mordi said, a little queasy at the thought of his father watching him on those damnable monitors.

Hieronymous swung his feet off his desk and leaned forward, long fingers drumming ceaselessly on the table. "Not sufficient? I created that device myself."

"Yes, sir. I know, sir." Mordi drew a deep breath, trying to harness enough courage to suggest that his father had done something with less than his usual precision. "But the device indicates only the general area. It doesn't pinpoint the stone."

Actually, considering what a vague location the device offered, Mordi thought he'd done a heck of a job just finding the rock. He'd located the shopkeeper and the girl on his own, before hiring the P.I. If that wasn't some quality gumshoeing, he didn't know what was.

Apparently, though, Daddy Dearest didn't agree.

"Father," he said, with a slightly submissive tilt of his head to ward off any particularly violent bouts of disapproval. "We know two things for sure. One, the stone is somewhere in Los Angeles. Two, by the nature of the prophecy, the stone may well find its way to Zoë."

His father's long fingers continued their tap-tapping, and the man frowned. "Go on."

"Right. Well. It seems only reasonable that I should focus my attention on Zoë. On keeping her from acquiring the stone. On wresting it away if she does. And this detective can be another set of eyes—eyes that are more accustomed to this sort of work."

Tap, tap. Tap, tap. Mordi watched his father's fingers, trying to gauge the man's mood from the movement. The tapping stopped.

"You little fool," Hieronymous said, and Mordi recoiled, anger and shame welling in his gut. His father pushed back from the desk and stood, practically filling the room.

"There's another reason for hiring the detective," Mordi squeaked, cringing.

"Explain."

"The detective appears to have an interest in my cousin—and she in him. If she finds the stone, Mr. Taylor will learn about it. And he, in turn, will tell me." He stared his father straight in the eyes. "And then I will go to retrieve the stone from Zoë. . . . Father, I *will* win that battle."

Hieronymous stroked his chin. "Yes. I would prefer to avoid such a confrontation altogether, but I believe you will prove the victor if you are forced into battle with your little cousin. Our entire future—my entire plan—depends on it. So I must believe in you."

"Thank you, sir." If that wasn't damning him with faint praise . . .

"I said I *must* believe. I did not say I intended to let blind faith dictate my actions."

So much for the hope he'd ever have a warm, fuzzy

relationship with his father. Hieronymous was as cold as steel and just as hard. No wonder Mordi's mother had left him—why would the woman want to risk raising a son who might take after the paternal side of his family?

Hieronymous turned, facing the monitors, their glass reflecting his face so that Mordi was suddenly under the scrutiny of twelve Hieronymouses, rather than just one. He pressed a large gold button on his desktop, and his smile reminded Mordi of the Grinch, back when his heart was still two sizes too small. "You keep that detective on retainer. Once Zoë is no longer around, he may be especially useful in helping to find the stone."

"Not around?" A chill ripped down Mordi's spine. It was one thing to beat her fair and square, to win the stone and fulfill the legend. But Hieronymous was apparently suggesting something much, much darker.

Still, if that was what it took to win his father's favor . . .

He shivered slightly. *Well, so be it.*

"Our hour is at hand," Hieronymous said. "And I think it is time that we stack the deck in our favor."

He aimed the remote at the monitors, all twelve of which immediately filled with an aerial view of Los Angeles. "I think it's time you took your cousin out of the equation."

From his perch on her window sill, Elmer watched as Zoë pirouetted in front of the full-length mirror, showing off her gold-belted little red dress.

"So? Whadaya think?" Deena asked. "I think the belt makes the outfit. Not bad for three bucks, huh?"

Elmer yawned. *It looks like you slapped a belt on a thrift-store dress*, he chittered to no one in particular.

The outfit didn't exactly look like Versace. And he should know. Hale dragged him to enough photo shoots. What a lucky ferret I am, he thought snippily.

"You don't think it looks tacky, do you?" Zoë asked, turning sideways. "Like I've slapped a belt on one of my mom's hand-me-downs?"

Yes.

"Hardly," Deena answered. Elmer wished he were human so he could roll his eyes. "You look hot," she enthused.

Zoë turned another circle, then ran her hands down her sides and over her hips. "I can't believe I'm going out in public like this. I mean, look at me. I've got curves."

So she did. Little Zoë Smith definitely had the family genes. If he weren't a ferret . . . well, zowie!

"I really look okay?" she asked again.

He nodded vigorously, but she wasn't paying attention.

"Hell, yes," Deena said. She cocked her head. "Still . . ."

Zoë's eyes went wide. "What?"

"I was just thinking that you could use a Wonderbra."

"Are you nuts? I've already got so much cleavage I could hide a bankroll. Besides, what exactly is he supposed to be wondering about?"

"Whether he's going to get some, of course."

"Deena! I told you. I'm not doing the dating thing. I'm not doing the relationship thing. And I'm certainly not doing the sex thing. Not anytime soon, at least. Leave it alone, okay?"

Deena shrugged. "Whatever."

Zoë turned sideways, and Elmer saw her reflection in

the mirror as she stood up straight and threw her shoulders back.

She ran her hands over the dress, and her eyes met Deena's in the mirror. "You're sure this looks good? Because I like it, and everyone knows I have no taste in clothes."

"Trust me, kid. You look great. With your figure you'd look great in a flour sack."

Just like he knew she would, Zoë turned to face Deena straight-on, and the blonde raised a hand in self-defense.

"Not that you *look* like you're wearing a flour sack. This dress is used, but it's chic." She reached out and fondled the material. "Raw silk. Can't beat that. And the belt is fab. Kind of retro cool."

When was ugly cool? Elmer squeaked in annoyance. There were times when not speaking human was downright inconvenient.

"It needs something, though." Deena dumped her purse on the bed, letting loose a shower of pens, paper, jewelry, paintbrushes, and other assorted stuff. "Earrings, maybe."

Elmer jumped off the windowsill to have a closer look. He'd never seen a mortal who hauled around so much junk.

Deena gave him a gentle shove as he got to close. "Do you mind? You're sitting on the jewelry." She looked up at Zoë. "When did you get a ferret, anyway?"

Zoë laughed. "He's my brother's. His name's Elmer, and he's got a knack for being in the middle of things."

"So I see," Deena agreed, digging once more into her purseful of junk. "Anyway, I still say you should go for it."

"For what?"

"*It.*" Deena waved her hand in the air. "You know. *Sex.*" Elmer's ears perked up.

"No way. We had this conversation yesterday, remember? I'm not ready." She shook her head. "Not happening. Uh-uh."

Good for you, kid. Stick to your guns.

"But you said that's because you hadn't found Mr. Right."

"No, that's what *you* said."

"Whatever." The blonde brushed the objection away like a gnat. "The point is, it was a brilliant observation." She finally came up with two matching earrings. "Yesterday you couldn't find Mr. Right. Well, now you—"

"—rented some guy I don't know anything about. No big deal."

Elmer's head shot up. Zoë looked over at him, her brows drawing together.

Deena paused, a sparkly earring dangling from her fingers. "What the hell are you talking about?"

"Just that Taylor's nothing more than some guy I hired for the evening. I mean, I just met him."

"No, he's not. He's Mr.—"

"George Bailey Taylor, private investigator." Zoë's eyes were wide, her jaw firm. "Good thing he's hard up for cash, huh? I mean, I needed to hire a date and this guy I hardly know needed the work. . . ." She glanced at Elmer, then back to her friend.

Deena scowled, then looked at Elmer, obviously confused by something. "Okay, fine. Whatever. He's just some guy you hired."

"Exactly."

"Nothing special there."

Zoë shrugged. "Nothing at all."

Elmer cringed. The girl was a lousy liar.

"So, you gonna wear your glasses?" Deena asked.

Zoë's eyes widened. Elmer nodded his little head, frantically trying to signal, *Yes, yes, by all means, wear the glasses*.

"Are you insane? Of course I am," she said, and Elmer breathed a sigh of relief.

Deena rolled her eyes. "Sweetie, you really need to take a walk on the wild side. You're at least going to take a peek."

"No peeking." Zoë crossed her arms over her chest and glared. "There's going to be absolutely no peeking." A tiny smile lifted one corner of her mouth. "Well . . . probably not, anyway."

Elmer crawled under a pillow. Hale was going to have an absolute fit, and, stone or no stone, the week was undoubtedly going to prove incredibly amusing.

"You're telling me she really jumped off a building?" Taylor watched Lane pour water into the coffeemaker as he swung a squealing Davy by one hand and one foot in a wide arc around the living room. "As in nosedive toward the ground? EMS? Broken bones and traumatized children?"

She wiped her hands on her jeans. "I told you—she didn't actually 'jump.' She wore some sort of special cape with these superstrong wires, and it worked like a hang glider."

"Uh-huh." He eased Davy to the floor. "Why am I not buying this?"

Lane shrugged. "What's not to buy? I saw it with my own eyes."

"And then you gave her the necklace—"

"Right."

"—but didn't get her name."

His foster sister sighed, screwing up her mouth in annoyance. "Bummer, huh?"

He laughed. "That's the understatement of the year."

"Ten grand . . . I can't believe it."

"Ten grand and then some," he added.

She ran her finger down an ancient refrigerator they'd just picked up at a garage sale. "Woulda been nice."

"Woulda been? It's not exactly over."

"Hello?" Lane said. "We don't have the necklace, remember?"

He shrugged. "Somebody does."

"And that somebody's not you or me. So how are we supposed to find it?"

He pointed at himself and tried to affect an insulted expression. "Remember me? Your multitalented brother? I'm a hell of an investigator. That's why this Mordon guy hired me in the first place."

"Well, yeah, but—"

"But nothing. We'll find her, and this rich loony bird can buy the necklace off her. Then we'll split the finder's fee."

Lane nodded, but didn't look too convinced.

"Come on. Trust me." He pulled a chair out from under her kitchen table, flipped it around, and straddled it. "Lane . . ."

She grinned. "I guess if anyone can find it, you're the man." She snorted. "Talk about turnabout. Eight months ago *I* was the one trying to convince *you* that you still had the stuff."

He cringed. Eight months ago he'd been released from rehab only to find out that the department was sticking him behind a desk and saddling him with an administrative job. Det. George Bailey Taylor, local hero, suddenly turned paper pusher.

After two months of sulking, he'd basically told them to shove the job and the damned disability checks. He'd struck out on his own—and was doing just fine, thank you very much. *Incapacitated, my ass*.

He rubbed his thigh, frowning. Of course, so far he hadn't needed to chase any thugs down dark alleys. But if it came to that . . . well, he'd show them. He'd do what needed to be done. Annoying limp and all. Nothing important had changed.

Nothing at all.

And it wasn't as if he'd be chasing any criminals tonight, anyway. At least, not any real ones. The only thugs after Zoë Smith were the ones living in her imagination. Though from what he could tell, her imagination was about as vivid as her hair.

"Taylor?" Lane was frowning. "You okay?"

"Fine," he said, his voice harsh to his ears. He shook his head, clearing his thoughts. "So we start with what we know. What did she look like?"

Lane shrugged. "She had on a hood."

"Strike one, but that's okay. They were filming a movie, right?"

"Yeah, *Boopsey Saves the World,* remember?" She grimaced, clearly not impressed with the title.

"Hmmm. I managed to catch someone at the *Hollywood Reporter*, and no one there knows anything about a movie like that in production right now."

Lane picked up Davy, who was tugging on her skirt. "Maybe it's a really small movie and the trades just don't know about it."

"Could be. But with this gizmo you saw, it sounds like they've got a decent budget."

"Yeah."

"Monday I'll call the city and see if they had a permit to film. Then I'll start calling all the production companies around town. Start big, work small."

Lane grinned. "I guess you do know your stuff."

"Aw, shucks, ma'am," he joked, and she rolled her eyes. "I'll also interview folks who work in nearby shops. Maybe they saw something."

"That sounds tedious."

"Sounds like detective work. Legwork. Same thing." Too bad his leg didn't work so well anymore.

"Cool beans." She looked at her watch. "Let me drop Davy at a friend's and we can start right now."

"Don't worry. I've got it under control."

She eyed him suspiciously. "*You've* got it under control? It was *my* necklace. I'm not going to let you do all the work and then split the money."

He opened his mouth to tell her he'd find her necklace and didn't need her help, but nothing came out. She only wanted to do some of the legwork, after all. And the damn thing had belonged to her originally. "Fine. *We'll* check out the shops."

To her credit, her smile wasn't overly smug. "Just let me grab my keys."

"We can't go now. I've got plans."

"Plans?" Her voice was incredulous, and he suddenly realized just how rarely he did anything even remotely social.

"Yeah, plans. You know? Where a person thinks ahead of time about doing something and then, when that time comes around, they actually do it."

"And who do you have these mysterious plans with?"

Oh, no. He wasn't getting into the date-no-date thing with Lane. That can of worms was going to remain firmly sealed shut. "No one you know. It's no big deal. Scour Hollywood by yourself if you want."

"No one I know, male? Or no one I know, female?"

He sighed. "Female."

Her eyes widened. "Oh, really? How very . . . interesting."

"In-tra-sing," echoed Davy.

Taylor rolled his eyes. "It's just a job, Lane."

"Is she pretty?"

"Hello? Didn't I just tell you it's a job?"

"Oh. Is she *normal?*"

Clearly there was no avoiding this conversation. "Very."

"This is sounding more and more promising by the minute."

"She *hired* me, Lane. Job, yes. Date, no."

"Too bad," said Lane, and Taylor had to agree.

Taylor drummed his fingers on the steering wheel, waiting for the light to change. How had a woman he barely knew managed to crawl so far under his skin?

Lane was right: he never socialized, never did the club scene, rarely even went out with a buddy for a drink.

But today he was going to a cocktail party, of all things. Correction, a *lawn* party. And damned if he wasn't looking forward to it.

Just what the heck was a lawn party anyway?

He ran his fingers through his hair, imagining himself and Zoë sipping wine, tasting various cocktails and appetizers on a big blanket spread out in a lush field. Next to them a giant umbrella was propped up against a lawn mower. *The softer side of Sears. Yes, indeed.* He was all for lawn-care products if they got him closer to Zoë Smith.

The woman touched something inside of him without even trying, without even lifting a finger. She was sweet and gentle, and had an air of innocence and a backbone of steel. Zoë Smith stood up for what she believed in—he'd seen that in the school library on the day he'd met her—and he wanted her to believe in him. To trust him. She made him feel alive, and he hadn't felt that way in a long, long time. And right now she needed him.

He could only hope like hell that she wanted him, too.

In his mind, Zoë was easing him down, lower and lower, until his back was pressed against a blanket. She was on top of him, warm and willing. She—

A horn blared behind him causing a surge of frustration to well in his gut, and he pounded the heel of his hand against the steering wheel. Primal and primitive his reaction to her might be, but damn if he could think of anything else.

Taken. The word taunted him. Why the hell did she have to be seeing another man?

Again the horn blared.

He closed his eyes, imagining her skin under his fingertips, the scent of flowers as he leaned in to press his lips against hers. Would she back away? Or would she lean forward to meet him, take his mouth with her own?

He opened his eyes, sighing. He could try. Hell, he had to try. Tonight might be his only shot. One gig playing the knight in shining armor and then they'd go their separate ways.

Not if he had any say in the matter.

Maybe a little seduction was in order. After all, what was the worst that could happen? He frowned. She could say no. Or she could slap the shit out of him. Or her boyfriend could.

But the best that could happen . . .

Well, the possibility of a long night with Zoë Smith was well worth risking a palm-shaped bruise on the side of his face.

And as for *Baywatch* boy . . . well, any man who would leave a woman like Zoë to fend for herself, who would leave her so desperate for an escort that she'd hire one, wasn't rowing with all his oars. Hell, Hoop hadn't even known Zoë had a steady guy, so he couldn't be too entrenched in her life.

In Taylor's book, that made the man an idiot. And if he was lucky, soon the idiot would be an ex, and Taylor could slide into the newly vacated slot in Zoë's life.

The little Toyota behind him honked again, and he glanced into the rearview mirror. A scruffy teenager with a mop of yellow hair was leaning on the horn, flipping him the bird.

He waved at the kid and moved into traffic. Time to get going anyway.

Time to go pick up his date for the evening.

Chapter Eleven

"If you don't sit still, you're going to end up looking like a clown instead of a beauty queen."

Zoë cringed as Deena leaned over her, brandishing a wand of mascara. "I don't want to be a beauty queen. I just want to be me."

"Same diff," Deena said.

Zoë pretended she hadn't heard, and hopped off the table. Deena had made her unbraid her hair first thing, and now Zoë twisted a strand around her finger as she walked from the sofa to the kitchen and back again.

"What is with you?"

Zoë nibbled on her lip. "I'm nervous. I'm really, really nervous." She glanced around the room. "We're sure Elmer's not here, right?"

"The ferret?" Deena asked. "Are you going to clue me in on what's with the ferret?"

"I'm just not real keen on him reporting back to my

brother with a full dissertation on the state of my nerves."

"Ah," said Deena. "Because, of course, the ferret talks to him."

"Right," Zoë said. "Hale's always dumping Elmer on me when he needs a spy. It's his passive-aggressive way of keeping me in line, and he thinks I don't realize."

"You've got a weird family, kid. But I'm not one to talk." She leaned back. "So. Does the ferret talk to you, too?"

"He talks. I don't understand. I'm not an animalinguist."

For about half a second, Deena looked a little disconcerted. Then she shrugged. "Fair enough. At least this explains that bizarro doublespeak in the other room."

Zoë grinned. Deena was nothing if not easygoing.

"At any rate, I don't see him anywhere," Zoë said.

"I wouldn't worry," said Deena. "He's probably in your bedroom having ferret phone sex or watching *Animal Planet*."

"Good point," Zoë said, managing to keep a straight face.

"Can we get back to the makeover? Taylor will be here any minute."

"I still don't see why—"

"If you're going to seduce a man, you might as well start out in top form."

"I am *not* going to sed—"

"Not that you don't look great even without makeup." Deena waved an eyelash curler like a small weapon. "But you'll want to look extra hot for Mr. Midnight."

"*Mr. Midnight?*"

A twinkle appeared in Deena's eyes. "Since Taylor's

the guy you've been lusting after, I'm assuming you think about him, you know . . . when it's dark."

"No comment," Zoë mumbled. Her friend looked smug. Of course, she had pretty much nailed the truth on the head with the nickname. For the past few days, Zoë's nights had been filled with Taylor—the imaginary version, anyway. Disconcerting, but oh so true. "Deena, I don't really want him to know I'm attracted to him. I mean, I spent the entire time I was at his office convincing him I *didn't* want a date-date. If I wear all of that"—she waved her hand over the cosmetics-covered table—"then surely he's gonna think I'm interested."

"Like I've been saying, just go for it. Damn the torpedoes, full orgasm ahead."

"Deenie . . ."

"Hmmm?" she asked, twisting up tubes of lipstick and inspecting the colors.

Zoë raised an eyebrow and tapped her foot.

Deena gave her an annoyed look. "Fine. Be a nun. But don't say I didn't try to help you." She sniffed a tube and tossed it aside. "At any rate, you should be prepared for the slim, minuscule off chance that something does develop. And a little sheer blush and extra-volume mascara never hurt anyone."

"You sound like a Revlon commercial."

"Hey, whatever works." She patted a cushion on the sofa. "Come on."

The fact was, Zoë did care about how she looked. This was Taylor, after all. Even if she wasn't going to do anything like *that* with him . . . well, she still wanted him to notice her. Wanted it a lot, actually.

Feeling rather pathetic, she sat on the coffee table in front of Deena. "Okay. Make me a new woman."

Preferably one who wasn't terrified of the prospect of getting close to the one man she desperately wanted to get close to.

"Don't talk. I'm going to do your lips. Do this," Deena said, then puckered.

"Should I—"

But she couldn't get the rest out, because Deena grabbed her mouth and made her pucker until she felt like a fish.

"You told me you can control your senses when you try, right?" the blond girl asked as she brushed on a thin layer of gloss.

Zoë nodded, since she was still pretty much lip-zipped.

"And you're doing it right now, right? I mean, I've got a hold of your cheeks."

True. And all Zoë felt was a rather uncomfortable squooshing sensation. She nodded.

"Well, see? There's no reason to spend your life hiding behind some invisible line. I mean, oatmeal and rice cakes . . . yuck."

"They're pretty tasty, actually," she managed, but Deena looked annoyed and squeezed her lips tight again.

"The point is, you just need to decide what you want and then go for it. Do you want to still be a virgin when you turn twenty-five, or do you want to get out there and go for it?"

"You make it sound so tawdry."

"Do I? I was hoping to make it sound fun."

Fun. Most women would probably agree. After all, she was going on a real date with a real man. A man she hadn't been able to get out of her mind for days.

Maybe she should let loose. . . .

Deena let go of her mouth, and Zoë massaged her cheeks.

"Careful of the gloss."

She stood up, then ran her fingers through her hair. She started to nibble on her lower lip, then stopped, remembering the makeup. This dressing-for-success thing was complicated. "What if I really can't handle it? His touch? What if it drives me crazy?"

"We've been over this, Zo. It's *supposed* to drive you crazy."

Maybe. But there was crazy and then there was *crazy*. And she wasn't sure she could manage either.

And that wasn't even her biggest fear. Knowing she was acting like one of the sixth graders with a crush, but unable to help it, she flopped back down onto the sofa. "What if he doesn't want me?"

"Zoë, please. Why wouldn't he?"

About a million reasons, not the least of which was that she had absolutely no idea how to act with a guy she actually liked. "I'm almost twenty-five and I've never even had a real date."

"You don't need to have had them. All you need is desire. And kiddo, you've got that in spades."

Maybe. But desiring and doing were two completely different things. And Zoë didn't intend to do anything about the *doing* part.

She heard Elmer stir far down the hallway, then heard him making his way toward the living room.

His little head appeared around the corner, and Deena waved. "Hey there, Elmer, you cute little ferret-face."

Zoë eyed the rodent, nibbling on her lower lip. There was no doubt in her mind that Hale had left Elmer to play chaperon—to cramp what little style she had while she went out on a date with a mortal.

A fresh wave of nervousness washed over her, and she fought to shake it before remembering that she had absolutely no reason to worry. After all, she wasn't going to do anything with the luscious Mr. Taylor.

Which meant there was nothing to be nervous about. Absolutely nothing at all.

A little voice in the back of her mind whispered, *Too bad.* Zoë sighed, wondering which was the bigger mistake—lusting after Taylor in the first place, or promising herself she wasn't going to do a darn thing about it.

Elmer was in no mood to be called cute or ferret-face, no matter how true either description was. He considered going back to the bedroom and watching another episode of *Hollywood Safari*, but Hale wanted him to keep an eye on Zoë. And from what he could tell, she needed some serious watching. The blond mortal was simply not a good influence.

With a grunt, Elmer climbed up the sofa and pulled himself onto the armrest. He perched there, watching the woman named Deena as she stared back at him.

"So he can understand me, right?"

Even if you speak Swahili, Elmer chittered snootily.

"As far as I know," said Zoë. "He always seems to understand what I'm saying. Don't you, Elmer?"

Oh, no. He wasn't about to do stupid ferret tricks for a mortal. He gave Zoë a stern look, then hopped onto the sofa cushion. If the girl was really going out on a date with a mortal, he'd stay and be Hale's spy, but that was all. He'd stay because that was his mission.

And also, of course, because he was stuck here. Since

ferrets couldn't operate motor vehicles, he wasn't exactly going anywhere else. Not unless he wanted to go out on the street to scratch out a *Hollywood or bust* sign and try to hitch a ride.

He didn't have to like this situation, but he was going to make the best of it. With a little hiss that he hoped conveyed how utterly bored he was by the whole thing, he turned in a circle three times, curled his tail under his chin, and tried to doze.

"I don't think he's feeling conversational," Deena said. She leaned down to peer at him until they were almost nose-to-nose. "I don't think he likes me."

Clever lady.

"Hale's not too crazy about me hanging out with mortals. His snobbery probably rubbed off on Elmer."

Elmer was thankful that got the blonde's attention, and she leaned up, removing her face from the proximity of his nose. "I thought you were half-mortal."

Zoë nodded. "Hale prefers the other half."

"I'm still unclear on what 'the other half' is. Hint, hint."

"I promised you an explanation, didn't I?"

"I'm all ears."

"Right," Zoë said, then sighed, and Elmer echoed her. Really, the girl shouldn't go around describing the history of the council to mortals. Rules were rules, after all.

Not that Zoë seemed to care.

He squeaked loudly, and Zoë scowled. "I know what you're saying," she said. "But Deena already saw me fly off the tower. She deserves an explanation."

Elmer wasn't too sure *deserves* was the word that leaped to mind. More likely she *deserved* to have her memory erased with one of those mysterious devices Zephron suspected Hieronymous was working on.

But Elmer was in no position to argue. And frankly he didn't care whether this Deena person knew the council's history or not. He just didn't want to see Zoë suffer. Hadn't Hale told him over and over again about how mortals didn't understand? Deena might have bought into the flying thing, but that was a far different matter from understanding the import of the council.

Zoë pushed herself off the couch, and he hopped up, trying to talk her out of it.

Don't do it, Zo, he chittered. She's not gonna believe you. You're just going to end up looking crazy.

Zoë shot him a look, but then ignored him. She paced to the bookshelf before turning back to Deena. Elmer grimaced, then hid his eyes behind his paws.

"How much do you know about mythology?" Zoë asked.

Elmer peeked and saw Deena's look of confusion.

"Some." Deena shrugged. "I've read a bit. School. That sort of thing."

"All those books on the mythological gods and goddesses . . ."

"Yeah?"

Zoë tossed Deena a copy of Edith Hamilton's *Mythology*. "My personal family history."

Oh, that's the way to tell her. Very subtle. Wouldn't want to freak her out or anything. Yeesh.

Deena dropped the book. "You're kidding."

"Nope. It's true. I'm part of a race called the Protectors. My branch of the family sort of started the Greek and Roman myths, but there're other branches as well.

If there's a set of myths out there, chances are there's a branch of my species that began it."

Deena looked at Zoë, then back to the book, then back to Zoë again. Then she shrugged. "Goddesses should *not* dress the way you do. Next week, first thing, we are getting you some new clothes. And your hair—every day with the braid. *Boring.* I think you need something a little more—"

"Deena . . ."

The girl looked up.

"I'm not a goddess."

"Oh." Deena frowned. "But you said . . ." She glanced at Elmer. "She said . . ."

"Protectors are just . . . different." Zoë shrugged. "And back then . . . well, I guess the whole god and goddess thing sounded like a really great cover story."

"Well, sure. Because if you're living back thousands of years ago and can see through walls or fly off mountains or talk to animals, you'd need a good cover story."

"Exactly," said Zoë. Elmer groaned. Apparently she hadn't noticed the tinge of sarcasm in Deena's voice.

"I guess it does make sense," Deena agreed. Elmer rolled over to get a better look at her. He peered at her face and, sure enough, the gal seemed to be buying it. Maybe that hadn't been sarcasm after all. Hale was never going to believe this.

Zoë twisted on the couch, then slid her hand under her rump.

"What?" Deena asked.

"It's like I'm sitting on a big lump." She reached between the cushions and pulled out a necklace. "There it is. I thought I'd lost it."

For just a minute it dangled from her fingers, the deep

181

green of the gemstone reflecting onto the far wall of the room.

Elmer let out a little squeal, then scrambled across the sofa, trying to get a better look.

Could it be? *Surely not.*

But it certainly looked to be. . . .

The stone! The gemstone from Aphrodite's girdle. He didn't know how it had ended up in Zoë's apartment, but there it was. And hey, who was he to question a legend?

Telling Deena the whole story pushed all of Zoë's problems front and center. Now she sighed, hoping she wasn't making a huge mistake by going out with Taylor. She should have picked someone who didn't make her insides all whooshy, someone not quite so rugged or intense. Someone whose eyes didn't look like they could see through her as easily as she could see through his clothing.

She wanted to walk on the wild side with Taylor, but she was too scared, too nervous, whatever, to invite him to come along for the ride.

Pathetic.

"It's actually not all that bad-looking," Deena said.

Zoë looked up. "Taylor?"

"You *do* have it bad. I was talking about the rock." Deena pointed to the necklace that still dangled from Zoë's fingers. "Are you gonna wear it tonight?"

She closed her fingers around it, surprised how warm the stone felt. "A green stone with a red dress? No, thanks. I'd end up feeling like a Christmas ornament."

"Mind if I borrow it?" Deena leaned forward, ready to take the necklace, when Elmer came running across the cushions, took a flying leap, and soared through the air—right smack into it.

Ferret, chain, and ugly gemstone tumbled to the carpet.

Deena and Zoë looked at each other and burst out laughing.

"Guess we know what kind of toys ferrets like," Deena said. She reached down to pick the chain back up but stopped as Elmer did a frantic little ferret dance, his fur all spiky as he bounced around on the floor. After a few seconds of that, he finally sprawled out, his eyes shifting from Zoë to Deena as though he were watching a tennis match.

"I have no idea what's getting him so excited."

Deena shrugged, then picked up the necklace. Elmer hopped back up, running in circles around the coffeetable leg. "I think you need to cut back on his caffeine."

"No kidding," said Zoë, wondering what the devil was wrong with him. Maybe it was the chain. Squirrels liked shiny things. Maybe ferrets did, too. She'd have to ask Hale. "Anyway, why do you want to wear it? I thought you hated the thing."

"I don't hate it. I said it's ugly. And it is. But in a cool sort of way. Hoop's taking me out tonight, and it'll go great with this green sweater I got the other day."

Zoë frowned. "Out? I thought you were coming to the Andersons', too. I have to do this alone?"

"No, no. We're doing both. The Andersons' first, and then Hoop's taking me to the Hollywood Bowl."

What was wrong with *that* picture? Zoë crossed her arms over her chest. "Your Hoop? Mr. I-think-*Vixens-In-Space*-is-great-cinema? He's going to the Bowl?"

Deena nodded, looking smug. "*Bugs Bunny on Broad-*

way. They show the cartoons and the orchestra plays the music live. That, Hoop can handle."

"Then by all means, you must have an ugly necklace for the evening," she said. Elmer's fur spiked up again.

Deena grinned. "Thanks."

Ding-dong.

Yikes. She caught Deena's eye. "I don't think that's the Avon lady."

"You'll do fine. Remember, deep breaths."

Zoë nodded and stood up. Right. Deep breaths. She could do that. *No problem.*

In front of her, Elmer was hopping back and forth, tail spiky, once again doing the funky ferret. It was probably all the rage in dance halls on Olympus.

She ignored him. If he'd figured out that she was going on a date with a man she really liked, she didn't want to know. If he just wanted to play, he could wait for Hale. Right now she had an agenda.

Right now she had to go let Mr. Midnight into her apartment—and her life.

Taylor paced in front of the closed door, swinging the bundle of roses he'd bought from the old man hawking flowers at an intersection. He licked the fingers on his free hand, then tried to control his cowlick, which always seemed to go the wrong direction.

He doubted he'd improved the hair situation, but with any luck, he still looked like a fine, upstanding citizen— the kind of guy any all-American girl would be nuts about. And from what he could tell, Zoë Smith was about as all-American as they came.

He cleared his throat and started to tighten the Windsor knot at his throat, then stopped himself. He'd done both—the throat clearing and the knot tightening—about a dozen times during the drive to her apartment. If he pulled the damn noose any tighter, he'd pass out and Zoë would spend most of their not-a-real-date reviving him with mouth-to-mouth.

Not a bad idea . . .

With a grunt of frustration, he shoved his free hand deep into his pocket. As appealing as mouth-to-mouth might be—and it was *very* appealing—passing out was not a good way to start a date. And even though a prone position would be great sometime before the end of the evening, he sincerely doubted that emergency first aid was going to get Zoë into his bed.

Absently he leaned against the door, trying to pull himself together. Suave, cool and collected—that was the ticket. After all, she'd made it absolutely clear that she didn't want the same things from the evening that he did. And since he was determined to work in some very datelike activities, that meant he needed to downshift to suave, pronto.

Shaking his head, he scowled at the door frame and finger-combed his hair. What was he doing here? A job? A seduction? Both?

He was still scowling and leaning against the door when it opened. Losing his balance, he tumbled over the threshold and landed in a heap on her hard tile floor, his dozen roses flying free to scatter all over the hall.

So much for a suave, sophisticated entrance.

Her hand flew to her mouth, her eyes crinkling behind her glasses and her body shaking with silent laughter. "Please," she finally said, amusement lacing her voice as she looked down at him. "Make yourself at home."

He scrambled for a clever retort—or even a ridiculous one—but his wit abandoned him. Instead he just sat up, leaning against the wall so he could take in every inch of the woman in the doorway. Had he thought she was beautiful before? He'd been a fool. She wasn't just beautiful; she was spectacular—the kind of woman that inspired poetry and love songs.

Too bad he was no poet. And his singing voice sucked.

Her smile faded as his silence continued. She leaned forward, squinting down at him. "Taylor? Are you okay?"

"Fine." He forced the word out, needing to move, to get past this stew of awe and first-not-really-a-date jitters. He reached out, pricking his finger on a thorn as his hand curled around a rose. He held it up. "My lady."

She took it, but didn't sniff it. Instead she let it hang at her side as she kept her fingers closed around the stem. *Okay.* Maybe his all-American Zoë wasn't the flower type.

With a grunt he climbed to his feet, then brushed dust off his rump. "Do me a favor," he said.

She tilted her head. "What?"

"Pretend I've just made an entrance worthy of James Bond—not Jerry Lewis."

Her mouth quirked. "Well, of course." Her blue eye twinkled behind those librarian glasses. "I just assumed you were trying to give any thugs who might be watching a false sense of security."

"Pretty clever of me, don't you think?"

"Brilliant," she said, then batted her eyelashes and pressed a limp hand to her forehead, Southern-belle style. "And I feel so much safer knowing you're here to protect me from the big, bad thuggies."

"Just doin' my job, little lady." It was a lousy John Wayne impersonation, but her smile grew broader, so he figured it had done the job.

He glanced around the entrance hall, bending down to check under a little table littered with her mail. "Seen any thugs around these parts?"

"Not a one," she said, closing the door. She leaned against the wall and smiled at him. She was sweet and innocent and perfectly polite—and all he could think about was tasting that mouth and getting her naked. *So much for chivalry.*

She licked her lips, and their eyes met. He took a step closer, wondering if that was a spark of interest he saw in her eyes. Hoping it was.

Her cheeks flushed and she looked away, clearing her throat. "Uh, no thugs at all." She grinned. "Unless you count Deena."

He blinked. "Deena?"

"My beauty consultant," she said. "It's a girl thing."

"Ah," he said, letting his gaze roam over her. Unlike the other times he'd seen Zoë, this time she was wearing makeup, and the deep red tint of her lips just about did him in. Every fiber of his body wanted to close his mouth over hers and kiss her—hard—until those glossy red lips were smeared under the onslaught. Until she melted in his arms and begged for more.

With a low groan, he forced his gaze away from her face. The red dress was like nothing he'd ever seen before, but on her it looked stunning. He didn't really care for the odd gold mesh belt—it looked like a reject from an Austin Powers movie—but on Zoë it looked perfect.

"Well, pay whatever she's charging. You look fantastic."

"Thank you." She held up the roses. "And thank you for the flowers."

"I thought you didn't like them."

She frowned. "Why would you think that?"

"You haven't even smelled that one."

"Oh," she said, glancing down at the single rose in her hand. "Right. I can't . . . I'm not . . . I'm—"

"Allergies," said Deena, stepping into the hallway.

Zoë exhaled, her shoulders dropping as if in relief. "Exactly!" she said. "I'm allergic. Talk about your rotten luck," she said, with more enthusiasm than he would've expected from one who was highly allergic. She pressed the rose into Deena's hands, scooting another one away with the toe of her shoe.

Deena stuck her nose down against the flower, then looked back up at Taylor. "They're lovely. Thanks."

"You're welcome," he said, feeling a tad bewildered. "Good to see you again."

"Oh, she's just leaving," Zoë said. She tilted her head toward the door. "Aren't you?"

Deena tossed a knowing grin Taylor's way.

"Practically out the door," she said, and then she was, the door clicking shut firmly behind her.

"Well," said Zoë. "I guess we're alone."

"Guess so."

Something clickity-clacked on the floor behind him, and he turned around. An oversize rat grinned at him, and he forced himself not to think it was bizarre. He turned back to Zoë, aiming his thumb behind him. "Who's the rodent?"

"Elmer." She glared at the little guy. "He's a ferret, and he's just leaving, too."

The ferret stood up on his hind legs, whiskers twitching. If Taylor didn't know better, he'd say that was an insolent look on Elmer's furry little face.

Zoë turned toward the ferret, almost prodding him with her eyes. "I said, he's just leaving, too."

The rodent squeaked, his fur bristled, and then he turned around and clickety-clacked back toward the rest of the apartment.

Taylor crossed his arms over his chest and grinned. "Well, well. If it isn't Zoë Dolittle. How long have you been talking to animals?"

"Oh, I can't—" She stopped, then scowled. "I mean, that's very clever."

"Right," he said, wondering what she wasn't saying. "That's me. Mr. Clever."

"No, you're Mr. Midnight," she said; then her eyes went wide and she slapped her hand over her mouth. "I can't believe I just said that," she said.

"Mr. Midnight?" He grinned, taking a step closer. "I kind of like the sound of that."

"It didn't mean anything. I'm just a little"—she waved her hand in a circle—"I don't know. Nervous, maybe."

As if to prove her point, she leaned back against the wall again and ran her tongue over her lips. It was definitely a nervous habit, but as habits went, this one was damned erotic.

He took a step toward her. "So tell me, sweetheart, just what do you have to be nervous about?"

The look she gave him just about ripped him in half. "Isn't it obvious? You."

"Me?" He tapped himself on the chest. "George Bailey Taylor me?"

She nodded. "George Bailey Taylor you."

He sucked in air, afraid this was some cruel joke fate was playing to teach him not to lust after beautiful women. "I'm probably going to regret asking, but why?"

She tilted her head until her glasses slid down her nose, then peered at him over the rim, her odd-colored gaze giving him the once-over. His body warmed as her eyes roamed over him—*all* over him—and he watched, knowing she was thoroughly checking him out.

One corner of her mouth curled up into a sensuous little smile that had his body tightening, and he couldn't help feeling a tiny bit smug.

"Because I need a date after all, Mr. Taylor." She exhaled—it was more of a sigh really—then lifted her head back up to look him in the eye. Her cheeks flushed, and, with a businesslike shove, she pushed her glasses back into place. "A *real* date. So tell me. Are you still game?"

Chapter Twelve

Zoë pushed her glasses up her nose one more time for good measure. *Oh, mother of Zeus.* She'd actually sneaked a peek at his underwear. Talk about lacking self-control. If there was a hell, a Hades, a whatever, Zoë was certain she was zipping that way faster than a speeding bullet.

Trying to ignore the wave of mortification that swept over her, she flashed him a weak smile, positive her cheeks were flaming red.

At least she'd managed to get a grip on herself before she'd peeked through that last little bit of material. She sighed, savoring the memory. Plain white cotton briefs. Simple. Sensible. And oh, so sexy.

She took a deep breath, then let it out slowly. *Oh, me, oh, my.*

Heck, she'd even throw in an *ooh-la-la.*

"Uh . . . Zoë?"

With a jerk she yanked her head up, suddenly realizing where her gaze was still aimed.

Oops.

Her cheeks burned hotter, and she pushed back from the wall, standing up straight and trying to pull herself together. "Right. Yes. Well . . ."

His gaze locked onto her, his brown eyes warm and inviting. When he took a step forward, she inhaled, her body humming with anticipation.

Nervous didn't even begin to describe the way she felt. *Terrified* was more like it. Still, it was just a date. She repeated the phrase like a mantra. *This is just a date. Just a guy and a girl going out.*

"What happened to Mr. Wonderful?"

She frowned. "Who?"

"You're taken. Remember?"

"Oh. Right. Well. *Taken* is such a vague term, really. Don't you think?"

"Vague? As in, Mr. Wonderful won't care? Or as in, there is no Mr. Wonderful?"

"He, uh, died." She met Taylor's eyes, saw pure passion burning there, then looked away again. *Oh, my.* "Very suddenly. Very tragic."

Taylor stepped closer, the heat from his body warming her to her toes, pooling in secret, intimate places. Teasing and taunting her.

She drew an unsteady breath. This dating thing was moving along a bit more quickly than she'd expected. "We'll miss him, of course, but life must go on."

"Of course," Taylor murmured. "So tell me, Zoë . . ."

She looked up. "Yes?"

"Why?"

"Why?" she repeated.

"Why did you tell me about Mr. Wonderful in the first place?"

"Oh, that." She licked her lips. "Well, he hadn't keeled over yet."

"Uh-huh."

"No?"

He shook his head. "Want to try again?"

She inhaled, then glanced down, breaking eye contact. "Maybe gorgeous men make me nervous."

He chuckled. "Oh."

She cleared her throat. "So this is okay with you?"

With a devious grin, he leaned forward, his face only inches from hers. She held her breath as he turned his head.

"This?" he asked, his mouth so close to her ear that his breath teased her.

She swallowed, searching for her voice. "A real date, I mean."

"Oh, yeah," he said, his voice low and dangerous. He leaned back to look at her, then reached out and touched her skin, his finger trailing down her cheek. "That's perfectly okay."

Oh, Apollo's apples, his touch. A firestorm of shocks ricocheted through her. Her chest constricted, her body warmed, and she felt faint. And then her body finally remembered that little detail about breathing . . . and she exhaled in a whoosh. Mildly mortified, she opened her mouth to say something, then shut it again when she realized her mouth wasn't too keen on sounding out vowels or consonants.

With a wink that suggested he knew exactly the effect he was having on her, he presented his arm for her to take. "Should we get going?"

"Mm-hmm," she managed, pleased to be able to form sounds. That, at least, was progress.

Sucking in more air, she slipped her arm through his, trying not to jump from the electricity that zinged through her when her skin brushed against his. Sooner or later she'd get used to his touch. Sooner, hopefully, because if she waited for later, all her nerve endings would likely be fried.

Somehow she managed to walk outside, down the stairs, and into the parking lot—all without her body dissolving into cinders and ash from the heat they were generating. That was convenient, really, since she didn't think a pile of charred flesh would make much of a hit at the party. And if she didn't go to the party, she had no legitimate reason to be with Taylor.

And she really, really wanted to be with him.

She frowned, realizing just how much that was true. He made her laugh; he made her insides flutter. He made her want to take risks.

Huge risks, actually. She nibbled on her lower lip, then stopped when she remembered Deena's words. Did she really want to lose herself to this man? Could she? Or was it more likely she'd lose her mind, since just the slightest brush of his skin against hers sent every atom in her body zooming into supercharged mode?

Insanity seemed like a small price to pay for everything she'd been denying herself for the past twenty-five years. This was Taylor, after all. The man she'd been fantasizing about for days during that soft time between waking and dreams. For this man she'd risk a psychotic episode.

She sneaked a peek at him out of the corner of her eye as they walked to the far end of the apartment complex's parking lot. He was about six inches taller than she was, had untamed hair that begged for her fingers to run through it, and a strong profile that made it clear this was a man who'd never let a woman down. He was Harrison Ford with a dash of Pierce Brosnan and an attitude.

At any rate, control didn't really seem to be a possibility here. Which meant that if they ended up in bed, she'd probably end up plastered to the ceiling or shooting for the stars or melting the box springs.

"You okay?" He'd maneuvered them in front of his Mustang, and now he was looking down at her from his six-inch advantage. His brow creased, and his brown eyes reflected so much concern that she almost melted.

How sweet. He was worried about her—and she was fantasizing about what he'd be like naked.

"I'm fine," she said, giving herself a mental shake. "Really."

He nodded, but didn't look too convinced, and she sighed. So much for that whole aloof tactic all the women's magazines promoted. Aloof she wasn't. Desperate, maybe.

Better to try to wrangle a little finesse into the situation, or at least try to carry on normal conversation. As best she could tell, in the dating world, desperate didn't equal desirable.

"Meet Francis Capra," he said, unlinking their arms so he could open the passenger door.

"Francis?"

"I wanted to name her Frank Capra after I finished her, but cars are female, and I didn't want to give her a complex."

"You rebuilt this car?"

"Yup."

"That must have been a lot of work."

"It was. But I loved every minute of it. Automobiles are different from other females. Women are enigmatic. But my car . . . I can take it apart, then put it back together until I know it backward and forward."

He ran his fingertip over the hood as he circled to the driver's side.

"And you can't know a woman that well?"

With a sidelong glance, he slid behind the steering wheel. "I didn't say that, sweetheart. I'd certainly be up for the challenge." He twisted in his seat to face her, one arm draped over her seat, completely casual and utterly intense.

She swallowed.

"For example," he continued, his grin revealing an adorable dimple. "I can imagine meeting a woman who intrigues me so much that I want nothing more than to make her come apart, to investigate her mysteries, to get to know every delicious inch of her."

She swallowed again, afraid to even hope that she might be worthy of such luscious scrutiny.

His smile broadened, reaching his eyes. "But even then, who's to say I'd learn all her secrets?"

Well, if that wasn't the understatement of the year . . .

"Like I said, women are enigmas," he finished in a wry voice.

"But would you want to learn all a girl's secrets?" she asked, knowing the answer. Not all secrets were created equal, and if he knew hers, he'd run. Just like Tessa had run from Donis. She'd never heard of even one mortal-Protector union that had lasted. Not one.

But that was okay, because all she wanted was a fling. Really.

He frowned, as if seriously considering her question. "There are some girls whose secrets are unknowable; they are complete and total enigmas," he said. "But there are a few with whom I'd be happy to spend years trying to work out the puzzle."

He grinned, and she was sure her face was on fire. Then he shifted in his seat and started the engine. It was about time, too. Who could have known that dating was going to be so much like a council meeting—eight different layers of meaning, nothing straightforward, and sweaty palms all the way?

But at least she knew one thing for certain. She snuggled back against the soft leather upholstery, trying not to let too satisfied a grin spread across her face. If nothing else, she was sure that—as much as she might be infatuated with George Bailey Taylor—he was just as interested in her.

Yes, indeed. She might like this dating thing after all.

Taylor was doing a piss-poor job of driving. The trouble was, he was a hell of a lot more interested in the woman next to him than he was in watching for red lights or paying attention to the other cars on the road.

And he'd bet Francis Capra that she wanted him as much as he wanted her. He'd seen it in her eyes, and it had thrilled him all the way down to his toes, which, considering he was a good three inches over six feet, was a heck of a long way down.

Hoop had called him charmed. Hell, maybe he was. This spectacular woman who'd been the center of his fantasies for days—no, for his whole life—actually wanted him. Even now—dead broke, off the force, his white-knight days long gone—still, she wanted him.

If that wasn't charmed, he didn't know what was.

"Uh, Taylor?"

"Hmmm?"

"Are you gonna pull over for the cop?"

Damn! Maybe not so charmed after all.

He tapped the brakes and turned off Sunset Boulevard onto one of the perfectly manicured side streets. Behind them, the siren *whoo-whoop*ed, the patrol car's kaleidoscope of lights dancing around like some bad disco memory.

"What did I do?" He swiveled around, trying to figure out what heinous traffic infraction he'd committed.

She'd switched out her regular glasses for sunglasses, but he could still see the corners of Zoë's eye crinkle as she laughed.

"I think the better question is, what didn't you do? You didn't stop at that light, you didn't yield at that intersection, and you certainly didn't pull over when the cop first tried to stop you."

"At least I'm thorough."

"Oh. Is that what they call it?"

A baby-faced cop with vivid green eyes walked up to the convertible.

"License, please."

"Problem, Officer?" Taylor asked, trying to sound innocent as he squirmed in his seat to fish his license out of his back pocket. Beside him, Zoë looked as though she had front row tickets to the best show in town. All she needed was a tub of popcorn and she'd be set.

Scowling, he handed the cop his license, keeping one hand closed over the steering wheel. Maybe it was unreasonable, but he was seriously resenting having his quality time with Zoë shortened by one of Los Angeles's finest.

"I'm going to have to ask the two of you to step out of the car."

Taylor scowled. That was weird. And certainly not protocol. What the hell was going on?

Another glance at the cop and the lightbulb pinged. A rookie.

"Look, Officer," he said. "We're running late. I used to be on the force. Give Captain Dodsen a call. He'll vouch for me."

The green eyes flashed. "I asked you to step out of the car."

"If you could just tell me what I did . . ." Taylor trailed off, his attention captured by the cop. Was he *shimmering?*

He squinted. Sure enough, the uniform had become almost transparent, replaced by a fine Italian suit. Everything about the man changed. Everything except those emerald green eyes.

And then, just as quick, he was a cop again, front and center and looking royally pissed.

Impossible. Clearly Taylor was long overdue for a good night's sleep.

He rubbed his eyes. For a moment there—not even half a second, really—the officer had looked exactly like his new client, Mr. Mordon. Weird. But explainable. Probably workaholic guilt. He should be working, after all.

"Now," said the cop, his hand closing over the door frame. "The girl, too."

Beside him Zoë stirred, and Taylor caught her staring

at the policeman. She was tense, wound up like a spring and ready to bolt. Hell, he couldn't blame her. This guy was even giving him the creeps.

"Chief Prescott's going to hear about this," he spat. "I promise you that."

"You can take it up with Prescott later," the officer said, his eyes darkening. "But first you're going to come with me."

The hell we are. He turned to Zoë, and she whispered just one word. *"Go."*

He wasn't about to argue. With a quick flip of his wrist, he turned the key and started the engine. The pseudocop made a grab and managed to lock his fingers onto Taylor's shirtsleeve, but Taylor floored the gas pedal and the car sped away, leaving him with a ripped shirt, but otherwise intact.

"What a strange—" He looked in the mirror and his jaw dropped. The cop was racing behind the car—on *foot*, for crying out loud—and he was gaining. "Who the hell is this guy?" Taylor muttered, wondering if they'd somehow gotten sucked into a *Terminator* movie.

Next to him, Zoë was rummaging around on his floorboard.

"And what the hell are you doing?"

Her head popped up, followed by the rest of her, and he saw that she was holding an empty commuter mug.

"Now's not really the time to stop at Starbucks," he joked.

She ignored the attempt at levity. "Fond of this cup?"

"Not particularly."

"Good." She heaved back and let it sail. Taylor checked the rearview mirror just in time to see it clunk the policeman square on the nose. The strange supercop began to lose ground.

"Nice shot."

"Let's just say I was on the varsity girl's softball team."

"You were?"

"No. But let's say so anyway." He opened his mouth to ask, but she turned back toward him. "Not to be a side-seat driver, but I'd get us lost if I were you."

A damn good suggestion. He floored the accelerator, then turned north toward the foothills and tried to find a side street that would lead up to Mulholland Drive. With all the little streets up in the hills, they should be able to lose their new buddy.

Their buddy? *No, no.* That was exactly the problem. Just who was the police officer after? Him, or the too-normal-to-be-real all-American girl in the seat next to him?

"Any idea who that guy is?" he asked.

"Nope," Zoë said quickly. "No idea at all." She shifted in her seat to face him better. "Thanks for going when I said 'go,' though. I . . . uh . . . had a bad feeling about him."

"You're welcome. But for the record, it wasn't just blind trust."

Her eyebrow went up. "No? Then why'd you haul off down the street? You can get into a lot of trouble for leaving after a cop stops you."

"If he'd been a cop, I wouldn't have left."

She smiled, broad and genuine. "How'd you know?"

"There is no Chief Prescott."

"Clever," she said, tapping the end of her nose.

"How did *you* know?" he countered. "You said you don't know who the guy is."

"I don't." She frowned and settled back into her seat. "But I told you in the library, I'm a good judge of character. That guy was weird."

"Uh-huh," he said, not believing her, but having no clue how to argue. He took a turn without slowing, then gave Francis Capra a nice pat on the dash before turning back to Zoë. "So, kidding aside . . . are there really thugs after you?" Or were they after him, and if so, why?

She sighed. "I haven't got a clue. I can't imagine why there would be."

"Zoë, I'm serious. I'm an investigator, remember? A bodyguard. That's the whole reason you hired me. Except that I thought we were joking."

"So did I."

He laughed. "You've never had a problem with your lies coming true, have you? Your dreams turning into reality?" He hummed a few bars of *The Twilight Zone* theme song.

She scowled. "Oh, mother of Zeus, not yet. That would be incredibly inconvenient."

He turned to look at her better. "I'm joking, you know."

At first she looked confused; then her face cleared. "Right. Of course." She smiled. "So am I."

Uh-huh. Something just wasn't ringing true, and he couldn't put his finger on it. Below them, the lights of Los Angeles twinkled on their right, a random pattern heading out toward the Pacific. To their left, the patterned grid of the lights of the San Fernando Valley winked at them.

Both order and chaos. Just like his life.

He turned off Mulholland and onto Coldwater Canyon, heading down toward the San Fernando Valley—as good a place to get lost as any.

He took his eyes off the road just long enough to glance at her. "Let's run through the scenario, okay, sweetheart?"

She nodded, looking a little wary, but not arguing.

"First you tell me you need an escort. Then you tell me you're being chased by thugs."

"Actually, you brought up the thugs."

"No, I didn't."

She nodded, twisting in her seat and tucking her leg up under her, revealing a luscious bit of thigh. He ripped his gaze away and focused on the twisting road.

"Yes, you did," she insisted. "Hoop said I need protection, and you said from thugs, then I—"

"Okay, fine."

She crossed her arms over her chest. "And your point is . . . ?"

He swallowed, not really sure, other than that he suddenly hoped that she hadn't really needed him. Just that she'd *wanted* him. Even if only a little.

"Taylor?"

He cleared his throat. "Well, maybe I'm wrong, but I got the distinct impression that you were a little attracted to me, and maybe *that's* why you'd started this charade in the first place." He twisted just enough to look at her out of the corner of his eye, his foot automatically easing up off the gas.

"I am." She flashed him a shy smile that almost melted his bones.

Fortunately his bones were in pretty good condition, and he managed to keep some semblance of control.

Otherwise Zoë and he might have just gone tumbling off into the canyon. "Oh." The warm feeling was back, despite the cool night air. "Good."

"But it wasn't."

He frowned. "Wasn't what?"

"The reason I hired you. I'm . . . attracted, yes. But I didn't know it was you when I came to ask your help."

That was true. She'd been as floored to see him as he'd been to see her. "So it was thugs."

"No. No thugs. Hoop made that up. Really." Her eyes were wide, her glasses making her look even more innocent. She took his hand and squeezed it, her touch making sensuous promises even though her lips remained silent. "Honest. Hoop just made up a story. Deena said he thought we made a cute couple."

"Well, I'm with him on that."

A light blush stained her cheeks. "I promise that fake cop has nothing to do with why I hired you."

It was an odd way of phrasing it, but he got her drift. "If you really didn't hire me to protect you from thugs, then why did you?"

"I told you. I need a date."

"You *need* a date."

"Right."

"After all this," he said, beating a near-dead horse, "I'm supposed to believe you hired me just because you needed a date for tonight?"

"Well . . . yeah."

What the hell. Stranger things had happened. Maybe that was the real story. "Okay. I'll bite. Why's this party so important?"

"It's because of my mot—"

Bang!

"Duck!" He reached out, pushing her head down with one hand as she struggled to sit up.

"Taylor! Let me up. It's the tire."

So it was. The back tire had blown out. "Sorry," he said, maneuvering the car to the shoulder. "I thought our friend had caught up and decided to try a little target practice."

"I'm pretty sure we've lost him."

"Convenient, since we're not going anywhere until we change that tire."

Fortunately he could change a tire in his sleep, and he had the car jacked up and the lug nuts off in no time.

"Taylor?" Zoë squatted next to him, the lug nuts collected in her open palm.

"Hmmm?" He pulled the tire off and balanced it with one hand.

"This is a great date so far."

He frowned. "Sarcasm isn't pretty."

She closed her hand, then moved closer, taking control of the tire from him. "No, I'm serious." Her eyes met his. "So far we've had a little flirting"—at that, her eyes darted away—"and a little intrigue, and now we've got some adventure." She smiled. "I can't wait to see what'll happen next."

"Can't wait, huh?"

"No," she said, her voice breathy.

He took that as an invitation and leaned close, trailing his fingertip over her shoulder and down her bare arm. She shivered and moaned, then pressed her back against the car as he moved closer.

"Zoë," he murmured, not even sure if he was saying her name out loud. He let his lips brush over hers in the slightest of touches, then pulled gently away.

205

"Oh, my. Oh, me, oh, my," she whispered. She rubbed the back of her hand over her mouth, then tilted her head to look him in the eyes. "I think my lips are numb."

"I never knew I had that effect on women."

The corner of her lips twitched, as though she had a secret she wasn't sharing. "Yeah? Well, you have that effect on me."

He traced his finger along her jaw, then over her lips. She closed her eyes and leaned her head back, her body rigid, as if she were fighting for control.

Damn, but she turned him on.

"Taylor?"

"Mmm?"

Her eyes opened, the passion there as clear as day, but something else was there, too. Fear? Hesitation? Well, why not? After all, they'd just fought off the possible leader of a not-so-imaginary gang of thugs. She probably had the right to be a little nervous.

He just hoped that he wasn't the cause of her nerves. "What is it, sweetheart?"

"The tire. I think I lost it."

He glanced down to her hand, where she'd been balancing the tire. Sure enough, it was gone.

"I think it may be all the way down to the valley by now," she added.

Unfortunately, considering the hill they were parked on, she might just be right. Any minute now, a single tire was going to go careening down Coldwater Canyon, turn onto Ventura, then stop to order a chili-cheese dog. His stomach growled. Clearly lust and hunger were making him delirious. Time to do something about one of those. And, being a guy, his first choice tended toward lust.

"Zoë?" he began, hoping to keep the "I'm desperate for you *now*" tone out of his voice. "I—"

"I'm sorry."

Well, hell. That really wasn't the reaction he'd been hoping for. He stood up, shoving a hand in his front pocket. "About what?"

She frowned, her brow crinkling in that adorable way she had. "Your tire."

"Oh. Oh, well." He doubted he'd ever been so thrilled about something so annoying in his life. "The spare's still in the trunk."

She stood up and dusted off her rear, the innocent action more than a little disconcerting. "We should probably get going. We're already late."

"About this party . . ."

"Yes?"

"How would you feel about a more private get-together?"

"I'd like that," she said, and Taylor felt like he'd just won the lottery. She took a deep breath. "Except—"

There went the sixty-million-dollar grand prize.

"—I tried to tell you earlier. My problem is that I really, *really* need you to meet my mother."

Chapter Thirteen

The Andersons' party was fabulous, of course. As Tessa looked around the perfectly manicured yard trimmed with tiny white lights, and the too-cute-for-words shrubs sculpted into a leafy wild kingdom, a fresh wave of envy washed over her. When Tessa had first met Linda June Anderson, she'd had to spend an entire afternoon practicing deep-breathing exercises just to fight off her not-too-ladylike reaction.

Even now she hated to admit it, but there it was—Tessa coveted Linda June's life.

Not her yard, really, though a yard bigger than a postage stamp would be nice. And not her banker husband who'd provided that yard, and not even the fabulous house with enough room to house five families. No, Tessa envied Linda's happiness.

Linda and Richard Anderson were desperately, hopelessly in love. At twenty-five, Linda had tossed caution to the wind and married a penniless salesman who'd adored her more than life. Unlike Tessa, Linda had gambled on love—and she'd hit the jackpot. That penniless salesman was now worth several hundred million, and he still thought his wife hung the moon.

Not for the first time, Tessa wondered what would have happened if she'd laid her happiness out there on red and let the roulette wheel spin. With a sigh, she shook her head. It was too late. She'd made her choice— for herself and for Zoë she'd walked away, and she'd insisted Donis disappear. And there wasn't any magic in the world that could tell her if she'd done the right thing.

Tessa just wanted the best for her daughter, and that included a perfectly normal life. Zoë needed to meet a nice young man—a doctor, maybe. A good man, a straight arrow. An average, run-of-the-mill man's man. They'd fall in love, live happily ever after in a house like the Andersons', and have a whole assortment of average, ordinary friends.

They'd be happy. They'd be normal.

That was what Zoë needed.

Tessa might have taken a wrong turn twenty-five years ago, but she was damn well going to make sure that Zoë found a husband and happiness. A man who'd love her as much as Donis had loved Tessa, but who wasn't carrying quite so much . . . well, baggage.

A single tear escaped, and she brushed it away, angry with herself for blaming Donis even after all these years. It wasn't his baggage—it was hers.

She'd been so scared. Scared she wasn't good enough, scared he'd get hurt or even killed. Scared of taking a backseat to obligations that included the entire rest of the world.

And so she'd clutched her fears around her like a blanket as she'd made him vow to stay away, thinking herself so clever for keeping her heart—and her daughter—safe.

But she'd never banked on being lonely. Not as long as her daughter—

A tuxedoed waiter passed by, and Tessa snagged a flute of champagne, then tossed it back, letting the bubbles go to her head. Maybe they'd scrub away her melancholy thoughts like those scrubbing bubbles attacked bathroom grime.

Trying to look nonchalant, she settled on a stone bench, watching the clusters of people who filled the huge lawn. The party was well under way, and the voices from over fifty guests drifted around her like a comforting lullaby.

After a while she closed her eyes, losing herself in snippets of conversation mixed with the jazzy strains from the band on the gazebo. A hand landed on her shoulder, and Tessa jumped, her eyes flying open.

"Sorry," Deena said. "Did I wake you?"

Tessa shook her head. "It's the eccentric old ladies who sleep at cocktail parties. Middle-aged eccentrics—that would be me—merely close their eyes and fade into the music."

"Right. Fade." Deena nodded. "Got it."

Tessa smiled. Knowing Deena, she probably really was filing that bit of information away for later use.

"Aw, hell, Tess," Hoop said. "Don't encourage her. Deena's already as eccentric as they come," Hoop said. "And she can fall asleep at the drop of a hat."

"But I'm not old or middle-aged," Deena countered. "I'm twenty-six, thank you very much, and I intend to stay right there until someone can prove otherwise."

"Don't worry," Tessa said. "I wouldn't even begin to try." She smiled at the girl, taking in her flower-print, gauzy dress that looked like a Woodstock reject, but seemed perfectly appropriate on Deena.

When Zoë had introduced her blond friend, Tessa had been uneasy. Zoë had grown from a solitary child who hated to be hugged into a solitary adult who rarely dated. And even though Tessa had always hoped Zoë would have friends, the friends she'd imagined had been of a more . . . average crowd. Deena was a far cry from average. Still, it had taken Tessa only about two minutes with her to know she was the perfect friend for Zoë.

She smiled at her. "I didn't realize you were coming tonight. Have you seen Zoë?"

"Nope. And we're not staying long," Deena admitted, plopping down onto the bench and forcing Tessa to scoot over or be sat upon. "We've got tickets to the Bowl."

Tessa looked from Deena to Hoop. "Classical music? I'm impressed."

"Animated," Hoop said.

"Pardon me?"

"She tells me there'll be cartoons. I figured, what the hell. How cultural can that be?" He shifted, looked around, then shrugged and sat on the grass, his rumpled slacks getting even more rumpled.

Tessa bit back a caution about grass stains. The man was in his thirties, after all. If he wanted an astronomical dry-cleaning bill, that was his business.

Deena pointed an accusing finger at Hoop. "He was actually going to blow this off and head straight for Hollywood just to get a decent parking space. Can you be-

211

lieve it?" The incredulity in Deena's voice made clear that she, at least, couldn't. "I mean, I'm dying to see Zoë and Taylor together. From what I saw this afternoon, there're some serious sparks brewing between those two."

"Taylor," said Tessa, deciding she liked the name. "I haven't met him."

"Oh, Taylor's great. A total looker."

"Deena," Hoop warned, but the grin told Tessa he wasn't quite as exasperated as his voice suggested.

"Well, it's true. He's a total hunk. And he's polite, and heck, he's even sort of a local hero."

"A hero?" The man her daughter was seeing was a hero? What on earth was the girl talking about?

"Deena!" Hoop repeated, but this time the censure was real.

Her eyes went wide. "Oh." She sucked on her lower lip, then shrugged. "Hell, Hoop, Tessa probably remembers it all. I mean, she's lived here forever."

Hoop rolled his eyes.

"Remembers what?"

"He's the one who busted that guy who killed his entire family. You know, the one who said it was a gang thing. Taylor solved it. That and a couple of other cases, too. They were all over the news."

"He's a police officer," Tessa said softly, vaguely remembering the news story. *How ironic. Like mother, like daughter.* Both fell for men who had dedicated their lives to fighting bad guys. Still, at least Zoë had picked the kind who carried a badge and actually worked for the government. That was a hell of a lot less complicated than falling for some guy who could have been part of the cast of a Saturday-morning cartoon.

"He quit the force. Now he's a private investigator."

"How serious are they?" Tessa asked abruptly, and Deena's eyes went wide.

"Who? Taylor and Zoë?"

Hoop snorted, then suddenly appeared to be fascinated with a grasshopper trying to climb over his shoe.

Tessa frowned. "Yes, you know—what we've been talking about. I'm guessing they must be getting serious. Zoë seemed pretty rattled when she told me she was bringing a date to this party."

"Well, that's unusual," Hoop said, his voice laced with sarcasm. "Zoë sounding rattled, I mean."

Tessa nodded. "She takes after me that way, I'm afraid." She grasped Deena's hand. "So tell me everything you know."

Deena frowned. "About you being rattled?"

"She means about Taylor and Zoë, babe. You having trouble keepin' track of the way the conversation's flowing?"

She stuck her tongue out, and he winked.

"Tell me everything," Tessa said, ignoring their antics.

"Everything, huh?" Deena parroted.

"You stepped in it this time," Hoop said, and it only made Tessa more curious.

"If Zoë is that serious about a fellow, I think I have the right to hear the relevant gossip," Tessa said. "How did they meet? How long have they been going out? Why didn't she mention this grand romance to her mother?"

"Right," Deena said, waving down the waiter with the champagne. "All good questions." She grabbed a flute off the tray. "Just give me a sec and I'll give you some good answers."

Hieronymous watched the yellow dot blinking on the third monitor from the left. Malibu. The stone was there, somewhere near the ocean.

And with Zoë out of commission, it would soon be his.

He sighed, imagining the breakers crashing on the beach. Perhaps a vacation was in order. Next week, when he was—*finally*—the supreme ruler, his first order of business would be to call a holiday. Hell, he might even go a little soft on those pesky mortals—might let them continue their ordinary lives—at least long enough for him to enjoy a week of R-and-R at a lush Club Med location.

He did so enjoy the islands.

A soft rap on the door interrupted his fantasies of drawn butter, lobster, and well-oiled mortal women to be used for his pleasure. "Enter."

"Mordichai failed, sire," said Clyde.

Ice formed along his spine as he turned to face the chief of his guards. "What did you say?"

"He failed, sire. They got away."

"*They?*"

"She was in a car with a human male. We assume it was a . . . date," he said, his face twisting with disgust. "The girl should have more pride. Just because she's a halfling, she needn't lower herself to dating a human."

"I am not concerned with whom she does or doesn't date. I *am* concerned that my son was not able to eradicate our little problem." He turned away from Clyde and stepped closer to the monitor, tapping the blinking circle with his index finger. "Clearly I underestimated my little niece by sending my son. I shan't make the same mistake twice."

"I understand, sire," said Clyde, looking a little green around the gills.

"Do you?" He clasped one hand in the other and cracked his knuckles. "Let me be absolutely clear. I think it is time to open the catacombs."

Clyde gasped and his eyes widened.

"Tell the guards to release my little pets."

The party was everything Zoë imagined a chic gathering in Malibu would be: a huge lawn that ended at a cliff's edge a few hundred feet above the ocean; strolling violinists plying the guests with music; and strolling waiters stuffing them with food and drink.

Zoë had no idea what the occasion was—her mom had simply announced that she'd be going and that Deena was invited, too—but the party certainly seemed exuberant. It was also exactly the kind of event that always made her feel out of place. Even more so today, considering she was no longer exactly looking her best.

She glanced down at her dusty red dress and the bit of axle grease still smeared across her ankle. At least she was hiding the sexy little outfit, and its state of disrepair, under Taylor's massive sportcoat. When she'd shivered from his touch, he'd offered the jacket. And, rather than explain that she wasn't actually cold, she'd willingly accepted, more than happy to be enveloped by his warm, musky clothing.

With a sigh, she ran her hands through her hair. So much for all of Deena's hard work. At least Taylor had seen the products of their labor, even if she'd managed to stay tidy for only a few minutes.

Frowning, she let her gaze roam over and through the crowd, trying to find the man of the hour. How long could it take to find drinks, anyway?

All the guests were perfectly coiffed, congregating in little groups that almost seemed color-coordinated. A gaggle of green here, a bevy of blue there, a pride of pink across the lawn. Finally Zoë caught sight of Taylor making his way past a flock of females dressed in fuchsia. He waved, his smile making her feel warm and safe.

He pointed toward the bar and she nodded, leaning against a stone likeness of one of her ancestors while she waited for him to return with something cold and sparkly. Despite the fact that champagne would probably make her mouth explode, she felt the need for something festive. Something that would hopefully lift the cloud that had been following her since Mordi had pulled them over.

She hugged herself, fighting a shiver. She'd seen the cop's eyes and suspected, but when the fluctuation had caught him, she'd been sure. He'd adjusted quickly, but the truth was clear: Mordichai was after her.

Why?

And why had he mugged that woman?

Only one explanation made any sense—the tests were beginning.

For years she and Mordi had gone head-to-head as the council assessed their skill levels as halflings. It only made sense that her application field test would be against Mordi. But still, that didn't answer the real question—what were they supposed to do? How was she supposed to beat him? Surely she wasn't supposed to have jumped out of the car and gone at it with him on the road? For one thing, Taylor would have seen. For another, she didn't have any reason to fight Mordi—at least, none that she knew of.

If they did fight, would the winner be automatically admitted to the council? Would the loser become an Outcast?

She swallowed, not liking that particular possibility. Her father had told her that Outcasts walked among mortals, but were neither mortal nor members of the council. It was like being in superhero purgatory, and Zoë didn't think it sounded like a good time at all.

Whatever the answer, she knew one thing for certain—Taylor was in the cross fire.

She needed to get rid of him. Needed to make him go home, go away. Somehow get him clear. Keep him out of danger.

She scanned the party, wishing her father or Hale would swoop down. She could really use some advice right about now. For every other test, they'd been right there with her, ready to offer their comments—whether she wanted them or not.

But tonight, when she really did want their help, they were nowhere to be found. Apparently, for her final exam, she had to go it alone.

An elderly woman stepped aside, and Zoë saw Taylor heading back to her with two flutes of champagne.

"Hey, beautiful," Taylor said, pressing a glass into her hand. "Miss me?"

"Of course," she said, meaning it, then immediately tried to figure out a way to end their date quickly. The thought of him getting hurt was enough to make her nauseous, and she sincerely doubted that Taylor was any match for the kind of creatures she might end up facing.

They stood next to each other, looking out at the glassy surface of the distant ocean. The sun had just started its descent, and sunbeams played across the water.

They stayed like that, in companionable silence, until Taylor slipped her hand into his. Suddenly the silence filled with the gentle tingle of bells and fairy songs, and Zoë realized she felt perfectly and completely at home. The feeling had nothing to do with her senses—it was in her heart, in her head. And it terrified her as much as it enticed.

She blinked and tugged her hand away, frowning. She wasn't supposed to feel like that. Not about a mortal, not when all she wanted was a fling. Not when the only thing she'd been planning was to take Zoë Smith and her supersenses for a test drive.

"Are you okay?"

When she looked up, she saw that Taylor was watching her, concern in his eyes. She tried out a smile. "I'm fine," she said, and it was the truth. She'd never been better, and the realization terrified her.

"What are you thinking about?" he asked.

"Emily," she said, only then realizing that the teacher had been on her mind. "My friend. The one you were trying to dig up dirt on. Why did you stop looking for her?"

"You."

Her eyes widened. "Me?"

"You," he repeated. "You were right. I didn't enjoy it. And I realized the only reason I was working was to pay the bills."

"That's a pretty good reason to work," Zoë admitted.

"I can't knock eating, but if that's all I wanted, I could have stayed with the police department."

"I don't understand."

He nodded but remained silent. Then he said sharply, "Why are you here? Why this big production for your mother, I mean?"

She frowned, not understanding where he was going. "Well, she worries about me. Dating. Alone in the big city." She shrugged. "You know."

"No, I really don't. I wish I did, actually."

She started to ask what he meant, but stayed quiet, somehow realizing that he was collecting his thoughts.

After a moment, he shifted, facing her more directly. "I never knew my mother. I grew up in foster homes, shuttled from house to house."

He picked up a stone and tossed it absently over the cliff. After a few seconds, Zoë heard it splash lightly into the water below.

"I didn't mind the moving," he said. "I minded not having a home, always tiptoeing about. Never feeling a part of anything that happened. I just had walls. But what's so special about walls?"

Without moving his head, he glanced at her. "I'd never even met my real parents, and yet I hated them. Ripping my life apart like that. Dumping me in the middle of a Wal-Mart like a toaster they wanted to return." He blew out a loud breath. "In my mind, they made a mess of my life before it even started."

Zoë nodded, silent. She couldn't imagine hating Donis or Tessa, but she understood what it was like to be ripped down the middle by events over which she had no control. And, Zeus knew, she knew what it felt like to not belong, to feel like a guest in one's own world.

219

Gently she took his hands in hers. For a moment they just stood there; then he flashed her a devilish grin, turning the moment lighter. "Of course, I wasn't the easiest kid in the world to deal with, either. According to my social worker, finding me a permanent home was harder than finding a hot-dog stand on the moon."

Zoë cringed, wishing she could give that social worker a nice, hard kick in the—

"Hell, he was probably right. But I ended up in a lot of not-so-great houses. Saw a lot of not-so-great things." He caught her eye. "Terrible things, actually. Terrible people doing terrible things, and I was just a kid. There wasn't a damn thing I could do about it."

He shrugged, shaking a bit, as if trying to shed the memories. "By the time I got out of school, I knew two things for certain: I wanted a real home, a real life. And I wanted to do everything in my power to stop people like the ones I'd grown up around." He shrugged. "Spying on folks like Emily Parker didn't exactly fit that bill."

For a moment he turned away, looking out toward the ocean, his eyes wistful. Then he blinked and his face hardened, but Zoë could still see the vulnerable boy beneath, and her heart wrenched.

"Well," he said, turning to her. "There's my life on the line. What about you, Zoë Smith? What is it you want?"

A good question. She nibbled on her lower lip as she thought about everything he'd said—everything he wanted, and everything he'd been denied. They were such simple goals, really: stopping the bad people, living the life his parents had denied him.

"I want pretty much the same thing," she said, realizing as she spoke that the words were completely true. She wanted exactly the same thing as a mortal. So maybe they weren't really that different after all.

"Just a normal life," she added. But the question still remained—what was normal for her?

"I thought so," he said with a smile. He stroked her cheek, and she shivered. "I hope you get it, Zoë Smith. I hope we both do."

As he turned slightly, his eyes widened, and then he leaned in toward the yard, squinting at something off in the distance. "Is that Hoop?"

Zoë glanced across the lawn. "That's him all right." She raised a hand to wave.

Taylor squinted some more. "Are you sure?"

"Positive."

He nodded, but didn't look convinced until Hoop came a few yards closer. "So it is, and he's coming over here. Damn. Company."

She laughed. "It is a party. I think we're supposed to mingle." Not that she would have raised serious objections to spending the entire night alone with Taylor. "Besides, we still have to deal with my—"

"Mother. I know. Not that I'm eager to share your company, but we are supposed to be playing the perfect couple for your mother." He squeezed her hand. "And I'm a natural for the role, if I do say so myself."

Hoop crested the small hill and joined them.

"What are you doing here?" Taylor asked. "Schmoozing?"

"I don't schmooze," said Hoop. "But I do accept invitations for parties where alcohol and tiny little sausages on toothpicks are being served." He offered Zoë a plate piled high with appetizers. "Munchie?"

"No thanks."

Hoop squinted at her. "Deenie did your makeup, right?"

"Yup. She pretty much insisted I wear some." She tilted her head back and smiled at Taylor. "You're the occasion, actually. Usually I go with more of an au naturel style."

"I think you'd look fabulous au naturel." Taylor winked. "Completely natural, actually."

Her cheeks warmed as Hoop laughed.

"My buddy Taylor's not one for subtlety," Hoop said.

Taylor shrugged. "Just telling it like it is."

Hoop nodded toward Zoë. "Well, if Deena was hoping to make you *Cosmo*'s new cover girl with that makeup job, I think she needs to put in a little more practice."

"What do you mean?"

Hoop tapped his forehead. Experimentally, she wiped her finger above her brow, then looked at her hand— black grease. She sighed and almost ran her hands through her hair before remembering that would only make things worse.

"A little bit of grease doesn't bother me," Taylor said with a laugh. "Still, it doesn't seem to be keeping in line with the other guests." He dipped the corner of a handkerchief in his champagne and moved closer, dabbing at her forehead.

She held her breath, forcing her body not to rip into a million pieces just because of his touch. *So far, so good.* Maybe concentration really was the key, because it seemed to be working. Instead of being on fire, she felt warm and safe. Instead of feeling like she needed to run, to burn off kilowatts of unspent energy, she felt secure and taken care of.

What a wonderfully nice feeling . . .

"Where is Deena anyway?"

Hoop ripped a little sausage off a toothpick with his teeth. "With yer muffer," he said.

"Excuse me?"

He gestured over his shoulder with his thumb, then swallowed. "She's with your mother. By the fountain."

"Deena?" Zoë said, sure her voice was squeaking. "With my mother? As in talking? Together? By themselves?" *Oh, Hera's handbag.* Why couldn't they have reached the party sooner? This had *disaster* written all over it.

Taylor looked at her. "What's the matter? Afraid she's going to reveal all your deep, dark secrets?"

"Actually, I just thought she'd tell my mom about our little arrangement." She bit her lower lip. "But now that you mention it . . ." She grabbed his hand and tugged. "Come on."

"Hell of a grip you've got there, lady," he said, limping a bit as he jogged alongside her.

She glanced at him, noting the way he favored one leg. "Are you doing okay?"

"I'm fine. It's sore, but fine."

"What happened?" she asked, then regretted the question as she saw his pained expression. It lasted only a second, but long enough for her to know she'd touched a nerve. "Sorry."

"No, I don't mind telling you." He drew in a breath. "I screwed up."

"How?"

"I was trying to protect a witness. I shouldn't have

223

moved her out of the safehouse, but I thought it had been marked. Her former boss managed to tail us, and I caught a bullet."

Zoë swallowed. "Was she killed?"

He shook his head, pointing to his thigh. "This was meant for her."

"Then you saved her." Her heart swelled as she imagined him risking his life for an innocent woman.

A flash of anger played across his face. "I shouldn't have endangered her in the first place. I was arrogant and stupid."

"It sounds to me like you were trying to keep her safe. You couldn't have known you were being followed."

He snorted.

"So you quit because of that?"

"Sort of." He glanced at her, as if considering saying more, then shrugged. "It's like I said earlier. They were going to put me into some administrative job. Research or some such nonsense. Have me work a desk until some other desk jockey gave me an okay to return to the field. Me. The guy who'd earned more commendations than anyone in the department. I told them to go screw themselves." He rolled his eyes. "Actually, I was a little more polite than that, but I left all the same."

"Is it that important to be in the field? I mean, most of being a detective is using your head, right?"

He gave her a wry grin. "It was that important to me."

"I'll buy that," she said. "But you only answered half my question."

He jammed a hand into his pocket. "You sound like Captain Dodsen." He scowled, his forehead furrowing. " 'Taylor, being a detective's about brains, not brawn.

Thrill to the most sensual, adventure-filled Romances on the market today...

FROM  LOVE SPELL BOOKS

As a home subscriber to the Love Spell Romance Book Club, you'll enjoy the best in today's BRAND-NEW Time Travel, Futuristic, Legendary Lovers, Perfect Heroes and other genre romance fiction. For five years, Love Spell has brought you the award-winning, high-quality authors you know and love to read. Each Love Spell romance will sweep you away to a world of high adventure...and intimate romance. Discover for yourself all the passion and excitement millions of readers thrill to each and every month.

Save $5.00 Each Time You Buy!

Every other month, the Love Spell Romance Book Club brings you four brand-new titles from Love Spell Books. EACH PACKAGE WILL SAVE YOU AT LEAST $5.00 FROM THE BOOKSTORE PRICE! And you'll never miss a new title with our convenient home delivery service.

Here's how we do it: Each package will carry a FREE 10-DAY EXAMINATION privilege. At the end of that time, if you decide to keep your books, simply pay the low invoice price of $17.96, no shipping or handling charges added. HOME DELIVERY IS ALWAYS FREE. With today's top romance novels selling for $5.99 and higher, our price SAVES YOU AT LEAST $5.00 with each shipment.

AND YOUR FIRST TWO-BOOK SHIP-MENT IS TOTALLY FREE!

IT'S A BARGAIN YOU CAN'T BEAT! A SUPER $11.48 Value!

Love Spell ✦ A Division of Dorchester Publishing Co., Inc.

GET YOUR 2 FREE BOOKS NOW—AN $11.48 VALUE!

Mail the Free Book Certificate Today!

TWO FREE BOOKS

Free Books Certificate

YES! I want to subscribe to the Love Spell Romance Book Club. Please send me my 2 FREE BOOKS. Then every other month I'll receive the four newest Love Spell selections to Preview FREE for 10 days. If I decide to keep them, I will pay the Special Member's Only discounted price of just $4.49 each, a total of $17.96. This is a SAVINGS of at least $5.00 off the bookstore price. There are no shipping, handling, or other charges. There is no minimum number of books I must buy and I may cancel the program at any time. In any case, the 2 FREE BOOKS are mine to keep—A BIG $11.48 Value!

Offer valid only in the U.S.A.

*Name*_____

*Address*_____

*City*_____

*State*_____ *Zip*_____

*Telephone*_____

*Signature*_____

If under 18, Parent or Guardian must sign. Terms, prices and conditions subject to change. Subscription subject to acceptance. Leisure Books reserves the right to reject any order or cancel any subscription.

A $11.48 VALUE

Get Two Books Totally
F R E E —
An $11.48 Value!

▼ Tear Here and Mail Your FREE Book Card Today! ▼

PLEASE RUSH
MY TWO FREE
BOOKS TO ME
RIGHT AWAY!

Love Spell Romance Book Club
P.O. Box 6613
Edison, NJ 08818-6613

Come back and do some good.'" He shrugged. "The thing is, I know I can still do the job."

"You can't do it from a desk?"

"I shouldn't have to," he said. "And anyway, now I'm doing it on my own." He shrugged. "So you wanna tell me why we were rushing?"

"Nope," she said, picking up her pace again. "A girl's entitled to a few secrets, right? Mind if we hurry back up?"

"Not at all," he said, huffing a little as he matched her stride for stride. "I take it your friend has a few secrets you'd rather not share with your mom?"

"Right you are."

"Or with me."

"Right again."

"But what if I'm curious about those secrets?"

She stopped, and he stumbled to a halt next to her. "Are you?" she asked, knowing the answer. The real question was how he'd react to the answers—answers she never intended to give. Not after knowing how her mom had reacted to Daddy's little revelation.

"Hey, I'm an investigator, remember? It's what I do. Figure stuff out."

"Are you going to try to figure me out?" she asked, the possibility both alluring and terrifying.

He framed her face with his hands, and she shivered— not from the contact of his skin against hers, but from what she saw in his eyes. Something wild. Something fiery.

And, Lord help her, it was a look she wanted to see again. Despite her fears, despite the danger, she wanted to see it again, *needed* to see it again.

"Sweetheart," he said, brushing the pad of his thumb over her lip. "I don't try. I do."

225

Chapter Fourteen

"It's past six," Tessa said, glancing at her watch. She took a long sip of champagne, then looked up at Deena. "Was she running late?"

"Nope. Early." Actually, Taylor had *arrived* early, but that didn't mean they'd left Zoë's apartment early—or even on time. She'd known Zoë for a while now, and never once had Deena seen her so worked up about a member of the opposite sex. And Taylor certainly hadn't been lacking desire, either.

In fact, considering the electricity zinging between the two of them—and considering everything she'd learned about Zoë recently—Deena was amazed she herself had managed to get out of the apartment without being hit by some fireball of passion. She wouldn't be at all surprised to learn that the lovebirds had lingered.

Damn, but she wished she were an animathingamajig. Then maybe she could talk to ferret-face and get the scoop.

Tessa took another peek at her watch.

"Don't worry," Deena said. "They'll be here." She craned her neck, trying to spot Zoë in the crowd. *Nothing. Damn.*

"Maybe they decided to go off on their own," Tessa said. "Young lovers, distracted, desperate to be alone?" She swung an arm wide, apparently trying to illustrate the joys of youth, and almost fell off the bench.

Deena caught Tessa's arm. "I'm sure they're on the way." After all the trouble they'd had finding Zoë a date for this specific party—to appease this specific mother— there was no way Zoë would have skipped out.

"Maybe they stopped for a bite," Tessa suggested, downing the last of her bubbly.

"I hope not. There's plenty to go around here." Deena's gaze swept the lawn, taking in all the little tables set up with food and drink. Her mouth watered, and she sighed, fantasizing about dainty cream puffs with gooey fillings. Before she and Hoop headed for the Bowl, she intended to do some serious appetizer sampling.

Tessa turned back to Deena, her face set. "You still haven't told me about Zoë's affair."

"Of course I have," Deena hedged.

Tessa released an exaggerated sigh. "Details, sweetie." She took Deena's hand. "We need to get down to the details."

"The details," Deena repeated dumbly. *Oh, God.*

"For example," Tessa said, cupping her hand behind her ear. "Do I hear wedding bells?"

Deena squinted, fighting the effects of the champagne she'd drank. *Just answer her questions. Answer the questions and don't volunteer information. If you keep your mouth mostly shut, you'll get through this just fine.*

She took a deep breath, trying to answer without telling a bold-faced lie. Instead, she'd just stretch the truth beyond recognition—like a comic strip on Silly Putty. "I doubt they've talked about marriage yet." That, at least, was one hundred percent true.

"Is he successful? What kind of husband would he make? Does he have a retirement plan?" Tessa turned, shifting on the bench until she was facing Deena head-on. "Most important, does he love my daughter? And does she love him?"

"You're putting me in a heck of a spot here, Tessa. I mean, Zoë's one of my best friends." And although Deena hadn't checked the manual recently, she was pretty sure that revealing a friend's secret lusts to her mother was a definite no-no.

"I just worry about her." Zoë's mom tilted her champagne glass back, then scowled when she realized it was empty. She set it aside, then leaned closer to Deena, as if to reveal her deepest, darkest secrets. "I worry about her and . . . *it.*"

Deena frowned, clueless. "It? What it?"

"You know. S . . . E . . . X."

"Oh! *It.*" Well, this was new. Deena'd done a lot of things in her life, but she'd never, ever discussed a friend's sex life with that friend's mother. She prided herself on being pretty open-minded, but this pushed even her envelope. New millennium or not, if these were the new rules, she'd like to go back a few centuries, thank you very much. This was embarrassing.

"I hope Taylor's patient," Tessa continued, apparently unperturbed. "Is he?"

Oh, dear. She downed the last of her champagne in one gulp. Despite the coolness of the liquid, her cheeks warmed, a rather disconcerting experience considering she rarely blushed. "Um . . . I guess so." She wrinkled her nose. "Why?"

"I told you, honey. *Sex.*"

Hopefully Tessa wasn't praising the virtues of a lover with a slow hand. Deena wasn't sure she could handle having *that* particular discussion with the woman. "I'm still not following you."

Tessa's brow furrowed, as if she were searching for words. "Zoë's never been big on physical inflection," Tessa finally said, and Deena wondered how many glasses of champagne she'd polished off.

"What?"

Tessa rolled her eyes, then looped an arm around Deena's shoulder to pull her close; they came nose-to-nose. "You know. *Psychical affection.*"

This was going to be a longer party than she'd expected. "Still lost," she said.

Tessa sighed as only a long-suffering mother could, then poked Deena in the arm. "Touching. She doesn't even like to be hugged."

Finally! Something that made sense. "Physical affection! Well, I'm not surprised," Deena mumbled, her mouth shoved up against Tessa's shoulder. "What with her sense of to—"

Uh-oh. She clamped her mouth shut, then pulled back out of Tessa's grasp.

Tessa leaned back, peering at Deena with determined eyes. "What?"

"What?" Deena repeated, stalling.

"You said something . . ." Tessa trailed off, scowling, her hand twirling. "About her sense of . . ." She shrugged. "Something."

"Oh!" said Deena. "I said she's *sensitive*. She's a very sensitive girl, your Zoë. That's why she's so great with kids."

Tessa practically beamed. "Yes, she is very . . ."

Deena breathed a sigh of relief as she mentally congratulated herself. One close call averted.

"But . . ."

So much for dodging crises.

"But what's that have to do with hugging?" Tessa asked.

"What?" Deena asked, falling back on what was fast becoming her standard response. Besides, stalling just might be a better plan than running away.

"What's . . . that . . . gotta . . . do . . . with . . . hugging?"

"Um . . . well . . . Zoë!" *Thank goodness!* Deena jumped up, practically tripping over her skirt, and waved frantically to her friend, who was speeding toward them with Taylor at her heels. Yards behind them, Hoop ambled along, lazily picking at a pile of goodies he had balanced on a paper plate.

Zoë stopped in front of them, not breaking a sweat and certainly not breathing hard. Taylor stumbled up next to her, clutching his side and gasping.

"I've got to get to the gym," Taylor wheezed. "I thought a year of physical therapy had done some good, but I don't think it did a damn thing."

"You must be Tiller," Tessa said, getting up off the bench.

"It's Taylor, Mom," said Zoë, eyeing the empty champagne glass.

"That's what I said." She flashed a grin toward Zoë as she held out her hand for Taylor to shake. "So tell me, Taylor, just what are your intentions toward my daughter?"

"Mom!" Zoë turned pink.

Taylor took Tessa's hand in both of his. "The best intentions, Mrs. Smith," he said, and Deena was sure he meant it. "The absolute best intentions."

The henchmen crouched under the bushes, peering out from behind a thick mass of leaves at the neatly trimmed lawn spread out before them.

Watching.

Waiting.

The fat one nudged the skinny one, pointing one of his sausagelike digits toward a stone bench. The halfling was there, the one they were looking for, cavorting with a group of mortals.

Silly little fool.

They'd strike with the advantage of surprise.

They'd strike for Hieronymous, and strike hard. They'd strike . . . and young Zoë would never know what hit her.

They looked at each other—snaggletoothed grins, drippy pug noses, little piggy eyes—and cackled as a flock of mockingbirds rose from the bushes, the thrum of flapping wings drowning out their laughter.

"Call me Tessa," she said, tugging him toward the bench. Taylor came willingly, already deciding he liked this woman. She sat down and straightened her skirt, then looked him straight in the eye. "So tell me about these good intentions."

"Mom . . ." Zoë looked at Taylor. "Sorry," she whispered with a shrug. "She doesn't usually do this."

He chuckled and shot Tessa an amused glance. She returned it with a wink. "You mean she doesn't usually interrogate your dates?"

Zoë's face reddened. "I've never . . . I don't really—"

"Date," put in Tessa as Zoë's color deepened. Tessa leaned back, tilting her head to look at him, her face intense. "You be good to my girl, you hear?"

"That's my plan," he said.

"Hello? I'm right here," Zoë said, waving frantically at them. "If you guys are planning my life can I be included?"

Tessa caught Taylor's eye and they both laughed.

"No, thanks, sweetheart," Tessa said.

"Really," he joked. "I think we've got your life well under control."

Zoë shook her head, managing to look both exasperated and amused.

Taylor knew he was grinning like a fool, but he couldn't help it. He'd never expected to become a co-conspirator with Zoë's mother, but he couldn't say he minded. Hell, it was clear after only two seconds that she adored her daughter—and that she'd have his hide if he hurt Zoë. All of which was perfectly okay by Taylor. Zoë had said she was trying to escape a rash of blind dates by making Tessa think Taylor and Zoë were a hot-and-heavy couple, but Taylor intended to make that bit of fiction a reality.

Tessa smiled up at Zoë. "I'm glad you finally made

it. We've been talking about you," she said, glancing toward Deena.

"Great," Zoë said. "I love being the topic of conversation." She caught Deena's eye. "I hope you didn't get too personal. I'd hate to think my ears were burning."

"Oh, no," Deena said. "Tessa just wants to know everything about you and Taylor." She smiled brightly. "Everything."

Taylor caught Zoë's gaze. "Looks like your mother and I have something in common."

Hoop shoved a chocolate-covered something into his mouth, presumably to muffle his laugh.

"Is she keeping secrets from you, too?" Tessa asked. "I thought *you* were the big secret. Your romance, I mean."

He aimed a smile at Tessa, then turned back to Zoë, delighted to find that her cheeks were pink again. "Well, our romance has been rather whirlwind. I'm sure she would have eventually gotten around to sharing her secrets with both of us. Especially now that our little affair is heating up."

Zoë's eyes went wide. She put a hand on her hip and stared him down. Even if he'd been telepathic, the message couldn't have been clearer. *Behave yourself!*

He curled the corner of his mouth up, hoping he'd managed to relay his unspoken question. *What do I get for being good?*

She must have caught at least an inkling of his message, because she aimed her eyes toward the sky and shook her head, the very picture of an exasperated schoolmarm. A very hot, very sexy schoolmarm.

He bit back a chuckle. Man, he couldn't wait to have a moment with her alone. Couldn't wait to run his fingers through that mass of hair, couldn't wait to kiss away that look of exasperation.

Couldn't wait to explore the *everything* that made up Zoë Smith.

Mordichai perched on the roof of the massive house, his coal black propulsion cloak draped around him, and scowled at the crowd milling about below. The green dot on his portable tracking monitor bleeped again— right over Malibu, right over this very neighborhood.

As he'd circled in for a landing, he'd counted the houses within a three-mile radius. Only ten. He could go to each one and search for the stone. But what was the point? Zoë was here; his hired detective was here. It didn't take a genius to know that meant the stone was here, too.

But which one of them had it?

More important, how could he get it?

He pressed his forefinger to his chin and considered his options. If Zoë had the stone, he needed to get it back before she returned it to the council.

On the other hand, the stone might be with the detective. Wouldn't that be poetic? Of course, paying the man was out of the question—Hieronymous would never agree to deplete his funds when other methods were available—but Mordi had no doubts about his ability to quickly and efficiently dispatch the mortal. Then the stone would be his, the world would be less one mortal, and Mordi could haul himself back to Manhattan and maybe, finally, see some smidgen of approval from dear old Dad.

Except . . .

He didn't know which one had the damn thing.

Attack the wrong one, and his plans could be foiled forever.

It was better to bide his time.

To watch, to wait.

To see if he could get the tracking device to work more precisely.

Sooner or later, the two would split up. And all he'd have to do then would be follow the little green blep.

Chapter Fifteen

"So . . . how's the seduction going?" Deena asked in a hiss, her eager expression making clear that only the dirty details would do. Tessa had insisted on having a moment with "her boys," so Deena and Zoë had been banished to the far side of the yard. Zoë'd been leery, but Deena had dragged her away, practically jumping at the chance to get her alone.

With a mischievous little grin, Zoë dropped down onto the grass. "Do I look like the kind of girl to kiss and tell?"

Deena immediately joined her, kneeling and leaning forward, her loose skirt draped more or less modestly over her legs. "You *kissed* him?"

"I—"

"How was it? Did your mouth explode?" She leaned closer, as if looking for lip shrapnel.

"No, we just—"

"What did it feel like? I bet it was like a billion of those little Pop Rocks candies fizzling in your mouth. But a good fizzle. Warm and tingly and—"

"We haven't really kissed yet. Just had sort of a lip-brush thing."

Deflated, Deena scooted back. "Well, damn. No tongue? Why not?"

Zoë shrugged. "It's not for lack of wanting, that's for sure."

"Oh, really?" Her voice rose with interest. "So you've decided to go for it?"

"*It*? No. I haven't decided to go for *that*." Her cheeks warmed. "But the kissing part ... well, I've decided to go for that."

Deena grinned. "I can see why he'd be hard to resist. He *is* a cutie, isn't he?"

"Not just that, it's the way he looks at me. Like I'm the whole world."

"I *knew* it. I knew you two would be perfect for each other." She bounced a little. "So why no smoochies?"

Zoë felt her cheeks heat. Why not indeed? Would that slight brush of his lips against hers have simmered into a true-blue, down-and-dirty kiss if it hadn't been for Mordi?

Would she have kissed him back?

Oh, yeah. Her lips might not have made it there yet, but her head was definitely well into the kissing part of the evening. And despite the significant probability of a serious Pop Rocks moment, Zoë was all for her lips catching up with her imagination.

But what would happen after, in that quiet time in his arms, when lovers were supposed to share secrets? If she couldn't share, maybe she shouldn't kiss.

Deena waved a hand in front of Zoë's face, then grinned when Zoë looked up. "Quit fantasizing and give me details."

Caught, she flashed a sheepish grin. "I'm feeling a little like a high school girl with a crush—not sure if he really likes me, and, if he does, not sure if I should do anything about it."

Deena made a show of shaking her head toward the heavens and rolling her eyes. "Hello? The answer to both questions is *yes,* and you know it."

Yes. She liked the sound of that. *Damn the torpedoes, yada, yada.* Except . . .

She shrugged. "It's easy when I'm with him to not think about the consequences, but when Taylor's not around, I start to wonder if it's the right thing to do."

"You mean because of your issues?"

Zoë nodded. Already she knew that walking away from Taylor would be hard. If they got even more serious, if these feelings of lust and wonder and affection turned out to be love, leaving Taylor would probably kill her. And the kicker was, she might not be the one doing the leaving. Tessa had left Donis, after all.

Mom's afraid of risks. Taylor isn't.

Maybe. But could she take that to the bank?

She glanced up and caught Deena watching her, one eyebrow raised. "Well?"

"I want him," Zoë said. "I really do. But I still don't know if it's the right thing."

"That is such a pathetic excuse. I mean, if you're scared to have sex that's one thing . . . and not hopping into bed with some guy just to get it over with is understandable too. But that's not really what's going on here."

Zoë couldn't help it; she laughed. "Gee, Deen, don't hold back. I mean, tell me what you really think."

"It's just that you two are perfect for each other. I don't want you to let something stupid stand in the way of true love and all that."

"Something stupid? Deen, haven't you heard anything I've told you? My world isn't normal. There's an opinionated ferret hanging out in my apartment. My brother can be invisible, my dad can change into a dog—"

At that, Deena's eyes widened, but Zoë didn't stop to explain.

"—I've got these powers, my senses. And I've got obligations. Save-the-world kind of stuff."

"So? Everybody's got issues. I used to see fairies and my sister-in-law's a cat."

"Excuse me?"

"Well, she's not a cat now, but she was when he met her."

Zoë tilted her head, not exactly sure how to respond.

Deena didn't give her the chance. "But that's another story. My point is, if you're looking for excuses, you'll find them. And if you're looking for love, you'll find it."

"I can't be in love with him. Not yet. I mean, I don't really even know him."

Those words were more to convince herself than Deena. Love at first sight might be all the rage in books and movies, but in real life it seemed a little dicey. This fuzzy feeling in her stomach whenever she thought about Taylor, looked at him, *touched* him . . . well, that feeling was nothing but lust.

The whole situation was frustrating. When she fought bad guys with Hale or her dad, she'd never had any fear, just an icy surge of adrenaline. But with Taylor—*oh, sweet Hera*—her knees went wobbly and her palms turned sweaty.

Apparently the whole superhero thing was a big zero when it came to fixing matters of the heart.

With a little sigh, Zoë stood up and brushed grass off her behind. "We better get back and rescue the guys. If we're not careful, Mom will have us both engaged."

"Works for me," Deena said. "I'm sharing the bathroom and the refrigerator, but I still haven't got the ring."

"Yeah, well, Hoop knows my mom. It's a safe bet he won't scream and run in terror. Taylor, on the other hand . . ."

She let the thought trail off, and Deena grinned. "You may have a point. We'd better go rescue your date before he escapes, and you don't get any snuggle time."

Zoë blushed, ashamed that she didn't feel more ashamed about wanting exactly that.

"And you still haven't answered my question," Deena said, as they trudged toward Tessa's bench.

"I haven't?" Zoë asked, trying to sound innocent. "What question was that?"

Deena scowled. "You know perfectly well," she said. "But it doesn't matter because I already know the answer. The question was, don't you want Taylor?"

"And the answer?"

"Is yes," Deena said, still trudging, but shooting Zoë a dirty look. "Isn't it?"

Zoë just hummed, sure she was driving Deena nuts, but having a pretty good time doing it.

"Zoë . . ."

"You win." Her cheeks did their flaming thing again. "The answer is yes."

"I knew it."

Zoë hummed louder, trying to sound innocent. "There's more, you know." She tapped the bridge of her glasses and grinned, wide and mischievous. "I took a little peek."

Deena stopped dead, grabbing Zoë's sleeve and pulling her to a halt. Her eyes widened and her mouth opened, but no sound came out.

Zoë fought back a burst of laughter. It took a heck of a lot to render Deena speechless.

She remembered fondly *exactly* what she'd seen during her sneak peek.

Yup . . . a whole heck of a lot.

"The girls are coming back," Hoop said.

Taylor spun around, the now-familiar warmth spreading through him as he watched Zoë cross back toward them from the far side of lawn. His sportcoat hung on her frame, revealing none of her dress, just her lovely legs, and creating the illusion that there was absolutely nothing else under that coat.

His mouth twitched. Maybe before the night was over, there wouldn't be.

She was sweet and genuine and beautiful, and maybe she wasn't as normal as—"You never did tell me how you and Zoë met," Tessa said, drawing Taylor out of his thoughts.

"Gee, I wonder why?" Hoop muttered so that only Taylor could hear him.

He shot his friend a stern glance, but Hoop only shrugged.

241

"Just askin'," he said.

"Tell me quick before Zoë gets here or else she'll make you stop," Tessa said.

Taylor blinked. "Why?" Other than the obvious reason that their relationship was imaginary. But Tessa didn't know that.

"Because I'm her mother and I'm nosy."

"No, I mean why will she make you stop?"

"Oh. That." Tessa scooted over on the bench and patted the space next to her.

Taylor moved toward it, but Hoop beat him there.

"You snooze, you lose," Hoop said, grinning.

Taylor rolled his eyes.

"Zoë's always been a private girl," Tessa said, ignoring their antics. "She likes to keep secrets. Even from her own mother."

Taylor nodded. He'd known Zoë for only a blink in time, and he'd already figured out that she liked being enigmatic. "That's okay. I'm good at learning secrets. It's what I do best."

"That's right. You're a detective."

"*Was* a detective. Now I'm a private investigator."

"And a damn good one, too," Hoop said.

"A private *detective*," Tessa said. "Same difference. All that sneaking around." She looked up at him, her eyes stern. "Do you work undercover?"

"Occasionally."

She tilted her head, and he had the impression she was studying him, like an art student might look at a Monet, or a math major might look at some particularly puzzling theorem. "Are you undercover now?"

Taylor balked, not exactly sure how to answer that. He was himself, true, but he was playing a role. Still, it was a role he wanted for keeps. "No. What you see is what you get."

She nodded, apparently satisfied, but her eyes looked a little sad. "Good."

He took her hand, and she smiled up at him. "Are you okay?" he asked.

"I'm fine. Your meeting?"

Taylor frowned. "Excuse me?"

"She wants to know how you and Zoë met," Hoop interjected. "Keep with the program, man."

"Right." He shot Hoop a "thanks for nothing" look. "Thanks," he said, then started trying to concoct a story. "Well, you see—"

"Taylor was hot on the trail of this kidnapped little girl," Hoop began.

"How awful," Tessa said, glancing between Hoop and Taylor.

"Right," said Hoop. "It was."

Taylor gaped, then mouthed, *Kidnapped?*

"Um," said Hoop, apparently backtracking. "Actually, it would've been awful, except it wasn't really a little girl."

"It wasn't?" asked Tessa.

"It wasn't?" asked Taylor at exactly the same time.

"Nope," Hoop said, sounding annoyed.

"Oh. Right," said Taylor, totally clueless, but willing to trust him. Not out of some sense of moral obligation, but just because he didn't have a better plan. "It *wasn't* a little girl."

Tessa looked from Taylor to Hoop and then back to Taylor again. "Well, then, what was it?"

"Ah . . ." Taylor began. He turned to Hoop. "You tell her."

"Right. I'll tell her." He frowned; then his face cleared. "It was a doll."

"A doll?" Tessa repeated.

Taylor opened his mouth to parrot her, then shut it tight when Hoop gave him a stern glance.

"Yes, a doll."

Tessa turned to Taylor, the question clear in her eyes. He shrugged, his smile watery. "Quite a story, huh?"

As soon as Hoop finished this absurd tale, Taylor was going to kill him. So much for trust.

"How or why would a doll be kidnapped? And what on earth does Zoë have to do with it?"

Hoop shifted on the bench and stroked his chin. "Well, that's the thing, see. One of the kids in Zoë's school said that her friend was missing. And, uh . . ."

"The school jumped the gun," added Taylor, deciding that Hoop's forte really wasn't fiction.

"And they thought the missing friend was a little girl, not a doll?"

Hoop hooked an arm around Tessa's shoulder and pulled her close. "Exactly."

Tessa frowned, then squinted at each of them in turn. Hoop caught Taylor's eye and moved his shoulder in the barest of shrugs. Taylor fought the urge to shake his head and sigh.

"But how does Zoë fit in?" Tessa asked.

"Ah, now we get to the meat." Hoop held out his arm, indicating Taylor. "Do you want to tell her, or should I?"

Taylor tried out a smile, hoping it didn't look too queasy. "You go ahead."

"Well, the police didn't have a lead—"

"I can imagine," Tessa said.

"—so they called in a private detective."

"That would be me," Taylor said, happy to have recognized his cue.

"He was supposed to meet Zoë when he was interviewing the staff. She knew there wasn't a kid, but no one would listen to her. So she avoided Taylor, and he had to follow her into the ladies' room, where she told him about the doll." Hoop was starting to look a little worried that the story wasn't ever going to end.

Taylor twirled his hand in the air, hoping to speed Hoop's bardish efforts along.

"Right. Well, then Taylor figured out who'd taken it, and they got the doll back, and everyone lived happily ever after." Hoop sucked in a deep breath, let it out, and grinned. "And the rest is history."

"Was it love at first sight?" Tessa asked. "From the moment you saw her in the bathroom?"

"Absolutely," Taylor said.

"Mmm-hmmm." She smoothed her skirt, her eyes full of both amusement and annoyance. "Do you think someday I'll get to hear the real story?"

Taylor stifled a chuckle and caught Hoop's eye. Clearly Hoop was trying just as hard not to laugh. They both lost the battle.

"Well, it could've happened that way," Hoop said between chortles.

"It was entertaining, anyway," Tessa said, with an indulgent smile. "That's okay. I can wait. Just tell me one thing."

"What's that?"

"The last part was true, right?"

"Which part?"

"About love at first sight."

"Definitely," said Taylor. It was what Tessa wanted to hear. And besides, he had the sneaking suspicion that it wasn't wholly untrue. Somehow, between the time he'd started his search for Emily Parker and this cocktail party, he'd fallen head over heels in love with Zoë Smith. Was that possible? he asked himself.

"I was young and in love once," Tessa said dreamily, interrupting his thoughts.

"I'll bet he was a cop," Hoop guessed.

Tessa nodded. "In a manner of speaking, yes."

"An undercover cop," Taylor said.

"Right again. I lit up whenever Donis was around. And he would have moved mountains for me." She laughed. "Even more than I knew." Her eyes misted as she remembered, a tiny smile touching her lips. "He was Zoë's father. I left him before she was born."

Hoop leaned forward. "Yeah? Why?"

She lifted one shoulder in the tiniest of movements. "I was young. I was stupid." She sighed. "But mostly I was scared."

Taylor nodded. Living with a cop wasn't easy. Thank God he hadn't been in a relationship when his leg had been shot. Lord knew he'd given Lane enough grief with his bitching and moaning. It would have taken a hell of a woman or a hell of a love to get through those months with him.

His mind conjured an image of Zoë. He barely knew her, yet the thought of losing her was enough to make his knees go weak.

He steeled himself, catching Tessa's gaze and looking deep into her eyes. "Don't worry, Tess. I'm not under-cover, I'm not scared, and I'm not going to hurt your daughter."

246

She smiled, but the melancholy look remained. Then she reached up and patted his cheek. "Darling boy . . . it's not you I'm worried about."

"Now?" asked the skinny one. He crouched, ready to spring.

The fat one threw out a meaty paw, walloping the skinny one upside the head. "Wassa matter with you?"

"What?" The skinny one rubbed his head. "What did I do?"

"We gotta wait. Too many folks around now. Would see us, they would. We follow now. We get the halfling later."

The skinny one scowled, settling back under the bushes. "I knew that. I did. I knew that all along."

The halfling and the human passed by, and they watched, eyes squinting.

"We go now. We change. We follow."

The skinny one sighed. "Now?"

The fat one shook his head, sending his rolls of fat jiggling. He reached up, pushed a fold of scaly skin out of his eyes, and scowled at his companion. "We gotta change. You change now."

The skinny one's flesh shimmered and shifted and stretched and pulled. Folds of skin faded away, globs of fat settled, tattered rags transformed into soft fur and a wagging tail. Suddenly, a golden-haired collie crouched under the shrubs decorating the manicured lawn.

"No, no, no," the fat one howled. "Not dogs. Human. We need to look *human*." He walloped the skinny dog in the ears. "Change now. I change, too." And he did, twisting and morphing into the rotund form of a cultured-seeming human male in a tweed jacket. Next to him, the collie had disappeared, and now the skinny one adjusted the sleeves on his tailored silk jacket.

"Good. We go now," the fat one whispered, shoving his way out from under the bushes.

The skinny one nodded and followed, and nobody noticed as they fell into step, keeping to the shadows as they followed the halfling and the human across the neatly trimmed lawn.

Chapter Sixteen

Zoë leaned against Taylor, watching as her mom slid into the taxi.

"You two be good," Tessa said with a wave.

He gave her shoulder a gentle squeeze. "Do we have to?"

"Taylor!" Zoë looked up at him, but he just smiled, his eyes dancing, as Tessa laughed. Instead of being entirely mortified, Zoë found herself grinning back.

The taxi disappeared down the Andersons' drive, and Zoë blew out a breath. How had she fallen so fast? In the blink of an eye, Taylor had gone from being an idle fantasy to being a reality. How on earth was she going to get herself centered? And did she even want to?

She was still wearing his sportcoat, but even so, a shiver racked her body, terrifying and enticing. Part of her wanted to run away. A bigger part of her wanted the valet to deliver the car, wanted to press Taylor up against it. Wanted to free-fall into the backseat, and do all those things she never did in high school.

Slowly, without even trying, Taylor was chipping away her defenses, melting the icy fear that usually accompanied even the thought of being touched like that.

She shivered again.

"Cold?" he asked.

"No, no." She swallowed, trying to gather her wits. "I'm fine."

"Well, I think you are, anyway," he said. "Fine, that is."

"Oh, that's original." Hoop sauntered toward them from the valet station, his arm around Deena.

"Maybe not original," Taylor said, looking only at Zoë. "But sincere."

"Good answer," Deena said, laughing, and Zoë felt her entire body blush redder than her hair.

She shook her head, clearing her thoughts, hoping to steer the conversation back to more manageable ground. "Sorry we had to leave you alone with Mom in marriage mode." She tried to shift her tone back to businesslike. "We're not engaged now or anything I should know about, right?"

A slow grin spread across his face, and a feeling like warm molasses ooched down her insides.

"Well, I don't know, sweetheart," he said. "What kind of *anything* did you have in mind?"

Oh, dear. The blush was back, its heat making her cheeks burn.

"Behave yourself," Hoop said.

"Unless you don't want him to," Deena whispered, her voice far too low for Hoop or Taylor. Zoë caught her eye, but Deena just grinned. "What? I didn't say anything."

Taylor and Hoop looked at each other.

"Did we miss something?" Taylor asked.

"You're men. You're supposed to be clueless," Deena said.

"That makes me the most manly man on the planet," Hoop said.

Deena kissed him on the cheek. "It certainly does."

Hoop opened his mouth and then closed it again.

"Good plan, Hoop," Taylor said. "Stay quiet. Otherwise you'll only dig yourself in deeper."

"Aren't you guys supposed to be getting a dose of culture right about now?" Zoë asked.

"Righto," Hoop said. "Where's the valet with the car? We need to get going." He grinned and sucked in a breath, then belted out, "Kill the wabbit! Kill the wabbit!" at the top of his lungs.

The few folks waiting at the valet stand turned, a half dozen pairs of eyes wide and curious.

Deena raised her eyes to the sky. "That's our cue."

"Thank goodness for that," Zoë said.

Hoop shrugged, the grin taking over his face. "What's the matter? You don't appreciate culture?"

"I guess I'm just a philistine," Zoë said.

Hoop nodded his head toward Taylor. "Don't do anything I wouldn't do."

"Well, that leaves my options pretty wide open," Taylor said, his intense look once again reducing Zoë to shakes and shivers. "*Is* there anything you wouldn't do?"

"A few things. Maybe. But if I say them out loud, I might get arrested."

Deena walloped him with her purse, and he held up

his hands to defend himself. They were still play-wrestling—the party guests watching them with amused expressions—when the valet pulled up in Hoop's battered Jeep. Hoop whisked Deena into his arms, planted a kiss on her mouth, then helped her up into the passenger seat before climbing behind the wheel.

Taylor swung his arm around Zoë's shoulder as Hoop pulled away, Deena riding backward in the open Jeep so she could wave and throw kisses. "They're quite a pair."

"Perfect for each other," Zoë agreed. She tried not to look at Taylor as she smothered a wave of forest green envy.

She wanted what Deena and Hoop had—that closeness, that playfulness, that sense of being almost one person. And the possibility that she'd never find it scared her.

She glanced up at Taylor, silently admitting that the possibility she'd already found it—but couldn't keep it—scared her even more.

It was amazing what one could accomplish at Radio Shack. While Zoë and her little human friend were downing cocktails on the lawn, Mordi had dashed to the nearest mall—not a long trek in southern California—and acquired a few key electronic components.

A few wires here, a transistor there, a capacitor hooked up in the middle, and voilà! One tracking device returned to prime working order. He hoped his dad was watching. At least somebody in the family knew how to work with electronics.

He watched the little green blip blinking right above the house where he again perched like an owl, his cloak draped over his shoulders. Zoë and Mr. Taylor were down there, along with their mortal friends. Eventually Zoë and the detective would split up—and Mordi would have his chance. He'd simply follow the bouncing green ball all the way back into his father's good graces.

Blip, blip, bleep.

He perked up. The blip was on the move.

Unfortunately, unlike his cousin, supersight wasn't one of his talents. Which meant he had to whip out his handy binoculars to get a visual on exactly who was moving—Zoë or the detective.

He pressed the glasses against his face and focused, the crowd changing from fuzzy relief to perfect clarity. He trained the lenses over the front porch, scanning the faces, until finally . . . he saw . . .

Both of them?

"What in the name of Pluto is going on?" he said with a snarl. With a jerk, he ripped the binocs away, lost his balance, and went scuttling down the roof, his heels and rear sending tile shingles flying. Reaching out, he grabbed hold of the rain gutter and hung there, suspended by just his fingertips, totally exposed to whomever might be looking.

He shouldn't have worried. Being a rather unobservant lot, the nearby mortals on the ground didn't even look up. And not one person noticed him literally hanging from his fingertips. Really, it was a wonder mortals had ever managed to drag themselves out of the primordial swamp.

Suspended four stories high, he swayed a bit, pondering his predicament. What to do? What to do?

Reconnaissance first. With his free hand, he pulled his cloak closed and fastened it. Then he grabbed up the

binocs. Surely he must have seen wrong. Either Zoë or
Taylor must have left. After all, the blip was moving.

He peered down, finally focusing in on Zoë. She stood
there, a little smile on her face, laughing a bit as she
talked to—he shifted his perspective a bit to the left—
the detective.

Damn!

The realization jolted him, and he clenched his fist to
pound it against the roof. Unfortunately it was the hand
that was holding on to the gutter, which meant that he
stopped holding on to the gutter. Which meant that he
fell. Four stories. All the way to the ground.

Bloody hell.

From behind the hydrangea bushes, he frowned in the
general direction of the driveway. If Zoë was there and
the detective was there and the blip was moving, that
could only mean one thing: someone else had the stone.

But who?

With a little grunt, he stood up, straightening his suit,
wiping bits of leaf and grass off the finely tailored Lon-
don original. He paused, his hand hovering over the seat
of his pants, wondering if he'd damned the situation too
soon.

After all, the little blip had been centered right above
Zoë. Zoë was still there, but the blip had gone bye-bye.

The mortal girl. The stone must be with Zoë's friend.
He smiled.

That had to be the explanation. And it made things
even easier. All he had to do was follow her with the
tracking device and then, when the moment was ripe,
make his move.

* * *

The flame from the gaslight at the end of the Andersons' driveway flickered and danced, splashing orange light across Zoë's hair. Taylor sucked in a breath, savoring the moment.

She looked ethereal, unreal. A goddess. *His* goddess.

When she smiled at him, his heart fluttered. Lord, how this woman made his soul sing.

"You're staring," she said.

"Am I?"

She nodded, then leaned up against the lamppost, mischief shining in her eyes. "What are you looking at, sailor?"

"The most beautiful woman in port."

Her cheeks flushed, and Taylor's body tightened in response. She was innocent, sweet, yet sexy as hell.

There was never a bed around when he needed one.

He mentally kicked himself. He wanted her in his bed—or her bed, he wasn't picky—but that wasn't all he wanted. Oh, yes, he wanted to seduce her, wanted her to want him just as desperately. But he also wanted to understand everything there was to know about her, and to explore those intimate secrets even she didn't know yet.

Oh, yeah, all that was what he wanted, all right. Where the hell was the damn car?

"You're still staring," she said, her delighted grin making it absolutely clear that she didn't mind at all.

"You're still beautiful."

If possible, her flush deepened, and she dropped her gaze. "Thank you."

He took a step closer. "Alone at last," he said, moving closer still, not touching her, but near enough that, if he concentrated, he was sure he could feel the desire thrumming through her.

She looked relaxed, but he knew she wasn't. He knew because he was wound up tight, just waiting for release in her arms, her lips. *Her.*

When she looked up, there was no mistaking the passion in her eyes. "There are still people waiting for their cars. I don't think we're alone."

Right then and there he decided he'd waited long enough for the damn car. He took her hand and she moaned slightly, her breath fluttery. "Come with me."

"Where to?"

"Somewhere where there aren't people waiting for their cars." He leaned closer to whisper in her ear. "Somewhere we can be alone."

"What about the car?

"Screw the car." He tugged her toward him.

"Why, Mr. Taylor, are you planning to seduce me?"

"As a matter of fact, I am. Do you mind?"

The burning desire shining in her eyes was real, and the shy honesty in her voice just about did him in. "I'd be disappointed," she said, "if you weren't."

The pathway twisted across the rocky slope, wending its way along the cliff above where the ocean beat against the shore. Zoë peered over the edge, watching froth leap and dance above the wave-polished rocks, the magnificent force of nature nothing compared to the tempest raging within her.

"A beautiful view," Taylor said.

"Yes, it is."

She turned to smile at him, then realized he wasn't looking at the view, but at her.

"I want to kiss you, Zoë."

"Then why don't you?"

"Maybe I'm afraid."

"I don't believe you're afraid of anything." She said it with a grin, but although he smiled back, there was something hidden in his eyes. He blinked, and his eyes cleared, leaving Zoë to wonder if she'd imagined it.

"But I *am* afraid," he said, the admission making her a little relieved she wasn't the only one. "Afraid that if I start to kiss you, I won't be able to stop."

She stepped closer, anticipating his lips on hers, steadying herself for the shock of his touch. With a little grin, she wrapped her arms around his waist. "Well, Mr. Taylor. What's wrong with that?"

"Oh, sweetheart." His words drifted toward her on a wisp of air, caressing her as softly as his hand gently cupped her cheek. She pressed her face against his palm, letting the warmth of his skin seep into her blood, letting her blood and his heat burn through her veins.

Her body lingered on the verge of ignition. Reveling in the torment, she turned her face, relishing the rough feel of his callused hand against her cheek, pressing her lips to his palm. He moaned, the soft sound sweeter to her ears than the purest musical note.

Except . . . there was another sound, too.

She twisted her head, trying to hear. "What was that?" Whatever it was, it meant *kissus interruptus,* and that was bad.

"What?"

"Do you hear that?" she asked, knowing the answer. The sound was too soft, too subtle. Even for her, it was almost inaudible. But it was there, low and threatening. Like a growl, or a low wail.

He hooked a finger under her chin and looked into her eyes. "I don't hear anything but you."

She smiled, but shook her head. "No, there's something out there."

He pulled back, immediately tense, ready to fight. His determination to protect her warmed Zoë to her very soul, even though she of all people didn't need a hero. "Something?" he whispered.

"Or someone." Then she saw it—a rustling in the brush off to the right. "There." She pointed, automatically stepping in front of him.

Just as automatically, he gripped her shoulders, pushing her aside and stepping in front of her. "What do you see?"

She sidled forward again, trying to get in front of him without being conspicuous, wanting to protect him. She squinted as she looked over the rims of her glasses, her nose wrinkling from a sudden stench, and once again Taylor moved in front of her. She stifled a grin at his persistent chivalry.

How in Hades could she describe what she saw—two creatures crouching among the leaves, one tall and thin, the other short and squatty. A greenish slime seemed to coat them both, and their mouths hung open, drool dripping off their big, pointy overbites.

On the round one, folds of scaled fat fell over more folds of fat. The skinny one had none, its skin seemingly clinging to pure bone, as if the fat one had taken his share. Their noxious odor drifted toward her, like rotten eggs mixed with curdled milk.

She bit back a gag and tried to decide what to do.

If Taylor could see these . . . *things,* she'd have some serious explaining to do.

* * *

"Those guys look strung out." Taylor stepped sideways, centering himself between Zoë and the two cretins in the bushes.

"Guys?" One eyebrow arched up.

"I realize it's giving them more credit than they deserve," he whispered. "But 'asshole junkies' seemed a little strong."

"Oh." She pushed her glasses firmly up her nose. "Right."

She sounded so confused, he turned around to look at her. "Don't worry. Just let me handle it and we'll be fine." He squinted. "Are you okay?"

"Fine. I'm fine," she said brightly.

But of course he knew she wasn't. How could she be? Hell, she was an elementary school librarian. Apart from that run-in with that police impersonator, Taylor was certain that the closest Zoë came to the wrong side of the law was chasing down people with overdue library books. And Taylor intended to keep it that way.

Her brow creased. "So you think they're just two guys hanging out in the bushes?"

"What I think is that we should get out of here." He took her hand and started heading back toward the Andersons' house. "If they are junkies, they probably wouldn't have any qualms about jumping us—not if they thought it might get them enough cash for their next hit."

His thigh ached, and he idly rubbed it. Whether she'd meant to hire him as a protector or a date, either way, he was there. And he didn't intend to let her down.

"Well, then," she said. "Let's get going."

He took her hand and hurried her down the path.

259

After a few seconds, she stopped.

"What?"

"Footsteps. Behind us." She started moving again, tugging him forward. "Let's get you—I mean us—out of here."

He slowed a bit, listening. "I don't hear anything."

She stepped behind him and nudged him with her shoulder. "Keep listening. You will."

Nodding, he moved on. Most likely she was just nervous, and wanted to get away as fast as possible. He would have been smart not to have said anything at all— to have just headed back to the house without clueing her in to their uninvited companions.

Now the poor girl was imagining footsteps and bogeymen. And no wonder. It wasn't as if she'd led a life of adventure, and here he was, dropping her into the middle of a situation that was decidedly *not* Capraesque.

He glanced over his shoulder and saw a shadow waver behind them on the darkened path. *Uh-oh.* Maybe Zoë was right. Maybe the whacked-out weirdos were following them after all.

He thought of the strange man impersonating an officer earlier and wondered if there was more to these druggie creeps than the need for a fix. Were these guys following them with a more nefarious purpose? And were they following him or Zoë?

Certainly not her. She'd seemed genuinely perplexed in the car. And he couldn't imagine anything in the life of a librarian that would attract such unpleasant attention. He, on the other hand, had recently been hired to locate a very large, very missing, very expensive gemstone.

Maybe he wasn't the only one looking for it. . . .

Damn it! He'd jumped so hard and so fast at the possibility of ten grand he hadn't even considered the consequences, had basically blown off Hoop's concern that it might be hot. And now he'd gone and embroiled Zoë in the twisted little plot.

Trying to hurry—without *looking* like he was hurrying—he took her elbow and moved her along.

"Are we hurrying?"

"Nope. Just strolling."

She sped up. "Let's hurry."

"Whatever you want."

They started walking faster, Zoë taking the lead and Taylor pumping hard, trying to keep up.

She took his hand and sped up. Taylor started trotting.

She sped up again. Taylor started running.

The trees started passing faster than they usually did when he jogged on the beach, and the wind cut into his face the way it did when he rode a roller-coaster. A stitch started in his side. His lungs burned; his thigh screamed.

He glanced over at Zoë, who looked about as winded as someone out for an evening stroll. "You . . . work . . . out, right?" he managed, sucking in air as they chugged along.

"Oh, yeah. Sure. Lots." She caught his eye. "Too fast?"

"No," he lied, clutching his side and gasping. He gave up. So much for being macho; this was the new millennium, after all. Coughing, he stopped, bent over, and sucked in gallons of glorious oxygen.

Air, God, how he loved the feel of air in his lungs.

"Sorry." Zoë stopped and jogged backward to him. "I get a little carried away."

261

"Hell, lady. You could qualify for the Olympics."

She laughed, but it sounded a little forced . . . and then her eyes went wide.

"What? Am I turning red? I do that when I'm winded sometimes." His hands were still perched just above his knees—his favorite gasping-for-air position—but when he looked up, he saw asshole junkie number one reflected in her glasses. And this was one fellow who definitely looked like there was more on his mind than a walk on the beach. He was lunging forward.

"Aw, hell." Whipping around, he kicked his leg out, ignoring the screaming of his thigh, his only thought of keeping Zoë safe.

"Taylor, *no!*"

His leg connected squarely with the fat one's jaw, but instead of the reassuring crack he'd expected, he heard an anticlimactic slooshing sound, a bit like he'd just karate-kicked a jellyfish. *Man, this is one drugged up son of a bitch who really needs to go on a diet.*

The slug sank to the ground, a nice imprint of the bottom of Taylor's shoe tattooed onto the side of his face. Flushed with victory, Taylor looked up at Zoë, whose eyes were still wide.

He had just enough time to say "What?" when it registered—he'd seen the fat one, but there had been a skinny one, too. And before he could do anything, a bony little arm locked around his neck.

In front of him, Zoë bounced up and down, looking like she wanted to jump into the fray.

"Stay back," he said, except with Skinny's arm pressing against his windpipe, it came out sounding more like *stray cats.*

"What?" She squinted, looking from him to Skinny,

then back to him again. And she was still bouncing, that "I really wanna help" look plastered on her face.

"Got . . . under . . . control," he managed to spit out, then realized with a bit of horror that his feet were no longer on the ground. The fact that he was about to pass out from lack of oxygen did not—*repeat, not*—mean that he was any less in control. *Nope, didn't mean that at all. Didn't, didn't, didn't.*

He realized what an odd-sounding word *didn't* was, and decided that maybe *control* was overstating things, especially considering he was getting a little loopy from lack of air.

Whizzzzzzzzzz! Something zinged over his head, and he heard a *thwack* as the something connected with Skinny's head. All of a sudden Taylor's feet were back on the ground, and his lungs were filling with oxygen.

Things were looking up.

One glance at Zoë confirmed that she was all right. More or less, anyway. She was staring—almost trance-like—at a point just over his head. Taylor whirled around, leading with his fist, and caught Skinny—who was standing there motionless like an idiot—square on the jaw. For a moment the junkie just teetered, almost as if he were drugged. Then he yelped and hightailed it down the path.

What a strange reaction to a punch, but the result was right.

He tossed a smile Zoë's way. "Guess that wraps up the fun for tonight. Join us for another mugging tomorrow. Same bat time, same bat channel." Then he sank to the ground.

* * *

He was making jokes. *Thank goodness.* She'd been afraid she hadn't acted fast enough and one of the nitwits had hurt him. Of course, Taylor'd managed to take care of Nit all on his own, but Wit's necklock hadn't exactly looked comfortable.

"Are you okay?" She knelt down beside him, checking his neck for bruising.

"Fine." His gaze swept over her, the inspection stirring her blood. "How about you?"

Not fine at all. But that had more to do with the way he was looking at her than what had happened with Nit and Wit. She forced herself to lie. "No problems here. You took care of them."

"I don't think they were junkies after all," he admitted. "I think they were after me."

She remembered the fangs and the drool and the really gross smell, and silently disagreed. Out loud she said, "Oh?"

What she really wanted to ask was, *Didn't you see the fangs? The slimy drool? The one eye instead of two? Do you really think those cretins were your average, everyday junkies?*

"Yeah. I just took on a new job. I'm tracking down an heirloom. Possibly stolen. Maybe they figure I've got a lead."

"Maybe." If he thought he knew where Nit and Wit came from, she wasn't going to argue. It guaranteed her secret was still safe.

She stifled a sigh. For Taylor, there was no drool, no fangs, just a couple of muggers out for a Sunday stroll.

"Well," she said, trying to sound chipper. "The important thing is you're okay."

"Okay? I'm great," he said. "Everyone says so," he

added confidentially and smiled. Then he stood up and helped her to her feet.

"Everyone?" she asked, looking at him pointedly and fighting a laugh.

"Oh, so now you're a detractor?" He said it with a grin, and she had to admit he looked pretty scrumptious.

"Well," she said, trying to sound grudging, but not succeeding very well, "I suppose you might be a little great."

"Great is an all-or-nothing thing."

She laughed. "Greedy, aren't you?"

He swung an arm around her and lowered his mouth to her ear. "Insatiable," he whispered, clearly pleased with himself.

Well, why shouldn't he be? He'd saved her from the bogeyman. Or at least that was what *he* thought.

The truth wasn't quite so straightforward.

He looped his arm through hers and they headed back toward the car in silence, Taylor most likely reliving his victory, Zoë definitely reliving hers.

Taylor had called them *men*. But they weren't men. Not at all. And when the skinny one had been dangling Taylor from one slime-covered tentacle thing, she'd been helpless. If she'd fought, if she'd lashed out and beat the bugger to a pulp, Taylor would surely have been suspicious. To say the least.

So she'd ripped a button off Taylor's coat and flung it at the beast, hitting the noxious creature square on the nose and stunning it. But then Taylor hadn't gotten away fast enough, and when the enraged beast was about to pummel him, Zoë had reacted on instinct, aiming a burst of concentration right between the dufus's bugged-out eyes.

And it had worked.

That was the truly amazing thing. Never in a million years had she thought that thinking really hard could rank up there on the list of top-ten ways to ward off ugly idiots. Who knew? She'd aimed her superstare in his direction, Wit had frozen, Taylor'd gotten in a solid punch, and the little creep had taken off, a groggy Nit following right behind.

Easy-squeezy.

Just a few days ago she could barely levitate a book. Now she was going all gonzo with telekinetic power. How cool was that? Except she shuddered to think what would have happened if the now fully functional Zoë Smith superstare hadn't worked. Either Taylor would have been monster fodder, or Zoë would have had to put some of her martial arts on display.

She shivered, and Taylor pulled her closer, smiling down at her. Automatically she smiled back, feeling absurdly safe just being in his arms. Absurd because Taylor didn't really up her safety quotient. Heck, she could lay the man out in two seconds flat, but still . . .

She sighed. There was something special about just being held by him.

"You sure you're okay?" he asked.

She tilted her head back, basking in the warmth of his luscious brown eyes. "Oh, yeah. I'm fine." But even more than before, she was sure Taylor was far from fine. If he got caught in the cross fire of her testing, if Nit and Wit decided to make an encore appearance . . .

She needed to send him on his way—safe back into Hollywood, where at least he was familiar with the bad guys. Where the bad guys were *guys*, not monsters in men suits. He'd never be safe with her.

They stopped in front of Francis Capra, the only car in the drive now that the guests had all left. She leaned against the back while Taylor opened the door for her.

"We ought to get you home. Some hot chocolate, some rest." He trailed a fingertip down her cheek, and it was all she could do not to gasp. "You've had a traumatic evening." He kissed his fingertip and pressed it against the end of her nose. "Maybe set you up on the couch, tuck a fluffy blanket around you, watch a funny movie . . ."

Oh, no. With sudden certainty, she knew that she wasn't about to settle for a PG-rated night with Taylor.

Heck, she wasn't even going to settle for R.

No, as scary as it was—as much as she was sure that she would practically explode from his touch, not to mention his kisses—Zoë knew one thing for sure.

Tonight, she wanted X-rated. Wanted it bad.

With what she hoped was a sultry smile, she reached up and stroked his cheek, banishing thoughts of Nit and Wit, pushing away worries about any of the council's tests. Right now she wanted only to think about Taylor. Gently, she turned his face toward hers. "No hot chocolate, no blankies. Just you."

"Zoë, we were attacked. This isn't—"

"You," she said with more force.

She hooked her arms around his neck and pulled herself up on her tip toes. She brushed her lips over his, calling on every ounce of concentration to stay focused when her lips tingled from the butterfly-soft kiss. "You can try to stop me, of course," she whispered. "I've never seduced a hero before, but I intend to go down fighting."

Taylor moaned, his hands caressing her back, pulling

267

her closer against him until her body burned with the heat of a thousand suns. "Sweetheart," he murmured. "I wouldn't dream of disappointing a lady."

Hieronymous drummed his fingers on his desk, his manicured nails click-clacking on the polished wood.

"They failed," Clyde said.

"I am aware of that." What should have been such a simple task—obtaining the stone, getting rid of Zoë and taking over the world—was becoming much too complicated.

"They were out of practice, they were," Clyde went on. "It's from being locked up so long."

"That is no excuse."

Clyde pulled himself up and to attention. "No, sir. Shall I dispose of them?"

Hieronymous tilted his head, considering. On one hand, the creatures had failed with a relatively simple task. On the other . . .

"No. They may still prove useful." He glanced at the center monitor, now displaying the Los Angeles skyline. "Depending on how Mordichai fares, they may still prove useful, indeed."

Chapter Seventeen

Box seats at the Hollywood Bowl went for over one hundred dollars; seats on the grass near the back could sometimes be had for free. Mordichai sat in neither, but he still had the best seat in the house—perched on top of the graceful white arc that rose like an upended teacup out of the Hollywood landscape.

Of course, he couldn't see the orchestra. For that matter, he couldn't see the cartoons being projected onto a screen inside the famous amphitheater. It was a pity, really. That wascally wabbit always cracked him up.

Bleep, bleep. The little green blip flashed, underscoring his purpose. He wasn't there to watch Bugs outwit Elmer Fudd. No, he was on a mission. And from his vantage point, he had a perfect view of his target.

The silly woman had no idea that tonight, when the music stopped, she was going to have an unfortunate encounter with one of those pesky Los Angeles mug-gers.

Deena clapped and bounced up, applauding like crazy, wishing she could fly out into the night with the music. "Wasn't that great? Aren't you glad we came?"

Hoop laughed and squeezed her hand, watching the last of the cartoons race across the screen. "I told you I'd like it. What I don't get is why the powers that be don't set all classical music to cartoons."

"I think it's the other way around. They scored the cartoons with the classical music."

Hoop shrugged. "Whatever. Point is, I like it." He nodded toward the exit as the encore finished. "Ready to battle the crowd?"

"Sure." She grabbed the hem of her oversize pullover sweater and yanked it up over her head, managing to get herself tangled.

"What on earth are you doing?"

She couldn't see him with her head in the darn thing. "I'm hot. And I'm stuck. Pull, would you?"

She could practically hear him rolling his eyes and shaking his head, but he grabbed hold and tugged, and the sweater slipped easily over her head and shoulders.

Something cold slid down into her cleavage and she shivered. Hoop shoved the sweater into the top of her tote bag. "Let's go." He stepped onto the pathway to-ward the exit, squeezing in behind a couple with four perky little kids. Deena followed, ignoring the stares as she groped at her chest and then her neck.

They had just about reached the exit when she stopped, realizing. "Oh, hell."

Hoop looked over his shoulder. "What?"

"It's gone."

He shrugged, looking lost.

"The necklace."

"Oh. When?"

"The chain must have gotten caught in my sweater. It's probably back in our box."

"Or smashed under someone's feet on the path, or someone picked it up, or—"

"I know," she said, running a hand through her hair.

"Don't worry about it, babe. It was an ugly necklace anyway."

She recalled the oddly twisted metal holding the green stone. "Well, I liked it. And so did Zoë. And it was hers, too."

"Right. I forgot." He shrugged. "We can wait if you want," he said, not sounding particularly keen about the idea.

"No," she said with a sigh. A swarm of people still meandered down the path, making it impossible to go back and search. "It's probably lost for good. And you're right. It was ugly." She shrugged. "Well, at least I've got the stone."

"You do?"

"It fell into my bra," she mumbled.

"What?" he asked, though his grin suggested he'd heard her perfectly well.

"My bra," she repeated with a smirk. "I guess it came loose from its setting and dropped there."

He chuckled, then took her hand and gave her a little tug toward the exit. "In that case, what say we head home? I'm thinking I should go on a search for buried treasure."

*   *   *

The trouble with X-rated was that Zoë didn't know a darn thing about it. Taylor was right there—right in front of her. Unfortunately he was in professional mode, scoping out the inside of her apartment for bogeymen hiding in the dark. Except for his not-so-subtle hints back at the car, he'd shown absolutely no interest in throwing her on the floor, ripping her clothes off, and ravishing her.

She considered tearing off her own clothes and throwing herself on the floor—just to jump-start the whole thing—but ruled it out as being a tad forward. *Bummer.*

So how on earth did she get him to move from point A to point bedroom?

For the first time, she wished she'd paid more attention in school. Not the geography, math, and social studies part, but the this-is-how-the-cool-girls-get-guys part. Not only had she pretty much flunked out in that department, she hadn't even gone to class. Which left her at a decided disadvantage when a gorgeous, sexy man was wandering through her darkened apartment doing the macho protection thing instead of the macho seduction thing.

He came back to the door, flipped on the light, and ushered her inside, the slight pressure of his hand against her waist sending her frantic atoms into meltdown.

"You're all set," he said. "The place looks fine."

His purely professional expression would've had her worried, except that she saw his eyes. Those eyes told a different story. Taylor's head might want to protect her from being ravaged by bad guys, but the rest of him wanted to be the one doing the ravaging.

She moved awkwardly into the apartment, making a point of brushing lightly against him as she passed. The slight contact set her body tingling, and she turned to face him, trying to pull herself back together. There was no sense in looking desperate and needy.

"Um . . . well . . . uh . . ." She grappled for an intelligent topic to discuss, and finally landed on coffee. "Want some?" *Oh, Zeus, what did I say?* "Coffee," she added, stumbling over herself to clarify. "Do you want some coffee?"

"Coffee would be great," he said, but his eyes said, *And how about getting naked with me in the bedroom?*

"Oh, yes." She blinked, realizing he hadn't said anything of the sort, then blushed even hotter.

"What?"

"Coffee it is," she said, while he squinted at her as though she'd lost her mind.

At least coffee was a reason to escape the living room. She hightailed it for her tiny kitchen and pulled a stack of filters out of the cabinet. Now the big decision—decaf or regular. She decided to go with the latter. Sure it would keep her up all night, but right now, being awake—and active—the whole night through sounded pretty darned appealing.

"Leaded? That'll keep us up all night."

His voice came from right behind her, and she almost jumped a mile. She whipped around, hoping he hadn't noticed that she'd jumped so high her hair really had grazed the ceiling.

"Sorry," he said. "I didn't mean to scare you."

She had no idea how he'd managed to get so close without her realizing—a testament to how distracted he'd made her—but there he was. Just three little inches of air separated them. Just air between her and those teasing lips and strong, firm hands.

273

"It's okay," she said. "Don't worry about it."

He moved even closer. The sound of his breath, the beating of his heart, the rustle of his clothes as he moved closer all made up a symphony of erotic sounds designed to drive her crazy. "Of course," he said, his voice low, "I don't have any problems with staying up all night."

He didn't move, and neither did she. He just looked down at her, his eyes warm and inviting. She waited for him to grab her around the waist, to pull her toward him, to kiss her senseless. . . .

Nothing.

She waited a little longer, their gazes locked, her breath quickening.

Still nothing.

No, not exactly nothing. But certainly nothing good, because now he'd broken eye contact and was staring toward the floor.

Well, heck.

With a sigh, she held her hands out to her sides. *In for a penny and all that.* "So," she said, "how about we get started on that seduction?" The second the words left her lips, she cringed. From the tone of her voice, she might as well have asked, *So, how about those Dodgers?*

Very smooth move.

Then again, maybe there had been a little method in her madness. When he lifted his head, the passion in his eyes was unmistakable. He moved closer, and she felt a surge of power that had nothing to do with her heritage and everything to do with being female.

He really wanted her. And right now, her feminine power put to shame every one of her piddly little superhero skills. Who really cared about flying when a

man like this could take her to the stars with one dark
and dangerous look?

"Is this a good idea?"

"What do you mean?" Her words came out as a
squeak, but she didn't care. She wasn't about to let him
back out on her now. "It's a fabulous idea."

He smiled, but his eyes were concerned. "I don't want
to drag you into this. If those guys really are after me,
I should leave."

"Why?" She shouldn't argue, not really. After all,
he'd be a lot safer away from her. But, Hera help her,
she didn't want him to go. It was selfish, but true.

His hands gripped her shoulders. "I want you, Zoë.
Oh, Lord, I want you. But I don't want to see you in
danger."

His eyes burned into her, and she swallowed, feeling
like a heel. He did want her, but he was willing to walk
away to keep her safe. She wanted him, and she was
ready to damn the consequences and go at it with Taylor
like bunnies.

Oh, dear. Maybe Hale was right. Maybe she was in
over her head. Maybe she really couldn't handle all these
wild, wanton, spinning, singing, zinging, and zipping
feelings storming around inside her. She should just let
this man walk away. Concentrate on passing her tests
and working up the courage to tell her mother. Forget
she was ever even remotely attracted to a mortal.

She tossed the idea around in her head, trying to decide if she was keen on the walk-away plan.

Um . . . nope.

So much for reason over emotion.

The sound of toenails clickety-clacking on tile echoed
from across the room, and she saw Elmer's furry little

face poke out from her bathroom. No question about it—
that was a scolding expression on his tiny rat face.

She ignored him. Best not to let one's life be ruled
by ferrets, after all. Especially not meddling, chaperon-
ing ferrets dumped in her apartment by her overbearing,
well-meaning big brother.

Switching her gaze back to Taylor—who apparently
hadn't heard the telltale toenail tapping—she sucked in
a deep breath and tried to summon some chutzpah.
"Look," she said in her best negotiating-with-eight-year-
olds voice, "nobody's here. And chances are nobody followed us, right?"

His nod was grudging, but affirmative.

"Which means that you're safe here for now. And so
am I."

He smiled, intense and provocative. "So we have a
wild night, I leave in the morning, and don't come calling, lest I lead the bad guys to your doorstep?"

"Well, yeah." She frowned, realizing that it sounded
like all she wanted was a wild night of passion to get
the man out of her system. Which was absolutely true—
really it was—but that didn't change the fact that it
sounded awful to put it so bluntly. She tried to soften
her tone. "What do *you* want?"

His examination started at her toes, and by the time
it reached her eyes, she was on fire. *Hera's hatpins.* This
man did things to her. Marvelous, erotic, wonderful, terrifying things.

"What do I want?" he repeated. "Let me tell you exactly what I want." He leaned forward until his mouth
was just a breath away from her ear. "I want to throw
you to the floor and make love to you until you beg for

more." The words were low, dangerous, and a shudder ripped through her soul.

"Oh."

With a look that told her he knew exactly the effect he was having on her, he moved in front of her. The heat from his body warmed her, pooling somewhere in her middle. He put his hands on her hips and pulled her closer and closer until she could tell just how much he'd meant his words.

"Oh," she repeated stupidly.

"What do you want?" He whispered the words, his breath hot against her ear, wicked and tempting.

She tried to answer, but her mouth had gone dry. She swallowed and tried again. "I . . . uh . . . want you to throw me to the floor and make love to me until I beg for more."

"Well, there you go. Looks like we're on the same wavele—Aieeee!" He ended with a howl, jerking away from her and hopping around on one foot while he held on to his other ankle. Below him, Elmer dodged, trying to escape being squashed by Taylor, the human pogo stick.

For such a tiny little ferret, he'd managed to put a pretty big damper on the moment. What had been shaping up like a really sweet Taster's Choice commercial was rapidly degenerating into a bad Fox Network special—*When Good Ferrets Go Bad*.

She glared at Elmer as he backed away, his head tilted up, abject innocence plastered all over his furry little face. "Oh, no, you don't. Hale's gonna hear about this."

"The little devil bit me."

"It was a love bite," she lied. "He's fond of you. Just a little overzealous."

277

"I'll say." Taylor rubbed his ankle.

Elmer hopped back and forth, his fur spiky, very clearly trying to communicate that *fond* and *Taylor* did not belong together.

"You just behave," Zoë said, scooping him up. "I have no idea what you're saying," she added in a low whisper, "but when Hale gets here, I'm gonna make sure he gives you a good talking-to."

She flashed her best hostess smile at Taylor, then shoved Elmer into the spare bedroom and closed the door. She went back into the kitchen wondering if she could salvage the moment.

"Look, Zoë. I'm incredibly attracted to you: I'm not about to deny it. But—"

There it was—the one little word that screamed *no salvage potential.*

"—considering, well, *everything,* maybe I should leave."

"You really want to leave?" Any minute, the world was going to crash down around her ears. She was sure of it. For the first time in her life, she'd met a man with whom she'd decided she could let go, could risk her heart and soul—and he was going to leave.

Well, that only proved Hale's point: Don't get involved with mortals; they just can't handle the lifestyle.

Except she hadn't intended to get *involved.* Didn't intend to. She needed to keep reminding herself of that. She was in this for the sex, pure and simple. Yup, there it was. Right there out in the open. She wanted sex with this man. One night of passion that would put her senses through the wringer and leave her breathless and sated. *Sure. That's all. Nothing permanent.*

They were lies, of course, but she tried to make herself believe them. After all, he'd never be able to handle a relationship, and she wouldn't have time for one anyway. Once the council finally processed her application, she'd have obligations, commitments. If she wanted to experience passion—and oh, yes, she knew now that she wanted to experience it—then it was now or never. After tonight she could walk away. Needed to walk away, actually, if she wanted to make sure Taylor stayed out of harm's way.

But for tonight, she wanted him in her bed.

"—so I don't *want* to," he was saying when she tuned back in. "God, Zoë, look at you. What I *want* is to run my hands all over your body and make you scream." He ran his hand through his hair instead of all over her body, then took a shaky breath. "But maybe it's best if I go."

"No!"

Maybe it wasn't the sophisticated thing to do—and she certainly wasn't playing it cool—but she flung herself at him. He caught her, lost his balance, and they both tumbled to the floor. She straddled him, her thighs pressed against his waist, her knees on the floor. Her face was right above his, her lips so close. . . .

"This isn't a good idea," he said, but the tone of his voice disagreed.

She brushed her lips over his mouth, slowly, experimentally, relishing the delicious sensation that whipped through her like hot chocolate for her soul, rich and enticing. "On the contrary," she whispered, "I think it's the best idea I've had in a long time."

"Zoë . . ." With one hand, he stroked her face, then tucked a stray strand of hair behind her ear.

She took off her glasses, tossing them onto the coffee

table, then scooted aside to look at him, awed by the raw strength of his mortal body. She ran her hand down his leg as she peeked through his clothing, stopping at the scar on his thigh, just one imperfection among infinite perfection. She kept her eyes away from *there,* somehow sure that looking now would be cheating. And she didn't want to cheat. Not with him, not ever.

He pulled her closer and she groaned, the pleasure of his touch nearly driving her mad. "Taylor, please."

"I guess I win," he said. His voice was still soft, but it was laced with humor, and she opened her eyes in question.

"What?"

His smile broadened. "We're on the floor. And you're begging."

She couldn't help it. She laughed, then tried to swat at his chest as she chastised him with a hearty, "You bum!" It was the swat that made her lose her control, and he flipped her over so that suddenly she was under him, with two hundred and ten pounds of pure, delectable male balanced right on top of her.

"Well, now you've gone and done it," he said.

"Done what?"

"Convinced me to stay."

"Is that bad?"

He lowered himself over her, his lips brushing against hers with the most infinitesimal of caresses—the tiniest of touches, yet enough to set off a chain reaction of pyrotechnic sensations that exploded through her body with the power of ten thousand bottle rockets. "You tell me," he whispered. "Is that bad?"

She couldn't talk, couldn't think. She could only shake her head and silently beg for his touch, wanting to lose herself in his heat, to be baptized in the living flame of his touch. Her skin tingled, the tiny hairs on her arms humming with electricity, her pulse throbbing against her skin.

"You're so beautiful." He was murmuring soft words as his hands skimmed over her body, her skin sizzling in his wake as he skillfully removed her from the clothing she no longer wanted, no longer needed. First his jacket, then—*please, soon*—the rest.

What was the point of clothing, anyway, if all it did was keep her body away from his? His finger grazed down the side of her neck, dancing over the curve of her collarbone, and she was burning up—sweltering in the thin summer dress. Her skin was flushed—as red as her dress. She felt so hot, so alive, she wasn't sure she could stand the sweet torment.

He leaned closer, his scent—earthy and primitive— assaulting her, sending her head reeling, urging her to let go and fly, to burn up in some sort of celestial flame.

Part of her wanted to run away, to get free, to calm down before she lost all control. Another part of her wanted to lose control. To lose it with this man. To believe—if only for a moment—that he could know all her secrets and still want her.

"I'm so hot," she whispered as her blood boiled.

His hand trailed lower still, stopping to cup her breast through the dress. "Do you want me to stop?"

She gasped. "Yes . . . no . . . never stop."

Sweet torment, yes, but somehow she knew that Taylor was the cure. That she would come near to incinerating before she'd be released from his spell. And—*oh, Hera*—how she wanted to burn.

An arctic cold rippled against her skin, the sensation

surprising her in the wake of such perfect heat. She shivered and realized he'd managed—she had no clue how—to get her wholly out of her dress. Now she lay before him in nothing except her bikini briefs. He had pulled away, taking his heat with him, and now he was kneeling over her, gazing down with something akin to wonder in his eyes.

Suddenly shy, she crossed her arms over chest, wishing she'd had the time to buy that Wonderbra after all.

"Don't you dare," he whispered, gently moving her arms to her sides. "I want to look at you. You're beautiful," he said. "You're a goddess."

"That's not important to me." She needed him to understand, but his hands were on her again, blazing paths down her sides, over her hips, making it difficult to think.

"What's not?"

"The goddess thing. I just want to be me."

"Who are you?" he whispered with a smile, surely not understanding what she meant.

She shrugged, trying to focus on his words despite the riptide building in her soul, urging her to break free and drift away. "I don't know." It was a lie. She knew perfectly well. She was somebody he could never have, would never really want.

"I do," he said. He leaned closer, his legs pressing against her hips. His hands grazed over her naked flesh, testing and teasing, drawing circles on her stomach until she wanted to cry out in frustration and demand that he touch her elsewhere . . . everywhere. "I know exactly who you are."

Those miraculous hands were on her breasts now, stroking and kneading, and through the rough material of his slacks she could feel the hard length of him press against her. A rainbow of colors shot through her—blue mating with yellow, red having its way with green—copulating colors, dancing and spinning like so many fairies, and oh, how she envied each and every one of them.

"Shall I tell you?" he asked, his mouth near her nipple, the caress of his breath softer than an infant's hair.

She nodded, mute, then gasped, her back arching of its own accord when he closed his mouth over her nipple, his tongue dancing on the sensitive skin. Rockets ignited in her soul—*T minus ten and counting. Oh, Hera.* She longed for liftoff.

He pulled away, but his hands continued to work miracles on her body. "You're sweet, and generous, and one of the most amazing women I've ever met."

She smiled at his words. But in the long run he didn't know her. And when he did—when he learned her secret, *if* he learned her secret—he'd run far and fast. But for now . . . for now she wanted to lose herself to him. Tomorrow she'd be alone again. After Tuesday he'd be out of her life. For now she wanted to belong to him.

Blinking back tears, she arched her back, raising her lips to meet his. "Kiss me. Make love to me. Make a memory with me that I can hold on to forever, no matter what happens tomorrow."

His arm swept behind her, pulling her closer. He pressed against her, his chest against hers, their hips rocking together, their lips joined as they shared breath and soul. When he laid her back against the carpet, tucking a throw pillow under her head, she moaned. His fingers played cruel, delightful games, dipping under the band of her panties, the sensation pooling between her thighs, warm and liquid and needy. She squirmed, trying to urge his fingers lower, needing to feel him inside her, on her, everywhere.

He moved to stand up, and she whimpered.

"What do you want?" he asked as he let his slacks and briefs drop to the ground.

She stared up at him. He was stunning. And he wanted her. That was certainly obvious. She fought a little smile, pleased that she hadn't peeked earlier, hadn't spoiled this moment. "I want you," she said, unable to remember ever speaking truer words.

The corner of his mouth lifted into the slightest of smiles as he lowered himself over her. "Good answer."

His fingers danced intimately along her skin, teasing her in places she'd only imagined being touched, igniting the fuel of a thousand rockets deep in her soul.

She couldn't speak, could only murmur soft sounds of pleasure as he stroked her secret places. Her body tightened as a rainbow swallowed her, reds and purples dancing on her skin, oranges and blues shooting from her fingertips, yellows and greens crackling and sparkling in her hair.

The rocket in her soul burned hotter.

T minus two and counting.

"Taylor." She grabbed his shoulders and pulled him closer, losing herself to the feel of his skin, his musky male scent. "Don't leave me," she whispered.

"Never," he said, rolling her over on top of him. His hands trailed down her back, his kisses covered her face, and she shivered, losing herself to the sweet sensation of his touch.

*　　*　　*

Lord, he was floating. Buffered by a haze of pure sensual pleasure, he truly felt as if he were floating on air.

Eyes closed, he trailed his hands along her bare back, caressing the sweet curve of her delicious behind. She moaned, the sound soft and satisfying and making him harder than he'd been just moments before. *Amazing. Man, oh man.* This woman did astounding things to his body. Unbelievable things. Just the way she writhed over him right now, trailing kisses down his chest, inching up to catch his mouth with hers . . .

He kept his eyes closed, unwilling to break the spell. He'd never felt so light before, so charged, so full of passionate energy. Like a live wire, his body tingled and hummed, and the only thing he could feel was the sweet press of Zoë against him, her body melded over his.

He shuddered and opened his mouth wider, hungrily devouring her lips, greedily sweeping his tongue inside her, needing to taste her, to possess her, to take her.

"I want you, Zoë," he said.

A shudder skimmed through her body, her reaction absurdly satisfying.

With a low groan, he rolled over until her back was against the floor again and he was straddling her. The back of his mind registered that his knees were pressed against the carpet, and he realized that they must have been on the floor the whole time. But—*oh, man*—this woman had him floating, and the feeling of being weightless in her arms was exquisite.

With something akin to reverence, he kissed her breast, kissed her belly button, and lower still, wanting to taste all of her. Wanting to know all of her secrets.

And he would, too. Zoë Smith would be his. Of that he was absolutely certain.

* * *

Zoë moaned as he kissed her intimately, his mouth moving lower and lower as her temperature spiked higher and higher. She was frantic, needy, writhing with desire. Silently urging him on. Silently begging him to touch her, caress her, take her.

The lightbulb in the kitchen blew out, and the television turned on, an old episode of *Love, American Style* playing softly in the background.

He was tasting her, and she shivered, burying her fingers in his hair, trying not to scream, but unable to stand it any longer. She urged him back to her and kissed him hard on the lips, running her hands over the strong muscles of his back.

"Now." His whisper caressed her, gentle but intense.

"Oh, yes." *Oh, yes, please.*

T minus zero and counting.

She spread her legs in a silent invitation, which he accepted with a low moan. A sharp burst of red exploded through her as he entered her, and she bit back a cry. She moved with him, slow and languid, trying to quell the pain of being filled by him.

"Zoë?"

"Don't stop," she whispered. The red was fading, the colors cooling, dancing on her skin. And then there was a different kind of red. Not pain, but heat and need. She arched against him, and he pulled her close as they moved together, more frenetic, more needy, and—*oh, dear Zeus*—how she needed him.

Now. Needed him . . . needed something . . . now.

And then, when she wanted it the most, he thrust again and found release. Their bodies melded together,

her soul bursting as a thousand bits of her exploded in a fiery mass.

Liftoff. She heard herself scream. A shudder ripped through her as the overhead light flickered on, then burned out with an explosive pop.

They drifted back to the floor and she sighed, thoroughly sated, thoroughly satisfied.

Zoë smiled.

Houston, we don't have a single problem.

Blip, blip. Bleep, bleep.

Mordi scowled at the tracker. He'd fixed it properly. He was sure of it.

And yet here he was in the park, and there was absolutely no sign of the mortal female. Irritated, he settled himself on a bench, then started drumming his fingers on its green metal. He stopped immediately, realizing what he was doing. The last thing in the world he wanted was to acquire one of his father's irritating habits.

He scowled at the sky, wondering if Hieronymous was watching him right now. Considering the council's intricate network of satellites, it was certainly possible. He glanced at his watch. And as far as he could tell, the major world markets were currently closed.

If Hieronymous wasn't watching the financial reports, he was probably watching his son.

Damn.

It was just past midnight on Monday morning. Only seventy-two hours before the eclipse, and still Mordi had failed to acquire the stone. A stone he didn't even want, all for a legacy of power that was his father's dream— not his own.

He shook his head, clearing his thoughts. This was his

287

golden chance. All his life he'd wanted his father to want him. To see him as a son, not a halfling. The legend had given him the chance to prove himself, and he intended to do just that. All that followed—the uprising of the Outcasts, the downfall of the mortals, the throne upon which he would sit next to Hieronymous—none of that mattered. Not really.

But if he could get the stone to Hieronymous in time for the eclipse, then surely he would feel worthy.

He sat up straighter, his resolve renewed.

He'd find the damn stone. No matter what he had to do, he would find it.

Frustrated, he lurched to his feet, the tracker held in front of him. Its green light blinked eerily in the dark. Where the hell was the female? According to the damn tracker, she should be right here. Right under his nose.

A mangy mutt padded by, stopped to sniff Mordi's shoes, then continued on. Mordi scowled, wondering at first if the dog was one of his father's little pets. But the dog was only a dog and it stopped in one of the landscaped areas and began digging, its paws churning with purpose into the soft earth beneath the birds-of-paradise.

Driven by a mixture of curiosity and boredom, Mordi approached the mutt, then glanced into the hole. Beneath a well-chewed bone, a glint of gold caught his attention. *Surely not . . .*

He dropped to his knees, digging with as much vigor as the dog until he could pull the chain free.

It was the necklace, all right, along with the intricate mounting to which his father had aimed the tracking device.

The stone, however, was nowhere to be found.

Chapter Eighteen

Lane paced outside Jerry's Scripts and Scraps, conveniently located across the street from the Tripoli Tower and right in front of where she'd been mugged just a few days ago. She still felt a little guilty not telling Taylor she'd been mugged, but what was the point? Taylor would only get obsessed and worry, and it wasn't like he could find the guy and arrest him.

She glanced at her watch: 9:58. It was only two minutes later than it had been the last time she'd looked. Frustrated, she grabbed hold of the metal gate and shook it. *For cryin' out loud*. This was Hollywood. Tourists galore. Why the devil couldn't these folks open their stores before ten?

So far the only area shopkeeper she'd been able to talk to was the owner of All American Donuts—open twenty-four/seven with specials every hour on the hour. After three cups of coffee and four glazed doughnuts, all Lane knew was that there wasn't a public bathroom in sight, and that the owner of the doughnut store hadn't seen a thing. Heck, the woman hadn't even realized there'd been a mugging, a movie crew, or a woman flying off the tower. Which meant Lane had sacrificed her thighs to four doughnuts for nothing.

She gave the gate another yank in frustration, and was still rattling the linked metal bars when a bearded man with a belly escaping over his waistband, headed toward her.

"You lookin' for me?" he asked, eyeing her suspiciously.

She unlocked her hand from the gate, smoothed her skirt, and tried to look respectable. "Are you Jerry?"

"Nope. Ain't Jerry."

"Oh." She waited for him to say something else, but he just looked at her and blinked. She blinked back, not sure what to do. This detective thing wasn't really her forte. But when she'd called Taylor's apartment, she'd only gotten his machine. And if they wanted to find that necklace, they needed to get started.

He held up a key ring. "You wanna step aside, lady?"

"Right. Sure." She stepped back. "This is your store?"

"Look, lady. I got a business to run. You wanna buy a script, I'm your man. You wanna chat on the sidewalk, you go find someone else."

Okaaay. She stepped back farther, giving him some space. Hell, who was she kidding? *Space, schmace.* She wanted a free path if she needed to turn tail and run.

Not-Jerry managed to open the door, and she followed him in. The second her nose hit the interior, she started to sneeze. The place was decorated in early American plywood bookshelf, and each shelve was crammed full with stack after stack of photocopied scripts. A glass case ran down the center of the room displaying more scripts, only these looked like the real deal, with autographs and lobby cards. In the layer of dust that coated the case, someone had written *clean me*.

"What can I do you for," Not-Jerry asked, suddenly all charm.

She sneezed again. And again. And one last time. Then she wiped her nose with the back of her hand and explained about looking for the two women working on the movie.

"What movie?" The voice was high and nasal and came from behind her.

Lane whipped around and found herself nose-to-nose with a surfer type wearing an *X-Files* baseball cap and a *What I Really Want to Do Is Direct* T-shirt.

"What movie?" he repeated.

"That's Boomer," Not-Jerry said, as if that meant something to her.

"Oh. Well, last Friday, there were some folks filming a movie here."

"Nobody was filming a movie here last week," Boomer said.

"Yes, they were. I was here."

Not-Jerry spread a newspaper open on the glass case, sending more dust flying. "If Boomer says they wasn't shooting, then they wasn't shooting. Boomer's my eyes and ears."

"I don't care if Boomer's your heart and soul. I was here. It was called *Boopsey Saves the Planet* or something. And I'm looking for the woman who flew off the tower." Even to her own ears, the story sounded crazy.

291

So much for that ten grand. No way were they going to find that mysterious flying woman.

The kid snorted. "Flying woman, my fat ass." Considering the kid was skin and bones, it wasn't much of a curse. "I want some of whatever you've been dropping."

Lane bristled. "I am *not* on drugs. A woman jumped off that tower. She had a cloak. She flew to the ground. She kicked a mugger. She saved my kid. I was there."

The kid held up his hands in a back-off gesture. "Whoa, there, baby cakes. Slow down. Don't get your panties in a wad."

"My panties are fine, thank you." She looked to Not-Jerry for help, but he just flipped a page of his newspaper and looked bored.

"Where'd you say this flying nun came from?"

Lane rolled her eyes and sighed. "The tower. She and her friend."

Boomer looked to Not-Jerry. "Coulda been one of them two chicks."

"Coulda been," Not-Jerry agreed.

Lane restrained herself from strangling them. "What chicks?"

"We see these chicks," Boomer said. "Every Friday. Blondie usually grabs a six-pack at the corner store. They hang out on the roof over there." He nodded vaguely in the direction of the Tripoli Tower.

So far, so good. "Do you know their names?"

Boomer looked at Not-Jerry, who shrugged. "Nope," he voiced for both of them.

"Ask at the tower," Not-Jerry said. "Maybe the guard'll know who your flying lady is."

"Right," she said, stifling the urge to kiss both of

them. It wasn't a very strong urge, so it didn't take too much effort to squelch it. Instead she smiled. "Thank you both so much."

She left Jerry's Scripts and Scraps with a spring in her step, and an old copy of an *I Love Lucy* script in her bag. After squeezing the info out of the store's owner, it had only seemed fair.

Whistling, she headed for the tower. Maybe she had a knack for this detective thing after all.

The morning light streamed in through the sheer curtains, tickling Zoë's nose and easing her out of the sweetest sleep. She woke to find herself trapped—but it was a nice trapped, safe and warm in the protective circle of Taylor's arms. Somehow they'd made it to the bedroom, and now he was sprawled out upon her king-size bed, managing to cover all but the tiniest sliver of mattress. Laid out on his back, softly snoring, Taylor was about the sexiest thing she'd ever seen.

Idly, she wondered if the newness would wear off after a while and the snoring and bed hogging would just be annoying. She didn't think so. Something told her she'd put up with a lot from this man.

Over and over last night she'd lost complete control, abandoning herself to this miraculous experience as her soul burst with the power of a million supernovas. And each time, she'd come back to herself to face the wonder in Taylor's eyes, the desire and passion reflected there nearly enough to bring her to tears.

Gently she extricated herself from his arms, propping herself up to look at him, and only then realized that she had a goofy smile plastered on her face. Well, after the night she'd just experienced, why shouldn't she smile?

Maybe this had started out as the Zoë Smith way of testing the sexual waters—but that didn't mean she couldn't feel something real now. Right?

Because she did. Hera help her, she really, really did.

Everything was moving so fast and furious. The wonderful man next to her. Her birthday. Her tests.

And the biggest mystery of all: what on earth were those drooling, fanged, smelly creatures Taylor had thought were men?

She could think of only one way to find the answer. With a little bit of trepidation, she sat up, careful not to wake him, and she glanced toward her dresser. There, under the silver box that held the rubber bands for her braid, were the recently delivered council publications. She'd started *The Venerate Council: A Brief History,* but had gotten bored at about page 320 during chapter four, "The Early Years." So far she hadn't even cracked the spine on *So You're a Halfling!*

Like she needed a book to remind her. But maybe . . .

Maybe the answers were in those pages.

As she slipped off the bed, Taylor groaned and rolled over, and her heart did a little somersault as he snuggled down against "her" side of the bed, his arm automatically closing around her pillow, seeking out her warmth even in sleep.

She drew in a ragged breath. Already she knew she couldn't bear to lose him.

She hauled the books off the dresser and snuggled down in her chair by the window, ready to settle in and find answers. With one final look at Taylor sleeping peacefully, she sighed, the warmth of her skin having nothing to do with the summer heat and everything to do with the man in her bed. She'd gone wading in a pool of emotion and gotten sucked in by a riptide of passion.

No, it was more than passion.

Hera help her, she loved the man.

Taylor awakened to the most beautiful sight in the world. "Hey, you," he whispered.

Zoë'd been reading some massive tome, and when she looked up, the pleasure dancing in her eyes gave him chills. Had anyone ever looked at him that way before? He doubted it. Not even his mother, before she'd dumped him. And certainly not any of his continuous cycle of foster parents. With a few exceptions, most of them had seen only an extra check every month, never a little boy.

But Zoë . . . she looked at him as if he were the whole world, and Taylor knew he had come home at last.

He wanted to say the kinds of pretty words women liked to hear, but he couldn't think. Not of words, not of sweet nothings, not of anything except touching Zoë again. Of sweeping his tongue inside her mouth and tasting her, of pressing her to the bed and burying himself inside her while she moaned his name, over and over and over.

She put down the book and moved to the bed, sitting beside him and stroking his hair.

He caught her hand and kissed her fingertips. "So why was I wrong?"

Her brow furrowed. "What?"

"I was wrong. You aren't taken. But I can't imagine why not." He brushed her cheek with his fingertip. "And why am I the first man who's ever shared your bed?"

She blushed bright red. "You're the first man I've ever wanted."

It wasn't until she said the words that he realized how much he'd wanted to hear them.

"I've never really dated."

"So your mom said."

Zoë cast her eyes skyward. "Uh-oh. I knew you spent too much time together."

Hooking his arm around her waist, he pulled her to him, unable to bear the distance between them any longer. "Just getting to know my woman and her family. Why didn't you date?"

"Like I said, I didn't really want to." She gave a tiny shrug. "But it was more than that. I guess I'm a private person." She twisted around to face him. "And the fact that my brother threatened to smash in the face of any boy that got near me . . ."

"Kinda put a damper on things, huh?"

"You could say that."

"I didn't even realize you had a brother."

She pulled away a little at that, ducking her head. "Mom doesn't know him." Her fingers toyed with the quilt. "I met my dad when I was just a toddler. And he had another kid. My half brother, Hale. They've been visiting me secretly all my life."

The image of a sleek black Ferrari drifted through his mind. "This brother doesn't look like a movie star and drive a fast car, does he?"

For a second she looked confused; then she smiled. "You were across the street."

"I thought he was your Mr. Wonderful."

"Nope." She snuggled close again, her heat burning into him. "That would be you."

He brushed his lips over the sexy curve of her ear, delighted when she shivered. "I thought I was Mr. Midnight."

"Mmmm." She melted in his arms, pressed up against him, warm and willing. "That you are."

"So is this brother still around?" He moved down to taste her neck.

"Oh, yeah."

He kissed her collarbone, thrilled when her breath came less steadily. "So how come you took the risk with me?"

"I already told you," she murmured.

"Tell me again."

She turned in his arms, then cupped his face with her hands, her eyes warm and sincere. "Because I wanted you."

His blood burned, and he wanted nothing more than to bury himself in her. "Do you want me now?"

"Oh, yes." A little smile danced on her lips, paying tribute to the desire in her voice. "Now would be very good."

Like a man starved, he took her mouth with his, tasting the ambrosia of her lips as she moved beneath him.

She was his. For now and—if he had his way—for always.

Elmer parked himself outside the bedroom door and tapped his little foot impatiently. Thank heaven Zoë had let him out last night, but she and Taylor had quickly shut themselves away.

They were still in Zoë's bedroom, and from the sound of things, they weren't going to be coming out anytime soon.

Well, wasn't that a pickle?

Hellooooo! Starving ferret out here! You wanna give me a hand with the can opener? Maybe throw a Hungry-Man meal in the oven? I mean, come on, people. It's well past noon here. . . .

No use. Zoë couldn't understand him, and even if she could, he had a sneaking suspicion that he wasn't her first priority.

When Hale got back, Elmer intended to give him a stern talking-to. What in Hades had he been thinking, leaving Elmer with people who would let him starve? Playing chaperon was one thing—not that he was any good at it, if the noises coming from behind that door were any indication—but that didn't mean he should go without breakfast. Or lunch.

The ferret scowled, suddenly sure that somewhere Hale was probably doing pretty near the same thing his sister was.

And Elmer was sure of one other thing, too. If Hale was holed up at the Beverly Wilshire with a king-size bed, room service, and satellite television while Elmer suffered here with Zoë Golightly and Mr. Studmuffin . . . well, there was going to be some serious hell to pay.

Tap-tap, tap-tap.

Mordi clenched his jaw, watching his father's fingers do their annoying dance on the polished wood.

"Let me see it."

He stepped closer, holding out the gold chain for his father to inspect.

Hieronymous held the chain up to the light, as if close inspection would reveal the current whereabouts of its stone.

"It's not in the park," Mordi said. "I looked everywhere."

"Had you retrieved the stone earlier—at the party, perhaps—this little incident could have been avoided."

With supreme effort, he clamped down on his temper. "The opportunity didn't exist. As I've mentioned, your tracking device was inadequate. I had to tweak it in order to pinpoint the location of the stone. Then, when I realized the stone had left with the mortal, it made more sense to follow it than to confront Zoë."

Hieronymous dismissed the comment with a wave. "No matter. After your pathetic performance as a police officer, I decided to take matters regarding your cousin into my own hands."

"You *what?*" He frowned, suddenly unsure of what he was doing, and why. Was Hieronymous so certain he'd fail?

Mordi sighed, wondering why he had let the red Mustang get away. True, Zoë's smack to the head with the mug had unsettled him, but surely he could have caught up again. If he'd raced forward, changing into something fast like a cougar, he could have paced the car. He could have easily caught them. Easily won.

So why hadn't he? Surely that would have been better than standing here now, taking it on the chin from his father.

"I told you I wanted the girl out of the equation. You failed. I released two henchmen." His father paused, and when he spoke again his voice was even colder. "Sadly, they were not successful."

Mordi shivered. "If the council finds out you have access—"

"They won't." He waved a hand to encompass his

wood-paneled office. "And if they do, so what? Am I on Olympus? Am I on the council? No. I've been an Outcast for years, stuck in this hell they call Manhattan with only my millions for comfort." He flashed an ironic smile. "There is nothing they can do to me now."

"Nothing?" Rumor was the punishment of out-of-control Outcasts was rather . . . well, *inventive*.

Hieronymous's mouth curved up in a thin smile. "I have certain . . . resources. I will be safe." He nodded, just a slight tilt of his head. "But thank you for your concern."

Mordi tilted his head, then straightened it when he realized he was aping his father. Resources? He knew nothing of such resources. For that matter, what did he really know of his father? A lust for power. A lust for revenge. And somehow his only son had become embroiled between the two. He was pretty much trapped between a rock and a Hiero place. *Oh, joy.*

When Hieronymous succeeded—when he usurped the council and enslaved the mortals—would he be satisfied? Did he truly want Mordi with him, helping him, being his right-hand usurper-of-the-council guy? Or would there be a new lust, a new desire? And would there still be the never-ending string of criticisms-on-parade?

Hieronymous rubbed his jaw, tap-tapping on the desktop with his free hand. "It appears that we are in a quandary, you and I. The stone is once again missing and the tracking device has nothing to track. Thus, we are left only with the legend to guide us." He looked up, his coal black eyes boring into Mordi's. "You will watch your cousin like a hawk. We are running out of time, and the stone will find its way to one of you."

Mordi nodded slowly, turning over possibilities in his mind. Either the stone was lost in the wilds of Los Angeles, or it was with the last person who had it—the blond mortal. That Deena person.

"I'll find the stone." He looked his father square in the eye without flinching. "And I don't need to spy on Zoë to do it."

For a moment, Hieronymous looked about to laugh; then he cocked his head, considering. "How?"

Mordichai held out his hand, an idea forming, as he recalled the subtle scent of the stone—a scent that surely lingered on the necklace. He could track it. He had to. It was his last chance. His only chance. "Let me have the necklace," he said. "I have an idea."

"Unbelievable!" Hale paced in front of Zoë's sofa. She was crouched there, her coppery hair wild and loose around her shoulders, her knees tucked up under her chin. She looked completely guilty and totally happy.

Her apartment looked like a tornado had whipped through it. An ugly red dress on the floor. Throw pillows strewn about. A gold belt dangling from a lamp shade. One sandal on the kitchen counter and its mate hanging from a ceiling fan blade. He shook his head, wordless.

"You can meet him if you want," she said, apparently oblivious to just how irritated he was. "He called a few minutes ago. He forgot his jacket, so he's going to swing by later today on his way to a meeting."

"Zoë . . ."

She dragged her teeth along her lower lip, frowning. "Then again, maybe you'd better leave before he gets here."

Hale nodded. Maybe he'd better. Especially considering that right now he wanted to really pound on the guy. And he didn't feel inclined to hold back.

This was absurd. Ridiculous. Unbelievably horrible. "You actually had sex with a mortal!"

A snorting sound emerged from one of the pillows next to Zoë, and Elmer crawled out, his eyes bleary with sleep. *Sex? Ha! They were going at it like bunnies, those two. I know! I heard! Just like you were probably doing across town. And did anybody think to feed the ferret?* He shook with rage, his entire body quivering. *Noooooo . . . And you know what else? I saw it with my own eyes. Zoë had the sto—*

Hale held up a hand to shut Elmer up, then ran it through his hair as he glared at his sister.

But—

"Zip it, Elmer. This is serious."

But the sto—

"Elmer!"

Harumph! The little rodent glared, then pointedly turned his back. *Well, fine. You abandon me during lunch . . . You-you can darn well let me know when you are ready to chat.*

Hale rolled his eyes. Great. Now he had both a self-destructive sister and a pissed-off ferret. This was not turning out to be one of his better weeks.

He caught Zoë's eye, and she just shrugged, a self-satisfied grin on her face.

Infuriating! He shot an angry glance toward the far side of the room, and the mirror over her writing table shattered. Zoë jumped, and Hale scowled, not in the mood to worry about keeping her furniture intact.

"Come on, Hale. It wasn't like—"

"You *promised* me."

"I never promised I wouldn't have sex with a mortal." Her eyes flashed, and he had to give the kid points for holding her own. "And you do it all the time."

"That's different," he said.

Can I just interject about the sto—

"Elmer," Hale yelled. "Hush!"

"How is it different?" Zoë asked.

"I don't fall for them." He quit glaring at Elmer to look at her tenderly. Dammit, she just didn't get it. He wanted only to protect her. And he intended to do whatever that took—interfering ferrets, threatening big-brotherly looks, whatever—to make sure Zoë stayed safe. All of her. Body and heart.

She didn't meet his eyes, looking instead at something just over his left shoulder. "I haven't fallen for anybody. It was just a fling. To see if I could handle it."

"And could you?"

She nodded, still not looking at him. Then she raised her head and her eyes shone clear, the blue and gray reflecting more than the light. "Yeah," she whispered. "I handled it just fine."

Oh, hell. She'd fallen even harder than he'd imagined. With a shake of his head, he sighed and dropped down onto the couch next to her, wishing he could figure out a way to talk her out of this little lust.

He took her hand and she gave him a watery smile. "So where is this mortal Casanova, anyway?"

"He left," she said, tossing one shoulder in a casual shrug. "I told you. It's no big deal." But the tears she blinked back told a different story, and when he squeezed her hand, she squeezed back, but didn't say anything more.

Elmer poked his head up. *If I can say something here,*

Mr. High and Mighty, without getting my head bitten off, thank you very much—

"What?"

She thinks she's protecting the mortal, keeping him safe in case she gets into another knock-down, drag-out.

"What are you talking about?" Hale turned to Zoë, cocking his head sideways toward Elmer. "What's he talking about?"

"I don't know. I don't speak ferret."

"Something about a knock-down, drag-out? What's going on? What happened."

"Just the tests. We were attacked." She shrugged. "Well, I was, anyway. Taylor was inconveniently located in the cross fire."

"Attacked? By who? When?" If Mordi hurt his sister, so help him, Hale would—

"Mordi, for one. But that wasn't any big deal. And then some henchmen."

He almost spit out his beer. He'd been expecting the first part of her answer. The second part came as a shock. "You know about henchmen?"

She held up a copy of *So You're a Halfling!* "Chapter six. Taylor thought they were men." Her face screwed up in disgust. "They were *so* not men." She sighed. "These field tests are intense."

Hale mumbled something noncommittal. The fact was, the tests were never supposed to be so dangerous, never this intense. This had Hieronymous written all over it.

Henchmen . . . Elmer shivered, then crawled back under his pillow.

"I thought it seemed pretty weird. Well, not so much just because we were attacked. I didn't know what henchmen were, then. But after I read the book . . ." She frowned.

Hale nodded absently, his mind swimming. All sorts of creatures roamed the earth in mortal guise, most unknown to mortals, seen as their true selves only by Protectors. And for centuries, the council had been tasked with locking in ancient catacombs those things that went bump in the night. When released, though, the creepy critters would do the bidding of whoever set them free.

"I think I understand how it works," Zoë said. "Protectors can see these creatures' true selves, right?"

Hale nodded.

"And since I'm a halfling, I'm just now starting to be able to do that."

"Right. It'll be strange for a while. You'll start to see them all over the place, but you won't always be able to fight them."

She cocked her head. "What do you mean?"

He shrugged. "Might draw attention. They're out there, more than you can imagine. Just wait. You'll start to see them. Politicians, cabdrivers. The guy at the movie theater who never gives you the correct change. You can't just take 'em out. Mortals wouldn't understand."

Zoë nodded, thoughtful. "Telemarketers?"

"Not as much as you'd think."

"Hmmm." She frowned. "So why am I being tested with henchmen? It seems a little extreme of a start."

He wished he could tell her. It would make this whole thing so much easier if he could just explain about the legend and the stone. His gaze drifted across the room, finally coming to rest on the ugly gold belt on the lamp shade.

It couldn't be.

He sprang across the room and plucked it up, turning it this way and that.

"Cool, isn't it?"

He couldn't answer. How could the belt have made it into Zoë's hands? Squinting, he examined it under the light, his hands shaking slightly. Then he noticed the flaking spots where the fake gold had worn off to the metal underneath. His shoulders sank. This belt was modern. Actually, it didn't even look much like the real one.

Damn. So much for returning to the council in triumph with a missing artifact. This cheap rip-off wasn't of any use at all.

Or was it? He cocked his head. If it were the real belt—Aphrodite's girdle itself—it would make its wearer invincible, not to mention incredibly desirable.

But maybe even a fake belt could make his sister invincible to dangers of the heart.

It was certainly worth a try.

He quashed a tiny pang of guilt. This was for her own good, after all. She'd only get hurt seriously by the mortal. No matter how much she cared for this Taylor person, Hale was doing the right thing.

Zoë squinted at Hale, who was still holding Deena's belt. "What are you doing?"

He waved the accessory in front of her face. "Do you know what this is?"

"A misguided attempt at fashion?"

He glared at her.

So much for levity. She tried again. "No. What is it?"

"Aphrodite's girdle."

"What?"

"You heard me."

Zoë blinked. "*The* Aphrodite's girdle?"

"Yup."

Aphrodite's girdle was the stuff of council legend, an ancient artifact with all sorts of mystical, magical powers. "Well, that's it, then." She smiled up at Hoop. "My test must have been to protect the girdle."

So maybe the tests were all over. Wouldn't that be nice? As soon as Hale left, she could call Taylor and maybe get another date in before the council ruled on her application. She grazed her teeth along her lower lip, considering.

Maybe even work up the nerve to confess the truth . . .

Hale cocked his head, studying her. Then he smiled, as though he'd just found the missing piece of a puzzle.

"What?"

"Were you wearing it last night?"

"The belt? Sure."

"Well, that explains it."

She had no idea what he was talking about it. "Explains what?"

"The mortal, of course."

She crossed her arms over her chest. "You wanna try again? I'm not following."

"What do you know about the girdle?"

She considered. "Well, it's pretty darn ugly with the wrong outfit, and it belonged to our ancestor, and it's been missing for hundreds of years." She shrugged. "That's about all."

"So you don't know about its powers? How it works?"

"Well, it's called a girdle. The only power that springs to mind is tummy control."

"Zoë—"

"Sorry. I know it has powers, but I don't know exactly what."

"Desire."

"Excuse me?"

"It makes the wearer irresistible to anyone she desires."

Not a bad trick. "Well, that's pretty cool. Boy, if some marketing firm couldn't make a mint off of—"

She looked at him as understanding dawned. "Taylor," she whispered.

His forehead furrowed. "I'm sorry."

"Sorry?" For some reason her brain had ceased to function. She stood up, running her fingers through her hair as she paced in front of him. "This belt?" Zoë plucked it out of his hand. "You're saying this ugly gold thing made Taylor wild with lust for me?"

"That's what the belt does," Hale said. "Why do you think the council's so keen on finding it again? Surely not because of some retro-fashion resurgence." He smiled, probably trying to make her feel better. It didn't work.

"I thought he liked me." She sank down, sitting on the couch's armrest. "I mean, I really, really thought he liked me."

He wrapped an arm around her. "I'm sorry, Zo. I really am. But isn't it better to know now?"

Was it? She didn't know. She just felt numb.

She sat there, empty and hollow. And then a tiny bit of hope flared. "But what about the first time we met? I didn't have the belt then." Not in the library. Not when sparks were flying from the mere brush of his fingers.

Hale's eyes darted away and he turned to pace the room. After a moment he stopped, his shoulders sagging. "The thing is, I'm not saying that *you* don't want him. I'm saying it's only the belt that makes him want you back." His eyes met hers briefly before turning back down toward the carpet.

"But . . . but . . ." Tears welled in her eyes and she knew she sounded like a blubbering fool. Her brother dropped down next to her on the sofa and slipped his arm around her. The touch did nothing. It was just pressure, and she idly realized that—slowly but surely—she was gaining complete sensual control. Under the circumstances, though, she wasn't exactly inclined to celebrate. "What about when he came to my house?" she asked, desperate to grasp on to even a shred of hope that he really liked her.

Hale squinted. "When was that?"

"The day you got to town. He'd been sitting across the street in his car. I saw him, and he said he'd come to ask me out." She twisted her sweatshirt in her fingers. "That he couldn't stop thinking about me."

"Oh. Well. Hmmm." Hale got up and started pacing the room. "Listen, kid, I don't want to hurt you. Really I don't. I only told you about the belt in the first place for your own good. You know that, right?"

She nodded, absolutely positive that Hale would never hurt her.

"The thing is, he probably is at least a little attracted to you. I mean, you may be my sister, but the fact is, a guy would have to be blind . . ."

"Thank you," she whispered, suddenly feeling the exact opposite. If she had to have the belt to get Taylor . . .

"So he probably did think you were hot, but since he was hiding and spying and everything before, don't you think that maybe he was working? You said he was a detective."

"He told me he *wasn't* there looking for Emily."

"And you believed him?"

She didn't answer, just swallowed. Had she been a fool? He knew where she lived, and he hadn't tried to ask her out before she caught him. He'd jumped on her flimsy excuse that she had a boyfriend. Sure, he flirted with her a bunch, but he hadn't wanted to take her to the party—and it had taken all of Hoop's and her cajoling to get him to agree. Only when she was dressed to the nines and decked out in the belt had he suddenly found her irresistible.

A stupid tear spilled down her cheek, and she wiped it away with the back of her hand. She looked up at her brother, unsure what to say, wanting something, but not knowing what.

Immediately he sat down beside her. "Hey, it's not like anything was going to come of this, right?"

She nodded. All along she'd known it wouldn't—couldn't—last. But some tiny part of her had still foolishly hoped.

Maybe it was better to know now. The closer she got to Taylor, the more it would hurt when she told him the truth—when she joined the council and he walked away.

"And besides," Hale continued. "This way you can concentrate on the rest of your tests."

She exhaled, trying to focus on her real problems. "More tests? You don't think I'm through?"

He shook his head. "Sorry."

She sighed. "Do you think they might send more henchmen after me?"

Hale nodded, and Zoë's insides turned cold. It was a cold of terror, but also of understanding. She'd made a decision. She wasn't sure when she'd made it; it had been brewing in her gut for a while. The henchmen just drove it home. More than just wanting to belong, more than not wanting to lose Hale and her father, she wanted to join the council to fight this evil that invaded the world and risked the lives of the people she loved.

She thought of Taylor and that bullet in his thigh. She thought of Tessa, who so wanted her to be normal, but also wanted her to be happy. She thought of Hoop and Deena and the little boy in the street. And then she thought of Taylor again, always Taylor. Even if he didn't really love her—oh, Hera help her—she loved him with all her soul. Loved all of them, and wanted to keep them safe.

She took a deep breath and made up her mind. She needed to tell Tessa and sign her affidavit.

And she had to do it soon.

Chapter Nineteen

Taylor whistled as he maneuvered Francis Capra down Ventura Boulevard. What a great day. What a glorious, wondrous, fabulous day. The sun was shining, birds were chirping, and even the smog had thinned out, giving him a stunning view of the mountains at the far side of the valley.

He zipped through the light at Coldwater and hooked a left, heading into the canyon and back toward the west side. Time to jump-start Mr. Mordon's little assignment. If someone else wanted him to find that gemstone, then dammit, that was exactly what he was going to do. Find it, hand it over to Mordon, and cut himself loose from the hounds of hell that had decided to stalk him.

Once Mordon had his rock back, those thugs would bother someone else, and Taylor could head back to Zoë, which was exactly where he wanted to be.

He punched the speakerphone and dialed the office,

humming a little as he waited for Hoop to pick up.

"Yo. I mean, Investigations. Can I help you?"

Taylor chuckled. "It's me. *Yo* works fine."

Hoop exhaled into the phone. "Damn, but we need a full-time secretary. I'm lousy at this."

"Yeah, well, you get the job for a few more minutes. I need you to call a florist for me." He remembered Zoë's allergies. "No. Make that a candy store." He remembered the way she'd avoided anything chocolate at the party. "Aw, hell, never mind. I don't have a clue what to send her."

"I take it the evening went well."

Oh, yeah. "She's fabulous. I'm crazy about her."

"Zoë's a great kid."

Taylor tapped the brakes, slowing as he approached a red light. "Lane's never going to let me hear the end of it, though."

"What's Lane got to do with your love life?"

"I told her I wanted a normal girl. No added color in my life."

Hoop snorted. "Zoë's a librarian. How much more normal can you get."

"That's what I thought." He drummed his fingers on the gear shift, trying to get a handle on the little oddities that had been niggling at him. "But there's some color there, too."

"Oh?"

"I don't get it. The girl's a magnet for weirdness. The first time I met her, I swear she was psychic—how else could she have heard me pawing through Emily's desk? And that stunt when she landed on the hood of my car— I mean, those kind of gymnastics would put Dorothy Hamill to shame."

"Hamill's an ice skater."

"Whatever. And I swear the guy in the Ferrari just disappeared. But she kept on talking to him."

"What guy?"

"Never mind. Not important. There's just all that, plus the cretins at the party, and the fake cop—who shimmered, by the way—"

"Shimmered?"

"—and on top of all that, man-oh-man, that woman can run!" He took a breath, realizing he was falling over his words. "And it's all incredibly odd stuff, but none of it bothers me in the least. It's *her* I'm interested in. And, Hoop, I am so very, very interested."

"So then just forget about the rest. Trust me. The weird stuff isn't what's important. My best friend married a cat and it didn't mess his life up any."

"Say again? There must have been static. I thought you said *cat*."

"Nothing. My point is that even normal people have quirks. I mean, hey, look at me."

Taylor laughed. "Now you're making me nervous."

"So? You want me to order chocolates?"

"Nah. I'll figure something out. Thanks for the free advice."

"You get what you pay for."

He hung up, grinning, as his fingers tapped a rhythm on the steering wheel. A few miles later, he realized he was smiling. Well, why not? He'd just spent the best night of his life with the most fascinating woman he'd ever met—warm and sweet and genuine.

He smiled again, remembering the fond way she looked at her mother, gently enduring Tessa's not-so-subtle attempts at matchmaking. The woman was special.

And she made him feel special, too.

The car phone rang and he punched the button for the speaker. "Taylor," he said, expecting Hoop.

"Well, hello, Taylor."

He grinned. Speak of the devil. "Hi, Tessa."

"I got your number from information and dialed your office. Where do you work? In a wind tunnel?"

"Sorry. Did Hoop patch you through?" He frowned, suddenly worried. "Is something wrong?"

"I don't know," she answered lightly. "Is there? Or is everything okay?"

He laughed, understanding dawning. He'd arrived at the post–first date checkpoint. "Everything's excellent."

"Is Zoë with you?" she asked hopefully.

He tried not to smile at the eager tone in her voice. "Just left her."

"And you'll be seeing her again when?"

Well, that was the tricky question. He imagined Tessa tapping her foot impatiently, standing in front of a calendar, and wondered what the appropriate premarital interval was. "I'm working a somewhat dangerous case. I don't want to accidentally get Zoë involved."

"I see."

"Well, the truth is I'm going to stop by later today." The thought of being away from her had chilled him, and he'd latched onto his forgotten jacket as an excuse. He didn't need the jacket, but he did need to see Zoë. Just one quick visit. There was some risk, true, but he could make sure he wasn't followed. Spotting and losing a tail were easy enough tasks, if you knew what you were doing.

"But after that, we're not going to see each other until this case is wrapped up." That was more to remind himself than for Tessa's benefit.

Silence.

"I want to see her. Believe me, Tessa, I want to."

More silence.

"Tessa?"

"Tomorrow," she said.

"Excuse me?"

"Zoë's birthday. You can take a break from your case and come, can't you?"

Pass up her birthday? Not in a million years. "I'd love to come," he said, realizing that he was now scheduled to see Zoë twice in the next twenty-four hours, despite having promised himself he'd stay far, far away.

So much for all his good intentions.

She gave him her address, "One o'clock sharp, then. And Taylor," she added. "Don't give up on her."

He frowned. "What?"

"Zoë," she said. "She's not your average girl."

"Believe me, I figured that out."

"Promise me."

"I'd sooner rip out my heart than give up on your daughter," Taylor said, absolutely certain it was true.

He could almost hear her smile from across the phone connection. "Well, then. That's all I wanted to know."

"This ugly retro belt?" Deena raised an eyebrow, the belt dangling between two fingers. "No way. If it were some ancient artifact with mystical powers, surely it wouldn't be so . . . well . . . *tacky*." She gave Zoë a confident look as she dropped it into her tote bag. "I think your brother is pulling your leg."

316

Zoë closed her eyes and leaned back against the lounge chair—they were sitting out on the deck near the apartment complex's pool—wishing Deena was right. But the truth was inescapable. She twirled a quarter between her fingers like a magician readying for a trick. With a sigh, she pitched the coin into the pool. "It's been missing for a while, and somehow that thrift store ended up with it."

Deena stood up. "Well, I'm going to go give him a piece of my mind. How the heck does he know what Taylor was feeling?"

Zoë grabbed the hem of her skirt and tugged her back. "Don't," she pleaded. "Hale isn't in the best of moods."

"Because you slept with a mortal?"

Zoë shrugged. "Well, yeah."

"That's the goofiest—"

"He's just trying to protect me."

"From what? Mortalitis? Is it catching? Are we not worthy?"

"It's not that." Actually, with Hale, it was. There were mortals, and there were Protectors, and never the twain should meet. "Mostly it's my parents."

Deena squinted at her. "Tessa?"

"She left my dad before I was born. He told her his secret, and she told him to get out." Zoë shrugged, blinking back tears as she tried to act nonchalant. "It's pretty common, actually. Throughout our history, I mean. Mortals don't stay."

"But Taylor's not like that. He adores you. I saw how he was looking at you."

"But that's just it," Zoë said, wiping away a renegade tear with the back of her hand. "He doesn't really. It's the belt. I like him, and so the belt made him want me, too. But it's not real. And if he knew the truth—the real truth—he'd run so far so fast." The damn tears were flowing now, and she turned away. "Just like my mom ran from my dad."

"Hey, come on." Deena took Zoë's hand between hers. "You don't know that. And I don't believe it. Taylor's a good guy. Hoop trusts him, and Hoop's one of the best judges of character I've ever met."

"He's a normal guy, Deena. He lives a pretty normal life. In case you hadn't noticed, I'm not normal." No matter how much she sometimes wished she were. "You should have seen him playing knight in shining armor when we were attacked at the party. I don't think he'll be too cool with the whole truth."

Deena's jaw tensed. "He'll get over it. Chivalry's cute and all, but *please*. This is the new millennium."

She swallowed. "But what if he's not cool? My mom wasn't, and that didn't have anything to do with chivalry. And the thing is, I don't want to give up the council. I want to make a difference."

"Then tell him. You shouldn't have to give anything up. Take a risk and tell him. He might surprise you."

Zoë wished like heck it were true, wished she had the strength to try. Not that it mattered anyway. Most everything he felt for her was a girdle-induced fake.

"I mean, even if he is a little weirded out that you can beat the crap out of him, it's not like he's gonna expect you to stay home barefoot and pregnant," Deena added.

Zoë grinned, idly wondering what NOW's position would be with regard to her little dilemma.

"Hey, look at the puppy."

Zoë followed the line of Deena's finger to the far side of the pool area. A gargantuan black Lab was sniffing around. "That's not a puppy. That dog's bigger than a Humvee."

"Hey, baby," Deena said. "You want a snack?" She rummaged around in her tote bag and came up with a bag of kitty treats.

"You carry cat food?"

"Long story."

Then Deena crossed over to the puppy. "Here you go, guy," she said, dropping a few treats in front of the dog.

It ignored the food, instead sniffing around Deena— all over her, actually. Zoë watched, frowning. Something about that dog . . .

She looked over the rims of her glasses, and the deep brown doggie eyes suddenly appeared a vivid green.

Uh-oh.

Deena bent over the dog, then whispered puppy nonsense in its pointy little ear. "Isn't it precious?"

"Why don't we go inside?" Why the devil was Mordi sniffing around Deena? It didn't make any sense. But the one thing she knew for certain was that she didn't want Mordi to know she was on to him. "I think I've got some leftover roast in the fridge," she said, edging toward the stairs and hoping Deena would follow. "Let's go get it and give him a snack."

"I think he likes me," Deena said.

"*Now,* Deena. Let's go."

Reluctantly, Deena stood up. "We'll be right back," she said. "You stay."

The Mordi-dog's ears twitched, as if he were trying to decide if she really was coming right back.

Zoë inched toward the stairs to her apartment, silently urging Deena along. With a flip of her skirt, Deena followed. *Thank goodness.* Zoë turned and was just about to head up when—

"Shit!"

At Deena's cry, she whipped around, and there was Mordi, doggie fangs bared, practically standing on Deena's chest as she struggled underneath him. Zoë lunged, flying off the stairs, and landed a good solid kick to Mordi's snout.

He jumped back, his head shaking like a cartoon dog's, the effect exacerbated by the shimmer of his change. In a blink of an eye he'd changed from doggie to gangmember, complete with baggy pants and attitude.

"What the—" Deena whispered.

"That's really not your best look," Zoë said, circling him, wary of the length of chain coiled in his hand.

"Cousin, you don't know me at all."

"Cousin?" Deena scooted further back, her voice raspy. "Okay. You really do win the dysfunctional family of the year award."

"Don't I know it," Zoë said, keeping a wary eye on Mordi. "What the heck are you doing, anyway?"

"That's the trouble with spending so much time with mortals, isn't it?" Mordi asked. "Like all that quality time you spend with your mother. And yet you never really know what's happening, do you?"

Zoë opened her mouth, then shut it again. What he said was true. Tessa didn't know about what went on with the council, the treaty between mortals and Protectors, anything. "Just being with my mom's important. She loves me."

"She won't when she finds out the truth." He sneered. "She'll dump you; they all do. But you already know that, don't you? Otherwise you would have already told her. Time's running out, after all. Just one more day."

"Tessa won't care," Deena said from behind Zoë. "Why the hell would she?"

Mordi whipped around, a ball of fire flying from his fingers. "What the hell do you know about it?" The fire exploded in front of Deena, and she jumped backward toward the swimming pool, unscathed but gasping.

He turned back to Zoë. "Mortals don't stay with us. You know it, even if you won't believe it." His eyes burned like green fire. "And Zeus knows I've seen enough to know it's true. Your mother won't, your Mr. Taylor won't—"

Zoë gasped. "What do you know about him?"

A sly smiled tugged at the corner of Mordi's mouth. "Trust me. I know plenty."

"You're wrong. Your—"

He held up a hand, his cold green eyes softening. "Wish I had time to chat, cousin. Maybe when this is all over we can have tea."

"When *what* is all over?"

"I'm sorry," he said, then leaped over her before she realized what was going on.

Deena's scream ripped the air, and Zoë whipped around, to see Mordi grabbing Deena by the back of her dress. Zoë launched herself, jumping onto his back and kicking like crazy.

"What are you doing?" she yelled. Her cousin had a hold of Deena's arm, but Zoë managed to pull him off, then kicked him in the gut with her heel. He went flying back, landing with a splat against the staircase.

When he got up, any hint of kindness in his eyes had vanished. They were cold. Cold and cruel and definitely not those of the little boy she'd grown up with.

321

"You shouldn't have done that," he whispered. "I don't want to hurt you."

"Then don't hurt my friends," she said, dropping into a crouch. If he tried to go for Deena again, he'd have to go through Zoë.

"I'm not interested in your friend," he said. "Just in what she has." With that, he lunged. Zoë leaped, catching him by the ankles as he pulled her over and over again. He landed on top of her, straddling her so that she couldn't get any leverage, his weight pressing down so she couldn't breathe.

And then she realized that his fingers were clamped viselike around her throat. She gasped, trying to suck in air, her lungs burning.

He was going to win again. Somehow Mordi always managed to win their tests. Too bad she didn't even know what this test was about.

The world spun. Thoughts darted about like minnows. *Deena, Hale, the belt, Taylor.*

Somewhere in the back of her mind she heard her name, and then there was air—cool, crisp air.

Coughing and confused, she sat up. Where was Mordi?

And then she saw him—and Taylor.

"No!" she screamed. She was on her feet, running to help Taylor, who was dodging the whip of ruffian Mordichai's steel chain.

"Stay out of this, Zoë!"

"But—"

"Dammit, Zo, let me handle this."

Her eyes darted to Deena, who mouthed the words, *Tell him,* and then, "Get in there and kick some butt."

Tell him? No way. And certainly not now. As for the

butt-kicking, that she itched to do even though it might show off her powers. For half a second she considered; then she took a breath and made the leap.

"Zoë!" Taylor cried.

She ended up plastered like a crab on Mordi's back, her arms wrapped around his face and her legs locked about his waist. It probably looked pretty silly, but with her strength, she knew she could hold on. And if he was struggling with her, Mordi wouldn't be able to get to Taylor or Deena.

He twisted and shoved and turned, trying to get her off, while Taylor rushed him, trying to get the chain.

"Stay back, Taylor!"

"The hell I will."

Hot. She was sweltering hot. She closed her eyes and hung on, trying to keep her grip despite the fire suddenly burning in her muscles. Her skin was slippery with sweat, then blistering from the intense heat.

"Jump, Zo!" Deena yelled. "His clothes are catching on fire."

Hopping Hades! So were hers. Already the heat was making her woozy.

Taylor was rushing at them both, and Zoë stifled the urge to shout at him to stand back. She needed to get them both safe, but how?

With all her strength she held on, ignoring the pain as she looked around, oblivious to Mordi's thrashing beneath her.

And then she saw it.

With a single jerk, she lunged away, but kept her hand deep in the flames, grabbing on to his collar. Mordi stumbled toward her and they both went tumbling into the pool.

Julie Kenner

A cloud of steam rose into the air, a faint hiss drifting away on the wind.

They went under then, rolling over and over until Zoë was sure she was going to be sick from being dizzy.

And then there was a big metal stick in front of her, but no Mordi—somehow he'd won again.

She gasped for air, looking into Taylor's eyes as he held the pole end of the pool skimmer out for her. "Where'd he go?"

"Took off that way," he said, nodding toward the front staircase. His face hardened as he helped her out of the pool. "Are you burned?"

She made a quick check, pleased that her halfling blood had protected her and kept her singe-free. "No."

"Good." He hugged her close, managing to soak his clothes in the process. "What the hell were you thinking?"

Deena crawled over. "Wow."

Zoë raised an eyebrow as she stood dripping on the concrete. "That's it?"

Deena shrugged. "I never thought I'd see me speechless, but wow."

"I don't think you answered me." Taylor leaned back, then kissed the tip of her nose. "So I'll try again. What the hell were you thinking?"

She stepped back, out of his embrace. "I was thinking of helping you."

He frowned. "Well, don't. I had it under control."

"Taylor, that's silly. I'm—" She stopped, not sure what she planned on saying.

"You're what? You're fine? Yes, you are. But only because you're lucky." He pulled her close again, wrapping his arms around her. "Jesus, Zoë," he whispered

324

into her hair. "Do you think I can stand watching you put yourself in danger? I'd rather die than see you hurt."

He pushed a soggy curl off her face. "Stay here. I want to make sure he's gone." He disappeared under the stairway, then returned immediately. "Nobody there. Just a big dog sniffing around."

Deena coughed, and Zoë flashed her a "be quiet" look as Taylor swung his arm around her shoulder.

"Let's get you upstairs," he said.

She nodded and let him lead her. Hale would be back any minute, but surely she could get Taylor out of her apartment before his return.

Because, truth be told, she wanted Taylor with her. Maybe she didn't need his help to fight her cousin, but she certainly wanted his strength after.

As for why she was fighting her cousin, or why Mordi was sniffing around Deena . . . about that, she had no idea. What did Deena have that he wanted?

Or maybe Deena was the subject of Zoë's tests—protect the mortal and make it into the council. She frowned. But that didn't really make sense either.

She glanced at her friend, still sitting on the concrete looking a little dazed. The fact was, she had no idea. But she did know one thing for certain—whatever was going on, it couldn't be good.

Mordi planted his rump on the sun-warmed sidewalk and scratched behind his ear with his back leg.

He didn't have the stone in hand, but still, it had been a successful encounter. He'd pulled the stone's scent off of the setting, and then he'd let his sensitive doggie nose go to work following his best lead—the blonde.

325

And his bet had panned out. The mortal still had the stone. He was certain of it.

Excellent.

Of course, Zoë might realize what he was after—first the woman at the tower and now Deena. The only thing they had in common was the stone. Would she make the connection? He let out a little doggie sigh. Best to focus on the good news. The stone was here, with the female mortal. By tonight it would be his, and Hieronymous would finally be proud.

All he had to do was wait.

After all, she couldn't stay in Cousin Zoë's apartment forever.

Hale glared at the mortal, not at all sure how to handle this latest bit of news.

"Don't look at me like that," Deena said. "It wasn't like I asked to be jumped by some shape-shifting doggie gangster."

Hale had to give the mortal credit. She hadn't burst into tears or run screaming from the room, swearing to never look Zoë in the face again. Not yet, anyway.

"Mordichai." He said the name like a curse. Damn their cousin for siding with his father. If the little worm had any backbone, there'd be no problem.

"What the heck did he want?" Zoë asked.

The stone, of course, but Hale couldn't tell her that. From what Zephron claimed, all hell would break loose if he did. Instead he shook his head in feigned ignorance.

"Even more," she added, "what did he want with Deena?"

"Probably trying to get to you. The tests and all."

"He seemed so sweet as a dog," the mortal said.

"He'd just as soon bite your head off," Hale said, just to shake her up.

"Hey," she said, staring him right in the eye. "I didn't say he was sweet, I said he *looked* sweet."

"Fair enough," Hale said, his estimation of Zoë's mortal friend increasing.

"Sweet or not, what was he looking for?" Zoë asked. Her eyes widened. "Of course! He wanted the belt." She looked at Deena. "He smelled it on you."

"You're probably right," Hale said, thinking fast. The fact was, Mordichai sniffing around Zoë meant one of two things: either Mordi had given up looking for the stone and was simply going to tail Zoë, figuring one of them would end up with it before the eclipse, or Mordi knew something the rest of them didn't.

Both options meant bad news for Zoë, and the best thing Hale could do was get back to Olympus, report in, and see if Zephron or Donis had learned anything useful. He glanced around aimlessly, trying to think up an excuse for leaving, and his gaze landed on Deena's overstuffed tote bag. "If he wants the belt, I should get rid of it," he said, pointing at the bag and urging the belt up and into his waiting hand.

"Cool trick," Deena said.

Zoë's brow furrowed. "Get rid of it how?"

"I'm taking this back to Zephron. I should have done it earlier." He shoved the belt into his backpack and headed for the door. He took a quick look around for Elmer, but the little guy wasn't to be found. The ferret had been hiding since he'd snapped at him earlier, and he was probably still sulking. Well, he'd just have to camp at Zoë's then, because Hale didn't have time to scour the place looking for him.

"Hale?" Deena said.

He turned to the mortal, his hand resting on the door-knob.

She smiled. "It was nice to meet you."

Hale stared at her, trying to decide what to say. He didn't have mortal friends, didn't want mortal friends. Didn't want or need any warm, fuzzy feelings for these creatures he'd sworn to protect.

But this one had stuck by his sister, so maybe he could make an exception. The world probably wouldn't come crashing down if he added one mortal to his list of friends. He sighed. "Yeah," he finally said. "It was nice to meet you, too."

Lane was waiting in the doorway to her apartment when Taylor got there. "Well, well, well," she said with a grin.

"What?"

She stepped into the apartment, tossing him a know-ing glance over her shoulder. "The clothes, hotshot. Those were what you were wearing yesterday. Guess the *job* went well, huh?"

He rolled his eyes skyward. "Lane—"

"Not that I'm prying or anything. I'm just glad to see you back in the saddle. So tell me, brother mine, is she *normal?*"

Shaking his head, he could only grin.

"All right, Taylor. Good going. Maybe I'll get a sister-in-law yet." She bent down to scoop up Davy, who waved at Taylor and then buried his face in Lane's shoulder.

"What's the matter, buddy?" *And thanks, kid, for helping me change the subject.*

The boy shook his head, but no smiling face appeared.

"He missed his nap," Lane explained, an apology in her voice. "It'll make it easier on Janet, though. He'll probably sleep the whole time we're gone."

"Did you talk to any of the store owners yesterday? Or is that on today's agenda?"

"Talk?" A wide grin split her face. "I did a lot more than talk. Big brother, I found our flying mystery woman."

"What?"

She nodded, clearly pleased with herself. "Yup. Managed to track down her home address and everything."

"How the hell did you manage that?" He stifled a sigh, suddenly feeling rather useless. First Zoë fighting like a banshee, then his sister doing all the gumshoeing, and doing it well.

"Easy." She took a deep breath. "Boomer figured she had to be one of the two girls who hang out on top of the tower, so I talked to the guard, and he told me their names—they have to sign in to get to the roof—and then I went to the school, but it was closed for the break, but the principal was there this morning, and I told her who I was looking for, and she pulled the file, and while it was on her desk, I read the address upside down." She'd rattled the whole thing off without taking a breath, and now she sucked in air. "That's it."

He blinked. He'd barely followed her speech, and he had no idea who Boomer was, but it had sure sounded good.

"So can we go talk to her? I've been waiting for you all morning, but you were otherwise indisposed." Her gentle smile told him that she'd forgive his tardiness since his love life was looking up.

"Let's go." He moved back out of the apartment and

waited while she passed Davy off to her across-the-hall neighbor.

"It's almost too bad you had a hot date last night," she teased as they headed toward Francis Capra.

"Yeah? Why's that?" Lord knew Taylor couldn't think of a reason in the world why his night with Zoë could even remotely be classified as "too bad."

She shrugged as he held the door open for her. "It's just that this woman—the one who flew off the building—is right up your alley. Normal, I mean."

"Flying off buildings is normal?"

"Well, not that part. But everything else about her sure is."

He circled the car and opened his door, amused by her smug expression. "Okay, give."

One eyebrow raised as the corner of her mouth curled up. "She's an elementary school librarian. Wasn't that just the kind of woman you said you were looking for?" Lane chuckled. "Her last name's even Smith. How much more average can you get?"

"You *jumped* off a building?" Taylor ran his hands through his hair as he paced Zoë's living room, confusion and fear clinging to him like dust.

She cringed and shrugged, wanting to explain. But she couldn't bring herself to tell him the truth. Not yet. "I—"

"She didn't jump," Lane said. "She flew. I told you." She grinned. "I still can't believe Zoë is your girlfriend. This is just too—"

"Lane." He held up a hand as Zoë warmed to the sound of the word *girlfriend.* "I'm trying to figure out what's going on." He turned back to Zoë. "Tell me. Sweetheart, what's going on?"

"It was no big deal, Taylor," Zoë said, her eyes darting to Deena, silently pleading for help.

"No big deal? Thirty stories is a very big deal." He looked from Deena to Zoë.

"What difference does it make to you?" Deena asked.

"What difference? The woman I love jumps off a building—"

Love? Zoë twisted back around to look at him.

"—and you think I'm just going to—" He snapped his mouth shut and closed his eyes, apparently realizing what he'd just said.

Lane clapped her hands and generally looked like she'd just won the lottery.

The room seemed to vanish as Zoë lost herself in his words. *Oh, Hera.* He loved her.

Then she remembered—the belt.

He didn't love her at all. Not really. No matter how much she might care about him, he just was feeling the after effects of what the belt had told him to feel.

She blinked back tears and looked to Deena, who managed to look both sympathetic and encouraging at the same time. Elmer padded over and pawed frantically at her foot. She swooped down and picked him up, hugging him tightly against her.

Taylor's eyes opened and the corner of his mouth twitched. His shoulder rolled in the slightest of shrugs. "It's true," he said, and she could see in his eyes that he really believed it. He ran his fingers through his hair. "I had planned on saying it under more romantic circumstances, but it's true."

"Oh, Taylor, I . . ." She trailed off. What could she say? She needed to tell him the truth. No matter how much she wished it were true, he really didn't love her.

Elmer twisted in her arms, and she scowled down at him. "What?"

He squeaked and fidgeted, but she had no idea what he wanted.

"Maybe he wants down," Deena said.

Taylor's eyes were still on her, ignoring the ferret's antics.

"Tell me the truth, babe. What's going on?"

Zoë shrugged and put Elmer on the back of the couch.

"There was no movie, was there?" Taylor asked, taking her hand.

"Not exactly. I, um, I—"

"Work part-time in R and D," Deena rushed to put in.

"Right," Zoë said, grateful Deena could still think. Zoë's brain was more or less fried.

"R and D," Taylor repeated.

"You know, research and development," Deena said.

"They did tell me it was some big experimental project," Lane admitted.

"That's the craziest thing I ever heard," he said.

"Let's back up," Zoë said. Too much was going on. She needed to focus, to get her head clear so she could decide what to do, what to say. She looked to Lane. "How did you know it was me who saved your child?" Then she looked at Taylor. "And how do you know Lane?"

"She's my foster sister," Taylor explained.

"But why was she—" She turned to Lane. "Why were you looking for me in the first place?"

"The necklace I gave you," said Lane. "That's the heirloom Taylor was hired to find."

*   *   *

Elmer lost his footing and tumbled off the back of the couch, landing upside down on the overstuffed cushions. Someone had hired Taylor to find the stone? That could mean only one thing: Mordichai.

"I asked around at the tower," Lane continued, "and they said you and Deena hang out there."

"I thought you said that necklace was junk," Deena said.

Lane shrugged. "Apparently jewelry appraisal isn't my thing." She looked at Zoë. "Do you still have it? Will you sell it back to the guy?"

Zoe looked at Deena.

"I kind of broke it," Deena admitted. "At the Hollywood Bowl."

"It's gone?" Taylor asked, deflating.

"Everything but the stone." Deena rummaged in the pocket of her skirt, then held out her hand, the green stone sitting like a lump on her palm. Elmer started to move toward it, then stopped, realizing that leaping for the stone just wouldn't work the way he wanted it to. Oh, why had he indulged in that snit earlier when Hale was around?

"You're welcome to have it back," Zoe said.

Deena tossed the rock to Lane, who caught it with one hand. Elmer danced back and forth from his front feet to his back. If the stone was here and Mordi was looking for it, that meant that Mordi would likely show up here, too. Or worse . . . *Hieronymous*. He gulped.

"Oh, no," Lane said, looking at the gem. "I can't take this back. I gave it to you."

"Of course you can," Zoe argued.

"But—"

"I'm serious. I wasn't expecting to be paid for helping

333

you, and you didn't know what you had. Keep it, and I hope you get a lot for it."

Taylor looked at Zoe. "You're sure?"

"Of course."

No, no, no, Elmer squeaked, but he was ignored as usual.

"Thanks," Lane said.

"But I should keep it," Taylor added. "Until this guy buys it off you."

Zoë shook her head. "She's perfectly safe, Taylor. Those muggers weren't after you. They wanted me."

"You?"

Elmer leaped up and started hopping around. He had to get their attention. *No, no, no! Don't send it out into the world with a mortal. Mordi won't have any trouble taking it off her!*

He hopped and hopped, and then hopped some more. But did anyone notice the ferret? *No, sirree.*

Yeesh. You'd think he was a hamster or something.

"Why would they be after *you?*" Taylor asked.

"The flying cloak," Zoë said. She frowned, dropping her gaze so she wasn't looking at his face. "And that belt I was wearing last night. They're both top-secret projects."

Poor kid. Poor, gullible kid. She actually believed Hale's belt story. Not that Elmer himself was any great mortalphile, but so far this Taylor guy seemed okay. And he sure seemed to really love Zoë.

Aw, hell. He'd been watching too many old movies on late-night cable. Love conquering adversity and all that. He was turning into a sap.

"Top secret?" Taylor repeated.

"It's all very hush-hush," Deena added.

"I guess it would be, if you can fly off a thirty-story building," Taylor said.

"That's how I knew Mord . . . uh, that fake cop was bad. I couldn't tell you then, but I did tell you to get out of there. Remember?"

Taylor nodded slowly. "Yeah. You did." His forehead creased. "Industrial espionage? We were being chased for your clothes?"

Zoë nodded. "I'm sorry I couldn't tell you. Nondisclosure agreement. I promise I didn't expect anything to happen that night. I wouldn't do anything to endanger you."

"Well," said Taylor, "I've heard of the fashion police, but this . . ."

"There's more." Zoë licked her lips. "We need to talk," she said, looking like she'd rather have major surgery without anesthetic. "Alone."

Taylor nodded. "All right." He dug in his pocket and then pitched Lane his keys. "Your choice. The car or the stone."

Elmer didn't think Lane could have looked more surprised if Ed McMahon had handed her a thirty-million-dollar check.

"Me?" Lane asked. "You're letting me drive Francis Capra?"

"Only if you leave the rock with me. Zoë can give me a ride." He looked at her, his eyes soft. "Right?"

"Of course she can," Deena said. "She'd be thrilled to give you a ride."

"Deena . . ." Zoë said, and Elmer could hear the note of warning in her voice.

A wide smile spread across Lane's face. "Hey, I'm no fool. I know when not to argue. It was great to meet

335

the real you, but now I need to go take my brother's car for a joy ride."

With a grin, she tossed Taylor the stone, and he caught it with one hand.

Elmer fidgeted beneath him, his eyes on the stone. And when Taylor dropped it into a silver candy dish on Zoë's coffee table, that was when he made his move. In a frenzy of flying ferret, he leaped and curled up on top of the candy dish, the stone tucked safely beneath him.

He might have screwed up and not told Hale where the stone was, but darn it, this time he wasn't letting the thing out of his sight.

"I think that's my cue to leave." Deena stood up and hooked her tote bag over her arm as Lane pulled the door open.

"You guys don't have to go so soon, do you?" Zoë asked. If they left, then Zoë was all out of excuses. She'd be all alone with Taylor. Her heart twisted. The man she'd fallen in love with.

The man who thought he was in love with her.

The man who wouldn't want her if he knew she could bench-press his car.

It was all fake—everything. She needed to tell him he didn't love her, needed to tell him they couldn't be together.

And she would.

Later.

Right now maybe they could just hang out. Play cards, charades, Pictionary. Something to keep them occupied so she didn't have to confess.

She flashed a perky smile toward Deena and Lane. "How about some coffee? We could watch a movie."

Deena rolled her eyes.

"Thanks," said Lane, "but I want to take Francis Capra out on PCH One before the sun sets."

"You guys are sure? I've got Monopoly."

Taylor flashed her a quizzical look.

"No, Zoë," Deena said firmly. "Thanks."

"Fine." She was stuck with Mr. Midnight. "At least let me walk you down."

"Zo, for cryin' out loud. You don't need—"

"In case my neighbor's dogs are still loose," Zoë said, trying to aim a meaningful look Deena's way.

"Oh," Deena said. "Right. Okay."

"I'll come, too," Taylor said.

"No!"

He frowned. "But if these dogs are vicious . . ."

Zoë looked to Deena for help.

"It's a code, Taylor. Girl talk."

Lane laughed as Taylor's cheeks went a little pink. "Oh. Well. Then I'll just walk Lane to the car. I need to get some stuff out of the trunk, anyway."

Zoë nodded, and they all left the apartment and trailed down the stairs, turning in opposite directions when they reached the sidewalk.

"I don't think I can tell him," Zoë said, the second Taylor and Lane were out of earshot. "What am I supposed to say?"

"Don't say anything," Deena said. "I don't believe Hale's nonsense for a minute, anyway."

"I don't know. . . ."

"Taylor loves you, Zo," Deena said as she opened the door to her car. "No matter what the fashion mags say, no piece of clothing was what made him feel that way."

"Maybe—"

337

"Holy cripes," Deena yelped, jumping back away from the poodle that had suddenly appeared and was sniffing her ankles.

"Hey!" Zoë swatted at it. "Get away!"

The dog looked from Zoë to Deena, a perky pink bow a counterpoint to its bored expression.

Zoë leaned in for a closer look. "Mordi?"

"Is it him?" Deena asked, her voice a low, worried whisper.

The dog snuffled a bit—testing the air for the scent of belt?—and then yawned.

"I can't tell," Zoë said. "I can't see its eyes. But it sure isn't acting like Mordi was earlier. And this dog's tiny."

The dog sniffed around the tires, then squatted and peed right next to Deena's whitewalls.

Deena and Zoë looked at each other. "Not Mordi," they said in unison.

Totally uninterested, the poodle trotted up the sidewalk toward Taylor as Lane peeled away from the curb in Francis Capra. The tiny dog sniffed around his ankles before turning up its nose and trotting across the street to disappear behind a building.

"Friend of yours?" Taylor called.

Zoë shrugged. "Never seen it before." At least it seemed to really be a dog. She hoped. She should have taken off her glasses. Still, it had certainly acted like a dog . . . and no matter what, it wasn't Mordi.

She shrugged, turning back to Deena. "Maybe it smelled Mordi on you."

"Who knows. Apparently I'm no longer all the rage in the doggie world, though. That poodle couldn't have been less interested."

And then she saw him—the green-eyed black Lab sitting next to a fire hydrant on the far side of the street.

"I think we spoke too soon," she said, nodding across the street.

"Uh-oh," said Deena. "Mordi?"

"Yup." She grabbed Deena's arm, ready to push her aside should the Mordi-dog attack. "Be careful."

The Mordi-dog yawned then—tail wagging—headed off down the street in the direction the poodle had taken.

How totally bizarre.

"Where'd he go?" Deena asked.

Zoë shrugged. "I don't have a clue. Maybe you should stay here."

Deena put a hand on her hip. "I don't think so. You just don't want to be alone with Taylor."

"But all these dogs—"

"Weren't in the least bit interested."

"Deen—"

"No. I'll call you when I get home."

Zoë sighed, defeated. "Fine."

Deena slid into her car. "And you need to call me tomorrow with a full report. Okay?"

Before Zoë could agree, Deena cranked the engine and pulled out.

Zoë just stood there a moment, trying to steel her emotions.

Time to go break the news to Taylor.

Time to go tell the man she loved that he didn't love her at all.

From the roof across the street, Mordi watched the detective and Zoë head up the stairs to her apartment. He'd sent one of his father's shapechangers on his little errand, and he'd come back empty-handed—no sign of the stone with Zoë, the detective, or that Deena person. Bad news, but at least he had his information. Maybe those disgusting henchmen were useful after all.

He drummed his fingers on the slate, irritated, then realized what he was doing and slapped his hand down hard.

Damn. She'd obviously passed the stone off. And that left only one from the usual suspects—the brunette who'd had the stone in the first place. She was the only one Lola hadn't sniffed.

Funny how fate worked.

He'd almost retrieved the stone from her before, but Zoë had interfered. This time he wouldn't fail.

Chapter Twenty

They were on the couch, and he was holding her hand, rubbing the pad of his thumb over her skin, sending shivers right down to her toes.

"I'm sorry about blurting it out like that," he said. "I was planning on candlelight and wine. I hope I didn't embarrass you."

"Oh, no. Nothing like that." *Sweet Hera.* How on earth did you tell a man he didn't really love you? She had no idea. And it wasn't even a conversation she wanted to be having.

"You're on spring break, right?"

She nodded, and when he kissed her fingertips, she blinked back tears.

"What would you say to a trip? Maybe a drive down to San Diego? Or up to the wine country?" His gaze locked with hers. "I feel like I've known you forever. I want reality to catch up with the way I feel."

"Taylor, I . . ."

Turning away, she pulled her hand free and settled it in her lap. Why did it have to be so hard?

"Zoë?" The unspoken question hung between them: *What's wrong?*

"If you don't feel the same . . ." he began. "I mean, I hope you do. But I don't want to pressure you. It's just . . . I thought . . ."

Not even trying to hide her tears, she spun back around to face him. "No, no! Taylor, I love you. I do. Heaven knows, I shouldn't, but I really do."

"Then what?"

She took a deep breath. "You don't love me."

He laughed, then kissed her on the forehead. "Sweetheart, you're priceless."

Whatever reaction she'd been expecting, it wasn't that.

"Taylor, aren't you listening?"

"I assure you, I do love you." His grin split his face. "I *knew* this would have worked better with roses and candlelight."

Argh! She pounded a fist uselessly into the sofa cushion. "No, no. Listen to me. You don't love me. You just think you do."

"Think I do, and *know* I do."

"It's not really love. It's an illusion."

"Then maybe we should take that vacation in Las Vegas. Maybe we could even get booked as an act."

She fell back against the cushions, exasperated. "You're not even trying to help."

"Well, no. Not if the goal is to convince me that I don't love you. I don't think I'm going to willingly help in that project."

"You're impossible," she said.

"Sorry 'bout that."

She took a deep breath, trying to steel herself. "You know that belt I was wearing last night?"

"Right. The ugly gold thing."

"You thought it was ugly?" She waved the question away before he could answer. "Doesn't matter. It's experimental. Like the cloak."

"You can fly when you're wearing it?"

"It made you fall in love with me."

He shook his head. "I don't think so."

She bounced off the couch and started pacing. "Yes. Yes, it did. It works . . ." *How?* How did it work? She ran her fingers through her hair, then started twisting a strand around her thumb. "Oh! Pheromones. It's loaded with pheromones."

"Fruit-fly hormones?"

"No." *Mother of Zeus.* The man was being intentionally dense. "Sex hormones. Desire. They've been all over the news. The birds and the bees. Attractors. You just got sucked in."

"Oh."

"You see?" Maybe he finally understood.

"No."

Hopping Hades! "Taylor, please." She ran both hands through her hair. "This is killing me. Please, please don't tease me. Try to pay attention."

He stood up, took her hands in his, then kissed the tip of her nose. In her Keds, her toes started to tingle.

"I'm not teasing you. I just don't buy it."

"But it's the truth."

He shrugged. "Oh, I believe the belt's weird. I mean, no self-respecting designer would put that ugly a belt

343

out into the fashion world, so something must be up with it." He stroked her cheek. "I just don't buy that it has anything at all to do with the way I feel about you."

"But—"

"I mean, you have lousy taste in clothes, and I still love you."

"Taylor, the glow's going to wear off in a few days."

The corner of his mouth curled up. "I think it's supposed to after a while. At least a little."

She sighed. "That's not what I mean."

He took her hand, tugging her down to sit on his lap. "Lane's great, isn't she?"

Zoë frowned, not at all sure where he was going with this. "Well, yeah."

"We don't share a drop of blood, yet I love her as if she were my own sister."

"You were in foster homes together."

"A lot of homes. She was the only family I ever had."

She nodded, not sure what she could say, not sure he wanted her to say anything.

"Do you know what our favorite thing to do was?"

"What?"

"Go to the grocery store."

She frowned, her brow pulling together.

"We liked to sit and watch the families. They'd come in, a husband, a wife, usually a couple of kids. And they'd just do their shopping. Sometimes we'd pick a family and follow them. You could see it in their eyes, you know? How much they cared, I mean. They'd laugh and joke and plan meals, and spoil the kids, and it always made my stomach hurt because I wanted so much to be one of those kids."

She blinked back tears, silent, as he pulled her closer.

"Now I want to be one of those parents." He kissed her ear. "I'm not knocking passion, mind you. I wouldn't even begin to guess what went on when those parents got behind their bedroom doors, but that's what I want. The kind of love those families in the grocery store had." He brushed a strand of hair off her face. "And I want it with you, Zoë."

She ignored her tears. "There has to be real love there in the beginning. Otherwise there's nothing warm and wonderful to fade into."

"Oh, sweetheart, there is real love. A millionfold. I promise you that."

"Taylor, you can't possibly love me. It's just the belt talking. You don't even know me."

"Don't know you? I think I do. You're a woman who's fiercely loyal to her friends, and who won't even rat on her acquaintances. A woman who loves her family and who's brave and smart, and has a wonderful sense of humor, and can forgive a man his stupid blunders."

She shivered. "You see all that in me?"

"A man can see a lot when he's in love."

Love. Oh, how she longed to believe.

"Zoë." He put his finger under her chin and tilted her face up until she had no choice but to look at him, blurry though he was through her tear-filled eyes. "I don't love you because of your keen fashion sense, and I'm not under any spell. I loved you the first moment I saw you in your library. You weren't wearing the belt then, were you?"

She shook her head.

"And you weren't wearing it when I was parked outside your apartment, right?"

She nodded. He was throwing all her arguments back, only this time they added up to truth.

"Take a chance on me, Zoë. Take a chance on us."

She nibbled her lip. Could it be true? *Oh, please Hera, let it be true.*

"Kiss me," he said.

"Oh, Taylor." She wrapped her arms around his neck and hugged him tight, then wiped her tears away on his shoulder. He tilted her head back and kissed her, hard and deep, and the one thing she knew for certain was that she felt more at home in his arms than she'd ever felt anywhere else on the planet.

"Taylor," she whispered, "I love you, too."

He was curled up asleep beside her as she tenderly leaned over to kiss his cheek, not wanting to wake him, but just to touch him. To breathe the musky scent of his skin, to feel the rough caress of his shadow of a beard across her lips. She moved closer, her lips brushing his skin, the sensation both tender and erotic.

Stroking his hair, she pressed her cheek to his. Her Taylor, her—

Ka-pow! Zip, blam, blooey!

Light and sound and terror exploded in her head. She sat upright, jerked away by the force of the image. Immediately she looked for Taylor, expecting him to have jumped up, alert and ready. But still he slept. How could he sleep? That force? That fear? *His* fear. She'd seen it, burning an angry red behind her eyes. She'd smelled the fear, as pungent as the sickly sweet smell of charred flesh.

She'd tasted terror, and now it hung bitter on her

tongue like rust on iron. Was it a sign? A coincidence? A portent?

What was going on?

Never before had she seen an image of the future, but she was certain that was exactly what she'd just experienced—Taylor, afraid and in danger.

Things were happening. And Taylor was right in the middle of it.

Dammit. Not if she could help it.

Steeling her jaw, she eased away from him. She didn't want to leave the circle of his arms—not now, not ever—but she needed to investigate.

Nothing was going to happen to this man. She intended to make damn sure of that.

Silently she padded to the computer and fired it up, then typed in the password she wasn't supposed to know.

The council headlines scrolled across the screen as she searched the site map for any information at all on visions. There had to be something, some information, anythi—

Aphrodite's girdle.

The image floated on the screen, and Zoë gasped. She leaned closer, her nose nearly pressing against the monitor. That belt didn't look a thing like the one she'd been wearing.

A chill chased up her spine.

Hale had lied to her. He'd lied. He knew what the belt looked like, and he'd intentionally tried to mess up her chances with Taylor.

A whirlwind of anger whipped through her, only to war with relief. She gnawed on her lower lip, wanting to be furious, but, somehow her anger kept getting overwhelmed by a wash of sadness. In the end, she couldn't keep the man anyway.

She cast a tender glance toward Taylor, her heart swelling as she watched the gentle rise and fall of his chest. No matter how misguided, Hale loved her. He didn't want to see her hurt. She remembered the stories she'd heard about how Hale's mother had died, about Tessa leaving, everything he'd warned her about mortal/Protector relationships.

Her brother just didn't believe in a happy ending with a mortal.

But she knew—with all her heart and soul—that Taylor was right for her. Just as Donis had been right for Tessa. Only this time it would work out. Taylor wouldn't run away. He was brave and noble and good. Surely together they could weather the storm.

Remembering her task, she scrolled down, past the image of the belt and its emerald green centerstone, taking in all the lore surrounding the belt and its gem.

One article caught her eye—about how the stone could harness unspeakable power at a certain location during a certain lunar eclipse. Tonight, and here in Los Angeles at the Griffith Observatory.

She swallowed, her eye moving down the screen. There was a legend, too. The stone would come to a halfling, but beyond that, the signs were hazy. Take one path, and the world continued as it was. Take the other, and the mortal population was enslaved, destined to serve the pleasure of the ruling Protector and his minions.

Zoë swallowed. She'd let it slip through her fingers. The fate of the world, and she'd haphazardly lent it out as jewelry.

She froze, the pieces coming together. Mordi had attacked first when Lane had the stone. Later he'd gone after Deena, who'd had the thing in her pocket all along. The poodle had sniffed around her and Deena and Taylor . . . which just left Lane.

She didn't have the stone, but Mordichai surely thought she did. After all, it wasn't a huge stretch to assume Deena had borrowed it, then returned it to Lane.

What in Hades had she done?

Taylor's hand on her shoulder startled her.

"Hey, birthday girl."

She whipped around, unable to think, just needing to get to Taylor's sister right then. "Lane," she said. "Danger."

Chapter Twenty-one

Taylor banged his hand on Zoë's steering wheel and cursed his stupidity. *Dammit!* Where were his instincts? He should never have let Lane leave by herself. And now, if what Zoë said was true, some badass thieves thought she had that jewel.

Idiot, idiot, idiot!

Ignoring the tow-away zone, he swung Zoë's tiny Toyota into a free space and bolted out of the car, the stone he'd wrested from the damn ferret weighing heavily in his pocket.

Zoë got out from the other side and ran after him.

"Wait here," he said. "I mean it, Zo. I don't want to have to watch out for both of you."

"But—"

"Zoë, please." He kissed her on the cheek, ignoring her look of exasperation, then dashed up the stairs to Lane's apartment.

The door was ajar. He burst in, then immediately stopped cold.

His employer, Mr. Mordon, presided over the room. "I think you have something I want."

"Just the opposite. Where's my sister?"

Mordon smiled. "She's fine. For now." He gestured across the room, and Taylor turned, looking into the shadows.

On the far side of the living room, Lane crouched on the floor, backed into a corner by two snarling dogs—a golden collie and ridiculously snarling toy poodle—that were approaching her from both sides. Her eyes were wide, pleading up at him.

"Stay still. Don't move." The toy poodle's jaws seemed enormous—as if they had grown somehow beyond normal proportions—and Taylor was certain the dog had a mean streak a mile wide. Maybe it was rabid, too.

Damn! If he attacked Mordon, the dogs would surely lunge. And even if he went for the dogs, there was no way to get them both in time. One would go for Lane's throat; he was sure of it. He wished he had his gun, but it was locked in Francis Capra, and Lane had the keys.

"A dilemma, isn't it," Mordon said, moving casually toward the sliding glass door. The man was wearing a perfectly tailored suit topped with a cape, as if he were trying to pass himself off as some English gentleman out of a Merchant Ivory film. "Perhaps I could see it, and we can arrange a trade."

"Just let her go." As he spoke, Taylor moved slowly, pulling the stone out of his pocket. "Call off the dogs and I'll toss you the rock."

Mordon's eyes narrowed. "No, Mr. Taylor," he said.

The stone moved in Taylor's hand. "I don't think so."

Before Taylor could grab the rock more tightly, it shot across the room to Mordon. He held it up, the green facets perfectly mimicking the color of his eyes. "You're far too obliging, Mr. Taylor." He tipped an imaginary hat. "So sorry about that finder's fee, but I'm sure you understand."

"You hurt Lane, and I'll kill you. So help me . . ."

"Ooooh. I'm shaking in my fine Italian boots," he said with a sneer. Then the sneer faded as something over Taylor's shoulder caught Mordon's attention.

Taylor whipped around, primed to do battle with some hideous ne'er-do-well. Instead he saw Zoë.

"Dammit, Zo—"

"Hello, Mordi," she said, ignoring him. "Happy birthday."

Confused, Taylor spun back around to face Mordon, who tipped an imaginary hat in her direction.

"Hello, cousin. You, too. It's ever so nice to see you again." He held up the gemstone. "I'd love to stay and chat, but my business is done, and I think you're my cue to leave." He smiled at Taylor. "You don't mind if I leave the puppies, do you?" He winked, this time at Zoë. "They're my father's little pets, and I borrowed them for this very occasion. Just in case you showed up." He nodded toward the dogs. "The poor things haven't had lunch yet."

As Mordon stepped backward onto the porch, Taylor lunged, but the man was gone. Poof! He'd leaped back, his cape fluttering. He'd hovered for a moment, then shot away, becoming nothing but a dot in the distant sky.

What the hell?

He spun back around to face Zoë. "What in heaven's name is going on?"

She opened her mouth, but didn't speak, her eyes darting toward Lane. She looked on the verge of leaping forward, tense, ready to spring. A panther on the ready.

"Taylor," Lane said, her voice tense. "Please."

The collie took a step toward her, it teeth bared.

"Stay still, Lane. We'll figure something out."

"Figure faster, okay?"

The poodle's muscles tensed, and Taylor saw Zoë crouch. What the hell did she think she was doing? This was no place for a librarian.

If he was going to keep both his girls from getting pulverized, he had to do something now.

Banking on one dog coming to the aid of the other, he jumped forward and grabbed the poodle, screaming in pain as its teeth closed on the soft flesh between his thumb and forefinger. He kicked the beast in the gut as Lane scrambled to safety and Zoë did a little backflip maneuver, ending up right next to him, a knife in her hand. She pressed the knife into his palm, then kissed him on the cheek.

"Just in case," she said.

What the hell?

The dog lunged at him again.

Blammo! Her leg shot out, hitting the beast square in the breastbone. With a single yelp, it flew across the room, landing with a *ker-thunk* against the kitchen cabinets. It slid to the floor, a twisted pile of mottled fur.

Zoë whipped around, her eyes meeting his with silent apology as her other leg shot out behind her. *Ka-pow!* The collie was down for the count.

As Taylor gaped, the collie shimmered and fizzled, as

it turned from Lassie into the skinny drugged-out attacker from the night of the party. Then he became an oozing, drooling, slimy creature.

"Zowie, Zoë," he whispered. "What the hell?"

"They're not really dogs."

"No kidding. What's going on?"

She held up a finger. "Just a sec."

As he parked his rump uselessly on the floor—his head spinning—Zoë scrambled to where the collie had fallen. She picked it effortlessly up by a leg; then she grabbed the other one out of the kitchen. On the balcony, she did a double windup, the creatures twirling at the ends of her windmilling arms. Then she released each one, sending them flying into the western sky. Taylor stood up just in time to see the distant splash in the ocean.

When Zoë turned around, he noticed that she wasn't even breathing hard. She didn't meet his eyes. "Um, I think maybe we need to talk."

"Yeah," he said, surprised his voice worked. "I think maybe we do."

Zoë finished her story, then tried to gauge his reaction out of the corner of her eye. He was tense, his hands gripping the railing so hard his knuckles were white. They were on Lane's balcony, looking down onto an alley, as Zoë threw bits of leaf out onto the wind, the casual gesture disguising the fact that she was twisted up in a million knots.

"Superheros, huh?" He said the words flat, as if all the emotion had been drained out of him. "That's . . . not something I was really expecting."

"What can I say? I've got an odd family."

"I guess so."

She shrugged, wishing he would touch her.

"So when you jumped off the building . . ."

"Not an R and D project," she said.

"And that cop?"

"Mordichai."

"And those two junkies?"

She shook her head. "Not really men at all." She nodded toward her apartment. "Not even dogs."

"Right." He nodded. "That's what you said. They were henchmen. Weird."

"Right." She sneaked another look at him, wishing she were telepathic, needing to know if she were going to lose him. With every minute that he didn't take her into his arms, she died a little death. If he didn't hurry up and kiss her soon, she was going to be nothing more than a crumpled pile of dust.

"So you can see these bad guys, huh? Just walking around day to day?"

"I'm starting to, yes."

He nodded to the alley below. "Any evil beings down there?"

She closed her eyes, terrified of where this was heading. Being tested by the council was one thing. If she passed, she'd belong. But what about Taylor's tests? Even if she passed, would she be out? Or especially if she passed? Her eyes welled, and she blinked back tears.

She knew the answer to that question. She'd known it all her life.

Summoning her courage, she looked down and saw the snarling beast below. "Yes," she said, pointing. "That one."

"The guy in the baggy clothes with the chain and the boom box? I could've told you that."

"No, he's okay." She pointed again. "The little old man working in the garden. See? He's hunched over in the poppies."

Taylor shook his head. "Guess I'm striking out all the way around."

"No! It's not you. It's—"

"Must have been pretty comical, huh? Watching me fight those guys."

Her stomach twisted. "Comical? I was terrified." She licked her lips. "Taylor, I don't want to lose you."

He gave a little laugh, but his eyes were sad. "Well, good thing you're around to protect me, huh? I mean, Lord knows I can't protect you. . . . Can't protect my sister." He pounded his fist against his thigh. "Can't even protect myself."

"I don't need you to protect me. I just need you to be with me."

He turned to her then and smiled, and a tiny bit of hope took root. His eyes were soft and warm as he reached out to stroke her cheek.

"I'm sorry," he said, and hope died in her heart. "I need to think. Need to get my head clear. I don't do this well. I wasn't . . . this isn't . . ."

He sighed, then ran his hands through his hair. "I just need to be alone right now. Besides, shouldn't you be out making the world safe for democracy or something?"

She opened her mouth to argue—the world *was* safe, until the eclipse. They had hours to sort this all out if only he'd stay. If only he'd talk to her. But the words didn't come, and instead of staying he left, marching down the stairs without even turning back.

She watched him go, a single tear tracing a path down her cheek. He was leaving her, and not one of her ridiculous powers could make him stay. He loved her, but he was leaving anyway.

Just as she'd always known he would.

Zoë walked into her mom's house, saw the chocolate birthday cake with the colorful sprinkles, and burst into tears.

In an instant, Deena and Hoop and Tessa had gathered around her, but she just dropped to the couch and buried her face in her hands. She was here, with her friends, with her mom—and yet she was completely alone.

"Oh, hell," said Deena. "He left, didn't he? I can't believe it."

"Taylor? I don't believe it," Hoop said. "He's head over heels in love with you."

Tessa sat on the sofa and put her arm around Zoë. "Did you two have a fight?"

Zoë shook her head. "He doesn't love me."

"Of course he does," Tessa said.

"Not the real me."

Tessa's eyes narrowed. "What do you mean?"

Zoë nibbled on her lower lip, then caught Deena's eye.

"You're gonna have to tell her," Deena said.

"Tell me what?"

"Yeah," said Hoop. "Tell her what?"

"Come on." Deena took Hoop's arm and steered him toward the back door. "Let's go check out the roses."

"I am *always* the last to know these things," Hoop grumbled as Deena steered him out the door.

Tessa tucked a finger under Zoë's chin and lifted until

Zoë had no choice but to look her in the eye. "Sweet-heart?"

"Oh, Mommy." She was eight years old all over again, and she wrapped her arms around her mom and held on for dear life.

"Hey, hey, come on, baby, what's the matter?"

She held on tight for a few more seconds, then pushed away. She had to tell—now—before she lost her courage. "There's something you need to know, Mom. Something I should have told you a long time ago."

Something flashed in Tessa's eyes as she took Zoë's hand. "It's okay. Just tell me."

And so she did. Everything. About Donis and Hale and the council. About her supersenses and her other fun little tricks. About the application and the legend.

About Mordichai and the stone and Lane, and how in a few hours she needed to zip off and try to save the world.

And, of course, about Taylor. It all spilled out.

"I'm sorry, Mom. I'm not a normal little girl. I never have been."

"Oh, baby." Tessa stroked her hair, rocking her back and forth, back and forth, making her feel safe and loved. "I thought . . . I didn't want to believe it, but I thought maybe it was . . ." She trailed off, then smiled weakly. "I'm so sorry. I was scared for you, scared of my memories. I didn't want to believe that you'd turned out like your father."

"I was afraid you'd leave me." Zoë sniffed. "Like you left Daddy. I didn't want you to think I was a freak."

Tessa's eyes went wide. "Oh, Zoë, no! I love you, sweetie. And I loved your father." She grinned sadly. "At first I thought he was . . . you know . . ." She twirled her finger at the side of her head. "But then, when I realized it was true, I was afraid for him. Afraid he'd get hurt, afraid he'd get killed and I'd be all alone." She frowned. "So many fears. I didn't want to take a back-seat to the entire world, either."

"That was just his job, Mom."

Tessa smiled. "Would it be just a job to you?"

Zoë shook her head. "No. More than a job." *Much more*. "But that doesn't mean I'd love Taylor less."

Her mom stroked her hair. "I know, sweetie. I know that now, anyway." She sighed. "But I didn't understand that then. . . . It was more than that, even. I couldn't believe your father really wanted me, or would want to keep me. What could I offer someone like that?"

"He loved you, Mom."

"I know. And I made a huge mistake. I let my fear get the best of me, and I walked away. Even worse, I made him promise to stay away." She pulled Zoë into a bear hug. "You listen to me, young lady. It doesn't matter who you are or what you do, I'm not going anywhere."

Zoë wanted to believe. "Taylor said he loved me. He left."

Tessa nodded. "Taylor doesn't have the benefit of twenty-twenty hindsight. And he's not your mom. He needs a stern talking-to." Tessa gave her a stalwart grin. "I wish somebody had been around to give me a stern talking-to."

"You're not planning on being the one who gives Taylor that talking-to, are you?" The idea of her mother chewing out her new now-ex-boyfriend made her more than a little queasy.

Tessa waved a hand. "Now what kind of question is that?"

Apparently a question to which she wasn't going to get an answer. Zoë considered pressing her mom, then decided against it. Taylor would do what he had to, no matter what Tessa or Deena or anybody said.

Zoë only hoped that, in the end, the one thing he had to do was come back to her. She couldn't talk or trick or anything him into it.

"You just do what *you* want. I left your father, and it nearly killed me. I loved him, but I forced him away, and it almost destroyed me." She stroked Zoë's cheek. "Didn't do you much good either, I'd say. I'm the one who's sorry, sweetie. Follow your heart, Zoë. Don't try to follow your head. It'll only confuse you."

Her heart. Her heart was with Taylor. Hera help her, she wanted him. Wanted his love, wanted his warmth. She'd always wanted a real family, and now she'd found a man who wanted one just as much. He'd thought she was the perfect woman, that they'd have a storybook life. Until she'd shoved her reality in his face.

And now . . . oh, now she wanted him back.

Even if that meant giving up her heritage? Was it worth the price to be safe in his arms again?

Oh, yes. He made her feel whole in a way being on the council never could. Being a superhero would make her feel useful. Being with Taylor made her feel alive.

"Sweetie? Are you okay?"

She flashed Tessa a weak smile. "I'm fine. I was just thinking about my cake."

Tessa squeezed her hand. "Your cake?"

She took a deep breath. "I've never really been able to handle chocolate. It kind of makes my mouth go all

360

crazy. I never got up the nerve to tell you."

Tessa laughed. "What some women wouldn't give to not be able to eat chocolate . . ." She hugged Zoë close. "That's okay, sweetie. I'm sure I've got some yellow cake mix somewhere. It'll only take a minute. Surely you have time for some cake before you rush off to save the world, right?"

"That's not what I mean, Mom." She remembered the Intent to Select Mortalization form sitting with her council materials and swallowed. For Taylor. For them.

For them, she'd sign it. She'd go fight Mordichai, and she'd win. She'd make her father and Hale so proud before she left them, and she'd fight like hell to keep at least one memory—even if they would make her think it was a dream. But in the end, she'd become mortal.

She'd be the woman Taylor wanted, and she'd have the family she always wanted. She wasn't going to make the same mistake as Tessa—wasn't going to give up on love and regret it forever.

And now, for one last time, she'd let her mouth tingle with the taste of chocolate. "No, Mom, you don't understand. The thing is, this time, I'd like an extra large piece."

"I don't understand any of this." Hale paced in front of Zephron's desk. "I mean, it's a freaking *legend*. Why now? Why'd this rock show up in Los Angeles after all this time?"

Zephron caught his eye. "Sometimes, even a legend needs a gentle nudge."

Donis stepped forward. "Are you saying the council—"

"Where the stone came from is not the point," Zephron said sharply. "Or why. Right now, our problem is that your daughter has lost it!"

"Maybe she wouldn't have if you'd let me go back and help her." Hale pounded a fist into his palm, trying to burn off nervous energy. Zephron and Donis had made him stay, planning for the worst—and he'd been going stir-crazy ever since.

"We must assume that Hieronymous will succeed."

"No way. My sister won't fail us. You saw her figure everything out, break into that Web page. . . . She knows the legend. She'll get that stone back!"

Zephron pointed to his viewing screen. "Your sister is forsaking her heritage. It would seem that we must now assume the worst."

Hale twisted around to look at the screen. There, larger than life, Zoë was signing her mortalization form. She looked up at the ceiling, as if she knew they were watching. "Okay, I signed it. I don't know who's supposed to come get me for mortalization, but you'd just better wait. It's not effective until after the eclipse. You hear me? I'll fight Mordi for you, but then I want to be with Taylor." She wiped a tear away. "The only thing is, can you make sure I see my dad and Hale first? One last time before I forget them?" She turned in a circle around the room, as if expecting an answer. "Please?"

The image faded as Hale caught his father's eye. "We need to help her. We need to change her mind."

A sad smile touched Donis's lips. "She's in love with her mortal, Hale. There's nothing you can do to change that. I sometimes wonder if I wouldn't have done the same, if I'd been given the chance."

Damn sentimental fools. Falling for mortals. It's absurd! He didn't get it. He just didn't get it.

He stalked around the room once more, trying to rein in his emotions. "Well, I'm going anyway. I'm not leaving her to face Mordichai by herself."

"There's nothing you can do," Zephron said. "We cannot interfere."

"Screw the rules. I'm going to be there for my sister." He looked at Donis. "Are you with me?"

"For my daughter? For Tessa's little girl?" Donis looked from Hale to Zephron, and then to the monitor. "Oh, yes. I'm going."

"You're an idiot." Hoop's voice filtered over him. "You know that, right?"

Taylor sat at his desk and rubbed his hands over his face.

"He's right," Deena said, pacing back and forth and shooting him dirty glares every time she turned. "You said you love her, and then you just up and left her?"

"I *do* love her." So help him, he did. "But how long do you think we'd last? I mean, how the hell can *she* love *me?*"

"Are you nuts? She thinks you hung the moon."

"I think that was her great-uncle Joe," Hoop said.

Taylor glared, and Deena tossed a pencil at him.

"Sorry. Bad joke."

"But that's exactly my point," Taylor said. Why the hell couldn't they understand? "She's a superhero, for crying out loud. Leaping tall buildings. Stopping runaway trains. I mean, hell, the girl's got X-ray vision—"

"Which is pretty damn cool, when you think about it."

"Hoop!" Deena screeched. "You're *not* helping."

Taylor pushed up out of his chair and started pacing. "Why the hell would someone like Zoë want to spend her life with someone like me?"

"Because she loves you, you foolish boy."

He spun around to see Tessa glaring at him for all she was worth, and suddenly he felt about four feet tall.

"Tessa. I'm sorry." What else could he say?

"You lied," she said simply.

The words found their mark. More than anything Hoop or Deena had been saying, Tessa's simple truth bored into his soul and festered.

"You promised you wouldn't give up on her. You told her you loved her. And now you're just going to abandon her?"

"Why would she want me?" he asked again, but it was a pathetic excuse, and he knew it. She did want him. God help him, that amazing woman loved him, and he'd hurt her more deeply than he could imagine.

Tessa stared him down. "Don't you play that game with me, George Bailey Taylor. Not ever with me. You need a good talking-to, and I'm here to give it to you."

"Tessa, she's—"

"Don't make the same mistake I did," Tessa said, ignoring him. "Don't you dare give up on that girl just because you're intimidated by everything she can do. That's only part of who she is. Just like that bullet in your leg is only part of who you are. And she loves you. If you really love her, too, I'd better not hear that you've let her down."

He tried to look chastised, but couldn't help the smile that fought to emerge. There was something so *right* about being called to the carpet by Zoë's mother.

Heaven help him, he'd been a fool. A damned arrogant fool.

More than anything in the world he wanted to hold Zoë, to tell her he was a jerk. To tell her he loved her and never wanted to lose her.

And he knew in his heart she'd forgive him. Hell, that was one of the reasons he loved her.

He couldn't lose her. Not now. Not ever.

He pushed out of his chair and his eyes found Deena. "Where is she?"

She shook her head. "I don't know. Something about a legend. She's off to save the world," Tessa said. The older woman smiled. "Get used to it."

"Save the world? Fine. Great. Wonderful. But I need to talk to her." He cursed his stupidity. "How the heck am I supposed to find her? She could be anywhere on the planet." With an angry sweep of his arm, Taylor wiped the top of his desk clean. "God, I'm such an idiot!"

"Wait!"

They all turned to Deena.

She smiled. "I just might know someone who can help."

Chapter Twenty-two

"Elmer?" Deena called, scrambling around on the floor as Taylor watched, baffled. "Come here, Elmer. Oh, little ferret, *please* be here."

He glanced at Hoop, then Tessa. They both shrugged.

"Deenie, my love," Hoop said, "what the hell are you doing?"

"The ferret," she said, rocking back on her heels. "He'll know where they are." She glanced up at the clock, and Taylor followed her gaze. It was already past eleven. They had to hurry.

"The ferret that buried his teeth in my leg?" Taylor asked. "We're looking for *him?*"

"He belongs to her half brother." She met his eyes. "Taylor, trust me."

He nodded. "Fine. Keep looking."

His eyes swept the baseboard as he moved around in Zoë's kitchen, around the countertop, and back into the breakfast area. He stopped by her table, letting his eyes scour the room, trying to think where he'd be if he were a ferret.

That was when he saw it—the official-looking piece of paper sitting under the salt shaker.

He picked it up and his blood ran cold.

"Taylor," Deena called. "Would you get with the program, already?"

"She's giving it up," he said, his voice barely audible even to his own ears. He read the words on the page, straining to make sense of the letters. After the eclipse, she was giving up her powers.

For him?

He closed his eyes. What the hell had he done?

Deena looked over his shoulder to the neatly printed form. She sucked in a breath and her eyes met his.

"We need to find her," he said, his voice low and tense. *"Now."*

"Then we need to find Elmer," she said, fear in her eyes. "He's our only chance."

He nodded. "I'll check the bedroom." As Hoop and Deena and Tessa crawled around on their hands and knees, Taylor headed to the back of the apartment. He ripped open the closet and started plowing through the piles of incredibly unfashionable clothes. An ugly jumper, a bright orange and gold dress, a tacky brown pantsuit, a—

Ferret.

Thank goodness. The little guy opened his eyes, blinked, then came wide-awake, jumping to his feet and hissing.

"Hey, hey, calm down." He glanced toward the door,

feeling rather silly. But he'd told Deena he'd trust her, so . . .

He put his hand out. "I'm sorry about throwing you off the candy dish to get the stone, but Zoë's in trouble. Will you help?"

The problem with mortals was that they simply weren't good at charades.

With much cajoling and bouncing about, Elmer finally got them to drop an atlas on the floor, and now he was doing a little dance on top of the West Coast.

"California?" Taylor asked. "She's still in California?"

Elmer jumped up and down, bobbing his head, and the mortals slapped their hands together and generally acted silly.

"In Los Angeles, still?" Tessa asked.

Again, Elmer bobbed.

"But we're still screwed," Hoop said. "Los Angeles isn't exactly Podunk, U.S.A. It covers a lot of territory."

"Here," said Deena, grabbing Elmer up and plunking him down in front of Zoë's computer. She logged on, typed a bit, and an image of Los Angeles and a list of activities popped onto the screen.

Elmer's whiskers twitched. Now they were cooking.

Rather roughly, she grabbed him under his forepaws and held him to the screen. "Point," she said.

A mite demanding, but he forgave her. They were all worried about Zoë, after all. He skimmed the words, stopping on *outdoor activities*. She hit a button, and the screen changed—popping up a whole list of things to do in Los Angeles.

His eyes glazed over . . . so much to do, so much to

see, and he hadn't even yet made it out of Zoë's apartment.

"Elmer!" That was Taylor.

He jumped. *Sorry!* He opened his eyes and focused on the screen. There it was, midway down the page—the Griffith Observatory. That's where Zephron had said this would all happen.

"You're sure?" Taylor asked. "The observatory?"

Sure I'm sure. Do I not look sure? he squeaked.

Taylor shrugged. "I'll take that as a yes."

Deena, Hoop, and Tessa all nodded and murmured agreement. *Zeus's zits, you'd think they'd teach ferret in those mortal schools.*

He squirmed, and Deena put him back on the floor as she grabbed her purse and ran for the door. Taylor was already gone, and Elmer ran after them, stopping at the threshold and bouncing up and down. *Come back! Come back this instant!*

After all that—all they'd been through together—and the dang mortals were just going to *leave* him? It just wasn't fair.

On the walkway, Taylor was sprinting toward the stairs. He paused, turned back, and his eyes met Elmer's. The corner of his mouth turned up as he nodded. "Don't forget to bring the ferret!" he called, and Elmer writhed with delight.

As the one called Hoop scooped him up, Elmer preened.

He just might take a liking to these mortals after all.

"Well, well," said Mordichai, standing near the Egyptian-looking stone obelisk that served as the focal point of the landscaped grounds fronting the Observatory. "Fancy meeting you here."

Zoë only nodded, too afraid to speak. In her stomach, a thousand butterflies had morphed into broad-winged bats. Behind them, the observatory glowed under the soft electric lights. Below, the sounds of Los Angeles drifted up.

The grounds were eerily empty, as if somehow the vibrations of the legend had kept the mortals away.

"Why don't we forget the whole thing?" he asked, holding up the stone. "You know you can't take it from me, and the eclipse will be here soon. All I have to do is hold this stone up, and my father will be able to speak to the Outcasts through me."

She looked around. "Uncle Hieronymous is here?"

Mordi frowned. "Not exactly."

"What's the matter? Is he too chicken to fight his own battle?"

"It's *our* battle, cousin." He took a step toward her. "Unless you'd care to join us? You know the council will never admit you. Your skills are"—his hand twirled in the air—*"lacking."*

"They're not going to admit me, anyway." She stood up straighter, trying to make peace with her decision. "I'm submitting to mortalization."

A look of disgust passed over his face.

"But not until after I get that stone from you."

"I wouldn't bet the ranch, cousin, dear."

She licked her lips, trying to find a way to win. Mordi was right. He *was* stronger. She could tell he'd been holding back all this time, knew he might have done much more harm than he'd actually managed. If she really had to fight him . . . "Why are you doing this? Why would you want to enslave all the mortals, anyway? Your mom's a mortal."

Mordi snorted, and Zoë realized that maybe that hadn't been the best argument.

"Why are you so keen on saving them?" he asked. "For that matter, why would you join them? Your precious Taylor? What makes you think that even if you become a mortal that he'll want to stay with you? Why would he want to? You're a freak, Zoë, and you always will be. We both are. My mother didn't want me any more than Taylor wants you."

"And Hieronymous does?" she spat. "Does he love you, Mordi? Or does he love what you can do for him?" If it weren't for that rock would he care about you in the slightest? He doesn't even really believe that you'll beat me, does he?" she asked, remembering Nit and Wit. "He's the one who sent those creeps to the party. Not you. He's afraid you'll lose, isn't he?"

"Enough!" Her cousin's eyes burned with green fire. "My father wants me at his side. *Me.*" His voice was shaking. "Mr. Taylor didn't want you. He wanted some pretty, normal mortal. Not you, Zoë. Never you."

"That's not true," she cried, but doubt niggled in her mind. She tried to push it away, but it fought back to the surface. She had risked everything for love, and she had no idea how anything would turn out in the end.

"It won't matter anyway," Mordi said, his voice stronger now. Firmer. "After tonight, mortals don't have much of a future." He swept his arm in a circle and a wall of flame danced up around them. "As they say in Rome, let the games begin."

* * *

"We've got to do something!" Hale watched, helpless, as Mordi whipped and spun and kicked in the circle of flame. Zoë was beaten back, time and again.

Midnight was fast approaching, and the moon had almost entirely disappeared. If Zoë didn't wrest that stone from Mordichai soon . . .

"Together!" Donis called, and Hale nodded. They linked hands, then burst forward, only to be thrown back by the living flames. They landed in a heap, Zephron standing calmly behind them.

"It's no use," the elder said. "We cannot even enter the circle. The eclipse has made them both stronger."

"She's better than this," complained Hale, flinching as a stream of sparks from Mordi's fingertips sent Zoë flying backward. "Why in Hades is she doing such a piss-poor job?"

"Your sister has never found focus. She seems to excel only when her heart is fully invested in the matter."

"She's not *invested* in preventing some lunatic relative from taking over the world?"

"I think she's distracted," Donis said calmly.

Hale spun to face him. "Well, maybe someone should remind her that she's not going to be able to spend any time with that *distraction* if Hieronymous unites the Outcasts."

"I don't think emotions are quite as pragmatic as you, son."

Hale shrugged off his father's platitudes and peered once more into the circle. "That's it, Zoë!" he yelled when she got in a particularly good punch. The trouble was, Mordi's powers were well developed. He could levitate, shoot pure energy from his fingertips, and even execute a really neat left hook.

372

Zoë, on the other hand, was a scrapper.

She was bouncing and dodging, but she wasn't holding her own. Little by little Mordi was wearing her down, and soon it would be too late.

"Zoë! Somebody help her, dammit!"

Hale turned toward the frantic voice and saw the mortal sprinting toward him, clearly favoring one leg. Behind him, Deena and Tessa and another mortal male struggled to keep up.

"Tessa," Donis whispered.

Hale sighed. He'd come expecting an action flick, but this was turning into a soap opera.

Straightening his shoulders, he turned to face Zoë's mortal. "You must be Taylor."

The man squinted. "And you must be Hale. Why the hell aren't you in there helping her? Afraid your picture-perfect skin will get bruised?"

Hale flashed him a look of disdain, then took a step into the flames. He was summarily tossed backward like so much garbage. Landing on his rump, he then looked up at Taylor. "Satisfied?"

Fear and frustration burned across the mortal's face, and Hale fought a wave of compassion. He didn't want to like this mortal; this was the man who was going to one day hurt his sister the way his father had been crushed.

Taylor paced, one hand running through his hair, the other keeping a death grip on a wadded-up piece of paper. He moved toward the circle. "Zoë! Sweetheart, it's Taylor!"

No response. Zoë couldn't hear him.

Taylor whipped around. "What the hell's wrong with everybody? Why can't we help her?"

"I thought she was some kick-ass superhero," the other mortal male said as Elmer peeked his head out of the man's jacket pocket. "How come that bastard's kicking her butt?"

"Hoop," Deena said, "I told you. It's like, she's in training."

Tessa's face tightened, her eyes never leaving Zoë, her terror obvious. Donis appeared next to her. Zoë's mother looked up, tears suddenly coming and leaving trails through her make-up. "I'm sorry," she whispered. Hale watched as, almost instinctually, his father gravitated toward the mortal. She held her hand out.

Donis moved closer. "Sorry?"

"About this. About everything." She looked away. "About making you—"

He took her outstretched hand, then pulled her close. They both focused on the circle then, and on their daughter fighting for all she was worth. Despite everything, Hale gave a small smile.

Nearby, Taylor kicked the heel of his shoe into the soft ground. "This is ridiculous. She's getting creamed! I don't intend to lose her. Now, somebody please tell me what the hell I can do!"

"Lose her?" Hale repeated, his anger flaring. "*You* lose her? She's giving up her heritage for you, buddy. *You* aren't the one who is losing her. That'll be her dad and me."

Cut the guy a break, Elmer said. *He's in love with the girl.*

Hale opened his mouth to answer, but Taylor got there first.

"You're not losing anybody," he said. "Not if I can help it." He held up the paper. "See this? This is bullshit." He turned toward the flames, shaking the paper as the fire leaped and curled outward.

In the circle, Mordi took a running leap toward Zoë. She jumped up into a backflip, managing to avoid Mordi's lethal legs.

"Yeah!" Hale screamed. "Way to go, Zoëster!" But he spoke too soon, and Mordi twirled around and caught her square in the back. She went flying forward, only to land in a crumpled heap.

"For crying out loud," Taylor yelled. "He's killing her."

He reached out, putting his hand in the flames, then immediately pulled back, cringing.

"It'll burn you, mortal," Hale said somewhat peevishly, "not just hold you back. Guess you're stuck out here with us."

"To hell with that," Taylor blurted. With his mouth set in a thin line, he looked at his mortal companions. Deena and Hoop eyed each other, fear in their eyes, but nodded their silent agreement. Then he turned to Hale, his face firm and determined. "If you aren't going to help her, I am."

"Are you brain-dead? I already told you we can't get past the circle. This is her battle."

He took a step toward the flame. "I . . ."—step—". . . am going . . ."—step, step—". . . to help her!" And with that, he leaped forward into the fire.

"No!" Hale lunged, grabbing the back of Taylor's shirt. Donis and Hale could stand the heat, but the mortal would burn to cinders. He tugged, keeping Taylor from sure death, but Zephron laid a hand on his shoulder and nodded toward the circle.

"Let the boy do what he has to do. If Zoë wins, he

will survive. If she loses . . . well perhaps death will be a blessing."

He didn't mean to, but his grip on the shirt weakened, and suddenly Taylor jumped into the circle. The flames leaped and danced, sucking him farther and farther into the fire.

She was going to lose.

She knew it; but, dammit, she couldn't accept it.

She'd been lucky recently, for her meager skills were no match for Mordi's years of training. Still, by Hera, she was going to go down fighting.

Across the circle, Mordi stalked her, biding his time. Above her, the shadow across the moon deepened.

It was almost time. . . .

Almost, and she hadn't managed to retrieve the stone.

She couldn't see anything past the circle of flames, but somehow she knew Donis and Hale were there. She wasn't going to let them down.

With renewed strength, she tore across the grass, launching herself at Mordi. His eyes went wide—comical—as if he'd never in a million years expected her to be so bold, or to take such an unsophisticated tack as a plain, old-fashioned football tackle. Arms locked, they rolled over and over until—*yes*—her fingers closed around the stone. *Thank goodness!*

She sprang backward, tearing the stone away, crouching like a tiger as Mordi retreated backward. He looked as if he was planning to leap at any moment.

Steady, steady. Just a few more minutes and the eclipse would pass. She just needed to hold on to the stone until—

Ka-thwang!

With just one look, he sent her tumbling, backward and backward, over and over, until she hit the wall of fire and fell forward onto the grass.

She opened her hand. . . .

Still there!

But Mordi was right there, too, a rather smug expression on his face. No question about it: her cousin was moving in for the kill.

Well, damn.

But she wasn't licked yet. She hauled herself to her feet, her fingers locked around the stone as she wondered if maybe the Zoë Smith superstare would work on Mordichai. She was just about to try when—

"Zoë!"

The familiar voice was far away, as if coming from deep within a well. She spun around, trying to find him, her blood running cold when she saw Taylor caught in the flames and writhing in pain. Just like in her dream . . .

As Mordichai raced toward her, she raced for Taylor, thrusting her hands into the white-hot fire to grasp his outstretched fingers. She barely had time to look into his eyes when she felt Mordichai's power lifting her up and away.

"No!"

She and Taylor yelled the word in unison, and, with a final tug, she broke free of Mordichai's hold and Taylor broke free from the flames. He burst out of the fire, and her heart leaped with joy when she realized he was unharmed.

"Zoë, look out!"

Ka-thwap! She twirled around just in time, catching an unsuspecting Mordi in the chest with the side of her foot and sending him careening to the far side of the circle. He slammed into the wall of fire and crumpled to the ground.

"Good job," Taylor said.

"Thanks."

He patted himself down. "What the hell? I'm not even singed."

She took her eyes off Mordi long enough to glare at him. "What are you doing here? You're in danger."

"*I'm* in danger? I'm here to help you."

She held up the hand holding the stone. "I'm fine. I just have to hold out a little longer."

On the far side of the circle, Mordichai climbed to his feet.

"And then what?" Taylor waved a piece of paper. "Become mortal? Are you nuts?"

Gnawing on her lower lip, she glanced at the approaching Mordichai, then turned back to Taylor. "I'm not sure now is the time. I'm a little busy at the moment."

Mordichai launched himself toward her, and they went tumbling to the ground. She twisted, trying to get out of his grasp. He was stronger than she, and Zoë struggled against his grip until, finally, she managed to spring away.

Taylor caught her, his arms strong and sure.

"Look out!" he yelled, and she whipped around, stopping Mordi's rush with an outthrust leg and shoving him back against the obelisk in front of the observatory.

Taylor rushed forward and landed a solid punch in Mordi's gut. Mordichai doubled over, but not before managing to shoot a couple of particularly nasty bursts of energy Taylor's way.

"Duck!" Zoë cried.

Taylor threw himself to the side, and Mordi's blasts scorched the grass instead of Taylor. "Don't you dare give this up because of me," he yelled as he climbed back to his feet.

A lump rose in her throat as she leaped backward to escape Mordi's lunge. *Dammit.* She didn't want to deal with her cousin, or stones, or legends. Here was the man she loved, and she needed to think. With a renewed burst of energy, she caught Mordi by the throat and held him firm against the obelisk as she turned to Taylor. "I don't want to lose you."

"I love you, Zoë," he said, tearing her Intent to Select Moralization form into tiny pieces. "*You.* And I'm sorry I didn't say it before, when you were so worried about how I'd react."

Could he really love her? Did he really?

"Excuse me," Mordi croaked. "This is all very heartwarming, but my father's waiting for results and I need to kick a little ass." He struggled under her grip, but Zoë's arm felt like iron.

"Zoë . . . don't give up on me because I was an idiot," Taylor shouted. "Let me love you. Hell, let me help you."

She watched as the little pieces of her mortalization form sparked and sputtered, disintegrating before her very eyes. He really did love her. She wasn't ever going to be June Cleaver normal, but he loved her anyway. It was there in his eyes, and she wanted so much to jump into his arms, to cry out for joy. Everything she'd ever wanted, right here, laid in front of her like candy. Love, a family, her heritage.

And it could all fizzle away in just a few minutes,

because there was still the little matter of Mordichai, who, at that very moment, had raised his head and was aiming a burst of pure energy right at her—

"No!" She cried as she was thrown clear.

Zing! With no warning, Taylor threw his body in the way, then was hurled by Mordi's blast into the wall of fire. Plastered against him, the living flames licked his body.

"Taylor!"

"I'm all right," he shouted, sounding surprised.

"For now," said Mordi. Rubbing his throat, he circled around Zoë until he was just below Taylor. Casually he looked up. "Apropos, don't you think? Once the ceremony is complete—once I win—those flames will consume him." He smiled. "Surely that will put me in good stead with my father."

"You're too late," she said, steeling herself, and hoping against hope she could hold out for the last few moments. "It's over. I've got the stone."

He merely smiled as a shiver rippled down her spine. Her hand opened, her fingers utterly ignoring her brain's desperate plea to close. The stone hovered for a moment, then zipped through the air to land with a soft thud in Mordi's black-gloved hand.

"And now you don't," he said.

She closed her eyes and sank to the ground. Over. It was all over, and she and Taylor hadn't even had a chance.

Tilting her head back to look him in the eyes, she whispered, "I'm sorry."

"Don't you dare give up," Taylor screamed, lashing out against the fingers of fire binding him.

Above them, the sliver of the moon faded to blackness. Zoë stared at Taylor with sorrow in her eyes.

"It's not over," he yelled. "You can beat him." He pounded his fist against the wall of flame. "Do something; do anything. Shoot him with your superstare, kick him in the gut, levitate something and throw it at him. *Anything!*"

The stone in Mordichai's hand started to glow as the darkness over the moon deepened.

"Ah," said Mordichai, "but my cousin has never quite mastered that. Have you, Zoë dear?"

She met his gaze, wheels turning in her head.

"Mastered? No." But she could manage—in a pinch, when it mattered.

Her eyes darted to Taylor. *Oh, sweet Hera.* It mattered now. But she needed help. She couldn't do it alone. Not and be sure. And time was running out. . . .

She met Taylor's gaze, silently imploring, and hoping beyond hope that what she saw in those deep brown eyes was more than just love—that it was understanding, too.

The stone glowed brighter. The circle of flame danced and leaped behind Mordi, the fire thinning with the fading moonlight. She drew a single deep breath, readying herself.

The stone burned, radiant with inner fire.

She focused, remembering little Patty in the library, the cafeteria, Davy . . . remembering Taylor, always Taylor. His touch. The way his kisses had her floating on air.

And when she felt it all—the emotion, the need, the desire, the *love*—well up inside her, that was when she looked at Mordi. With all her strength, she caught him in her gaze and concentrated like she'd never concentrated before.

"I can, Mordi. When it matters, I can levitate anything."

"Way to go sweetheart," said Taylor.

Mordi must have heard Taylor's voice right behind him—an unusual fact, considering Mordi had pinned him to the wall of flame a good five feet above the ground—because he tried to twist around, stumbling a bit when he realized his feet were no longer connected with anything solid. As Zoë fought a victorious grin, Taylor yanked his foot back and let loose with a kick that would have made an angry mule proud. His foot struck pay dirt, slamming into Mordi's arm and sending the stone flying out into the night.

Zoë exhaled, and Mordi fell to the ground. Immediately he started crawling around on his hands and knees, searching for the lost gem.

The circle of flame vanished, and suddenly Taylor was right there, sprawled at Zoë's feet, battered and bruised from fighting the flames. She threw her arms around him and held him close as he rocked her back and forth.

She had no idea where the stone had landed, but it didn't matter. A sliver of moon peeked out from behind the shadow.

It was over.

She'd won.

She smiled at Taylor, cradling him in her arms. He squeezed her hand and smiled back.

No, she amended. *They'd* won.

From across the circle, Hale saw Mordi look furtively around, then stoop down and pick something up.

Please, Zeus, no. Not again. Not this soon. If Mordi had the stone . . .

It might be over for now, but what about tomorrow? The next eclipse? Some other ancient prophecy? Zephron had said the stone had many mysterious properties, and Hale had seen more than enough of them.

Was he supposed to stop Mordi now? Was the testing, the legend, through?

He shivered. He'd had his quota of legends, and somewhere out there was a Greek beach with his name on it. If only fate would cut him a break.

Mordichai's eyes glowed in the returning moonlight as he moved toward him. Hale stood ready, tense. He'd fight if he had to. He certainly wasn't going to let Mordi destroy Zoë's victory.

Mordi stopped right in front of Hale, his eyes sad and deep as the ocean. He seemed broken by his defeat. "She was right. It was never about the power, never about the council. Not for me. All I ever wanted was for my dad to believe in me." He looked behind him toward Zoë, who was helping Taylor to his feet. "That mortal, he didn't even understand what was at stake, and yet he risked everything for her. I didn't expect that."

"Neither did I," admitted Hale warily. As soon as Mordi turned to walk away, Hale would jump him and get that stone.

Mordi nodded, then held out his hand to shake. "Your sister fought the good fight."

For a second Hale hesitated, smelling a trick. Then he nodded curtly and pressed his hand against his cousin's. As Mordi pulled his hand away, Hale felt something cold against his skin. He looked down, his eyes widening as he saw the green stone that had been pressed into his palm.

"If my father ever finds out I gave this to you, I'll hunt you down and kill you. He'd probably find some use for it, even now."

Hale nodded, speechless, as he watched the stone glow and shimmer in his hand. When he looked up, he saw a real smile begin in Mordi's eyes for the first time in years. "Good to see you again, too, cousin," Hale said.

With a curt nod, Mordichai faded back into the shadows, then was gone with the night.

Zoë came over, a battered Taylor right beside her.

"So how's our hero doing?" Hale asked.

She kissed the mortal, and Hale didn't even flinch. *Amazing.*

"He's doing great," she said.

"Need a hand with him?"

"*Him* can do fine on his own," Taylor said, taking an unsteady step forward.

Hale rolled his eyes. "Mortals. They're a damn stubborn lot."

Zoë smiled and kissed Taylor on the cheek, her eyes brimming with love. "Yes, they are. A very stubborn lot."

"You're okay with this?" Zoë asked Hale as her gaze drifted to Taylor, who was propped up against the obelisk nursing his leg. A few yards away, Deena and Hoop snuggled in the grass, Elmer curled up between them.

"Mortals, mortals, everywhere," Hale mumbled, looking in the same direction.

"Hale . . ." She put her hands on her hips. "Well? Are you?"

He turned to face her, his face serious. "Would it matter if I wasn't?"

For half a second, she hesitated, not wanting to irritate her brother. But the truth won out. "No."

"Then I guess I'm okay with it," he said. His voice was stern, but the way the corner of his mouth twitched told her he'd come around soon enough—if he hadn't already.

"Besides," he added, "I'm pretty much outnumbered." He nodded toward the parking lot, where Donis and Tessa were perched on Francis Capra, deep in conversation.

"They look really good together," she said, her heart swelling at the sight of her mom and dad together for the first time in her entire life. "They've both waited a long time. This is kind of weird."

Hale took her hand and they started walking toward Taylor. "You really love him?" he asked.

"Oh, yes."

"Well," he said grudgingly, "he seems okay. For a mortal, I mean."

From Hale, that was high praise indeed. "Thanks, Halester. I think so."

Zephron stepped out of a shadow, seeming to materialize from the darkness. "You did well, young Zoë."

"Thank you." She swallowed, remembering everything she'd done wrong, all the skills she still didn't have down. "I . . . I never quite—"

"Your admission packet will be at your apartment tomorrow," he said. "You may bring your mortal to the swearing-in ceremony if you like."

385

Her pulse jumped. "Really?" She looked from Hale to Zephron. "I'm in?"

His weathered face remained stern, but his eyes were warm and grandfatherly. "You're in."

Hale caught her in a tight hug and swung her around. "I knew you could do it!"

"What about Mordi?" she asked, a little breathlessly, as soon as Hale put her down.

"Your cousin is in a somewhat different position," Zephron said. "But he did pass his test—he didn't succumb to his father's demands." He held up the stone, and its facets reflected the silvery light of the moon. "Mordichai will be admitted to the council should he request it, but his admission is probationary. I fear he has a few more hurdles to face before he becomes a full member."

"Sounds fair to me," Hale said. "After all the grief he put Zoë through."

Zoë nodded absently. He had put her through a lot over the last few days, but in the end, he'd done the right thing. And she hoped he passed the rest of his tests, whatever they might be.

"What about Uncle Hieronymous?"

"Ah, yes. He is already an Outcast, you see. And to be honest, he has done nothing we did not expect—or want—him to do. But I assure you that we are watching him. If he seeks to interfere again, we shall surely intercede." Zephron patted her hand. "But your ordeal is over. And your mortal is waiting for you."

Impulsively, she stood on her tiptoes and kissed Zephron's cheek as Hale gawked. She wasn't too surprised. It wasn't exactly proper protocol to kiss the high elder.

But if the flush on the elder's cheeks was any indication, he didn't mind too much.

"Halflings," she heard Hale mutter as she raced away.

"Hey, babe," Taylor said as she ran to him, the corners of his eyes crinkling as he smiled.

"Hi, yourself."

"I was thinking that maybe next week we could just stay home with a video."

"Sounds good to me."

"Something tame. Like *Die Hard*."

"It's a date." She knelt in front of him and ran her fingers through his hair. "Thank you," she whispered.

"Anytime," he said, his voice low and inviting.

"I don't need any more rescuing. Not tonight. But I was wondering if . . . well, if you'd like to come home with me."

"Sweetheart, I can't think of anything I'd like more." He pulled himself to his feet, grimacing as his hurt leg took his weight. "I've just got one question."

Zoë nodded, a tiny bit of dread welling in her. "What's that?"

His furrowed brow accentuated its sexy scar, and he winced as he took a careful step toward her. "I don't suppose you could fly us there?"

She laughed and moved closer, hooking her arm around his waist to steady him. "Darling Taylor, if you want, I'll even fly us to the moon."

"We don't need to go quite that far. Just someplace quiet." He leaned closer, brushing his lips against her ear. "Someplace with a bed."

Tilting her head back, she looked into his eyes, which

were dark and deep with passion. Her body hummed with anticipation, tiny shock waves rippling through her. "Yeah," she said, a trifle breathlessly, "I think that can be arranged."

Epilogue

"It'll all fit, but the letters will be tiny." Deena squinted at the newly turpentined door, her paintbrush poised.

Zoë considered the frosted glass, trying to picture how their stenciled names would look.

"Well, we need to get it all on there," Hoop said. "Zoë's been working here for the last two months, and her name's still not on the door."

Taylor looped an arm around her shoulder, and she leaned against him, turning her face up to receive a quick kiss on the nose.

"She's been doing a damn good job of it, too. For us and for the council."

"I like this undercover assignment," she said honestly. "Being a librarian was fine, but being a private investigator's much better." She smiled up at Taylor. "And being your partner's the best of all."

"Hey!" said Hoop.

Zoë smiled. "Your partner, too." The three of them had joined forces, and Hooper, Taylor, & Smith, Investigators, had been doing reasonably well. Certainly Taylor wasn't surviving on peanut butter, any more than Zoë was living on rice cakes.

"That's better," Hoop said. His stomach growled.

Deena rolled her eyes. "He must have run out of Twinkies. Got any of those PTA candy bars left?"

Zoë shook her head. "I finished the last one off last week during a stakeout."

"I'm impressed how well you're handling chocolate," Taylor said. He flashed a smile that warmed her straight to her toes. "Then again, I'm impressed how well you're handling a lot of things."

Long nights—and some equally long days—snuggled up with Taylor drifted through her memory. "Yeah, well, practice makes perfect." Not that she was completely used to her senses yet, but she was getting closer. She frowned, thinking back to her birthday. "I'm still amazed the council admitted me."

"Why?" Deena asked. "You kicked butt. You pretty much saved the world, right?"

"Well, yeah. But I had help," she said, smiling at Taylor.

"Maybe that was the point," he said. "Sometimes you have to ask for help."

"Is that right?"

"Yeah," he said firmly. "That's right." He gave her hand a gentle squeeze. "But it doesn't have anything to do with our immediate problem," he said, nodding meaningfully at the door.

"Right," Zoë said.

"Right," Hoop echoed.

Deena tapped her foot. "Well, what do you want me to paint on this door?"

Taylor tapped his index finger against his chin. "I think it's too long."

"I know it is," Deena said. "That's why I need to use smaller letters."

"I don't like the smaller letters," Taylor said, casting a look Hoop's way.

"Me, either," Hoop said.

Zoë caught Deena's eye. "Men."

"I do have one suggestion," Taylor said.

Deena sighed, clearly exasperated. "Well spit it out."

"Hooper and Taylor Investigators, fits just fine."

"Absolutely," Hoop said. "Nice and classy-looking."

"But—" Zoë protested.

"What about her?" Deena finished. "She's a partner, too. You can't just—"

"I thought maybe you'd be interested in expanding our partnership," Taylor said, his eyes locked on Zoë's.

"Our partnership?" Zoë repeated stupidly. Her pulse picked up tempo. She tried to calm herself, afraid she was hearing something he wasn't saying. "I'm not . . . I don't know. . . ."

"What the hell are you talking about?" Deena asked, one hand resting on her hip.

"I'm trying to propose here."

"Oh," said Deena. "Well, then. Get on with it."

"Maybe a little privacy?" he asked, looking meaningfully toward the far end of the hall.

Deena looked at Hoop as Zoë tried to keep from floating off the polished wood floor.

"No problem," Hoop said, dragging Deena away.

"Thank you," Taylor said, then turned to face her better. As he took her hands in his, every cell in her body started doing a happy dance. "How about it, sweetheart? We're already partners at the office. How about being partners in life, too?"

She nodded, mute, then threw herself into his waiting arms, planting kisses all over his face.

He laughed. "Can I assume that's a yes?"

"Oh, yeah," she said. "That's very much a yes."

The Cat's Fancy
Julie Kenner

Straight-laced Nicholas Goodman's life is going just fine. A hotshot attorney in a huge law firm, Nick has money, success, and a girlfriend whose father just happens to be his biggest client. All the aspects of his life are tucked neatly into nice little corners, just the way Nick likes it. Until he opens his door and finds a completely naked, slightly befuddled green-eyed beauty on his doorstep.

Maggie has found the man of her dreams—Nick Goodman. He is smart and sexy, and she knows he loves her. Maggie's only problem is . . . well, she isn't entirely human. But Maggie is determined, and through the power of love she is given a chance—and a lithe woman's body. She has one week to convince Nicholas to admit that he loves her. One week to prove that a guy like Nick can fall for "a girl like Maggie." One week to prove that a cat's fancy can be the love of a lifetime.

____52397-3 $5.99 US/$6.99 CAN

WICKED ANGEL SHIRL HENKE

A gawky preacher's daughter, Jocelyn Angelica Woodbridge is hardly the type to incite street brawls, much less two in one day. "Holy Hannah," as those of the *ton* call her, would much rather nurse the sick or reform the fallen. Yet ever since a dashing American saved her from an angry mob, Joss's thoughts have turned most impure.

The son of an American Indian and an English aristocrat, Alexander Blackthorne has been sent to England for some "civilizing." But the only lessons he cares to learn are those offered by taverns and trollops. When a marriage of convenience forces Jocelyn and Alex together, Joss knows she will need more than prayer to make a loving husband of her . . . wicked angel.

___4854-X $5.99 US/$6.99CAN

Alicia's Song
Susan Plunkett

For Alicia James, something is missing. Her childhood romance hadn't ended the way she dreamed, and she is wary of trying again. Still, she finds solace in her sisters and in the fact that her career is inspiring. And together with those sisters, Alicia finds a magic in song that seems almost able to carry away her woes.

In fact, singing carries Alicia away—from her home in modern-day Wyoming to Alaska, a century before her own. There she finds a sexy, dark-haired gentleman with an angelic child just crying out for guidance. And Alicia is everything this pair desperately needs. Suddenly it seems as if life is reaching out and giving Alicia the chance to create a beautiful music she's never been able to make with her sisters—all she needs is the courage to sing her part.

___52434-1 $4.99 US/$5.99 CAN

✦the Mermaid of Penperro

Lisa Cach

Konstanze never imagined that singing could land someone in such trouble. The disrepute of the stage is nothing compared to the danger of playing a seductress of the sea—or the reckless abandon she feels while doing so. She has come to Penperro to escape her past, to find anonymity among the people of Cornwall, and her inhibitions melt away as she does. But the Cornish are less simple than she expected, and the role she is forced to play is harder. For one thing, her siren song lures to her not only the agent of the crown she's been paid to perplex, but the smuggler who hired her. And in his strong arms she finds everything she's been missing. Suddenly, Konstanze sees the true peril of her situation—not that of losing her honor, but her heart.

___52437-6 $5.50 US/$6.50 CAN

Dorchester Publishing Co., Inc.
P.O. Box 6640
Wayne, PA 19087-8640

Please add $2.50 for shipping and handling for the first book and $.75 for each book thereafter. NY, NYC, and PA residents, please add appropriate sales tax. No cash, stamps, or C.O.D.s. All orders shipped within 6 weeks via postal service book rate. Canadian orders require $2.50 extra postage and must be paid in U.S. dollars through a U.S. banking facility.

Name_____
Address_____
City_____ State   Zip
I have enclosed $_____ in payment for the checked book(s).
Payment <u>must</u> accompany all orders. ❏ Please send a free catalog.
CHECK OUT OUR WEBSITE! www.dorchesterpub.com

. . . and coming
May 2001
from. . .

Moonshadow

PENELOPE NERI

"Lillies-of-the-valley," he murmurs, "the sweet scent of innocence." Yet his kisses are anything but innocent as he feeds her deepest desires while honeysuckle and wild roses perfume the languid air.

"Steyning Hall. It is a cold place. And melancholy," he warns, "almost as if it is . . .waiting for someone. Perhaps your coming will change all that."

Wedded mere hours, Madeleine gazes up at the windows of the mansion, stained the color of blood by the dying sun. In the shifting moonshadows she hears voices calling, an infant wailing, and knows not whether to flee for her life or offer up her heart.

___52416-3 $5.99 US/$6.99 CAN

A Passionate Magic

Flora Speer

Sent as an offering of peace between two feuding families, Lady Emma is prepared to perform her wifely duties. But when she first lifts her gaze to the turquoise eyes of her lord, she senses that he is the man she has seen in her most intimate visions. Dain of Penruan has lived an austere life in his Cornish castle on the cliffs, and he doesn't intend to cease doing so, regardless of this arranged marriage to the daughter of his father's hated rival. But though he attempts to disdain Lady Emma, the lusty lord can not ignore her lush curves, or the strange amethyst light sparkling from the depths of her chestnut eyes. Perched upon the precipice of a feeling as mysterious and poignant as silvery moonlight on the sea, Lady and Lord plunge into a love that can only have been conjured by . . . a passionate magic.

____52439-2 $5.50 US/$6.50 CAN